VIKRAMADITYA VEERGATHA
BOOK 2

THE CONSPIRACY AT MERU

VIKRAMADITYA VEERGATHA

BOOK 2

THE CONSPIRACY AT MERU

NATIONAL BESTSELLING SERIES

SHATRUJEET NATH

JAICO PUBLISHING HOUSE

Ahmedabad Bangalore Chennai
Delhi Hyderabad Kolkata Mumbai

Published by Jaico Publishing House
A-2 Jash Chambers, 7-A Sir Phirozshah Mehta Road
Fort, Mumbai - 400 001
jaicopub@jaicobooks.com
www.jaicobooks.com

VIKRAMADITYA VEERGATHA: BOOK 2
THE CONSPIRACY AT MERU
ISBN 978-81-8495-887-4

First Jaico Impression: 2016
Fourth Jaico Impression (New Cover): 2021

Page design and layout: R. Ajith Kumar, Delhi

Printed by
Trinity Academy For Corporate Training Limited, Mumbai

To old friends
Manoj, Viji, Hari, PK, Raja,
Santhosh, Shankar, Suresh & Paul.
May we always stay one step ahead of our sins.

The Marusthali
Matsya
Viratapuri
R. Yamuna
Kosala
Sravasti
Pragjyotishpura
Arbuda Mts.
Kausambi
Girivraja
Vatsa
Magadha
Udaypuri
Sristhali
R. Kshipra
Dandakabhukti
Vanga
Avanti
Riksha Mts.
Ujjayini
Tamralipti
Dvarka
Anarta
Heheya
Vindhya Mts.
Odra
Mahishmati
Uttara Tosali
R. Payoshni
Aanupa Marsh
Bhrigukaksha
Tosali
Kalinga
Dandaka Forest
Sindhuvarta

Index of Major Characters
(In alphabetical order)

Humans

THE KINGDOM OF AVANTI

Aatreya	merchant of Malawa
Amara Simha	councilor of Avanti
Angamitra	captain of the samsaptakas
Aparupa	girl in Udaypuri
Atulyateja	garrison commander of Udaypuri
Brichcha	father of Shanku
Chirayu	lackey to Governor Satyaveda
Dhanavantri	councilor of Avanti and royal physician
Ghatakarpara	councilor of Avanti; nephew of Vikramaditya and Vararuchi
Kalidasa	councilor of Avanti
Keeri	Warden of the Stables
Kshapanaka	councilor of Avanti; sister of queen Vishakha
Kunjala	physician at Avanti's palace

Mahendraditya	late king of Avanti; father of Vikramaditya, Vararuchi and Pralupi
Mother Oracle	Shanku's grandmother; head of the Wandering Tribe
Pralupi	sister of Vikramaditya; Ghatakarpara's mother
Satyaveda	governor of Malawa province
Shanku	councilor of Avanti; granddaughter of the Mother Oracle
Udayasanga	samsaptaka warrior of Avanti
Upashruti	mother of Vikramaditya and Pralupi; second wife of Mahendraditya
Ushantha	mother of Vararuchi; first wife of Mahendraditya
Varahamihira	councilor of Avanti
Vararuchi	councilor of Avanti; half-brother of Vikramaditya
Vetala Bhatta	chief councilor of Avanti; royal tutor
Vikramaditya	king of Avanti
Vishakha	wife of Vikramaditya; Kshapanaka's sister

The Kingdom of Magadha

Asmabindu	councilor of Magadha
Bhaskara	councilor of Magadha
Daipayana	general of the Magadhan army
Diganta	councilor of Magadha
Kapila	second son of late king Siddhasena
Shoorasena	king of Magadha; elder son of late king Siddhasena
Siddhasena	late king of Magadha
Uttama	councilor of Magadha

The Kingdom of Vatsa

Chandravardhan	king of Vatsa; ally of Avanti
Himavardhan	brother of Chandravardhan; father of Ghatakarpara
Shashivardhan	son of Chandravardhan
Yashobhavi	councilor of Vatsa

The Kingdom of Kosala

Bhoomipala	king of Kosala; ally of Avanti
Gajaketu	travelling musician
Pallavan	envoy and councilor of Kosala

The Kingdom of Heheya

Harihara	king of Heheya; ally of Avanti
Rukma	daughter of Harihara
Sumayanti	queen of Heheya

The Kingdom of Matsya

Baanahasta	king of Matsya; ally of Avanti

The Anarta Federation

Manidhara	chieftain of the Anarta Federation
Yugandhara	chief of the Anarta Federation; ally of Avanti

The Republic of Vanga

Sudasan	chancellor of the Republic of Vanga

Devas

Agneyi	apsara and chief of the fire-wraiths
Brihaspati	royal chaplain of the devas

Dasra	captain of the Ashvins; twin brother of Nasatya
Gandharvasena	a deva
Indra	lord of the devas; king of Devaloka
Jayanta	son of Indra
Manyu	palace keeper of Devaloka
Menaka	apsara of Devaloka
Narada	envoy of Devaloka and advisor to Indra
Nasatya	captain of the Ashvins; twin brother of Dasra
Shachi	wife of Indra; Jayanta's mother
The Ashvins	elite cavalry of Devaloka, led by Nasatya and Dasra
The Maruts	the seven sons of Diti
Urvashi	apsara of Devaloka and mistress of Indra

Asuras

Amarka	asura general; son of Shukracharya
Andhaka	the blind rakshasa
Chandasura	asura general; son of Shukracharya
Diti	sorceress and matriarch of the asuras
Hiranyaksha	lord of the asuras; king of Patala
Holika	sister-consort of Hiranyaksha; witch queen of Patala
Shukracharya	high priest of the asuras
Veeshada	the asura who stole the Halahala

Others

Ahi	the serpent-dragon
Kubera	lord of the yakshas
Shiva	the Omniscient One
Tribhanu	lord of the kinnaras

Glossary of Indian Terms

(In alphabetical order)

aguru	oil of agarwood
agnikantaka	a fire catapult or flamethrower
apsara	a beautiful, supernatural female being in Hindu mythology
ashoka	a rain-forest tree
babul	prickly acacia
badi-maa	elder mother; a form of address
chaturanga	an ancient Indian strategy game; ancestor of chess
chausar	an ancient Indian board game; precursor to Ludo
chillum	tradition Indian clay pipe
danava	a mythical race
Dasa-Mahavidyas	Wisdom goddesses; the ten aspects of the Divine Mother Kali
devadaru	a species of cedar
ganjika	cannabis
garuda	a large, mythical, humanoid bird

ghat	steps leading down to a body of water such as a holy river
gurudev	master or teacher; also a form of address
jamun	black plum; Java plum
kalasha	a traditional Indian metal pot
kamandalam	a traditional Indian water pot
kashayam	a brewed Ayurvedic medicine
katari	a fist dagger
kimpurusha	a legendary tribe in Vedic India
kinnara	a legendary tribe in Vedic India
ksheera	traditional Indian rice pudding
mahaguru	grandmaster or teacher; also a form of address
mahisha	buffalo
mandala	a spiritual and ritual symbol in Hinduism representing the universe
modaka	a sweet dumpling
mriga	deer
naga	a legendary tribe in Vedic India
narilata	a mythical orchid
neem	a tree common in India
paduka	traditional Indian sandals
parijata	coral jasmine
peepal	the sacred fig tree
pishacha	a mythical flesh-eating demon
pranaam	salutation
rajasuya yajna	ritual sacrifice performed by ancient Indian kings before being anointed emperor
raj-guru	royal tutor; also a form of address
rakshasa	a mythical humanoid being
sambrani	a balsamic resin used as incense
samrat	emperor or overlord

samsaptaka	a tribe of mythical warriors
shrikhand	a sweet dish made from yogurt
soma	Vedic ritual drink
suvarnaka	golden shower tree
tambulam	paan; a betel leaf and areca nut preparation
urumi	a longsword with a flexible whip-like blade
vaidyanath	physician; also an honorific and form of address
vajra / vajrayudha	thunderbolt; Indra's weapon of choice
vyala	a mythical beast
yaksha	a mythical spirit

Contents

Smoke

He is staggering through the smoke, hardly able to breathe, barely alive.

The smoke is everywhere. Swathes and swathes of it, pressing in on him, crowding him out. Obscuring the sky above, fuzzing out the ground below. Smarting in his eyes. Catching in his throat. Corroding his nostrils. Looking for ways to snuff him out.

Hot. Pungent. Filled with the smell of burning wood. And the reek of charred flesh.

Something tells him he should never have been here. That he should have made off when he had the chance to. But that doesn't matter now. He is here, in the smoke. So he pushes on, gagging and choking, blind in the smother of grey-white. Blind, but not deaf.

A woman's scream, shrill and fraught with fear, rips through the smoke. But it is silenced almost immediately by another sound, softer but more ominous – the ka-chunk *of a battle-axe coming in contact with flesh and bone.*

The acrid fumes get the better of him and he sinks to his knees, his skin grazing on the flinty gravel underneath. He sways uncertainly for a moment, one part of him wanting to give in to the smoke's embrace. But there's another, more defiant part that wants to go on. This is the part that had wanted to know – needed to know – *what was happening; that had led him into the fire and smoke and prevented him from fleeing.*

Snorting and coughing, he wills himself to crawl forward on all fours.

The screams have been dying down around him slowly. Even the tumult of running feet has receded, though he senses someone issuing commands far away. He presses on, dragging himself over ground that is slick with blood in places. There is an instance where his groping hand grabs something cold and fleshy – a man's arm, severed from the shoulder down, the blood still glutinous and congealing around the open mangle of tissue and bone. His stomach heaves and pitches, but fighting the nausea back, he pushes on.

He emerges from the smoke onto a broad, muddy pathway. The pathway isn't entirely free of smoke, but it is a big improvement on the place he has just exited. Rising on wobbly legs, he stands in the middle of the road, bent at the waist, gulping in large mouthfuls of air. Every breath is a struggle, his stomach knotted tight with anxiety. Tears run freely down his cheeks.

Taking slow, shallow breaths, he wipes his watering eyes, rubs the spittle and snot off his mouth and chin, and surveys his surroundings.

The road is deserted, curving away to his left into a wood. To his right, it rises toward an embankment shrouded in shifting wisps of smoke. From beyond the embankment comes a faded murmur of voices.

He pauses, listening. There is a sudden change in the

direction of the wind, and he hears more agonized screaming from the direction of the embankment.

Clinging to the shoulder of the pathway, just outside the reach of the pall of smoke, he steals toward the embankment.

Almost at the top, he drops to a crouch, then goes down on his stomach, slithering the rest of the way to peek cautiously over the lip into the crater-like depression beneath.

Through the drifts of smoke, he sees half a dozen buildings in this small, basin-shaped valley. Save for one, all are in flames. Soldiers wielding spears are herding four manacled figures into the one untouched building – a granary. Though he can't make them out clearly, three of the captives are women, wailing and pleading for mercy. The fourth, a man, appears to have lost the faculty of speech altogether.

Closer to the embankment, a man sits astride a horse, observing the soldiers. The horseman has his back to the embankment, his face concealed from view. But there is something vaguely familiar about his build, the way he sits on his saddle, the slight slouch of his left shoulder…

The soldiers shove their terrified prisoners into the granary, slamming the door shut behind them, locking them in. At a sign from the horseman, one soldier takes a burning torch and sets the granary alight.

Lying atop the embankment, watching the granary catch fire and burn, his throat parched with fear, he no longer needs to know what is happening.

He knows.

He has seen enough. It is time to make an escape before he is detected.

A sudden shout echoes behind him, followed by more shouts and curses, and the pounding of feet on earth.

It is too late. He has already been found. There is nowhere to run, nowhere to hide.

Too petrified to move, capture and death now inevitable,

he stares wild-eyed into the depression as the heavy thud of approaching feet draws near. He stares at the horseman, a phantom of a figure in the softly swirling smoke.

Drawn by the shouts and cries, the horseman is turning his head, glancing over his shoulder, in the direction of the embankment. And again, something about the man – the fall of his jet-black locks, the shape of the uncovered head, the set of the shoulders, casual and self-assured – stirs a memory, remote and elusive, yet tantalizing in its persistence.

He has to know who the rider is.

With a rising chill of anticipation, he waits for the horseman to turn around and face him…

Messages

It had been another long and cheerless day for the ten-odd men employed at Ujjayini's cremation ground. For five days at a stretch, they had been piling logs, building pyres and laying the dead to rest, before clearing the debris of old pyres to set up fresh ones. It was hard, backbreaking work, and it stirred uncomfortable memories of a time in the not-so-distant past, when the savages from the Marusthali had held sway over Sindhuvarta, and the pyres of Avanti's dead had burned for months on end. So, at the close of each day, the groundskeepers had borne their fatigued, soot-stained bodies homeward in the hope that that day was the last. That on the next, there would be no more boats ferrying corpses from Ujjayini across the Kshipra.

Yet the dead from the three attacks on their kingdom kept coming, bringing a trail of mourners in tow, many as dead in spirit as the ones they had come to bid farewell to. By the third day, the men had stopped keeping count of the bodies they helped dispose of. They simply went about their task, maintaining stoic expressions in the face of all the misery around them.

The nature of their work being what it was, it was hardly a surprise that the men failed to notice the stocky figure of Shukracharya make a surreptitious appearance at the cremation ground on the fifth evening. The high priest of the asuras arrived a little before sundown, but instead of revealing himself straightaway, he lurked around the brambly woods bordering the ground, watching the weary, dispirited attendants finish up for the day.

It was only after the sun had dipped under the horizon – and the ground was almost empty of mourners – that he stepped into the open, moving tentatively, his keen eye sweeping right and left, ensuring he had the place to himself. Even then, he waited until the last three attendants began their trudge back home, before venturing amidst the smouldering pyres, their grey smoke smudging the orange-pink sunset like the manifestation of an ugly curse.

Threading between the pyres, Shukracharya made for his destination – the lone banyan tree that stood in the middle of the cremation ground. It was tall and leafy, but young in years. Its aerial roots were still forming around its trunk, most of them stringy clusters no thicker than a grown man's wrist, swaying in the light breeze. But the tree had majesty. More than majesty, it had the promise of growing into a fine old specimen – a giant, grandfather of a banyan.

For Shukracharya, though, the tree held a different sort of promise.

There was scarcely a moment during the last four days when the tree wasn't uppermost in the high priest's mind. He had been desperate for this trip, but the casualties from the Maruts' attack had kept him in Ujjayini – his services had been much in demand, summons and pleas to attend to the wounded coming from homes and hospices in every quarter of the city. Eventually, to ease the burden on the Healer, the samrat had had a makeshift hospice erected on the palace grounds, where the maimed could be brought for treatment.

This, however, had proved an even bigger impediment to Shukracharya's plans, tethering him to the precincts of the palace. But to neglect Ujjayini's citizenry at this stage would have meant having his motives questioned, an ill-advised move. So the deva had endured the delay, dispensing care, biding his time.

Even when there were no wounded to tend to, he was compelled to stay back in the palace to monitor Queen Vishakha's progress, which could neatly be summed up in one word – *remarkable*!

On the second morning following the Maruts' attack, the queen had demonstrated the ability to recollect more of her childhood in the kingdom of Nishada. By the same evening, she was able to piece together snatches of her more recent past, from the time she had first come to reside in the palace of Ujjayini. The next day, she had improved enough to recognize Kshapanaka and Queen Mother Upashruti as older versions of people she remembered vaguely – though she still couldn't establish their relationships to one another or to herself. And hours later, she had limped out of her bedchamber for the first time in two years and hobbled along the palace galleries, staring inquisitively into some rooms, pointing with mild excitement at others that she recalled.

Shukracharya had received a severe jolt upon observing Vishakha's rapid recovery. At this rate, he knew it wouldn't be long before everything came back to the queen, a prospect that alarmed him. It meant his losing purchase over Vikramaditya, losing the edge he held over the human king while negotiating the matter of Veeshada's dagger. To have control over the king, control over Vishakha's condition was imperative.

He understood that the queen's progress was the effect of

the Regeneration Spell he had cast over Ujjayini the night the Maruts had come for the Halahala. Without his meaning to do so, the spell had begun the task of reconstruction, illuminating the fog-bound spots in Vishakha's mind, repairing bridges between isolated patches of her memory. So the high priest had set about retarding the process, drawing the curtains back down. Under the pretext of curing her, he invoked dark mantras and cast spells that brought the shadows creeping back into the recesses of the queen's mind. The effort required was considerable, but it showed signs of working – there were no new additions to Vishakha's memory over the last two days.

The high priest had also made certain the queen spent much of her time asleep, incapable of active thought, leaving clear instructions that she was not to be disturbed from slumber.

Secure in the knowledge that Vishakha wouldn't awaken before daybreak – and knowing he wouldn't be missed in the palace in a hurry – Shukracharya had braved this visit to the cremation ground. Treading with caution, he now approached the banyan, casting his eye around for anyone who might see him on this errand.

Shukracharya came to a halt under the tree's spreading canopy, a jumble of dark leaves against a purple sky. He stood at its base, scouring its trunk and branches, taking in every little cleft and fork in the wood. He walked around it in circles, examining the ground around its roots, looking for telltale signs of the earth having been dug recently. He ran his hands over the rough, calloused bark, feeling for hidden cracks and crevices.

Nothing.

He stepped back two paces and looked up at the tree in frustration. Somewhere at the back of his mind, he had always suspected this to be a foolish quest. With a sinking heart, he saw that his intuition was being proved right.

But the bones had never been wrong. Had never *ever* been wrong.

It is in the banyan that holds up the field of endless pyres.

The answer had jumped at him the night he had posed the bones his question on the whereabouts of the dagger. And for four consecutive nights thereafter, the answer had been the same, whichever way he framed the questions.

Yes, Veeshada's dagger was very much in Ujjayini. No, the devas had not taken possession of it yet. But the dagger was not in the palace. It was in the banyan that holds up the field of endless pyres.

All the arguments that had been nagging him against what the bones had foretold came rushing back to Shukracharya. How and where could a dagger be hidden in a tree in a way that guaranteed it would never be found, even by accident? Why would the human king choose to leave the Halahala unguarded in a desolate cremation ground, miles from the protection of the palace? And what assurance did the king have that such a hiding place would never be discovered by the devas and the asuras?

But the bones had never been wrong...

The thought of Indra and Brihaspati sitting in Devaloka and plotting to lay their hands on the dagger instilled a sudden sense of purpose in Shukracharya. The Ashvins and the Maruts may have been beaten, but he knew Indra well enough to realize that the defeats would only have incited the deva's anger. Indra would want to strike back, and whenever he did, it would, in all probability, end disastrously for Avanti. He couldn't let that happen, at least not until he had resolved the riddle of the dagger and the banyan tree.

It was time he took the devas' minds off the dagger, gave them something else to worry about instead.

With renewed purpose, the high priest walked the dozen steps to the nearest pyre. Crouching down by the still-smoking pile of burned wood, he sifted through the warm ash at its base until he had uncovered the jet-black soot that lay, layer upon layer, underneath. He scooped a small portion of the soot into the palm of his hand before returning to the tree, where he squatted on his haunches. He then began softly dabbing the soot on the ground with his index finger.

With sure strokes, he drew a series of lines and smears in the likeness of three birds, muttering incantations as he worked. Then, closing his eye, he scattered a handful of mud over the crude drawings. Instantly, the birds sprouted black plumage and came alive – three crows, sooty smudges in the darkness, ruffling their feathers at the foot of the banyan.

The high priest reached a hand out, calling to the crows. Two of them jumped onto his hand, their claws digging into his wrist and forearm. He murmured a few words to them, and they spread their wings and flapped into the foliage overhead. Shukracharya followed their flight with a satisfied smile. The two birds would be his sentinels, watching over the banyan. They would let him know if the king – if *anyone* – showed undue interest in the tree again.

He turned his attention to the third crow. Once it had answered his beckons and perched on his hand, he began whispering into its ear. These instructions were long and detailed, and it was some time before the bird rose into the air and headed in a southerly direction.

Gaining his feet, Shukracharya watched the dark shape melt into the night sky, sending a prayer in its wake. That bird had a long journey ahead of it, and was bearing a message of great import to the asura lord Hiranyaksha.

A message to unleash a preemptive strike on Devaloka.

* * *

The sky was an indeterminate grey, filled with banks of patchy, shapeless clouds that kept muddling into one another, shuttled by the winds. But closer to the earth, there was hardly a hint of breeze, and even without the sun, the mid-morning air was warm and mildly stuffy, causing Vikramaditya, the Acharya and Kalidasa to perspire as they sauntered along the walkway on top of Ujjayini's eastern wall.

They were out inspecting the extensive repair work underway all over the city. Every day, a steady stream of carts was converging from the towns of Lava, Bhojapuri and even faraway Viswapuri, loaded with the lumber, stone and sand needed to rebuild Ujjayini. Brick kilns, smithies and stone-breaking yards had sprouted around the city to cater to the spike in demand, and carpenters, stonemasons and brick makers had been drafted from all over the kingdom. Still, there was a dearth of experienced hands for the work involved, and progress was slow.

The fortification of the city's ramparts and its four main gates was consuming more than a fair share of manpower and materials. At one level, this was deemed necessary and made perfect sense. Had it not been for these defences, the Ashvin cavalry would have ravaged Ujjayini in no time; the walls and the gates had held the devas back, limiting their damage to the perimeters of the city. At the same time, it required no great intelligence to see that walls and gates were no answer to rakshasas that dropped from the sky in bolts of lightning. So, there was an unspoken question over the wisdom of their upkeep, particularly when they were such a drain on resources.

"We will be ignoring the wall at our own peril," said Vikramaditya, drawing to a halt near the northeastern corner of the walkway. The samrat's face was drawn, his eyes stormy, mirroring a mind preoccupied with a hundred thoughts concerning the safety of his city and his subjects.

"I agree, Vikrama," replied Acharya Vetala Bhatta, his tone gentle and reassuring as he considered the man who had once been his pupil and was now his king. He couldn't help notice how the samrat had aged over the last week. "Walls are a city's greatest defence. We are doing right in strengthening ours."

"Right now, Chancellor Sudasan could do with some stout walls around Tamralipti," said the samrat, stroking his moustache pensively.

It took the Acharya a moment to make sense of the sudden change in topic. Catching the samrat's train of thought, he nodded. Late the previous night, his spies had brought news of Magadhan troops under General Daipayana's command capturing the mining town of Dandakabhukti. The spies had also reported that Prince Shoorasena had visited Dandakabhukti, and had commissioned Daipayana and Kapila to push further into the Republic of Vanga and wrest control of the port of Tamralipti.

"How would you rate Vanga's chances against Magadha, raj-guru?" Vikramaditya cocked an eyebrow at Vetala Bhatta. "Do you think Tamralipti could be defended?"

"Not highly," the chief councilor chose to reply to the first question. "Vanga has an army of sorts, but it consists essentially of militia drawn from its eighteen principalities. It is sizeable in numbers, but is semi-trained and no match for Magadha's efficient troops. Moreover, Vanga's central armoury is in Dandakabhukti – which is now in Magadha's hands. So..."

"Tamralipti will inevitably fall," the samrat completed the sentence, his hand straying involuntarily to the pommel of the sword strapped to his waist. Vetala Bhatta and Kalidasa were also similarly armed; after all these years, wearing weapons had once again become the norm in Ujjayini, the Acharya couldn't help thinking.

For a while, the three men were quiet, contemplating the full impact of Magadha's move against Vanga.

"With Dandakabhukti, Magadha controls the supply of

iron ore, and with Tamralipti, it holds the access point to all trade with the kingdoms of Sribhoja and Srivijaya," said Vikramaditya. "Shoorasena can hold all of Sindhuvarta to ransom if he chooses to."

"It explains why the prince was quick to snap ties with the rest of us," Vetala Bhatta smiled sardonically. "You can't hold friends and allies to ransom, and if you've got only friends and allies around you, it's in your interest to drop a few of them."

"At least we now know why King Siddhasena was killed. The old king would never have approved of Shoorasena's plans, and he was sure to have exposed his son when he realized he was plotting against the rest of us." The samrat paused a moment. "Let's just hope Councilor Pallavan is able to find the men who were loyal to Siddhasena and convince them about what happened to their good king."

"Speaking of allies, any fresh updates on how King Chandravardhan is keeping?" the Acharya enquired.

Captain Angamitra and his posse of *samsaptakas* had returned from Kausambi three days earlier, bringing with them the report of the paralytic stroke that Chandravardhan had suffered. The news had unsettled the royal palace. Since King Mahendraditya's time, Vatsa had been one of Avanti's staunchest allies, and not only did Vatsa and Avanti share blood ties, Chandravardhan was a man who could be relied on in times of crisis.

"Nothing." The samrat's reply was distracted, his gaze lingering over the wall, staring at something further to the south.

Turning around, the chief councilor followed the king's line of sight to see two bullock carts rolling out of the city gates, making for the flat countryside. Both carts were precariously stacked with household items, women and little children seated in whatever spaces were left available. The menfolk and the older children walked beside the carts. It was plain that this was a final departure. The spectacle held little novelty, though. Scores of families, scared and scarred by the attacks, had quietly been leaving Ujjayini in much the same way over the past few days, uprooting themselves, dismantling their lives to move from one uncertainty to what they hoped would be a less frightening uncertainty.

Glancing back, Vetala Bhatta saw a pained expression flit across the samrat's face, and his heart went out to the king. He knew the reports of citizens fleeing Ujjayini were eating away at Vikramaditya, and that the samrat was holding himself responsible for bringing this on his subjects, for not being able to protect them. Yet it was beyond his power to put an end to his people's misery. He could say nothing to hold them back, give them no assurances, make no promises he couldn't honour. So, helpless and distraught, he was letting them go.

With a determined shake of his head, Vikramaditya tore his eyes away from the bullock carts and looked at the Acharya. "Nothing," he said again. "We can only pray for the king's recovery and wellbeing."

After a brief pause, he added, "At least Prince Shashivardhan doesn't appear to have been cast in the same mould as Shoorasena, which is a huge relief. From what Angamitra says, Shashivardhan and Councilor Yashobhavi pledged assistance to Avanti should the need ever arise."

"Which is a lot more than what Kalidasa got from King Harihara," the Acharya turned inquisitively to the giant, who had stationed himself a little to the left and behind Vetala Bhatta.

"Uh, what?" Kalidasa looked at the chief councilor in confusion. "My apologies, raj-guru, but I didn't quite get that."

The Acharya peered at Kalidasa with narrowed eyes. There appeared to be something bothering the giant for the last few days. Though not given to speaking freely, Kalidasa had been uncharacteristically reticent ever since the night he had fought the rakshasa into the palace lake. He had hardly uttered a word all morning, tagging along quietly like a shadow. And this lack of alertness to what was being said around him – that wasn't typical of Kalidasa.

"Is everything alright?" the chief councilor's voice was tinged with concern.

"No... I mean, yes. I mean no... there's nothing," Kalidasa brushed his forehead lightly, as if clearing a cobweb somewhere. He then looked at the Acharya. "You were asking about King Harihara?"

"Yes." Vetala Bhatta decided to accept Kalidasa's answer for the time being. "I was saying Harihara wasn't a model of friendship when you paid him that visit."

"He definitely wasn't." The giant's face darkened and he suddenly looked like the Kalidasa of old, focused and ominous. "He kept whining about how his kingdom had suffered so much at the hands of the pishachas for no fault of theirs. The way he went on and on about how Heheya is now in danger of being attacked by the devas and asuras, one would think we had burdened him with the sole responsibility of protecting the Halahala."

Now that he had been properly riled, there was no stopping Kalidasa. "He had the audacity to ask what Avanti wants from its allies. This, after we took the trouble of disposing of Kulabheda for him and giving him back his throne. I had half a mind of tossing him out of the window of his chamber and returning to Ujjayini with that chest of gold we gave him. King Harihara doesn't deserve a single coin from Avanti's mints."

Kalidasa's reaction brought faint smiles to Vikramaditya and Vetala Bhatta's lips. The giant's unwavering love and loyalty toward Avanti was both endearing and reassuring.

"Don't be so harsh on King Harihara, brother," the samrat chided, still smiling to rob his words of any offence. "The old king means well. It is just that the pishachas came perilously close to Mahishmati, and that must have shaken Heheya. And lest we forget, the pishachas did cause them harm – for no fault of theirs."

"You are too trusting, brother," countered Kalidasa. "I was watching the king. Yes, there was fear in his eyes, which I understand. But I also saw ingratitude and selfishness. Harihara was thinking of nothing but himself and Heheya. It was..."

A clatter of approaching hooves from the streets below brought the conversation to an abrupt halt. Craning their necks, the king and his councilors looked down, and were rewarded with the sight of two men on horseback coming round a bend at a brisk pace. One of them was Vararuchi, while the other appeared to be a common soldier.

The horses drew up at the foot of a stairway, and moments later, Vararuchi and the soldier emerged from the well. Stepping onto the walkway, they approached Vikramaditya.

"Salutations to Samrat Vikramaditya," said the soldier, bowing deeply.

"My salutations to you, soldier," the king replied, switching a quizzical gaze from the man to Vararuchi.

"The soldier is a rider from the command centre of Sristhali, samrat," the king's half-brother explained. "He bears a critical message from Councilor Amara Simha."

"Amara Simha is in Sristhali?" Vikramaditya stared at Vararuchi in surprise. "I thought he was in Udaypuri, and that he was on his way back to Ujjayini."

"He is on his way back here, samrat," said Vararuchi. "But he was in Sristhali a week ago, when he dispatched this message for us."

"*One week!*" Vetala Bhatta's eyes bored into the rider's. "What took you so long to bring us this message?"

"Your honour, I delivered the message to the palace five

days ago," the rider answered. As the king exchanged puzzled glances with Kalidasa and the Acharya, the soldier spoke again. "I delivered it to Commander Sadguna the night the rakshasas attacked us; just before the attacks began."

"He came to the palace and asked to see the samrat, rajguru," Vararuchi looked at the Acharya knowingly. "But the samrat was... busy. He then asked to see you, but you were also occupied. So was Kalidasa, and I wasn't there either."

"I didn't know what to do, your honour," the rider butted in, eager to explain himself. "Councilor Amara Simha had instructed me to deliver the message without delay, so I shared it with Commander Sadguna. The commander assured me he would share it with the samrat, but he also asked me not to breathe a word to anyone else. It was only this morning that it struck me that Commander Sadguna had died that same night. That's why I decided to bring this to your notice."

Vikramaditya and the councilors exchanged glances and nodded. It was obvious that the late chief of the Palace Guards had had neither the time nor the opportunity to relay the rider's message to anyone in the council.

"What was Amara Simha's message?" the samrat asked the rider kindly. Not only had the soldier exonerated himself, he had displayed the presence of mind to return to the palace instead of assuming that the message had reached the king's ears.

Quickly, but without missing out any details, the rider filled them in on the capture of the Huna scouts near Sristhali, the suspicious death of one of them from snakebite, and the revelations made by the other on the Huna plan to attack the Anarta Federation by sea.

"Councilor Ghatakarpara departed for Dvarka the same morning as I did to warn Chief Yugandhara of the threat to the Anartas, your honour," the soldier concluded. "My instructions were to deliver the same update to the palace."

"You have done well, soldier," Vikramaditya nodded. "You may leave now. But keep all this to yourself."

Once they had the walkway to themselves, the king looked at the Acharya questioningly.

"What do you make of what we have just learnt, raj-guru?"

"It may seem farfetched, but only because the Hunas and Sakas have never displayed any skill in naval warcraft before," Vetala Bhatta shrugged.

"Even so, the possibility of such an attack cannot be entirely overruled," cautioned Vikramaditya. "The Hunas may have learnt a trick or two over the years."

"I agree. And as Amara Simha rightly points out, the Hunas have successfully drawn the troops of Sindhuvarta to the frontier, leaving the Anartas exposed and vulnerable. If it is a strategy, it is an ingenious one. Amara Simha did well in sending Ghatakarpara to Yugandhara's court."

"The Mother Oracle has made no mention of any of this so far," ventured Vararuchi. "If I remember correctly, she had only spoken about a wall of dust rising in the Great Desert. Could the two be connected?"

No one made a move to answer the question. The indecisive silence was broken by Kalidasa.

"Maybe we should ask the Mother Oracle about the ships. She might be able to verify what the scout told Amara Simha."

Leaning his hands on the parapet, the samrat nodded, his eyes trained on the distant horizon, deep in contemplation. At last he pushed himself upright and turned to his councilors.

"We should have a word about this with the Mother Oracle. If the Anartas are at risk, we must prepare to send in reinforcements. We can't let the Federation fall to the barbarians."

Seeing he had the full attention of the men in front of him, Vikramaditya continued. "And though I doubt it, it would be nice if the Mother Oracle could learn who killed that scout in his cell in Sristhali. It had to be an inside job. Which means the threat from the Hunas is a lot closer than we expected – it is already well inside the boundaries of Avanti."

* * *

For the fifth time in probably as many minutes, Governor Satyaveda reached for the quill sticking out of the inkwell on his table. Extracting it, he brought its sharpened nib to the blank stretch of palm leaf lying in front of him with the intention of putting his thoughts into words, but his hand merely hovered over the leaf, fingers idly twirling the quill, as he struggled to compose a coherent message.

The governor's problem was that he didn't know what to write and what to leave out. Rather, he admitted to himself grudgingly, he had very little to write about, and what he did have to say was of no use to anybody.

However, later that evening, he was scheduled to meet the merchant Aatreya – his and the Huna chieftain's go-between – and he had to have an update ready. That was the understanding under which the pouches of coins were delivered to him, week after week. So, Satyaveda stared across the rooftops of Udaypuri and once again made an assessment of the facts at his disposal.

He knew that in spite of his best efforts, things had gone drastically wrong in Sristhali. By some confounded stroke of misfortune, right after his departure from the command centre, Amara Simha had somehow unearthed a second Huna scout. Satyaveda had learnt of this only when Amara Simha had returned to the fort of Udaypuri with his prisoner, who was immediately placed under the guard of an elite unit of the Imperial Army.

He knew with surety that something was afoot when he discovered that no one other than Commander Atulyateja and Amara Simha himself had access to the scout. Added to that was the mysterious absence of Ghatakarpara – when Satyaveda had probed the matter, Amara Simha had been evasive, saying the prince had stayed back in Sristhali to gain experience in coordinating troop movements. But some clever snooping by Chirayu, his wily and ever-reliable assistant, had revealed a different story. The king's nephew had left Sristhali with an escort of ten guards, and had headed for Dvarka!

Then the reports of the rakshasas' attack on Ujjayini had arrived, along with a call to Amara Simha to return to the capital.

The sight of Amara Simha leaving the fort had brought the governor immense relief. Even when he had served in Ujjayini as a courtier at the palace – *before the Acharya had deviously plotted his transfer to the wilderness of Malawa, he reminded himself bitterly* – Satyaveda had been in mortal fear of the brusque and overbearing councilor.

But the fact that Amara Simha had taken the scout with him to Ujjayini was worrying. And try as he might, the governor was unable to get anything out of Atulyateja on what the scout could possibly have spilled to the councilor.

So here he was with the knowledge that a Huna scout had been apprehended near Sristhali and brought to Udaypuri, where he had been placed under heavy guard, before being taken to Ujjayini. Had the scout revealed anything of importance to Amara Simha? Did Ghatakarpara's unscheduled departure to the Anartas have anything to do with the scout? He didn't know, and he didn't believe he would learn the truth about either question.

All he knew for a fact was that the garrison of Udaypuri was no longer under the command of Amara Simha. And that Ghatakarpara was returning to Udaypuri later in the day. He guessed that the prince would now probably take charge of the garrison along with Atulyateja...

Satyaveda sat upright in his chair, gripping its armrests tightly, his eyes shining as he stared at a large, embroidered map of Malawa province that hung on the facing wall.

What had he been thinking when he had told himself he had nothing of significance to share in his weekly report!

The garrison of Udaypuri was likely to come under the command of a buffoon who had yet to shake off his adolescence and get rid of the airs of the palace. Satyaveda had observed enough of the prince to know it was easy to pander to the boy's ego. He was naïve and impressionable, and craved approval. Ghatakarpara was ripe for the picking.

Best of all, there was no interfering Amara Simha to mind over him now.

Almost humming with energy, the governor reached for the quill.

Promise

The palace of Amaravati wore a disconsolate air, its broad passageways and galleries strangely empty of courtiers and palace hands, the halls and antechambers missing the usual song and mirth of the delectable apsaras. Silence lay everywhere, heavy and funereal, broken now and then by the eerie lament of the wind as it slipped over the towering cliffs and cascaded into the chasm that engulfed the palace on all sides.

Jayanta, first-born son of Indra, padded quietly along one of these deserted galleries, heading in the direction of Urvashi's boudoir. His manner was furtive, eyes darting around to see if he was being watched, even as his ears strained against the wind, struggling to pick up a hint of Urvashi's voice.

All he got in return was the echo of the gloom that had enveloped the palace.

The atmosphere had stayed that way ever since news of the Maruts' rout had reached Indra's ears. Five times thereafter, the sun had risen, but it had failed to bring warmth and cheer; the palace only seemed to sink lower into the shadows of the surrounding abyss. Its inhabitants had remained cloistered in their chambers rather than risk crossing Indra's path, their voices rarely rising above muted undertones. The king of the devas himself, though, had hardly ventured out of his own bedchamber, opting for solitude over company.

Then, earlier that afternoon, a garuda had appeared from the east and alighted on Indra's balcony to confer with its king. Moments after the garuda had departed, spreading its large wings in elegant flight, the lord of the devas had sent summons for the apsara Menaka, and asked that Airavata, his battle elephant, be put in harness. A hundred pairs of curious eyes had watched Indra and Menaka emerge from the palace stockade astride Airavata – a humungous, albino woolly mammoth, its six big curling tusks sharpened to points. Concealed behind the curtains of his bedchamber, Jayanta had followed the mammoth as it traversed the moat and turned toward the cleft in the hills that opened to the road heading east.

Knowing his father was safely out of the way, Jayanta turned the corner that led to Urvashi's chambers in the fervent hope that he would find the apsara in her lodgings. It had been days since he had had a glimpse of her svelte figure, and he longed to see her, hear her, breathe in the heady scent of her youth... hold her close.

And pleasure her with kisses as they drowned in passionate lovemaking.

The image of Urvashi spread deliciously on soft cushions, smiling up at him, arms and legs thrown open in invitation, welcoming him, sent bolts of lust shooting through Jayanta's veins. With quickening steps, he approached the apsara's room – and was immediately rewarded with the chime of her irrepressible laughter. Clear and bubbling like a mountain stream, brimming with love, overflowing with life, casting aside the dreariness that was saturating the palace.

Giddy with anticipation, his pulse tripping over itself, Jayanta reached the heavy door to the apsara's bedchamber before the significance of what he had heard dawned on him. The laugh meant Urvashi was not alone.

Jayanta pushed the door gently open. Poking his head around it, he caught sight of Urvashi lounging against silken bolsters at the far end of the covered terrace abutting the chamber, her back to the door. He drank in her reclining form with greedy eyes, trailing the contours of her body; the soft alabaster neck and shoulders; the slip of her smooth back; the narrowing of the waist, encircled lovingly by a delicate girdle of woven gold; and the supple, rounded heave of her hips.

Conscious of the flutter in his stomach and the stirring in his loins, the prince transferred his gaze to the second apsara, whom he now recognized as Yavika, a pretty handmaiden of Urvashi's. Yavika sat facing Urvashi, a game of *chausar* spread on the floor between them. Decked all around the apsaras were large ferns and sweet-smelling blossoms in big copper urns, the leaves and vines swaying and bobbing in the wind.

The sight of the two nymphs, sparingly clothed, emboldened Jayanta. Stepping inside, he shut the door and strode across the expanse of the bedchamber, even as Yavika rolled the two wooden dice, which struck the marbled floor with a loud clatter. Observing the dice, Yavika squealed in exultation – to the accompaniment of an exasperated chuckle from a male voice!

Already halfway to the terrace, Jayanta stopped short, his self-assured smile falling away in big chunks. Disappointment crashed against his chest in high-crested waves.

The male voice was one he recognized.

Just then, one of the large fronds of a fern moved in the wind to reveal what Jayanta was already expecting to find – the handsome profile of Narada. The chief emissary of Devaloka occupied the third arm of the *chausar* board, flanked to his right and left by the apsaras, his position concealed from view by the urn he was leaning against.

"Not again," Narada rued, shaking his head good-humouredly. "Destiny is not playing fair with me today and you two shouldn't be taking advantage of that."

"Hush, your honour," replied Urvashi, placing a flirtatious hand on Narada's knee, her tone placatory, yet ripe with mischief. "We haven't even started yet. We'll soon have you begging for our mercy, won't we?"

She shot Yavika a wicked glance, and with another laugh and a toss of her head, reached her hand out for the pair of dice.

Giving a coy smile, Yavika looked up at Urvashi. Her eyes strayed over her mistress's shoulder, looking further into the bedchamber... and she spotted Jayanta, shuffling from one foot to another indecisively.

"Oh, our lordship," she uttered a small gasp, pushing herself upright, licking her lips in nervousness.

His feet heavy as lead, Jayanta took a few half-hearted steps forward. He watched Urvashi turn and throw him a lazy glance over her shoulder.

"Ah, what brings *you* here?" she asked, her large, beautiful eyes regarding him coolly.

Before the prince had a chance to answer, Narada craned his neck from behind the urn and looked at him.

"Come, come, my lordship," the court diplomat invited, pointing to the empty seat opposite him. "Would you care for a game or two?"

Glancing from Urvashi to Yavika, Narada continued addressing Jayanta. "These two have taken all my gold and have now begun stripping me of my belongings. Help me win back what is rightfully mine, will you?"

"I am not here to indulge in silly games," Jayanta answered harshly, drawing himself erect to stare down at Narada, his lips curling in disdain. Aware of three pairs of eyes assessing him, he added, "How can you be jesting here when Devaloka has been put to disgrace by the humans?"

The ensuing silence warmed Jayanta's heart. He knew he had succeeded in pushing Narada into a corner, making him uncomfortable, and he watched the courtier squirm for a suitable answer.

"Then what are you here for?"

The question came from a totally unexpected quarter – from Urvashi. Jayanta looked at the apsara, who continued to appraise him over her shoulder as if he were some lowly palace hand. Tongue-tied, he glanced at Narada, who was now observing him with twinkling eyes. The prince saw that Urvashi's question had not just given the diplomat an honourable exit, it had turned the tables on him, wresting the initiative out of his hands, putting him firmly on the defensive.

"I came... I wanted to know if... if Menaka said anything of where she... *they* were going," he stumbled through a face-saving explanation while cursing Urvashi at the back of his mind.

The apsara gave a dismissive shrug. "I didn't meet her, so she didn't say."

Jayanta caught Narada's eye and the diplomat shook his head in helplessness as well. Seeing the handsome courtier sprawled next to the apsaras, the thought of him touching them, cavorting with them, brought the prince to a sudden boil.

"How come you don't know anything of this?" he snapped accusingly at Narada. "Shouldn't *you* be aware of what's happening in the palace? Isn't that one of your duties?"

"You are correct, my prince," Narada's reply was equanimous. "But there are times when a king chooses to keep his counsel. My duty is also to respect my king's decision to keep his thoughts private."

Jayanta was still working out a good retort to this one when Urvashi spoke.

"If you were so keen on finding out where they are heading, why didn't you ask the king yourself?" she asked tartly. "Wouldn't a father have humoured a son with an explanation?"

Lashing out like a flail, stinging him, tearing his self-esteem to shreds. Why was she doing this, the prince wondered through the haze of confusion and dismay that was settling around him.

This time, the pregnant silence stretched even longer as the diplomat and the two apsaras waited with sadistic pleasure for Jayanta to respond. A part of him wanted to run out of the room, but the prince knew that was no option. So he stood rooted to the spot, sullen and slouched in despondency, Urvashi's words smarting in his ears.

"I think his lordship would like to be left alone in the company of Urvashi," Narada spoke at last, his eyes locking with Jayanta's. Turning to Yavika, he added with a winsome smile, "Come dear, let us revive our little duel elsewhere – though this time I believe luck will be in my favour."

Retrieving his shawl and turban from the floor, Narada rose to his feet. As Yavika busied herself with gathering the *chausar* board, the shells and the wooden dice, the diplomat stepped in front of Jayanta.

"Thank you for interrupting our game and rescuing me from ruin, my prince," he said, gesturing to the shawl that was now draped over his forearm. The courtier was smiling, but there was a calculative coldness in his eyes that unnerved Jayanta. "With your permission..."

Narada began bowing with the intent of taking his leave, then stopped and looked at the prince as if a thought had struck him.

"I think you must know this, your lordship. I am *always*

aware of what's happening in the palace. I see, I hear, I observe, I deduce. I don't always reveal everything I know." The diplomat paused, as the subtle menace of his words swept the room like an undercurrent. "My silence should never be construed as ignorance."

A shiver went through Jayanta as he watched the door shut on Narada and Yavika. Turning back to the room, he saw Urvashi leaning against the parapet of the terrace, gazing up at the ring of cliffs. The sun was well on its westerly course, and the wind had gained a stiff edge, moulding Urvashi's clothes to her shapely form. Fallen blossoms and leaves, driven by the wind, skittered and rustled over the marble floor of the terrace.

"Why do you treat me this way?"

The prince took a few tentative steps toward the terrace, but stopped when Urvashi turned around to scrutinize him, her eyes flashing.

"How else do you expect me to treat you?" the apsara countered angrily. She leaned back on the railings and crossed her arms across her chest, accentuating the swell of her breasts. Even in the state she was in, she couldn't help being beautiful, Jayanta thought.

"I... I want you to treat me nicely... with... with dignity..." he began weakly, but the apsara cut him short.

"Why? Why do you deserve any dignity?"

"I... because..." Flustered, Jayanta groped for words. "Because I am the son of Indra, lord of Devaloka."

"There you are!" Urvashi threw up her hands as if she had just proved a point and smirked. "You have just admitted who you really are – a *nobody*. You hold onto Indra's name like a crutch, because without that, you amount to *nothing*."

"That's not true..." Jayanta whined in rebellion, but the apsara again interrupted him.

"Do you really think I don't know what brought you to my chambers today?"

The prince dropped his gaze, but Urvashi wasn't done yet.

"You talk of being a man, but you lack the courage of men. You wait for your father to leave the palace before slinking down here to profess your love for me. You stand around making silly excuses in front of mere maids like Yavika instead of speaking boldly, as is wont of a prince. Your behaviour speaks neither of courage nor passion nor love."

"Oh, I love you, Urvashi. I swear I love you." Jayanta took a few more faltering steps toward the apsara, his voice choking and floundering with emotion. "My passion for you runs far deeper than you think. Far deeper than my father's ever can..."

"Now really?" The apsara mimicked the prince's tone. "What makes you believe so?"

"I have been thinking of nothing but you these past few days. I couldn't bear the wait to see you, and every moment was agony. But look at father – he banishes you from his chamber because the Maruts have made fools of themselves in Sindhuvarta. You call that passion? And look how he's gone off somewhere with Menaka. With *Menaka*, not you."

Detaching herself from the parapet, the apsara walked toward Jayanta, her hips sawing seductively, her face softening in the shadows of the approaching sunset. For a fleeting moment, the prince thought he had made some headway, gained a hold on her affection. Then he saw her eyes and realized he was wrong.

"Our king has been thinking of nothing but the pride of Devaloka these past few days. And you? All *you* did during that time was think of me. How can you even compare yourself to your father? On top of that, you had the gall to suggest that Narada and I were *jesting* here. Listen to yourself – how selfish and petty you sound."

"That was meant only for Narada, not you..."

Before Jayanta could essay any further into another

tremulous defence, Urvashi snapped her fingers under his nose, silencing him.

"Enough," she reprimanded. "If you want to be treated with dignity, learn to be half the man your father is. You want to take your father's place in my bed. First go and get the Halahala from the human king. Be of some use to the devas, prove your worth, then come to my bedchamber. Else return to your mother's lap, callow boy."

Jayanta stormed out of the chamber, slamming the heavy door behind him, sparing no thought for the deep reverberations that echoed through the quiet palace. He rushed headlong through the maze of passages, blinded by grief and anger. Bursting into his own room, he hurled himself on the bed, burying his face in a velvet pillow as the first fat tear broke free of its shackles and rolled down his cheek.

He didn't know for how long he lay there weeping his heart out, but when he finally surfaced, red-eyed, the chamber was almost dark, the cliffs outside his window a black silhouette against a deep purple sky riddled with dozens of silvery stars.

Callow boy, she had called him, addressing him the way his father had not long ago, when dismissing him after he had offered to lead an army to Sindhuvarta to get back Veeshada's dagger.

Sniffling and wiping his eyes, Jayanta sat up in his bed.

Yes, he would bring the dagger to Amaravati. He would bring the dagger and heap humiliation on his father, the great Indra. And on Narada and on all the Ashvins and all the Maruts – and on all the devas and apsaras who had dared snigger at him.

He would uproot the human kingdom from its foundations if the need arose, but he would find the Halahala and bring it, he swore to himself.

* * *

"So the king wants to know if the barbarians now commandeer ships."

"We have reason to believe that the Hunas might be amassing ships to attack Sindhuvarta through the Anartas," Shanku said by way of explanation.

"The Anartas," the Mother Oracle's voice inflected with surprise and mild admiration. "By sea... That's clever of the barbarians."

The two women were seated on a wrought-iron bench, high on a knoll in a wooded reserve a little to the north of the palace. The bench overlooked a small portion of Ujjayini, and the palace and lake were partly visible through a break in the shrubbery. The park itself was full of tall, shady trees where birds and squirrels nested, and peacock, black-naped hares and chital frequently sauntered onto the intersecting bridle paths. The spot afforded peace and seclusion, and had become a favourite haunt of the Mother Oracle; she had told Shanku, plainly and quite insistently, that she preferred it here to being anywhere in the palace.

It was obvious to Shanku that her grandmother was having trouble adjusting to Ujjayini.

The first couple of days hadn't been so bad, when the grandeur of the palace, the lake surrounding it, and the bustle of Ujjayini itself had captivated the Mother Oracle's interest. Then the attacks had occurred, and she had been escorted into the safety of the Labyrinth along with the rest of the royal household. After an entire night spent deep in the bowels of the palace, hot and claustrophobic, she had emerged in the morning in a foul temper – one that hadn't entirely left her since.

To top it all, there was hardly any distance between her and the palace dungeons, where Brichcha, the son-in-law she so utterly despised, languished.

It was to take her grandmother's mind away from the

palace that Shanku had suggested a visit to the park. The Mother Oracle had been delighted to discover it, so every evening they came and sat on the bench watching the sun go down. Shanku liked the company of the old woman, listening to the tribe's adventures and hearing stories of her mother, whom she now barely remembered.

"Will you be able to find out about the ships?" she asked.

The Mother Oracle shrugged. "If the birds and the clouds tell me."

"You will ask them, won't you?" Shanku probed.

"Isn't that why I am here?" the Mother Oracle turned and peered at her granddaughter. "To ask these questions on behalf of the king?"

Shanku nodded and turned away, struggling to decipher the oracle's mood. She detected grudging reluctance – probably even hostility – in her grandmother's words. It disquieted her.

Sensing her confusion, the Mother Oracle's voice softened. "Of course I will, my child. The Wandering Tribe always keeps its word." She reached a withered hand out and stroked the girl's hair softly. "Does it still hurt?"

Shanku still wore a bandage around her head, the effect of her fall the night of the attack.

"A little, but not much," she smiled at her grandmother. "Dhanavantri says the wound is healing well and I should be fine in a day or so."

"So you didn't go to the one they call the Healer?" The Mother Oracle looked closely at Shanku.

"No. The Healer has had to tend to so many of our severely wounded that I didn't have the heart to go to him for something as small as this." She looked toward the city, which was turning golden in colour. "Ujjayini owes the Healer so much."

"I fear when the time comes, the price he will exact

from Ujjayini will be adequately steep," remarked the Mother Oracle.

"Why do you say that?" Shanku swung around sharply.

Instead of replying, the old woman sniffed and changed the topic. "Don't you remember how you did it... the disappearing, I mean?"

The girl looked down at her hands and shook her head.

"You must... remember *something*, child," the oracle's tone was gentle, helpful. "What did you feel at that time... what you were thinking... *something*."

"I saw the demon's foot coming down on me and I desperately wanted to be somewhere else."

"Where?" The Mother Oracle pressed.

"*Anywhere*. I... just wanted to not be where I was."

"Then you must try to do it again, child."

Shanku stared at her grandmother in puzzlement.

"It is a gift that you have. Like the gift I have of being able to read signs. We all have gifts, though most of us sadly never discover it for ourselves. It's not a choice, we just have it. But knowing you have a gift and doing something useful, something good with it – *that* is a choice. That is why you must learn to master your gift, child. Master it, control it, and wield it with wisdom."

Grandmother and granddaughter sat in silence for a while, watching a flock of egrets sail over the city, returning home to roost. The sun was turning orange, bleeding its colour into the sky, and overhead, the bats had begun stirring.

"There is another thing the king would like to know," said Shanku. "Last week, a Huna scout we had captured near the frontier died in his cell in Sristhali under suspicious circumstances. We believe he was killed by someone from our side, a traitor who didn't want us to learn anything from the scout. Do you think..."

She stopped on seeing the oracle shake her head.

"For that, I would probably need to visit Sristhali, and even that might amount to nothing. And this incident happened last week, you say." The Mother Oracle shook her head more definitively. "No, I don't think I can be of help here."

She began to rise from her seat and Shanku reached over to help her. As she grasped her granddaughter's arm for support, the oracle spoke again in a voice that, to Shanku's mind, was layered with hidden meaning.

"But if the purpose is to find out if the enemy is near, then yes, the enemy is near. I think your king is already aware of that."

* * *

Vikramaditya was about to set foot on the terrace when he heard her laugh.

It was a clear, liquid sound, filling and lifting into the air. It mingled with the fragrance of the jasmines blooming nearby, and intertwined with the soft moonbeams that shone down through the tatters in the clouds, a concoction of delight and enchantment that made the breath catch in the samrat's throat.

It was the first time he had heard Vishakha's laughter since that fateful morning when she had set out to ride with her sister. She had come to their bed to wake him, and when he had drowsily tried to grab her and pull her to him, she had slapped his hand away in play and leaped out of his reach. He remembered having mumbled something about it being unfair to have woken him and deprived him of a kiss, to which she had laughingly retorted that if he wanted a kiss from her, he would have to come after her.

He hadn't gone after her. He had snuggled back to sleep, instead. Vishakha had punished him for that with two years of cold, indifferent silence.

Vikramaditya had lost count of the number of times he

had wished he had risen to Vishakha's bait that morning, and accompanied her and Kshapanaka to the meadow. If he had been with them, perhaps he would have prevented Vishakha from accepting her sister's challenge to try riding her mount. And even if he had let Vishakha ride Kshapanaka's horse, perhaps he would have ridden by her side to make sure the unpredictable beast behaved itself. Perhaps he would have sensed the horse's impatience with its new rider, and would have stepped in before it reared and threw his wife off its back. Perhaps, even after her fall, he would have been able to rush Vishakha back to the palace quicker so Dhanavantri could attend to her sooner...

Vishakha's laugh issued from the terrace once again, a softer lilt that infused the king with warmth and hope, making the day's cares and worries drain magically off his shoulders. Vikramaditya ached to catch a glimpse of his wife's smiling face, the sparkle of mirth in her eyes, the carefree toss of her head whenever something struck her as being funny. Yet he hung back in the shadows of the doorway to the terrace, reluctant to take a step further for fear that he might disturb the moment, making it unravel and fall apart like an illusion.

"You have to be with her, Vikrama," the samrat heard Queen Upashruti's words echo in his head. "You have been with her all the while she wasn't there. Now that she is coming back, help her make that journey. Be brave, my son, because Vishakha needs you to be brave now more than ever."

Steeling himself, the king took a deep breath and walked onto the terrace. His mother was right. It didn't matter that his wife still didn't recognize him. It didn't matter that this broke his heart and crippled his spirit. The only thing of consequence was that he loved Vishakha and would wait for her to rediscover her love for him.

Vikramaditya didn't have to look to find Vishakha. Two large and wide ornamental swings nestled in one corner of the terrace, partially concealed by a cluster of hibiscus shrubs. A low murmur of voices came from the direction of the shrubs, and as the king approached, he could tell that Vishakha had Kshapanaka for company.

It was probably a footfall that gave him away, but by the time the samrat rounded the corner, the two siblings from the erstwhile kingdom of Nishada had fallen silent and were looking expectantly in his direction. In the light of the four decorative lamps suspended from the swings' crosspieces, Vikramaditya could tell that the sisters had been threading red and pink hibiscus flowers into garlands as they sat chatting. The king sensed a twitch of jealousy, unreasonable yet overwhelming. He felt like an intruder, unwanted, unwelcome.

"Samrat, what a lovely surprise!" Kshapanaka's eyes lit up with genuine delight on seeing Vikramaditya, and her tone was inviting. "I didn't know you were back in the palace. Come, sit with us."

"I..." Seized by uncertainty, the samrat fell back again. He glanced at Vishakha, who met his gaze for a moment before looking at Kshapanaka. The queen then dropped her eyes to the garland lying on her lap.

"I didn't know you were here," the king fumbled. "I was... it wasn't my intention to bother the two of you."

"Oh, it's nothing. We were just making garlands." Kshapanaka looked at her sister briefly, and even in the dim light, Vikramaditya could see the glow of affection in the councilor's face. When she turned back to him, Kshapanaka's eyes wore a thoughtful expression.

Leaning to her right, the councilor looked down at the floor of the terrace. There, by the side of the swing she sat on, was an open clay bowl used to burn incense. The samrat could see that the bowl was full of cold ash.

"Oh no, it has gone out again." Reaching down, Kshapanaka

picked up the bowl. "Why don't you sit, Samrat? I will go and find someone to fill in some more *sambrani* and charcoal."

"You don't need to go. You could summon a servant to do it," the king offered a token suggestion, knowing his words sounded hollow and insincere. He realized what Kshapanaka was doing, and he felt ashamed at having let jealousy take hold of him, however fleetingly.

"No, I'll do it," Kshapanaka smiled as she got off her swing. There was decisiveness in her tone and manner as she walked tactfully away, leaving neither Vikramaditya nor Vishakha with an opportunity to lay a protest.

As the councilor's footsteps faded away, Vikramaditya stood awkwardly by the swing, knotting his fingers. He stole a glance at Vishakha, who sat with her head bowed, twirling a hibiscus between thumb and forefinger.

"Can I... sit?" The samrat pointed at the empty space on the swing beside his wife.

Vishakha raised her head, looked at him and nodded.

Vikramaditya lowered himself down and began swaying back and forth in gentle arcs. The space between the king and his queen quivered with stilted silence, overpowering them both, stretching across the terrace as if it intended to take a hold over the entire palace and the lake. It amplified the faraway clomping of horse hooves on the palace causeway, which lay at the end furthest from the terrace. To the samrat, it felt as if the palace was holding its breath, listening in on what he had to say to Vishakha.

"Lovely moonlight," Vikramaditya looked up at the sky.

Vishakha followed his gaze, nodded again and looked down at her lap.

Seeing he was making no headway with small talk, the king took a different tack. "What were you and Kshapanaka talking about?"

"We were... she..." Even though the light was low, the

samrat observed a blush steal across Vishakha's face. "She was telling me how we were afraid of the king, how we used to hide from him. It seems she once jumped into the palace lake because the king rode onto the causeway and she had nowhere else to run. I used… she says I used to tell her the king would kill us if we didn't behave ourselves."

"Which king is this?" Vikramaditya framed the question nonchalantly, but his eyes were sharp as they considered the queen.

"King Mahendraditya."

"Do you remember him?" the samrat asked.

"He was a big man," Vishakha nodded. "He had a loud voice and a big, black beard. I think that was what scared us. But I also seem to think of him as being very kind."

Vikramaditya nodded. There had been nothing small about King Mahendraditya. Burly in build, his father was prone to exaggerations – a boisterous laugh, a roaring rage, and a large heart that always had room to spare for friends. Legend had it that when Avanti's soldiers had found Mahendraditya lying mortally wounded on the battlefield, his stomach cut open by a Saka sword, the first thing their king had asked for was his battle-axe, so he could hunt down the Saka warrior who had inflicted the grievous injury.

The samrat also recalled his father being the antithesis of King Vallabha, Vishakha and Kshapanaka's father and the late king of Nishada. Vallabha had been a gentle, soft-spoken man full of civilities, so it was only natural the sisters found the loud, hard-swearing Mahendraditya intimidating. It had taken Mahendraditya over a year to earn the young girls' trust and confidence – that too only after he had followed Kshapanaka into the palace lake to save her from drowning. Later, after Vallabha and his court had been publicly executed by the invading Huna army, Mahendraditya had emerged as a surrogate father to the girls, building a deep, affectionate bond with them that lasted until the day the king left the palace gates one last time, borne on four shoulders to the cremation ground across the Kshipra.

"Who else do you remember?" Vikramaditya tried to keep his tone gentle despite his eagerness.

"My mother and my father. And Itti *tai*." A sadness crept over Vishakha's face. "Kshapanaka tells me they are all dead... that they were killed by invaders." Then, as if realizing the drift of Vikramaditya's question, she looked directly at him. "By who else... you mean *here*?"

The king shrugged and inclined his head vaguely, reluctant to force the conversation where he wanted it to go.

"The queen... the king's wife... Queen Upashruti, I mean."

"Anyone else?"

"There was the raj-guru..." Vishakha paused for a bit. "Kshapanaka pointed him out to me this afternoon. He doesn't look like the raj-guru who used to tutor Kshapanaka, me and the other children in the palace. This raj-guru is thinner and older."

Vishakha tilted her head and frowned, as if something was bothering her. "I suddenly seem to remember another man," she said. "Very strong, massive forearms and shoulders, with a thick red beard and huge earrings. Very fierce looking. I don't know whether he was here in the palace, though I think he was."

The samrat's heart skipped a beat.

Amara Simha!

"What about the other children in the palace whom the raj-guru tutored?" he pressed. "Do you remember any of them?"

Vishakha shook her head and looked away.

The samrat could feel a heavy weight crush his chest. "You don't remember me?"

Vikramaditya posed the question in spite of himself, in spite of knowing what her answer would be, knowing he was setting himself up for disappointment.

Vishakha didn't answer for a long time. She just sat on her end of the swing, staring down at the hibiscus in her hand, caressing its petals softly between thumb and forefinger.

"I was told... Kshapanaka tells me you are... we are married." Vishakha finally raised her head to look at Vikramaditya. Her voice was timid and unsure, her eyes large and filled with fear. "You are... my husband. But I don't remember... I am sorry."

The samrat raised a hand to reach out to Vishakha, but he changed his mind and let the hand drop limp by his side. Instead, he nodded and gave her a smile of reassurance, which he knew was crumbling at the edges. As he looked away, the queen spoke again.

"Will you help me remember?"

Vikramaditya turned sharply to Vishakha. This time, in her eyes he saw more than fear. He saw hope and expectation. He saw a search for promise.

"I will." The king couldn't trust himself to say more without breaking into sobs of relief. He felt the tears stinging his eyes as he stretched to pat Vishakha's hand. The queen instantly gripped his hand, squeezing, seeking comfort in touch.

"What if I don't – what if I *can't*?" she whispered, her lips trembling. "What if... this is the way it will be until the very end?"

"*I* will help you remember." Not willing to consider that possibility, Vikramaditya forced resolve into his voice. For the first time in years, Vishakha had reached out to him – he wouldn't let this moment pass. "I will do everything it takes. I will fight death itself, if need be, but you will remember. It is a promise."

They had hardly sat a minute in silence, holding hands, when they heard the shuffle of approaching footsteps. Looking up, they expected to see Kshapanaka returning, but instead, they were rewarded by the sight of the Healer.

"Ah, so you are *here*!" the Healer exclaimed on seeing Vishakha. Then, on finding the king seated by her side, he stopped abruptly as if in confusion. "Oh... oh, I didn't know you were here too, Samrat."

"It is a wonderful moonlit night and we were admiring its beauty," Vikramaditya replied.

"Indeed it is." The Healer looked down at their entwined fingers. "It is late. The queen should be resting. Come, child. Let us go inside."

Vishakha looked at the king, who nodded once. Releasing his fingers, the queen rose.

"Come, don't dally," the Healer's manner appeared brusque, even agitated, as he waved his hand, urging speed. "You shouldn't be out here so late. You should be asleep. Come now."

As Vikramaditya gained his feet, Vishakha cast one last look back at him, and the king knew she wanted to stay. The Healer, however, was already herding his patient away into the palace. Watching the retreating figure of the Healer, something stirred and squirmed its way forward in the samrat's mind.

It was the morning Vishakha had started recollecting bits and pieces from her childhood in Nishada. Despite the overarching gloom wrought by the rakshasa attack just two days earlier, the palace of Ujjayini had burst with hope and excitement on learning about the improvement in the queen's condition. Palace Guards were dispatched to fetch the Healer from the hospice in the palace ground, and much of the royal household was crammed into Vishakha's bedchamber, waiting with bated breath for the Healer to show up.

The Healer had eventually arrived and made an assessment of Vishakha's progress – and that was when Vikramaditya noticed it. For a fleeting instant, the Healer had looked more shocked than excited or pleased with the evidence in front of him. The expression on the Healer's face had passed in the twinkling of an eye, but in its passing, like an inefficient servant, it had left a trace of itself behind in Vikramaditya's memory.

Now, allowing the scene to unspool in his mind's eye, it struck the king that more than just being shocked, the Healer had appeared positively perturbed and worried – even panicked – at the change he was witnessing in Vishakha. Perhaps, in that fraction of light and shadow where indecision nested, the Healer's eyes had even betrayed fear.

And besides fear, something else – *greed*?

As he followed the Healer and Vishakha out of the terrace, the samrat pondered over what the Mother Oracle had said to him the morning he had gone to see her.

Beware of the stranger in the palace, wise king.

Gift

Shanku's first instinct was to duck for cover.

Seized by a frenzy of panic, her eyes darted about her, looking for a place to hide, but out on the open steps of the palace bath, there was nothing to offer her concealment.

Standing exposed in the middle of the steps, rooted to the spot with five steep stairs behind her and four in front descending to the large, rectangular bath, Shanku realized that no matter what she did, she would be discovered by either Queen Upashruti, or by one or the other of the maids attending to the Queen Mother.

Turning red with embarrassment and wondering what explanation she could proffer for her unexpected appearance at the royal bath, the girl watched as one maid oiled the queen's hair, while another slathered sandalwood paste on the queen's arms. A third maid was busy laying out a fresh set of clothes, while the Queen Mother herself sat on the edge of the bath, her feet dipped into the water up to the knees. None of the women by the pool was looking in Shanku's direction – but a subtle tilt of the head or even a slight raising of the eyes was sufficient to reveal her presence to them.

A sudden flutter of wings from the pigeons roosting amid the rafters overhead startled Shanku. And as if that was all that was needed for her brain to kick into action, it occurred to her that she knew precisely what she had to do to escape from the bath undetected.

She just had to concentrate on being somewhere else.

The thought was still making its way through her mind, when Shanku felt the bath blur and dissolve before her eyes. The sensation made her head spin mildly, forcing her to blink a couple of times.

When her vision stabilized, Shanku found herself staring at a fat, white silkworm crawling across a broad, bright green leaf with serrated edges. The worm and the leaf were just inches away from her nose, making Shanku jerk her head back in revulsion as the worm arched its back and reared on its stubby hind legs, stretching and waving to grab at a tight bunch of black mulberries that overhung the leaf.

"You will rely solely on your senses of smell and hearing, is that clear?"

Shanku froze, before realizing that the words had come from a fair distance away, and given their context, couldn't have been directed at her. She recognized the voice as Angamitra's.

"Listen to the wind and the small changes in its pitch as the birds fly past," the captain of the *samsaptakas* continued in a high, clear tone infused with authority. "Still your breathing so you can catch the whisper of a leaf falling to the ground."

With great economy of movement, Shanku turned to her left and peered through the leaves of the mulberry bush. She had already guessed where she was – in a training camp in the western quarter of Ujjayini, used exclusively for the training of young *samsaptaka* recruits. Pushing a branch gently aside, she peeked out in the direction of Angamitra's voice to see the captain standing in front of a row of seven young men wearing blindfolds. The *samsaptakas* were nearly fifty yards away, in the middle of an open field, out of earshot. Shanku's eyes flitted right and left, taking in the heavily wooded training ground with its camouflaged mud pits and ingenious rope traps, before returning to Angamitra and his seven blindfolded cadets.

"Teach yourselves to tell the smell of a horse from that of a mare," Angamitra instructed the new recruits. "To discern the smell of fear from the smell of excitement in a man's sweat. Master the senses of smell and hearing, for these are the skills of the predator. Master these and you can fight even if you have been blinded."

Letting the branch fall softly back in place, Shanku exhaled in relief. It was sheer luck that she had ended up behind this dense thicket of mulberry bushes. She could well have appeared somewhere in that open field, in plain view of Angamitra, which would have left her with a lot of explaining to do.

You must learn to master your gift, child. Master it, control it, and wield it with wisdom.

Shanku frowned at the thought of the Mother Oracle's words. The previous night, standing before the tin mirror in her bedchamber, she had tried using what her grandmother had termed *her gift*. She had wanted to see if she could disappear from where she was and appear in her bed. At first, nothing had happened – and then, suddenly, Shanku had found herself on the uppermost terrace of the palace, looking down over the lamp-lit causeway and the black waters of the lake.

Rattled by the experience, she had quietly returned to her room, but daybreak found her filled with the resolve to have another go. Once again, she had tried to move herself from one end of her bedchamber to another – only to end up on the steps of the palace bath, almost under Queen Upashruti's nose. And now she was here, in one overgrown corner of the *samsaptaka* training camp, miles away from the palace.

She was nowhere near controlling her gift, much less mastering it. And at the rate she was going, she would end up making a complete fool of herself, appearing somewhere unannounced and uninvited, an embarrassment to herself and those around her. She knew she had to exercise more care and caution while experimenting with her gift, but she had no idea how.

"How are the new recruits faring? Are they learning anything, or are they just a waste of your and Angamitra's time?"

Shanku jumped on hearing Vetala Bhatta's voice.

"The new recruits are... yes, I think they are okay," Kalidasa's voice sounded more distant to Shanku's ears, probably on account of a shift in the early morning breeze.

Both voices had come from the direction of a path that wound through the trees, leading away from the training ground toward a forest of wild trees and shrubbery. The path bordered the thicket where Shanku was concealed, and followed the natural curvature of the mulberry bushes. Taking utmost care not to make a noise, planting her feet softly on the dew-damp grass so her anklets wouldn't chime, the girl edged over to the bushes adjoining the path.

"What I meant is, will they make good *samsaptakas*?" Shanku detected an undercurrent of impatience in the Acharya's otherwise calm tone.

Crouching to see through a small gap in the leaves, the girl observed Kalidasa and the chief councilor standing in the middle of the pathway, watching the cadets as they went through their exercises.

"We will know only after their training is complete, raj-guru," the giant answered with a shrug and a mild note of resignation. "We can only hope they will. We lost nearly a dozen *samsaptakas* during the asura attack, and good *samsaptakas* are hard to replace."

"At least you have a larger pool to choose from now," Vetala Bhatta countered. "The last I heard, the number of soldiers volunteering to join the *samsaptakas* has doubled ever since the asura attack. You are an inspiration for Avanti's soldiers, Kalidasa."

"I agree." Shanku heard Dhanavantri speak moments before the physician's broad bulk stepped into her line of vision, almost blotting out the Acharya's lean frame. Though he had his back to her, Shanku could tell the physician was grinning.

"I reckon half of Avanti's soldiers want to become a Kalidasa by throwing an asura into the palace lake," Dhanavantri continued with a chuckle. "As long as the other half doesn't get it into their heads to start writing poetry, it should be fine with me."

As a small bubble of laughter burst and scattered along the path, Shanku caught herself smiling at the mental image of Avanti's barracks filled with dreamy-eyed soldiers scratching on palm leaves with quills. The councilors on the path eventually fell silent and returned to observing the cadets of the field.

"I presume the two of you didn't come all the way here to discuss how my new recruits are faring," Kalidasa turned and looked down at his companions. "May I know what brings you here?"

Though couched in the mildest of terms, the bluntness of the question had plainly stumped the Acharya and Dhanavantri. Noticing the two councilors exchange glances, it dawned on Shanku that she shouldn't be eavesdropping on this conversation. Yet, by moving around, she risked exposing herself. She was also certain she didn't want to try using her *gift* once more – there was no telling where, and in how much awkwardness, she would end up. Two near disasters were enough for one morning, she decided.

Moreover, her curiosity had been piqued.

"We are a bit... concerned about you, Kalidasa," the raj-guru spoke gently.

"Concerned about what?" the giant looked puzzled.

"You haven't been your usual self of late. You look distracted, as if something is weighing on your mind."

Kalidasa turned to consider the field, deep in thought. "Well, I haven't been sleeping too well," he offered almost grudgingly.

"Why is that?" asked Dhanavantri.

Kalidasa kept staring into the field for a moment longer before turning his attention to the physician.

"My sleep is disturbed because I see things while I'm asleep. And I don't fall asleep easily because of the things I see flash through my mind."

"You are disturbed by dreams?" asked the Acharya.

"I don't know if they are dreams," the giant replied.

"What do you see?" asked Dhanavantri.

Kalidasa didn't answer immediately. Instead, he ran his fingers through his hair, brushing it back, knotting it into a ponytail. Shanku could see his eyes looked troubled.

"The things I see don't make much sense. Sometimes, I am on a horse, charging across an open plain. I know there are others behind me, all on horses, all galloping, but I have no idea who they are. Everyone is shouting. Don't ask me how I know this, but there is a lust for blood in the air. And there is this man riding right behind me. He is after me, and when I turn to look, he raises a bow with an arrow nocked in place. He points the arrow in my direction, draws the bowstring back and shouts at me."

"You don't recognize this man?"

"It is too hazy," Kalidasa shook his head. "He somehow

seems familiar, but I am almost sure I haven't seen the man before."

"What does he say when he shouts at you?"

"I don't understand a word of what he says."

"What happens then?"

"Nothing. That is the end of it. But this image keeps coming back to me, sometimes when I am asleep, sometimes when I am awake. I can't say if it is something I dreamt that comes back to me when I am awake, or if it is something I imagined when I was awake that returns to haunt me in my dreams."

"There are others like this one?" the Acharya placed a gentle hand on Kalidasa's arm.

"A fire has been lit and people are sitting around it," the giant nodded. "Again, I don't know who these people are. Everything is hazy. I know I am there, and I know the fire has been lit for me. Why? I have no idea, but I know the fire has something to do with me. One of the figures by the fire stands up and he – it looks like a man – is holding a dagger. I instinctively know the dagger is meant to hurt me. I can feel its cutting pain, the fear surging up my throat, my heartbeat going faster... Then there is nothing. It just ends."

"Are there any more?" Dhanavantri probed.

The way Kalidasa paused for just a fraction of a second, Shanku could tell he was in two minds. He turned and started ambling slowly down the path.

"There are more, but... they aren't as persistent, so I can't remember them."

Shanku thought the giant wasn't being entirely honest and it made her wonder why.

"Since when have you been seeing these sequences?" Vetala Bhatta fell in step beside the giant. The physician joined them a moment later.

"The past few days. They just flash through my mind when

I am least expecting them. They come..." Kalidasa snapped his fingers, "...and they are gone."

The three councilors slipped from Shanku's view, their voices and footsteps fading as they drew away. She shifted on her haunches to keep them in sight, but the shrubs restricted her vision.

"I shall give you something to calm your nerves and induce sleep," Dhanavantri's words, assured and reassuring, floated to her ears. "Let us watch for a few days and see if..."

A thieving breeze blew the rest of it away.

* * *

"Are you sure you are going through with this decision of yours?"

King Harihara, seated on a thick cotton quilt and bent low over a writing table, paused shuffling between a stack of palm leaves, his face clouding with annoyance. For a moment he was quiet, sour-face, shoulders hunched, elbows pressed against his ribs, hands holding the palm leaves perfectly still, contemplating the inkwell on the table. He gave the impression of a stork caught in an unexpected cloudburst – stiff, awkward and unhappy.

Queen Sumayanti stared back at her husband, her delicate features rid of all expression. She was a small woman with a plain face that was ageing gracefully, imparting her with a charm and dignity that youth had denied her. Sitting upright on the edge of her chair, legs crossed, hands clasped daintily over an upraised knee, she was a picture of poise and self-possession.

Faltering under her steady gaze, Harihara looked away. "We cannot have another Kulabheda raising his vile head inside this palace," he mumbled. Laying the palm leaves on the table, he reached for a quill. "Rukma is gaining in years, and her place is in her husband's house."

"I presume you have communicated your decision to Vikramaditya's court as well?"

Harihara's head snapped up, his eyes hot and indignant. "Why should I?" The flat monotone of her voice notwithstanding, he was wise enough to guess that the queen had presumed no such thing. "Rukma is *my* daughter. What business is it of anybody's where I choose to give her hand in marriage?"

"You won't even let the son of your oldest ally in Sindhuvarta know?" For the first time, there was an inflection in Sumayanti's voice, chiding, barely a ripple in satin.

"I will... when the time is right." Again, the king avoided his wife's eyes.

"Vikramaditya is the only reason why Rukma escaped Kulabheda's clutches." The queen's words were now underscored by an accusatory tone. "Vikramaditya is the only reason why you and I are sitting here, breathing in the fresh air and soaking in the warm sun, instead of wasting away in the stale dungeons below. And you act as if you owe him nothing."

Harihara threw the quill down in exasperation.

"Look, I have work to do." He thrust his hands toward the tabletop piled with palm leaves. "The garrison of Payoshni lies in ruins, and four villages need to be built from scratch. Our Minister of Revenue is awaiting my approval on increasing taxes and levies, and I have to go through this proposal of his. So stop bothering me now."

Reaching for the quill once again, he added as an afterthought, "And lest we forget, Avanti is the only reason the kingdom of Heheya had to suffer the wrath of those pishachas. Look at the losses we have incurred," he pointed his quill in the general direction of the palm leaves.

"You can't be serious," Sumayanti looked aghast at the suggestion. Seeing her husband squirm, she added, "And if I am not mistaken, Vikramaditya has offered more than just his regrets for what Heheya had to endure. I am told Kalidasa brought a chest of gold with him for our treasury."

"So? What about that?" Harihara eyed the queen combatively. "One chest of gold doesn't go far to compensate for our losses."

"It isn't about a chest of gold. It is about what allies do for one another."

"I have lent three thousand of my infantry and a thousand of my cavalry to help protect Avanti from the Hunas," the king grumbled. "Don't go around lecturing me on what allies are supposed to do. Now if you will leave me, I can get back to work."

Sumayanti rose, but instead of leaving, she walked across the room to an east-facing window. Reaching up, she pulled the drapes drawn across the window apart, allowing the morning sunlight to flood the chamber. The sudden surge in brightness made Harihara flinch.

"What are you doing?" he protested, blinking and raising an arm to ward the light off his eyes. "Please shut it."

Ignoring the plea, Sumayanti stared out of the window that overlooked an orchard of mango, papaya and neem trees.

"What made you suddenly decide this was a good match for Rukma?" she asked.

The king peered at Sumayanti. Bathed in the golden-white light of the morning, he felt she had acquired a soft translucence that reminded him of the mother-of-pearl statuettes that formed the pieces on his *chaturanga* board. The thought of the *chaturanga* set with its exquisitely carved war elephants, chariots, cavalry and infantry – a gift from King Mahendraditya on his coronation as king of Heheya – made Harihara uncomfortable.

"Why isn't it a good match?" he countered. "As queen of a powerful kingdom, our daughter will enjoy the status and respect reserved for the most privileged of Sindhuvarta."

"This despite what is supposed to have happened in the palace of Girivraja?"

"Rumours," Harihara waved a hand dismissively. "Mere rumours. Who is to say what actually happened?"

"There was a witness..."

"Humph!" The king snorted, cutting Sumayanti off mid-sentence. "Since when did we begin to trust the word of a common musician over that of a king?"

The couple stared at one another for a few moments, the deadlock stretching and humming balefully in the ether between them.

"Now, with your permission, can I get on with these?" Harihara waved the two palm leaves in his left hand, his voice laced with sarcasm.

Without another word, Sumayanti turned on her heel and left the room. Harihara watched her depart until the door had closed firmly behind her, before returning to his revenue calculations. However, barely a minute later, he looked up distractedly, unable to focus on the numbers. The morning had passed off on a decidedly unsatisfactory note, and the king could sense a foul mood brewing in him. If he had to go through the rest of the day on his terms, he knew he had to reassert his authority over what remained of the morning.

Placing the quill back in its stand, Harihara tugged a tasseled bell rope that hung nearby. A tiny bell chimed somewhere, and almost immediately, an attendant appeared from an anteroom, bowing deeply.

"Fetch me some buttermilk," he ordered. "Make sure they don't spice it up with too many curry leaves, though. What they served yesterday wasn't fit for stable boys. Also, draw those drapes before you go. This infernal sun is blinding me."

As the servant began drawing the drapes, Harihara addressed him again. "I want you to inform the royal scribe and the court calligrapher to present themselves here this afternoon, after my siesta. Instruct them to come well prepared – they need to draft a very important letter intended for a king."

***

The goblet was large and heavy, made of tempered brass and bound by an inlay of iron that formed an intricate pattern along its smooth, rounded surface. It was big enough to sit smack in the middle of Indra's palm, bulging and spilling outward from the curl of his thick fingers.

Yet, ever so slowly, it changed shape.

First narrowing at the mouth, then progressively losing its roundness, it crumpled from the sides as Indra exerted greater and greater force on the hard metal, crushing it in his inexorable grip. The deva's knuckles turned white and the tendons in his forearm shivered under the strain, but the grasp around the goblet grew tighter still until the cup imploded, sending a splash of red soma over the lip and running down Indra's fingers.

The touch of the cool, tingling wine snapped Indra out of the black pit of rage he was sinking into. With a jerk of his head, he looked up and about him, his gaze barely registering the open sweep of the misty garden that rolled out from the foot of the wide terrace where he stood. Eventually, sensing the soma trickle down his forearm and drip on his toes, the deva glanced down at the twisted remains of the goblet.

A red-hot bolt of anger erupted and surged up his chest once again.

Taking a firm grip on the cup, his lips stretched in a grimace, Indra drew his arm and flung the goblet out across the terrace. The cup sailed through the air, a high arc of yellow metal, spinning and glinting as it went over the parapet. It fell on the marbled pathway that led down to the nearby lake, bouncing twice on the stone steps before disappearing into the shrubbery that bordered the pathway. As the sharp, echoing ring of metal on stone died in the soft folds of mist, a voice spoke from behind Indra.

"You must be patient, my lord. I am doing everything I can to please Kubera."

Indra turned, his cold blue eyes settling on the gorgeous apsara who stood leaning against the arched doorway that connected the terrace to the splendid lake house with its steeply tiled roofs, water curtains, porcelain wind chimes and lilting water music. The apsara was a delight to behold, sumptuous in form, her milky-white skin gilded with the blush of dawn. She had deep black eyes, pools of subtle seduction in a face that could melt iron, and her lips almost pleaded to be caressed and kissed.

"I don't doubt that, Menaka," Indra's voice rumbled in his throat as he struggled to quell the rising tides of passion the apsara was stirring in him. Averting his gaze, he added, "And I hate him all the more for that."

"Hush, my lord," Menaka placed a theatrical finger on her lips as she stepped onto the terrace. "We are the yaksha's guests and it is bad form for guests to speak ill of their hosts."

"*He* hasn't had the courtesy to call on me or invite me to his palace," the deva glowered moodily at the lake. "He hasn't even acknowledged my presence here. It is as if I don't exist. How is *that* good form?"

It had been three days since Indra and Menaka had arrived on the misty shores of Lake Alaka. The mist-wraiths that manned the ferry crossing had welcomed them without question or challenge, and once Airavata had been entrusted to the care of an old yaksha elephant keeper, the deva and the apsara had been escorted, unbidden, to the lake house on its tiny island. Neither Kubera nor any of his yaksha ministers or lieutenants had put in an appearance, though Indra guessed that Kubera knew about this sudden, unscheduled visit – and possibly even the reason behind it.

The deva also knew that the passage into Alaka wouldn't have been as easy – or the welcome as cordial, if it could be called that – had Menaka not been by his side.

The morning after their arrival, a narrow boat had materialized out of the surrounding mists and nudged the steps leading up to the pathway to the house. Upon investigation, Indra and Menaka had found that it was empty, and constructed to seat just one person under its small, sloping roof. The moment Indra made to get on board, the boat drifted away from the shore, but when Menaka attempted to get on, it bobbed in the water, docile and willing.

It was plain that the boat had come to claim Kubera's gift.

Since that morning, the boat had routinely made an appearance two or even three times a day, bearing the apsara away into the mist before bringing her back hours later. On two occasions, Indra had tried to force his way into the boat, but both times the boat had easily slipped his strong grasp and receded into the mist, returning to the shore only for Menaka.

So the deva had reconciled to waiting, quaffing soma and chaffing at the delay, stewing with anger while the sensuous apsara kept Kubera company. He loathed the solitude and isolation of the lake house with its eerie music and its silent mist-wraiths who fulfilled every wish before the wishes were even clearly articulated. He had all the comforts he needed, yet he felt like a prisoner, confined to his island, held captive by the cold water and the clammy mist. He knew that the lake was dotted with hundreds of islands that housed palaces, markets and the yakshas' magic-foundries, but he couldn't help feeling lost and lonely in this strange, alien land that Kubera had claimed as his own so many years ago.

"Perhaps the yaksha king is hard to please," Menaka

offered by way of explanation. "Pardon me, my lord, but I will strive even harder."

The sincerity in the apsara's voice made Indra flinch just a bit.

"This is not about you, Menaka. This is just his way of trying to prove how superior he is. He knows I am here for a reason, and he wants to revel in the knowledge that he can make me wait for an audience with him." What the deva left unsaid was that the delay in granting an audience also prolonged the time the yaksha spent with the apsara. "Kubera is a sadist."

A sudden squawk came from just above Indra's right shoulder, startling the deva. Glancing up, he eyed a wicker cage hanging from a bough of the cherry tree, the parrot inside it observing him with its beady, black eye. The first morning Menaka had been to Kubera's palace, she had returned with the bird, a gift for her from the yaksha king.

"Stupid bird," Indra spat in annoyance. "I have half a mind of wringing the silly thing's neck."

The parrot shuffled away a few steps, ruffled its feathers and cocked its head, as if waiting to see if the deva had any more niceties to add.

"Don't say that," said Menaka, opening the small door to the cage and crooking two fingers toward the bird, enticing it to come to her. The parrot responded immediately by hopping onto the apsara's hand. "It is a beautiful bird. I've never seen one quite like this before."

Jealousy sputtered and burst inside Indra, making him choke on his words. "There are lots of these in the hills around Devaloka. Nothing so special about this one. I could have got you a dozen of them had you said so."

Feeling a sudden craving for soma, he regretted having thrown the goblet away. At that very instant, out of the corner of his eye, he sensed a mist-wraith appear near a low table placed next to the doorway. In the twinkling of an eye, the wraith placed a fresh goblet on the table and vaporized.

The deva made for the table. "Hasn't Kubera given *any* indication of when he will see me?" he threw the question over his shoulder.

Picking up the newly filled goblet, Indra gulped a large measure of its contents down. As the spicy liquid sizzled its way past his gullet, the deva heard Menaka reply.

"All he's ever said to that question is that when the time comes, you will be informed, my lord." After a slight pause, she added, "He has also instructed me not to rob the joy out of our lovemaking by nagging him."

Flush with indignation, the king of the devas spun around to face Menaka, his heavy bearded face livid at the thought of the apsara and the yaksha together in bed. He knew the pangs of envy were bizarre and misplaced – stupid even, considering his purpose behind bringing Menaka here – yet he couldn't help feeling he was being cheated. He opened his mouth to retort, but the words caught in his throat as he observed the apsara put the parrot back into its cage. Her back was to him, and as she raised her hands to steady the swaying cage, the supple spread of her waist beckoned invitingly. His eyes trailed the curves and folds of her body, the sight filling him with a rush of passion that descended over him in an avalanche.

"What is it, my lord?"

Indra blinked and stared at the apsara. The parrot was back in its cage, and the apsara now stood looking at him with large doe-like eyes, the soft mist swirling around her softness, making her irresistible. The deva swallowed hard and remembered to exhale.

"I cannot let the yaksha have you all for himself." Placing the half-empty cup on the table, Indra took two steps toward the apsara, his eyes burning with desire.

"The yaksha doesn't have me at all, my king," Menaka

replied, stepping forward, opening her arms to embrace the deva. "In my heart and my mind, it is always you."

The deva and the apsara came together in a tight, hungry clasp, hands groping over bare flesh, seeking purchase, fevered breaths escaping through wet, parted lips, nostrils flared to soak in the heady scents of love and lust. But as Indra dropped his head to plant a kiss on Menaka's exposed shoulder, a harsh, grating, jarring squawk issued from the birdcage.

"Damn that bird," Indra said through gritted teeth. The parrot seemed to be watching them with a great deal of interest. Staring back at it balefully, the deva took Menaka by the shoulders with the intention of guiding her into the privacy of the lake house. "Come, dear."

The apsara was about to give in when she stopped and tensed. "Look, deva," she whispered, placing a finger on his arm to stay him.

Indra followed Menaka's gaze to the lake. Through the heave and flow of the mist, he saw the boat glide through the still waters, cutting through the white curtains and making straight for the steps at the bottom of the garden.

The deva's brow knotted in anger and dismay. "Let him wait," he growled. He hated the idea of being robbed of his pleasure thus. "We will *make* him wait. Let us show him he can't always have his way."

He began tugging at the apsara, urging her indoors, but instead of following her king, Menaka resisted. "No, my lord. I must go." Seeing the frown deepen on Indra's brow, she said, "What if he wants to tell me that he is prepared to see you? And because we delayed him, he changes his mind?"

With great reluctance, Indra loosened his grip on Menaka's shoulder. He watched her cross the terrace and go down the garden path – an exuberance of musk and nectar, slipping beyond his reach. The apsara waded into the water, which swirled and lapped at her slender legs in arousal. Her clothes clung and wrapped around the lushness of her hips, while the mist caressed her bare back and shoulders with soft, playful fingers. The very elements were eager to make love to her, Indra thought with bitterness as she climbed aboard the boat. He followed her departure until she faded into the embrace of white.

Draining the soma down, Indra cursed Kubera profusely for the indignities that the yaksha was heaping on him. Then, suddenly, the root cause of his predicament – of *all* his recent sufferings and setbacks – came up to him, floating slowly to the surface like a bloated corpse in water.

Vikramaditya.

It struck Indra that death would be too easy, too light a penalty for the human king. He needed to exact a greater, far more satisfying revenge, one that left the human pleading for mercy, for death, for release.

Vikramaditya would have to pay for all this humiliation in ounces, in slow drips of pain and agony and despair.

***

The air along the steep, winding stairway was thick with the smell of burned cannabis, growing heavier and more overpowering with the climb. It filled Jayanta's lungs as he inhaled harder with every stair mounted, making him momentarily giddy, forcing him to place a palm on the curving stone wall to steady himself. The draught, if one was there at all, did little to clear the atmosphere of staleness and decay that leeched through the stairway's cold, drab walls.

Jayanta nearly had to drag himself up the final flight of two dozen stairs, and when he ultimately made it to the landing, he leaned his back against one wall, out of breath from the long, arduous climb. The landing was large but poorly lit, with only one patch of oblique light shining through a high-set casement. The light had neither brightness nor warmth, and illuminated the centre of the landing like a weak spotlight, barely holding back the shadows that washed down the walls like a murky tide.

Set against one of these walls was a carved wooden door, a shadow within shadows, almost indiscernible in the musty gloom. As he stood recovering his breath, Jayanta considered the door with mixed feelings. He liked what was behind it – it was one of the few islands of comfort he had in an otherwise hostile palace. He could always withdraw to that door knowing he would be welcome, knowing he wouldn't be judged and jeered at. Still, whenever he came away from that door, he brought back with him an intolerable sadness that clung to him – like the smell of cannabis – for days on end. He had often gone past that door in search of solace, only to return with an even greater longing to be consoled.

But today was different. He wasn't here to give or seek comfort. Today was about stealth, about cunning.

The prince walked to the door and pushed at it, knowing it wouldn't be locked. As the door swung silently on its hinges, he was met with a rush of cannabis smoke that made his head reel and his nose twitch in irritation. The next moment, he let out a big, rollicking sneeze.

"Is that you, my son?"

"Yes, mother," he replied sniffling and blinking the last of the sparks from his eyes.

"Shut the door, will you? It gets cold here."

The prince did so, before stepping deeper into the room. The chamber was both large and lofty, relatively well lit by three tall, east-facing windows. But much like the landing and the staircase outside, it was cold, the marbled floor icy underfoot. The highlight of the sparsely furnished room was a giant four-poster bed, overflowing with faded sheets and woollen blankets, pushed against one wall. The only thing that occupied the chilly expanse between the bed and the windows was a tall wooden easel and a high stool placed in front of it.

The woman who stood at the easel was tall and regal in her bearing, yet her disheveled appearance was at odds with her natural poise. There was something careless about the way she wore her clothes, as if in disdain of palace etiquette, and her hair, streaked with grey, fell down to her waist in an unkempt, tangled mass. More striking, however, was her gaunt, pallid face, with its sunken cheeks and black, haunted eyes.

That face was now turned in Jayanta's direction, and for just a moment, a flicker of joy flared in those hollow eyes.

"Jayanta, my darling child," the woman waltzed halfway across the room, then stopped as if distracted. "Have you closed the door? It can get cold if it is left open."

"I did, mother."

The prince waved away a few stray tendrils of smoke that wafted before his face and glanced to his left. There, flush against the wall, concealed in the shadows cast by the windows, he discerned the outline of four heavy ironwood chests, bound and riveted with copper and iron bands. Jayanta's pulse quickened at the sight of the chests – what had brought him to the chamber was in one of them.

Apprehensive that he might have accidentally let slip his motives, the prince jerked his head around and back at the woman. Blushing faintly, he studied her eyes to see if she suspected anything, but the woman merely stood there, staring at him with a blank face.

Relieved, the prince transferred his attention to the woman's palms and fingers, black and grubby with soot. In her right hand, she held a small piece of charcoal that she kept rolling between her fingers. Following Jayanta's gaze, the woman looked down at her hand, and her face brightened.

"Let me show you what I am drawing today. Come, come."

Jayanta wanted the woman to take him into her arms,

embrace him and lock him away from all that was wrong with his world, but instead, he allowed her to take him by his elbow and lead him to the easel.

"Look at that!" Eyes shining with excitement, she pointed at the stretch of white cotton fabric drawn tight across the easel. "What do you think of it?"

Swallowing hard at the lump forming in his throat, Jayanta looked at the easel. The drawing was only half done, but he could see a reproduction of one part of the cliff that surrounded the royal palace. A part of the cliff that was visible from the chamber's three windows; two towering crags with a deep cleft down the middle, the crag to the left sharp and pointed, its sister to the right rounded and subdued.

"What do you think?" the woman asked again.

"It's lovely, mother," the prince cleared his throat.

"It is, isn't it? I decided to make it just this morning."

Jayanta's eyes drifted to the walls of the chamber. On every wall, there were drawings and paintings, dozens of them, some made from charcoal like the one on the easel, others from inks and still others from vegetable dyes. Some were black and white, some in soft tones of brown and pink, while the rest were a profusion of colours.

But every one of them depicted the same scene of the two craggy cliffs with the cleft down the middle – from the same perspective of the room and the three windows. Apart from the colours and the shading, nothing ever changed from painting to painting.

That had been the way with Shachi and her paintings since the time she had withdrawn into this remote corner of the palace, becoming a recluse, pulling the chamber around her like a cloak, like a prison. She painted the cliffs – her last remaining contact with the world outside – almost every day, transferring her passion onto cloth and canvas, treating each painting she made as if it were unique, without once realizing that every effort of hers only resulted in capturing the monotony of her view of the world.

"It is nice," she said, admiring the sketch.

As she reached out to apply a few light strokes of shading to the cleft, she added, "I thought the cliffs looked very nice against the rising sun, so I had to try this one. I meant to..." she paused to look at Jayanta. "Did you shut the door after coming in?"

"Yes, mother," the words left Jayanta's lips in a small sob. Fighting to keep the tears from his eyes, the prince put his head on his mother's shoulder, hiding his face in the crook of her neck, trying to lose himself in the jumble of her hair. Not for the first time, he mentally cursed his father for what had become of his mother.

Sensing something was the matter, Shachi raised her left hand to stroke her son's face gently, smearing charcoal across his cheek. "Are you alright? Do you want to eat or drink something? There should be something to drink somewhere..."

Her eyes looked around the room uncertainly, and then she lost interest, her hand dropping back to her side.

"No mother, I'm not thirsty or hungry." Remembering what he had come for, Jayanta took a hold over his emotions. Lifting his head, he steered his mother toward the bed. "Come, sit down. I have brought something for you."

Jayanta extracted a small silken pouch, tied at the mouth with a drawstring. He glanced at Shachi, and seeing her eyes widen in anticipation, he nodded.

"Pass me your *chillum*, mother."

Shachi reached for the short, conical clay pipe that rested on a side table, and handed it to her son. "I hope you closed the door..." she began again, but Jayanta interrupted her.

"I *have* closed the door, mother," he said. Conscious of the harshness that had crept into his tone, he gave Shachi a lopsided smile. "Don't worry. Just sit back and enjoy this. It is the best *ganjika* available in Devaloka."

An unearthly stillness infused the room as Jayanta began filling the *chillum* with a mixture of cannabis seeds and leaves. Once the preparation was ready, the prince handed the pipe to his mother, and fetched a small charcoal brazier that burned in one corner of the room. Putting the *chillum* to her thin lips, Shachi lit the cannabis with the brazier. Inhaling deeply, she let the smoke run out of her nostrils as she leaned back against a pillow.

"Aah," she let out a satisfied sigh and smiled. "This *ganjika* is indeed divine."

Seeing that rare look of contentment on his mother's face, Jayanta was reminded of his early childhood, when his mother was generally content with life. Of the time when Shachi was still very much a part of the royal palace, and not a piece of its forgotten history, dwindling away in her chamber like an overlooked footnote.

Shachi's betrothal to Indra was the sorry outcome of a treaty struck between the devas and the asuras after a series of attacks and counterattacks had left both sides bloodied and gasping for relief. The devas and asuras negotiated a truce under which neither would attack the other nor covet the other's territory, and as a token of good faith, Puloman, who was then the lord of the asuras, offered Indra his daughter Shachi's hand in marriage.

Indra was compelled to accept Shachi as his wife in order to keep the covenant intact, and so she came to Devaloka as its queen, where she soon gave Indra a son – Jayanta – as his heir. There was no real affection between the king and queen, though. Theirs was a marriage of convenience, a fact that Shachi accepted, allowing her husband to pursue his amorous pleasures with the many apsaras in his court.

Not many years after Jayanta's birth, the armistice between

the devas and the asuras started buckling. Both sides alleged that the other was infringing into their territory, and before long, the war of words led to increasingly violent skirmishes. The bickering left Shachi torn, with both the devas and asuras questioning her loyalties; Indra even offered to return her to her father's dominions. Shachi, however, roundly refused to leave Devaloka, insisting that her place was by her husband's side.

The pact between Devaloka and Patala ultimately ended when the asuras launched a surprise attack on Amaravati. The devas were caught napping, the palace was on the verge of falling, and though the threat was repulsed in the nick of time, the devas suffered grave losses in the long and gory battle. Before the blood spilled on the palace courtyards had a chance to dry, whispers sprung up like ghosts and floated through the halls of the palace, suggesting that the attack was the handiwork of a traitor, whose unseen hand had guided the asuras to the palace. Fingers were pointed at Shachi, first in private, then openly. She and Puloman were accused of having plotted her marriage to Indra, so she could come to Amaravati and send its secrets back to her father.

Jayanta still remembered the day when Indra had come to Shachi's bedchamber and demanded to know the truth. Cowering behind his mother, clutching at the hem of her shawl in terror, Jayanta remembered watching Shachi plead her innocence as Indra cursed and ranted at her. Indra finally had to accept his wife's word for lack of evidence, but he had his revenge by banishing her to her chamber and barring her from setting foot in his court again.

That was the beginning of Shachi's hermitic existence. With no confidants or well-wishers around her, she spent all her time in her chamber, reading and painting, with only Jayanta and a few servants for company. She was still sane in mind, but even that didn't last long, for one day, news arrived of Puloman's death at the hands of his son-in-law. Indra had invited Puloman to Mount Meru to discuss another truce, but in reality it had been a trap – Puloman and his entire entourage were slaughtered in cold blood by an army of devas, with Indra himself driving a sword through Puloman's heart. The news of her father's murder sent Shachi over the edge, setting the spiral of cannabis addiction and cliff painting in motion.

The last of the cannabis was smouldering in the *chillum*. Jayanta reached across and took the pipe from his mother's nerveless fingers.

"Was it as good as you had hoped for, mother?" he asked.

"Mmmh," Shachi didn't even bother forming words. Her eyes had acquired a glazed, faraway expression. Just to be sure, the prince waved his hand in front of her face and flicked his fingers, but Shachi didn't flinch.

Jayanta rose from the bed and went over to the chests. Given his mother's usual state, he knew he could have tried to go through them without resorting to drugging her. But there was always a chance that she wouldn't have approved, and would have tried to stop him, raising a fuss that could have drawn the attention of servants. That, in turn, would have called for a lot of explaining...

He couldn't afford any of that.

He had first heard of Ahi from his mother. This was after her exile from Indra's court, living as an outcast in her chamber, dedicating all her time to reading ancient parchments salvaged from the vaults of the palace library. Shachi read a lot, and as she had only Jayanta around her, she often ended up telling the child about the fascinating things she had read.

"Its name is Ahi and it is counted among the worst possible curses in all three worlds." Jayanta still remembered his mother's words. "It is so ancient that most of those living today have forgotten about it – which is good, because we are safe as long as it slumbers."

"Where does it slumber, mother?"

"At the bottom of an unknown ocean, my child. It can be awakened only by a secret mantra, that too only if uttered by someone with asura *and* deva blood flowing in his veins."

"How come no one knows about Ahi or the mantra that can awaken it?"

"Because no one bothers to read these old texts anymore," Shachi had replied, pointing to the chests. "They just lie rotting in the library. Nobody values old things, old knowledge."

Jayanta knelt before the first of the four chests, recalling that conversation. It had come back to him the night before, as he lay on his bed, wide awake and burning with the desire for vengeance.

Pushing the lid right back, Jayanta stared into the open chest. It was filled with palm-leaf scrolls and parchments, some bound together with yellowing cotton yarn, some just a loose scatter of leaves. Everything inside was decaying and crumbling; everything was covered by a thin layer of dust that came away on his fingers as he pushed and prodded at the pile.

Dusting his fingers, the prince realized there was a lot of work to be done. The text with the mention of Ahi could be in any of the four chests, each packed to the brim with palm-leaf manuscripts. He would have to open every scroll and scour every leaf before he found the relevant text – if he found it at all. Then, even if he did find the text, there was no guarantee it would contain the mantra needed to raise Ahi.

It all amounted to a great deal of effort, but an effort worth taking if Ahi was, indeed, one of the worst curses in all three worlds.

Sisters

The white mare nuzzled Vishakha's hand in the hope of finding another handful of grain. Upon discovering that the hand was empty, the horse snorted and gave a small, dissatisfied shake of its head, but it allowed the queen to continue stroking its long, smooth neck.

"You are such an adorable creature," Vishakha spoke to the horse softly, brushing its cheek with the tips of her fingers. Her voice was tender, full of affection, and her eyes shone with pleasure at the sight of the magnificent beast. Kshapanaka stood a few paces away, watching her with an indulgent smile.

The sisters were inside the royal stables. Outside, the bright, sunny morning was full of stable noises – horses neighing and whinnying, stable hands whistling and chitchatting while they pitched hay and groomed the animals, the heavy roll of carts bringing in hay and grain – but within the building, all was quiet.

"Greetings, my queen," a male voice abruptly broke the hush. "And my greetings to you too, Councilor Kshapanaka."

Both sisters turned to see a wiry man standing respectfully

by a door. Attired in the uniform of a palace official, he additionally sported the badge of the Warden of the Imperial Stables on his arm. The Warden's skin was the colour of bronze, his hair that of silver.

"Is that you, Keeri?" Vishakha squinted at the Warden doubtfully.

"I take it as an honour that the queen not only recognizes me, she even remembers my name," the Warden smiled and bowed, his chest swelling with pride.

"What happened to your hair?" Vishakha clapped a hand to her mouth in amazement. Her words rang with old warmth and familiarity. "It's all *white*."

"Age lays its claim on each of us in different ways, my queen," Keeri replied with another smile. "In exchange for my youth, it brought me a gift of silver." After a brief pause, the Warden added, "I was told you are here to..." He hesitated, his eyes flickering to Kshapanaka as he tried to assess the mood.

"Yes," Vishakha's tone was matter-of-fact. "I am here to see the horse."

Keeri shuffled his feet and cast another doubtful look in Kshapanaka's direction. The councilor, for her part, kept her face expressionless, but the Warden could see she would rather have been elsewhere.

"Are you sure about this?" Kshapanaka spoke at last.

"I am," her sister gave a firm nod.

Seeing the councilor give a faint shrug, the Warden swept his hand down the aisle. "Kindly step this way, your honour."

The three of them walked down the aisle that turned twice at right angles. Stalls filled both sides of the aisle, nearly half of them occupied by horses munching on hay. Grooms ran about, some fetching water while others washed horses or cleaned out the stalls. The Warden and the sisters took a narrower aisle and walked some distance, slowing down as they approached the stalls at the far end.

Keeri didn't have to point the horse out. It was in its stall all by itself, the adjacent stalls lying vacant. The horse was a big, grey stallion with a long face and black, doleful eyes. Its black hide was visible through its silvery coat, and its mane had started yellowing with age. Perking up its ears, it stared at the visitors with a mixture of interest, misery and malice.

"Please be careful, your honour," the Warden said softly. "Don't get... too close..."

Unmindful of Keeri's warnings, Vishakha walked up to the horse. As the Warden drifted to a lame stop, Kshapanaka observed her sister take out a handful of grain from a small bag. Vishakha extended her hand, and the horse instantly snuffled up the offering. One more handful, and the queen slowly reached out and stroked the stallion's neck and shoulder. The animal responded by stretching its neck forward, and Kshapanaka blinked as the beast lay its chin on top of Vishakha's head.

For a fleeting moment, the councilor imagined she saw remorse and repentance in the steed's big, black eyes.

"Why don't you come here?" Vishakha invited Kshapanaka. "It is *your* horse, after all."

"I don't think I can. It took too much away from me for too long."

"It is only an animal," the queen reasoned. "I'm sure it didn't mean any harm."

Kshapanaka shook her head and turned away to hide her tears. The green meadow, the golden sunlight, Vishakha sitting astride the horse – this grey beast, *her* mount – the exhilaration in Vishakha's laughter, the laughter choking and dying in a sudden screech of panic... Her life had come apart that morning and it was all because of this horse.

"Take good care of him," Vishakha said to Keeri, giving the horse a pat on the neck.

"In spite of everything, you forgive him too, your honour?" the Warden looked incredulous.

"What is there to forgive? He didn't ask me to ride on his back. It was my decision, so how can this poor beast be faulted for what happened?"

"It is true what they say of you and the Samrat sharing the same heartbeat, my queen," Keeri bowed. Inclining his head at the stallion, he added, "I shall take good care of him. You have my word."

Emerging from the stable, the sisters picked their way back toward the palace, choosing to walk instead of taking the palanquin.

"What did Keeri mean when he said the Samrat and I share the same heartbeat?"

"He meant it in connection to the horse." Noticing the queen's bemused expression, Kshapanaka said, "After the accident, everyone in the palace – maybe even everyone in the city – was of the opinion that the horse should be put down."

"You mean killing the poor beast?" Vishakha looked horrified.

The councilor nodded. "But Vikramaditya wouldn't allow it. He said the horse was innocent, that killing it would be the lowest form of vengeance. He insisted that no matter how deep our love for someone was, that love should never colour our judgment of what is fair, just and right."

Vishakha lapsed into a brief silence. When she spoke next, her voice was subdued. "He loved me a lot, didn't he?"

"More than anything else; he still does. There wasn't a day he didn't come to your bedside and speak to you." Kshapanaka paused and looked her sister squarely in the eye. "You remember the horse; you remember *Keeri*... but nothing of Vikramaditya? There has to be a faint memory of the Samrat *somewhere*..."

"I am trying my best, sister. I swear I am."

Noticing the tremble of self-doubt and guilt afflicting Vishakha's voice, Kshapanaka put an arm around the queen's shoulder and drew her close. They walked in that fashion up to the causeway, and were about to step onto it when Vishakha spoke, her tone wistful.

"I wish the white mare hasn't been claimed by anyone. I would love to have her as mine. Maybe then I could ride to the meadow and see..."

"We can make enquiries about the horse, but why do you wish to visit that awful meadow?" Kshapanaka asked sharply. "I fail to see why that terrible place fascinates you so much. Even my horse, for that matter. Why did you insist on seeing him? What morbid fancy has struck you?"

"I..." The queen stopped and swallowed. "I want to go back and see everything that happened that day. Who knows what memory that might trigger? It might just help me remember the Samrat."

"Oh, I didn't see it that way," the councilor's head dropped apologetically. "But I doubt if the Healer will allow you to ride a horse just yet, that too all the way to the meadow."

A curtain fell over Vishakha's face at the mention of the Healer. "Where did the Healer come from?" she asked.

"Nobody really knows. He says his home is on the banks of the Lauhitya, in faraway Pragjyotishpura. We are just lucky he came to Avanti when he did."

"There are times I am afraid of him," the queen said timidly. "The way he looks at me... I get the feeling he doesn't want to cure me. I feel he wants something else that has nothing to do with me... that he wouldn't care about me as long as he got what he wanted."

"The Healer scares you?" Kshapanaka looked at Vishakha in surprise and let out a small laugh. "There is nothing to fear from him, sister. His remedies have worked on half of Ujjayini's citizenry, and he has brought so much of you back from the darkness. It is just your mind up to some tricks – trust me, he means none of us any harm."

"You are probably right," the queen gave a small, broken smile as they reached the end of the causeway and entered the palace.

* * *

"What do the physicians treating him have to say?"

Councilor Yashobhavi didn't reply immediately. Instead, for a moment, he stood with his arms crossed in deference, observing the drops of rain that fell from the eaves and spattered on the waxy green leaves of the lemon shrub that grew just outside the balcony.

"They say it is possible he might recover a bit, your honour," he said with a noncommittal shrug. "But then, at other times, they also say the paralysis may be permanent."

With a shake of his head, King Baanahasta turned away from the councilor. Leaning his elbows tiredly on the balcony's wooden parapet, he took in the sweep of Kausambi, with the Yamuna meandering away far to his right.

"What about you?" the king looked back at the councilor. "Have you noticed an improvement in Chandravardhan?"

"I like to think I am seeing a change for the better, your honour. But you have seen the king for yourself. I doubt there has been any improvement, to be honest."

Baanahasta nodded faintly. The report of the calamity that had befallen Chandravardhan had reached Matsya three nights earlier. Baanahasta had left for Kausambi immediately, riding almost without cease to look his friend up. The alliance between Matsya and Vatsa went back a long way, and he and Chandravardhan had been friends much before either of them came to inherit their thrones. Vatsa had been a rock of support in the early stages of the Huna-Saka invasion, and along with King Mahendraditya, it was Chandravardhan who had convinced Magadha, Kosala, Heheya and the Anarta Federation to join the war against the barbarians.

Yet, the moment he had been ushered into the palace and been escorted to Chandravardhan's bedchamber, Baanahasta had regretted coming.

The sight of his friend, broken and helpless – an empty husk of the man who had once embraced life in a bear hug – had not just saddened Baanahasta; it had also made him painfully aware of his own lengthening years. Mahendraditya had been the first to go. Four years ago, Chief Jayandhara, father of Yugandhara, had died in his sleep. King Siddhasena was also no more now, and here Chandravardhan lay in a precarious condition. It was disheartening to imagine that in a matter of time, this generation would pass entirely into Sindhuvarta's history.

"Where is Shashivardhan?" Baanahasta asked, pushing himself erect and looking around. "I haven't seen him since I came."

"The prince has gone to Prayaga, your honour. A boat capsized in the Yamuna yesterday morning. Eight of Prayaga's citizens drowned, six more went missing." Yashobhavi paused. "The prince did the right thing by going personally to offer his condolences."

"He went unsupervised?" Baanahasta raised an eyebrow.

"I had to stay here to welcome you." If the councilor understood the implication behind the question, he made no sign of it.

"How is he… faring?" Baanahasta raised his hand, fingers curled around an imaginary goblet, twice toward his lips in rapid succession. The gesture and its meaning couldn't be confused for anything else.

"He needs encouragement from time to time," Yashobhavi nodded with a sigh.

"He needs to take responsibility," Baanahasta was firm. "One day he will be king of Vatsa."

"I don't know, your honour..." The councilor let the sentence trail, inconclusive.

"What do you mean by that, councilor?" Baanahasta looked at Yashobhavi sharply. "He *will* be king of Vatsa."

"I guess he will, your honour." Again, a pause. Except for the patter of the rain, the afternoon was silent. The palace household appeared to be in siesta.

Yashobhavi finally turned to Baanahasta, but owing to his squint, the councilor appeared to look over the king's shoulder at something behind him.

"I sometimes fear for Vatsa, your honour," Yashobhavi's stoicism seemed to melt a little. "The time that lies ahead of us – it is going to be rough. It will demand men of steel. The prince... he is kind, well intentioned. But he is a king for fair weather and peaceful times."

Even as he inclined his head, a shadow passed over Baanahasta's face. He knew exactly what the councilor meant. The same thought had been troubling him ever since he had received news of Chandravardhan's illness. Deep in his heart, he too feared for Vatsa.

And that fear, in turn, stoked in him a greater fear for Matsya's own future.

At that moment, Baanahasta heard the creak of a door opening some distance away. Turning around, the king looked up in the direction of the first-floor balcony from where the sound had come. He saw a woman step out of a room, shut the door, and walk away from them.

"That's... Princess Pralupi, isn't it?" Baanahasta asked.

"Yes, your honour."

"What's she doing here? I would have thought she would have left for Ujjayini. You know... considering what her city has been through."

"As soon as we heard, Prince Shashivardhan offered to have her escorted to Avanti, your honour. But she chose to stay here."

"Really?"

"She said with King Chandravardhan being in the state he is in, being the only daughter-in-law of the palace, her place was in Kausambi." There was something cryptic in Yashobhavi's tone that Baanahasta couldn't quite decipher.

"That was pretty nice of her, I suppose."

The councilor nodded, but his expression remained unreadable.

Suddenly, an idea flashed through Baanahasta's mind. He looked at Yashobhavi with bright eyes.

"Just occurred to me – why don't we ask Vikramaditya to have Dhanavantri sent over to take a look at Chandravardhan?" he snapped his fingers in excitement. "Dhanavantri is possibly the best physician we have in Sindhuvarta."

"A good idea, your honour, but I doubt if the Samrat will be able to spare us the services of Dhanavantri. We could ask, and the Samrat might even agree in his kindness, but after the three attacks on Ujjayini, it would be selfish on our part to take this request to Avanti."

The king looked out over the wet courtyard once again, deep in thought. A few days ago, an emissary from Vikramaditya's court had arrived in Viratapuri, bringing news of the first two attacks and their cause – the Halahala and the samrat's word to protect it. The account of the Halahala had dazzled Baanahasta, filling him with pride, and though he worried that Vikramaditya had incurred the displeasure of the devas and the asuras, he felt reassured that the young samrat had been entrusted the task by none less than the Omniscient One.

Now, however, there had been a third attack on Ujjayini, one severe enough to cripple the city. It was true that the attack had been rebuffed and the rakshasas repelled. It also proved that the samrat and his Council of Nine were still very formidable, and that the Omniscient One had chosen his warriors wisely.

But the third attack also alerted him to something that was worrisome for the other kingdoms of Sindhuvarta.

Baanahasta didn't doubt Vikramaditya and his councilors' commitment to keeping Sindhuvarta safe from the invaders, but he understood that the dagger with the Halahala had inevitably changed everything. Hereafter, Vikramaditya and Avanti's attention would always be divided – and it would increasingly fall on the rest of Sindhuvarta to keep the barbarians from the Marusthali at bay.

The rest of Sindhuvarta would have to bear the penalty of the samrat's promise to Shiva, Baanahasta thought glumly.

* * *

By the time the caravan of fifteen trade carts rolled out of Amaravati's eastern gate, the sky had purpled from horizon to horizon, and the stars were winking awake. Merchant devas rode on horseback alongside the trade carts, each laden with goods as diverse as spices, silks, dyes and *ganjika*, while hairy, dwarf-like kimpurusha minions trotted in front, holding torches and lighting the way. Three palanquins bearing apsaras were also part of the caravan, which was bound for the town of Devaprastha, the old capital of Devaloka, far to the east and under the shadow of Mount Kanchanshringa.

The devas guarding the east gate gave the caravan no more than a cursory glance. None of the guards even registered the rider who brought up the rear, a nondescript figure in a crumpled cloak who stooped over his horse, head down and face averted from the torchlight. It was only after the caravan was well past the gate that the rider risked a quick, sly peek over his shoulder at the guards, who had returned to their idle chitchat.

The rider stayed with the caravan, waiting for the night to draw around them as they headed into the sparsely forested countryside. He kept to himself, discreetly lagging behind so he wouldn't attract attention; to his relief, none of his companions seemed particularly interested in him. They rode that way for a few miles, until the road meandered into a dense thicket of wild ashoka trees. The rider slowed his horse's pace even more, before drawing to halt at a sharp turn in the road.

Cocking an ear, he listened to the receding squeak and rumble of the carts' wheels and the clip-clop of hooves. He waited until the caravan was out of earshot, before wheeling his horse around and riding back in the direction of Amaravati. However, on reaching a fork in the road, instead of continuing due west, the rider picked the narrower path that led away in a northwesterly direction.

The rider pushed his mount hard, paying scant regard to the fact that the scorching pace would only tire the beast quicker, and when the moon finally rose behind him two hours later, he had put many miles between him and Amaravati. The horse, however, was in need of rest, so he was forced to slow down. When they came across a mountain stream, he reined in and dismounted to let the beast quench its thirst and catch its breath.

The rider knelt over the bubbling stream, scooping out handfuls of water to splash on his face. As he straightened, the moonlight shone on the soft, fleshy features and mean, narrow eyes of Jayanta.

It had taken Jayanta three visits to Shachi's chamber – and three rounds of sedating her with *ganjika* – before he had finally excavated a text that mentioned Ahi. He had read the text with a sinking heart, for though it had much to say about Ahi's destructive powers, there was nothing about the mantra needed to wake the monster. Jayanta was on the verge of despair when it occurred to him to go through all the chests anyway. After two more visits and much meticulous searching, he had finally brushed the dust off a bunch of palm leaves buried at the bottom of the fourth chest. Moments later, eyes moist and shining with delight, he had clasped his mother in a tight embrace of gratitude for having preserved the texts that she had once borrowed from the vaults.

Finding the text with the mantra was just the beginning. There was still a lot of work left, a lot of ground to cover, before he could initiate the rituals that would raise Ahi. And time was short – Jayanta wanted to be back in the palace before his father returned to Amaravati. Yet, because this was to be a surprise – *an awakening, a slap in the face* – to all those who thought so little of him, he had to adopt great secrecy every step of the way.

The prince didn't expect anyone in the palace to take much note of his absence. No one there ever cared what happened to him – *though that would change when he presented his father with Veeshada's dagger* – as long as he kept out of trouble. But he still had to guard against the garudas. They missed very little, and if one of them were to observe what he was up to, the news would travel quickly to Narada and Brihaspati's ears, and they would send someone to stop him. For the same reason, relying on any of the conventional means of leaving Devaloka was out of question – someone was bound to notice and become suspicious. That left him with just one resort: this detour.

Getting away from the palace had been easy enough, and Jayanta was certain no one had recognized him as he had slipped into the market and joined the caravan to Devaprastha. Now all he needed to do was use the cover of darkness to get to the mountains to the north where the kinnaras dwelt.

There another challenge awaited him – finding and convincing a kinnara to take him to Sindhuvarta and the kingdom of Vikramaditya.

Vyala

The rain and the dark were like co-conspirators, Pallavan decided as he sloshed through a trench of knee-deep water, his head bowed under a thick shawl. Working in tandem like a pair of tricksters, they were doing everything in their capacity to lead him astray, keeping him from the path that led to his journey's end.

The rain, of course, had set in much before the dark. It had started as a light drizzle in the afternoon, steadily gaining force as the day wore on. At sundown or thereabouts, it had crossed the line into malevolence, covering the whole of Girivraja, flooding its streets with water and driving its people into the safety of their homes. In fact, around the time Pallavan had set out on his mission, the floodwaters were reaching up to the threshold of many low-lying houses, and threatened to seep into the caravanserai where he was putting up.

Pallavan now picked what he assumed was the right direction and pressed forward, pulling the shawl low over his head. The shawl had ceased offering protection from the rain ages ago, but at least it still hooded his face from curious eyes

– not that there had been any on the streets in a long while. For good measure, he had disguised his face under a theatrical beard made of goat's hair, but he could feel the beard coming unstuck at his left temple, the glue undone by all the water that had been raining down.

Moving from street to lane, lane to alley, the councilor headed toward what he hoped was the quarter that housed Magadha's palace officials and members of the Magadhan royal council. He ploughed on through the swirling waters, slowly losing track of time, the nibble of despair and hunger growing inside him with every passing moment. Then suddenly, fortuitously, he turned a corner to find himself at a junction where the street he was on bisected an avenue.

Much to his joy, Pallavan espied the tiered dome of Girivraja's main Kali temple rising to his left. Sighing with relief, he turned right. As long as he counted correctly, he could now easily locate Uttama's house.

Ten minutes later, the councilor stood in a small, dimly lit backroom, toweling himself dry as Uttama stared at him with a mixture of amazement and suspicion. He had been let into the house by Uttama himself, but not before he had peeled the false beard off and thrust his face to the light of the lamp in Uttama's hand for minute inspection.

Changed and dry, Pallavan was finally escorted to a guest room. "Be seated," said Uttama, waving his hand at a low divan. Uttama then filled a goblet of soma from a side table. "Can I offer you some soma as well?"

"Would you have any firewater instead?" Pallavan replied. "So much the better to fight the cold with."

"Excuses, excuses... I can see your tastes have badly declined from the last time I saw you," Uttama wrinkled his nose in mock contempt. Still, he clapped his hands, and when a maid appeared, he instructed her to bring in a pitcher of firewater.

"I didn't expect you to land up in this rain," Uttama said, once the maid had left. "Of course, had you not come, I would have throttled you for making me miss the banquet at the palace."

"You had a banquet to attend tonight?"

"The royal council had sent personal invitations on behalf of King Shoorasena," Uttama nodded, seating himself.

"*King* Shoorasena?" Pallavan cocked an eyebrow. "So is it formal now?"

"It will be, soon. The news is being shared with the subjects of Magadha tomorrow; the coronation will happen as soon as the king returns from Tamralipti."

"Shoorasena is in Tamralipti?" Pallavan's eyebrows stayed in firm contact with his hairline. "Tamralipti has been captured by your army?"

"A couple of days ago," Uttama nodded. The maid had returned bearing the firewater. "The details are still awaited, but yes, Vanga is now virtually under Magadhan control, my friend. What do you think tonight's banquet was in celebration of?"

Pallavan studied Uttama as the latter accepted the pitcher, dismissed the maid and went about filling a goblet. Short and slightly built, the man had changed little over the years. Only his beard, which had once been jet black, was now fully grey, making his smooth brown skin stand out even more starkly. As always, the beard was carefully cultivated, a neat growth that came down from the temples and ran along the jawline to end in a sharp point at the chin.

They had met as young men many summers ago, training in accounting and diplomacy under the same tutor at Prayaga, in the principality of Kasi. Having similar temperaments and worldviews, they had struck up an instant friendship – one that had endured long after Uttama had accepted an offer from King Siddhasena's court to serve at Girivraja, while Pallavan had moved to Sravasti as an understudy at Bhoomipala's court. Now, as chief envoy of Kosala and tax administrator of Magadha, they hardly had time to meet, but Pallavan believed if there was one person he could trust in Magadha, it would be Uttama.

"But enough of the banquet," said Uttama, planting the goblet of firewater in Pallavan's hands before returning to his seat. "Tell me what brings you here... *like this*." The tax administrator paused to peer at Pallavan's face. "What a ghastly beard! Was all this secrecy necessary? This disguise, the letter you had delivered to me through the fruit seller..." Then, as a new thought occurred to him, an expression of concern swept his face. "Are you in some trouble? Are you fleeing Kosala?"

"I'm quite alright and very much in the good books of King Bhoomipala, my friend," Pallavan replied, pressing the beard at the temple where it was coming loose. "I couldn't risk being seen and identified in Girivraja – unfortunately, there are enough people here who recognize me. I don't want anyone reporting my presence in the city to your royal council."

For the first time, a shadow of apprehension crossed Uttama's face. "Why is that?"

Pallavan took a long pull from his goblet, allowing the firewater to burn down his gullet and settle in his stomach. Then, dropping his voice to a murmur, he recounted everything to Uttama: his visit to Girivraja to meet Shoorasena, the musician who had come to him seeking asylum, the musician's disclosure of what had actually happened on the stairs of the palace, their flight to Sravasti, his subsequent visit to Vikramaditya's court...

Uttama listened without interruption, his face turning ashen at the point where Pallavan revealed what the musician had witnessed the morning of Siddhasena's death. When Pallavan was finally done, the administrator drained his goblet in one big quaff and slouched back in his seat with a troubled expression.

"How can we be sure this musician..." Uttama paused to look at his visitor. "Does this musician of yours even have a name?"

"Gajaketu," answered Pallavan.

"Okay, so how do we know this fellow is speaking the truth? People are known to say crazy things to attract attention... He might not even be a musician for all we know."

"We have been making enquiries to ascertain his credibility. Everything checks out."

"But he could still be making up all the stuff about... about what he says he saw," Uttama insisted as he refilled his goblet with the sterner firewater.

Pallavan allowed his friend to drink down some of the firewater, before replying.

"Why would he lie about something like this?"

"Who knows... maybe he has some axe to grind."

"Against who? Shoorasena? Magadha?"

Uttama sat back in silence, cradling his goblet.

"Tell me, do you really believe the Kikatas were rising in rebellion against Magadha with the support of Vanga?" Pallavan stared closely at his host.

The administrator shifted in his seat uncomfortably, still saying nothing.

"I have always admired you for your intellect, my friend," said Pallavan, reaching for the pitcher and replenishing his own empty goblet. "I urge you to use it now. The old king held nothing against the Kikatas, and he would never have approved of an invasion of Vanga. But now the Kikatas are victims of a campaign of hatred, and war has been successfully waged against Vanga. Ask yourself if any of this would have been possible if Siddhasena were alive today."

Uttama eyed the councilor cautiously, his face betraying the doubts coursing freely through his mind.

"There is always a possibility that Gajaketu is lying, but we fail to see what he could gain from it," Pallavan persevered. "But if, only for a moment, we give him the benefit of doubt, it becomes plain what Shoorasena gains by killing the king and the loyal Sajaya."

"He gets a justifiable reason to invade Vanga and capture Tamralipti." Uttama spoke in a whisper, his attention seemingly on the contents of his goblet.

He sat still for a while before raising his eyes to appraise Pallavan. "So Bhoomipala and Samrat Vikramaditya now want to bring Shoorasena to justice, is it?"

"What my king and the Samrat want is of little relevance, my friend. I remember the day in Prayaga thirty-five years ago, when you got the invite to come to Girivraja. I remember it like yesterday – the joy in your eyes at serving in Siddhasena's court. Siddhasena was *your* king. So all that matters is what *you* want now."

"We will have to make subtle enquiries, somehow get to the bottom of this," Uttama replied. "But we will have to be careful. I will have to find people whom I can trust, people who would want to uncover the truth, people who..."

"People who loved the old king," Pallavan completed the sentence.

A little while later, the two friends stood at the door of Uttama's house. Outside, the rain had finally stopped, but a chill wind blew, casting ripples on the floodwater in the streets.

"You're sure you can find your way back?" the administrator looked doubtfully into the dark. "I can get someone to escort you..."

"No, it's too risky for both of us. Also, now onward, we shouldn't meet here. Pick a better place. I will be in touch through my friend, the fruit seller."

Pallavan was on the verge of taking his leave when he stopped, one hand on the door. "Wouldn't your absence from the banquet have been noted by the royal council?" he asked. "How are you going to explain it away, should someone ask?"

"Worry not, my friend. When I got your letter, I declined the invitation feigning indigestion." Uttama's face clouded over. "Though, after everything you've just told me, I fear indigestion will not be merely an excuse for me tonight."

* * *

"Do have some more *ksheera*, my prince." Satyaveda pushed a large bowl in Ghatakarpara's direction, his voice all honey. "I remember you had loved it the last time you visited, so I had my cooks prepare it especially for you."

"Indeed, it is excellent," the young councilor nodded with enthusiasm, reaching for the ladle to replenish his plate. "And you, sir, have a very good memory."

"Ah, it is nothing." Smiling cloyingly, Satyaveda brushed off the compliment with a wave of a hand. "I do it out of sheer selfishness, my prince. The small joys of hosting the Samrat's nephew."

Atulyateja, sitting across the table from the governor, watched this exchange with troubled eyes. They were in Satyaveda's house, a grand old mansion in the heart of Udaypuri that had once served as the palace for the kings of Malawa, before the Hunas and Sakas had laid waste to the kingdom and its last ruling dynasty. The building was now the official residence of Malawa's governor, yet it struck Atulyateja that he had hardly ever seen it from the inside before.

Not exactly a surprise, considering Satyaveda had never before extended him an invitation to visit, in all the time he had been commander of the garrison of Udaypuri. Leave alone invitations, Satyaveda had barely acknowledged him and the soldiers of the Frontier Guard with routine inspections of the garrison, preferring, instead, to have reports tabled before him at his office every week. The governor was not much into mixing with the rabble, it was obvious.

That was then, of course. Now, though, things had taken a marked upswing, with Satyaveda displaying a willingness to fraternize that was both alarming and off-putting. There were moments when Atulyateja sincerely wished Satyaveda would revert to his earlier, snobbish version, which was, bizarrely enough, easier to deal with.

Blessed with a sensible head, the commander understood that his recent rise in stock was attributable solely to his friendship with Ghatakarpara. Even so, he had been surprised when, earlier in the afternoon, the governor had dropped by the garrison to invite him for dinner in the company of the prince. Atulyateja had not known what to expect, but courtesy demanded that he go, so here he was, sitting in front of a mid-sized feast, watching Satyaveda butter up his friend.

He also finally had an inkling of why he had been pressed into coming.

"The command centre of Madhyamika is already under the control of Brihatsa, a very capable captain of the Imperial Army, sir," Atulyateja returned to the topic under discussion. "My going there will be of no practical use. The frontier will be better served by my staying in Udaypuri."

"However capable this Brihatsa might be, he is only a captain of the Imperial Army. You, on the other hand, are a garrison commander of the Frontier Guard. Who knows this terrain and landscape better – you or this captain?" The governor stared across the table in challenge. "A commander of the Frontier Guard, or a soldier from Ujjayini?"

"Councilor Amara Simha holds Brihatsa in high esteem, sir," Atulyateja spoke softly to take the edge off the subtle pulling of rank. "The councilor told me as long as Brihatsa is in charge of Madhyamika, we are free to focus our energies elsewhere."

"Alright, perhaps you don't have to *go* to Madhyamika," Satyaveda picked up a cup of buttermilk in a huff. Draining half the contents down, he carefully wiped his lips with a thumb and forefinger. "But the borders to the north still need overseeing by someone who knows the lay of the land. You know those parts, and you can liaise with the soldiers guarding Gosringa so that the borders of both provinces are secure."

"I just paid that border a visit..." the garrison commander began, but Satyaveda interrupted him.

"It is not about paying a visit," the governor paused and eyed Ghatakarpara, who was polishing off his plate. "Much as I recommend the *ksheera*, please do leave some space for the *shrikhand*, my prince. I assure you it will rival anything you have savoured in Ujjayini."

While Ghatakarpara grinned in abashment, Satyaveda turned his gaze back to Atulyateja. "Where were we? Yes... I was saying it is not good enough to *visit* the border. The border needs constant monitoring. As soldiers, the two of you will know more about this than I do, but won't you agree, my prince?"

"I suppose so... I mean, yes." Roped unexpectedly into the conversation, Ghatakarpara fumbled for answers. "Borders need to be monitored."

"Precisely," the governor leaned back in satisfaction. "I am sure even Councilor Amara Simha would agree."

"Even I agree," said Atulyateja with a sigh. "But were I to expend all my time and energy in the north, what about the garrison here, and frontiers to the south? Those are also my responsibilities."

"Why, you have the prince here for that!" Satyaveda gave the garrison commander a bemused stare, exaggerated by the arching of the shoulders. The governor's expression suggested exactly what he thought of Atulyateja denseness. "Didn't that obvious possibility strike you, commander?"

Atulyateja studied Ghatakarpara as the prince looked at the governor with raised brows, surprised by the suggestion. He noticed the delight spread from Ghatakarpara's eyes to his lips, spreading out in a smile. The prince turned to him, beaming, a why-not expression plastered on his face. The commander's shoulders sagged in relief at finding his friend free of artifice.

"Don't you trust the prince, commander?" the governor pressed. "Do you doubt your friend's ability to carry out the task?"

"No, I don't," Atulyateja squared his shoulders. "I have never had reason to doubt the councilor, and I am sure he will never give me reason to. It is just that he is new to these parts and unfamiliar..."

"He is not going to be alone. There is the whole Frontier Guard, and platoons of the Imperial Army with him, not to mention the local militia. What's there to worry about?"

"The governor is right, brother," Ghatakarpara placed a hand on Atulyateja's shoulder, giving it a reassuring squeeze. "You also forget that I have been up to Sristhali. I know what this part of the frontier looks like. If we split up, we can do a better job of keeping a vigil over the frontier. You to the north, me to the south."

The commander looked at his friend, with whom he had spent so many afternoons raiding mango orchards, stealing firewater and hoodwinking assorted traders, separating them from their wares at no cost. Despite being of royal descent, Ghatakarpara had always tried to lead the normal, everyday lives of his friends, sharing their small joys and pains.

Atulyateja was pleased to see that this aspect of Ghatakarpara had not changed. Now that he was at the frontier, the prince was keen to live the life of a Frontier Guardsman.

"If you so wish it, my prince," he smiled at Ghatakarpara.

"Excellent decision," Satyaveda grinned and clapped his fingertips lightly in a theatrical display of delight. "Very wise of you, commander. Very wise."

* * *

The cry was grotesque and chilling, a high-pitched, rasping half-scream like the strangulated crow of a rooster, only many times louder and more ominous. It filled the frigid night air, setting the teeth on edge. It made the dim torches that lit the pathway waver violently, and sent the flurries of snow, drifting gently through the torchlight, into a panicked twirl. It made the two mahishas snort and toss their giant, horned heads in alarm.

"Hurr... tchk, tchk, tchk," the asura minion steering the cart flicked his whip lightly across the mahishas' flanks, fighting to control the reins that went around the beasts' thick necks. His eyes flickered involuntarily to his left, ill at ease.

The minion was not the only one drawn to the cry. Toward the rear of the cart, seated on a broad, high-backed chair, the asura lord Hiranyaksha also peered into the night, his naturally golden eyes burning bright orange in the torchlight. He was not alone at the back; flanking him were two figures, the light reflecting off the heavy helmets and visors over their heads and faces. Judging by their bulk, the width of their shoulders and the set of necks, they were gigantic in build, and looked the wrong sort to cross in battle.

The cry rose into the night once again, quivering with primeval rage. It seemed to shake the very ground, making the mahishas wrench away in fright, causing the cart to lurch and skid on the snowy pathway. The three passengers grabbed whatever support was available, as the minion hauled and wrestled with the reins. Fortunately for those in the cart, the cry was cut off abruptly, its echo bouncing off some distant, invisible ridge.

The bisons finally quieted and fell back to a steady trot. Hiranyaksha and his companions stared in the direction from where the cry had emerged.

"Why are we moving so slowly?" the asura lord demanded, blinking through the falling snow into the impenetrable night. "Where exactly are we?"

"We're almost at the vyala pit, my king," the minion replied. "Pardon me, lord, but the snow lies heavy and slippery on the ground. I cannot risk going any faster."

Even as the minion spoke, the lighted pathway swerved to the left, and the low roar of rushing water replaced the silence of the night. Moments later, the cart was on a narrow bridge, and the rush of water was engulfed by the drumming of hooves and the heavy rumble of wheels on wooden planks. The bridge creaked and swayed under the combined weight of the mahishas, the cart and its occupants, and Hiranyaksha was acutely aware that a small misstep from either bison could send all of them tumbling headlong into the Patala Ganga raging far below. Yet, for all the unsettling swaying, he knew the bridge itself would hold up, protected as it was by an ancient charm of the forest-dwelling danavas who once ruled Patala.

Despite the snowfall, the darkness and the giddy rocking of the bridge, the crossing was accomplished without incident, and the cart came to a grinding halt before a strong gate, where a posse of asura commanders had gathered to receive their king. As Hiranyaksha and his companions disembarked, one of the waiting asuras stepped forward.

"Salutations, my king," he bowed deeply to Hiranyaksha before nodding at the two hulking figures beside the asura lord. "And my respects to the brave Chandasura and Amarka."

The two giants acknowledged the greeting in silence,

waiting for Hiranyaksha to speak. The asura king still towered over his generals by a hand, the majestic ram horns on his head sweeping upward and back.

"The vyala..." Hiranyaksha's thumb jerked upward into the night, his voice gruff. "Why was it allowed to scream?"

The asuras shifted uncomfortably. "We don't know, your honour. We have been down here all this while."

"Never mind, let's get on with it."

The asuras parted for Hiranyaksha, but instead of heading for the gate, their lord strode toward a broad, open platform that swung a little off the ground to one side. The platform was rigged with thick ropes and pulleys, with two ropes rising into the darkness above. Hiranyaksha stepped onto the platform, followed by Chandasura, Amarka and a pair of asura commanders. At a command, four mahishas harnessed to an enormous winch began drawing on the ropes. The winch groaned and turned, and with a shudder and a jolt, the platform lifted, first in unsure jerks, and then smoothly, as the bisons found their momentum.

Yard upon yard, the platform was hoisted up along the sheer face of a hill. Gradually, a blush of orange appeared far over the asuras' heads, the glow growing in colour and strength with every yard gained.

"You know what to do when you reach Devaloka," Hiranyaksha looked from one to the other of his generals. "The message that the crow brought from your father was clear. We are to attack Amaravati with force," he drove his right fist into his left palm with a smack, "and inflict as much damage as possible. However, we are not to claim or hold any deva territory. The idea is to harry the devas and take their minds off Veeshada's dagger, that's all."

"We will do as our father has commanded, lord," one of the helmeted giants answered.

The wind tore at the asuras as the platform neared the

hill's summit, snow whipping across their faces, biting and cold. Yet, a strange warmth enveloped them the closer they got to the orange glow, fuzzy and suffocating and filled with the smell of sulphur.

The platform bumped and came to rest by a rocky landing not far from the hill's crest. The asuras got off, and with Hiranyaksha in the lead, they made the short way up the gradient, until they came to the edge of a large, bowl-shaped crater that fanned out over a huge section of the hilltop. The glow originated from within the crater, lighting the asuras' faces bright orange.

Amarka and Chandasura unfastened their helmets as they joined their king at the lip of the crater, their bared faces revealing a contrast not often seen in blood brothers. While Amarka was swarthy, heavily bearded, and had a profusion of unruly black hair that sat low on his forehead, Chandasura was yellowish in complexion, completely bald, with a smooth, round face to keep the head company. Whereas Amarka's eyes flashed big and mutinous under furry eyebrows, Chandasura's were small and slanted amid the hairless folds of flesh around his forehead and cheekbones. The brothers had nothing in common except for their fierce muscularity – and the cold glint of malice in the depths of their eyes.

There was also eagerness and excitement in those eyes as they stared into the pit in front of them.

The crater wasn't very deep, its floor a mass of black, igneous rock. The rock was broken in many places, and molten lava oozed between the slabs in small rivulets, forming swirling puddles of bubbling magma. Noxious sulphur fumes rose from these puddles, and here and there, small tongues of blue-green flame licked the air, as if savouring the melting drops of falling snow.

Standing amidst the burning-hot rivulets and pools were the vyalas. Dozens and dozens of them.

Bearing a crude resemblance to ostriches but many times larger and heavier in build, the vyalas had round, powerful bodies covered in an armour of black, oily scales that glinted in the light of the lava. Each vyala had a pair of long and strong avian legs, each leg ending in three sharply curved talons the size of small sickles. There was nothing distinctive about the rear portion of their bodies, which ended abruptly in small and disproportionate stubs instead of tails.

In contrast, the arresting feature of the vyalas was at the other end of their bodies; their long necks – *five necks for every vyala, all light grey, bare and wattled* – twisting and rising from their shoulders and swaying about in the air.

Five necks for every vyala, branching out abominably in all directions, each neck ending in a big, scaly head adorned with two beady eyes and a massive, hooked beak.

The vyalas' beaks had been forced shut with ligatures, the knots held together by magic mantras that could only be undone by specific commands. So tight were the ligatures that the only sound to escape from the muzzled creatures was the occasional, high-pitched hum of a smothered shriek – irascible and filled with loathing.

The asuras stood for a moment watching the five-headed monstrosities as they writhed and coiled their necks in ill temper. Not only did the vyalas peck at one another, at times two heads of the same vyala got into a spat, slapping into each other in rage, poking with their sharp beaks in rapidly escalating conflict.

"These are going to be a nasty surprise in Devaloka," Amarka flashed a snarl of a grin.

"Indeed," Hiranyaksha returned a wide smile. "A pity I won't be with you to savour the shock on the devas' faces."

Noticing the company above, a vyala stretched one neck, then a second in the direction of the asuras. While both heads rose up from the crater, one was more adventurous and snaked close to Hiranyaksha, Chandasura and Amarka, peering at them in curiosity. Suddenly, without warning, the head lunged at Chandasura, striking at his face with its beak. The asura, however, grabbed the attacking head with one large hand, capturing its throat and squeezing it tight. Wriggling furiously, the captive head uttered a throaty croak, and instantly, the vyala's other four heads sprang up from its shoulders, ready for a fight.

Chandasura, however, used his free hand to draw a dagger from his belt, and in one swift stroke severed the head he held in his other hand.

"You want a fight?" Chandasura challenged. "Come with me and I will give you one. Obey me and you can fight to your hearts' content." He flicked the head he had cut into the crater, where it bounced off a rock and sank into a lava pool with a meaty sizzle.

The vyalas appeared to sense what the asura said, and the multitude of heads eyed one another with enthusiasm, tittering excitedly. The four heads of the vyala that had attacked Chandasura sank back, even as the mutilated fifth neck began sprouting a new head, soft, pink and fleshy. By the time Chandasura had wiped his dagger clean and sheathed it, the vyala's new head had begun maturing, becoming hard and scaly, the beak bulging and curving as it grew.

The unrestrained beak promptly opened wide, a cry building at the larynx from where a short, dagger-like tongue of red-hot fire protruded, growing longer with every passing moment. Before either cry or flame could fully emerge from the back of the vyala's throat, an asura stepped forward. With a sharp command, he conjured up a fresh ligature, which slipped and wound itself tight around the beak, clamping it shut with a snap, trapping the beast's lethal tongue in and snuffing the terrible cry out.

"You should be going," said Hiranyaksha. With a chuckle,

he added, "You have promised the vyalas something, and they are not the most patient of creatures. Go before they change their minds about you."

Amarka and Chandasura extended their hands in the direction of the two asura commanders who had accompanied them up the hill. One of the commanders handed Amarka a battle-axe, while the other gave Chandasura a heavy, flanged mace. The brothers then went down on their knees, bowing their heads before Hiranyaksha.

"Bless us, lord."

"More than mine, you have the blessings of the mahaguru," the asura king replied. "Fight well, and let the vyalas rain terror over Devaloka."

Watching the sons of Shukracharya and the sorceress Urjaswati descend into the crater, Hiranyaksha felt his nape prickle at the thought of the assault on Amaravati. The brothers had both deva and asura blood in their veins, making them uniquely powerful; asura blood made them bold and fearless, deva blood rendered them immune to most tricks the devas resorted to. Chandasura and Amarka were a fearsome prospect in any battle. At the head of a legion of vyalas, they would be terror incarnate.

The asura lord almost felt bad for the devas.

Chandasura and Amarka joined the army of asuras waiting at the floor of the crater. Each of them mounted a vyala, thrusting their feet deep into the stirrups and taking a firm grip on the reins. At a command from Amarka, the chains that had kept the beasts shackled to the crater floor were unclasped. At another command, the first vyala stretched its broad, scaly wings and leaped into the sky. Taking their cue, the other vyalas followed suit, beating their heavy wings and rising above the crater in ever-widening spirals.

Butterflies

The lamp had nearly gone out, encouraging the shadows to leave the walls and encroach upon Shanku and the Mother Oracle, circling the two women like a pack of jackals, inching ever closer as the lamp's wick guttered and charred in its bowl.

The Mother Oracle lay on a thick cotton quilt spread over a mat woven from palm leaves, her eyes closed, her breathing deep and regular. Shanku sat on the floor beside her sleeping grandmother, propped against a wall, her head slumped to one side in deep slumber. Black hair fell over her elfin face, which was drawn and tired. The girl held an embroidered straw and silk fan in her right hand, both fan and hand inert in her lap. Outside, the night was quiet, except for the soothing gurgle of water falling from a three-level fountain nearby.

The Mother Oracle's eyes slowly fluttered open. She lay on her quilt for a while, staring into the gloom gathering around her. Then, slowly she turned toward Shanku, her face softening at the sight of her granddaughter. Reaching out, the oracle placed a hand on the girl's knee and gave it a gentle shake.

Shanku stirred in her sleep before jerking into wakefulness. She blinked and stared about her in confusion – and then, as realization dawned, her eyes dropped to her grandmother in concern.

"How are you feeling, grandmother?" Leaning forward, Shanku placed an open palm on the oracle's forehead. "There's no fever. Are you still nauseous?"

"Only weak," the old woman muttered drily with a tired shake of her head.

Shanku scrambled to her knees. "Let me fetch Councilor Dhanavantri. He asked me to inform..."

The Mother Oracle caught the girl by the wrist, staying her. "I'm feeling alright," she croaked again. "Just very thirsty. Get me some water, child."

Shanku hastened over to a window where a clay carafe sat on the windowsill, cooled by the gentle night breeze. Filling a goblet, she returned to her grandmother's side. Kneeling down, she propped the Mother Oracle up with one arm; with the other, she helped the old woman sip from the goblet.

"I am sorry I went off to sleep, grandmother. Were you awake long? You should have woken me earlier."

"I am alright, child," the Mother Oracle sighed as she subsided onto the quilt. "I just awoke. How long was I asleep?"

"Since early evening." Shanku placed the goblet on the floor, then leaned over to pour a measure of oil into the lamp from a small brass *kamandalam*. She adjusted the wick, and the lamp burned with renewed vigour, sending the shadows scuttling back up the walls. "Everyone was worried. The Samrat came twice. Councilor Dhanavantri was here past midnight to monitor how you were faring."

"Very kind of him. And of the king."

The sun was still setting over Ujjayini when the Mother Oracle had complained to a maid of heartburn. At first, though, the oracle had taken a tribal nostrum of betel leaves dipped in honey, and lain down to rest, insisting that the pain would ease. However, within half an hour, she had begun retching violently, and a mild fever had taken her over. Worse, of course, had been the growing pain in her stomach, accompanied by cramps. Shanku had been informed, and she, in turn, had notified Dhanavantri. The councilor and his assistants had tended to the oracle all evening, administering her with *kashayams* and unctions until her condition had stabilized to Dhanavantri's satisfaction.

"Councilor Dhanavantri says it was acidity induced by indigestion."

"The palace food is the culprit, I suppose. Too rich for the tastes of the tribe." The old woman adjusted her head in a search for a comfortable position. Then, as a new thought occurred, "I would like to see the tribe. I miss them."

Shanku knelt by the oracle's side, looking down at her. "You can't leave here, grandmother. You need to rest. But yes, I will have word sent to my cousins. The clansmen can come to Ujjayini to see you."

"Can you do that, child?"

"Tomorrow, at first light," the girl nodded. "Now I really must inform Councilor Dhanavantri that you have woken. He won't be happy if..."

"In a while, my child," the Mother Oracle registered her protest in a weak voice. Patting the floor by her side, she continued. "Sit here a while with me."

Unsure, Shanku considered her grandmother for a moment. Then she decided to do as the oracle bid her. Reaching across, she picked up the fan and started stirring the air over her grandmother's head.

"I tried doing the thing you told me about... in the park, remember?" Shanku spoke with hesitation. "The... the disappearing thing, I mean. I intended telling you earlier..."

"How did it go?" The Mother Oracle raised her head off

the quilt in eagerness, her eyes widening, and then narrowing as she peered at the girl.

Shanku shook her head. "I have no control over where I end up going."

"You will get used to it. This is a wonderful gift to have, my child."

"I suppose so, though unless I know how to control it, it is a pretty useless gift."

"You will learn," the oracle patted the girl's hand gently. "Learn to concentrate..."

"I do concentrate," Shanku insisted. "I focus so hard on where I want to be, but every time I fail miserably."

"But that is precisely why you have failed," the oracle said mysteriously. "The trick is to focus on where you *need* to be and not where you *want* to be. Your heart knows where you need to be. Shut out what your mind says and heed your heart. Do that and you will discover the true value of your gift."

Shanku lapsed into silence, meditating on what her grandmother had just said. The breeze blowing outside picked up, rustling through the trees. A small moth, probably borne by the breeze, flitted into the room and began orbiting the lamp in a frenzy of erratic ellipses.

"I'm so thankful the royal physician was in the palace. I'd have hated to have the other one prescribe me any of his loathsome remedies."

Consumed by her own thoughts and the moth's jumpy flight, the abruptness of the oracle's statement – and the sudden change it ushered in the direction of their conversation – confounded Shanku.

"The one you call the Healer," the crone clarified. "Curse his soul."

Shanku gave her grandmother's hand a reassuring squeeze. Even as she had heaved and retched and writhed in agony, the old woman had been insistent – even *vehement* – that she did not want treatment from the Healer. Between winces and hacking coughs, she had made it clear to her granddaughter that no matter what happened, the Healer was *not* to be summoned to attend to her. She would much rather submit herself to the care of the least experienced of Dhanavantri's apprentices, she had said through gritted teeth.

"Why won't you allow the Healer to take a look at you?" The girl asked gently after letting a few moments pass.

"I don't trust him, that's all." The oracle frowned, finding strength in her stubbornness. "There is something sinister about the man. I don't want his shadow falling over me."

Silence enveloped the two women once again. Seeing that the oracle's eyes were growing heavy with fatigue, Shanku laid the fan down. "I must send word to Councilor Dhanavantri, grandmother. He will want to see you."

The Mother Oracle nodded and released her grip on the girl's hand. However, as Shanku stood up, she spoke.

"I don't know how much time I have left in this world, child. So before you go, listen to what I learnt from the clouds this evening – before the heartburn set in. The clouds that blow from the west speak of a thousand black butterflies following the Dark River that bleeds the Great Desert. Go and tell that to your king. A thousand black butterflies following the Dark River, all heading south."

Shanku stared at the old woman for a moment before nodding. "Thank you, I will." But again, just as she turned on her heels, the oracle addressed her.

"I have a message for you as well, child. I found it woven in the patterns of the spider webs that infest the Labyrinth. I... I didn't want to believe it... maybe I still don't. Nevertheless, you should know of it."

Shanku paused in mid-stride and turned. She could sense

that the Mother Oracle was struggling to share whatever she had learnt during the time the palace household had sought shelter in the Labyrinth.

"The spider webs speak of repentance in the dungeons. They speak of... atonement. So, when the time comes, you will have to choose between punishment and forgiveness. It is your decision to make, not mine. Whichever you choose, I will always feel sorry for you for having to make that hard choice, my child."

* * *

Daylight had just broken in the east when Shukracharya's head emerged from the depths of the cold, dark water.

For several minutes, though, from his cheekbones down, the rest of him remained submerged underwater as he held his breath and meditated on the Dasa-Mahavidyas.

Slowly, the high priest broke through the water's surface, eye still closed, his palms joined in obeisance. When the water had reached waist level, he bowed his head in a deep *pranaam* to the rising sun – which, at the moment, was little more than a tentative blush – before wading out of the pool and stepping onto the old laterite steps of the bath.

Located in the northeastern corner of the palace, the bath was one of the three reserved exclusively for the male members of the palace household. It was large and rectangular, walled in on three sides and open to the sky. A set of steep stairs, cut into the rock and caked with moss and lichen, led down the open end to the water's edge. A huge peepal growing nearby cast two heavy branches over the bath, offering both shade and cover to bathers. Being a little out of the way, the bath wasn't heavily frequented, which suited Shukracharya nicely – particularly on mornings such as this one, when his mind was a churn of ragged-edged thoughts tearing at one another, clamouring for priority. The solitude of the bath was just the antidote for the night gone by.

The high priest had hardly slept a wink, and when he did, his sleep was riddled with dreams that he couldn't recall now. Much of the night had passed in tossing and turning, wrestling with thoughts about Indra, Vishakha, Veeshada's dagger...

He was getting increasingly flustered with the bones' cryptic but unwavering response to the whereabouts of Veeshada's dagger. The crows he had left behind at the cremation ground had had nothing to report so far; evidently, no one had shown the least interest in the great banyan. Shukracharya was finding it hard to believe that the human king would leave the Halahala unattended for so long... yet the bones were steadfast in their answer.

It is in the banyan that holds up the field of endless pyres.

Then there was Indra in Alaka, chaffing with impatience, but waiting at Kubera's door like a beggar. Was he planning to enlist the yakshas in an assault on the human kingdom? Or did he intend employing the yakshas' potent magic to locate the Halahala? The high priest knew the deva was up to something, even bringing Menaka as an enticement for Kubera, but what Indra sought from the yaksha king was right now beyond even the bones.

In all this uncertainty, the planned attack on Devaloka was one spot of solace for the high priest. His instructions to Hiranyaksha had been delivered, and any time now an asura army would descend on the demoralized and leaderless devas. Toweling himself dry on the bath's steps, Shukracharya's mouth twisted with vindictiveness at the thought of the terror that lay in store for his unsuspecting kinsmen – his own blood brothers who had betrayed him by choosing a lesser being as their guru.

Every strike on Devaloka was his revenge for the insult the devas had dealt him eons ago.

Engrossed in his thoughts, head bent as he mounted each steep stair, the high priest was tracing his way back to his chamber when, halfway up the steps, a voice called out, startling him.

"Greetings, Healer!"

Looking up, Shukracharya saw a tall, lean figure standing at the top of the steps, silhouetted against the flamingo-pink dawn.

"I see you have intended to start the day early," the man exclaimed, his tone mildly sardonic. He descended a step and stopped.

"There is much to heal in this world, raj-guru," the high priest kept his voice even. "The sooner we begin, the better."

"Indeed," Vetala Bhatta inclined his head as if in agreement. "And how is the business of healing going?"

Shukracharya didn't answer until he had climbed the penultimate step and drawn level with the chief councilor.

"Better than I could have asked for," he said finally, pulling the eye-patch over his left eye and knotting it carefully behind his head. Looking the Acharya in the eye, he added, "You only have to look around you to judge for yourself. Hardly an injury left to cure, hardly a bone left to mend."

"One couldn't quarrel with you on that," Vetala Bhatta inclined his head again, accompanying the gesture with a thin smile. "It's not without reason they call you the Healer. The citizens of Ujjayini believe there's magic in your touch."

As Shukracharya gave an offhand shrug, the Acharya looked sharply at the high priest from under his grey eyebrows. "But what about the one that gave you entry into this palace… the one that earned you a welcome here?"

Shukracharya darted the councilor a defiant glance. "If you are referring to the queen, you would be pleased to know that she now recognizes you, raj-guru. You *would* count that as an improvement, I presume?"

"Oh, most certainly," the Acharya's air was one of exaggerated magnanimity, his tone still needling. "But my question was about when she would be fully cured."

"A few weeks ago, she couldn't move or talk or feed herself. Today..." the high priest threw up his hands in a theatrical shrug.

"But you can't say by when she would be cured?" the chief councilor persisted.

"Despite everything they might say or believe, I am a healer, *not* a magician," Shukracharya drew himself up to his full height and stared up at Vetala Bhatta. "All I can say for certain is that when the queen is cured, she will be the first to know, and you will know it from her. Now, if I have your permission, I will take my leave. I need to see the queen shortly."

Frustration stacked up inside Shukracharya, layer upon impenetrable layer. It choked him, bolting all his thoughts together into a knot of rage that he fought to contain in the pit of his stomach. He knew the Acharya disliked and distrusted him – had distrusted him from the first day he had walked into Vikramaditya's court and offered to revive the queen. What irked the high priest was that despite knowing this, he had walked into the raj-guru's little game of thrust and parry, and allowed himself to be flattered before being forced to beat an inglorious retreat.

Yet, more than Vetala Bhatta, Vishakha was the cause of the frustration now mounting inside Shukracharya. In spite of everything he was doing to slow her recovery, the queen was steadily picking up the threads of her lost past and joining the dots with alarming frequency. She already remembered Vetala Bhatta, Amara Simha and Dhanavantri, and the previous afternoon, she had surprised the royal household by identifying Shanku as the daughter of Brichcha, disgraced Warden of the Imperial Stables.

Whenever he got the opportunity, the high priest heaped

dark incantations on Vishakha, but such was the force of the Regeneration Spell he had cast that every time she seemed to emerge stronger and more clear-headed in her journey of self-discovery. The other night, Shukracharya had nearly reeled at the sight of the king and Vishakha seated on the swing, holding hands. To his great relief, he had gathered that the queen still didn't remember Vikramaditya – but he knew it was only a matter of time. The idea bothered him, *scared* him. For his plan to succeed, he had to prevent that *one* link from falling in place, but how could he fight the Regeneration Spell and manipulate so many aspects attached to the queen's memory –

The high priest froze in mid-thought.

For his plan to succeed, he had to prevent that one *link from falling in place.*

That link! That was the *only* link, the only aspect to the queen's memory that mattered. None of the others were of any consequence. Not to him and his task of gaining the Halahala.

Shukracharya smiled at his own stupidity. For the first time in many days, he smiled in a way that let the light shine within him. For the first time in many days, Shukracharya felt in control of things.

* * *

When Amara Simha shouldered past the heavy council room door, the council was already underway.

"...the threat that the Anartas face is severe and needs to be –"

The samrat, seated at the head of the council table, facing the door, stopped in mid-sentence to see who was coming in. Heads immediately swiveled to the door, and as Amara Simha stepped inside, eyes lit up in delight.

"Ah, look who's here!" Vetala Bhatta rose from his seat,

smiling fondly at his old friend. "What took you so long getting back?"

"Long story," Amara Simha shook his head as he embraced the raj-guru. "That bloody scout we'd captured near Sristhali – the one who revealed the Huna plan to attack the Anartas…?" he paused to see if the others were getting the context of what he was saying. Heads nodded vigorously. "Well, the fellow tried to make an escape near Lava. Almost succeeded, the little devil."

Amara Simha had the attention of everyone around the table. "Under the pretext of relieving himself, he gave his guards the slip," he explained, lowering himself into a chair. "Happened at night, so we had no idea which way he had gone. That too in the middle of a forest."

"Then?" Vararuchi, seated to Vikramaditya's right, prompted.

"Then what!" Amara Simha spread his hands as if stating the obvious. "We launched a hunt for him."

"And you found him," Varahamihira didn't frame his words as a question, but the implication was clear.

"Of course we did." The burly councilor jerked a thumb over his shoulder. "He is in the city garrison under lock and key."

"Where was he hiding?" the samrat asked.

"In the hills, north of Lava," Amara Simha smiled and leaned back in his seat. "The sly little fox tried to outsmart us by fleeing north. Thought we would head back west in the direction of Udaypuri and the frontier, looking for him."

"How did you know he had gone north?" Kshapanaka's voice held both curiosity and admiration.

"We didn't."

"Then how did you find him?" the Acharya raised his eyebrows. "You had an escort of what – a dozen soldiers?"

"Ten, to be precise," Amara Simha replied. "I told the

men that they'd have a pouch of gold coins to share among themselves if we found him. I also made it clear to the two guards who had lost him that if we *didn't* find him, they would spend the rest of their days in the Forest of the Exiles. Greed and fear can make all kinds of magic happen."

"Amazing!" Vikramaditya shook his head in marvel.

"Yes," Amara Simha agreed. "Took us three extra days, running around in the heat and dust, but it was worth it."

"Someone should teach the scout to hide better while he's here," said Dhanavantri with an irrepressible grin. "But for his incompetence, you would still be out there chasing him, and we would have been spared the sight of your surly face for a few more days. Look at you – you look like something that's walked out of a nightmare."

"Maybe *you* should have been the one chasing him, my friend," Amara Simha shot back, as the councilors rocked back in laughter at the familiar ribbing. "Would have helped you shed some of that weight. Look at you – any fatter you get, and we could just roll you onto the attacking Hunas and send them scattering."

"Peace, brother, peace," the physician chuckled, his jowls and shoulders quivering in mirth.

"And I am sorry if my appearance insults your exquisite tastes, but I happened to ride into Ujjayini very late last night and barely got a few hours' rest... while you were busy enjoying your beauty sleep," Amara Simha was reveling in his repartees, his eyes twinkling at Dhanavantri.

Sobering up, he looked from the raj-guru to Vikramaditya. "In fact, I was awakened early by a message saying we are to convene here to discuss a matter of high importance."

The lively mood dispelled in an instant. The samrat heaved a sigh and drew himself up on his chair.

"Well..." the king paused and shot a glance at Shanku, who was at her usual place close to the foot of the council table. "When we received your dispatch from Sristhali about the possibility of the Hunas attacking the Anarta Federation by sea, we thought it would be wise to consult the Mother Oracle. The oracle read a sign in the clouds yesterday evening."

"What did the sign say?" Amara Simha asked.

The samrat caught Shanku's eye and nodded.

"The clouds coming in from the west told the oracle that a thousand black butterflies are following the Dark River," the girl said softly. "And all the butterflies are moving south."

"Butterflies?" Amara Simha stared around the table in confusion.

"Imagine you are a cloud floating high above, and you look down at a river, which appears full of black butterflies," said the Acharya. "What do you think you are seeing?"

"I don't know – black butterflies, I presume."

"How would you know they are butterflies?" prodded Varahamihira.

"By their wings, of course. How else can one tell..." Amara Simha paused, his cocksure tone waning as light finally dawned. "*Sails*. Black ship sails!"

"Precisely," the raj-guru said. "A thousand black ship sails following the Dark River's course south. And where do you think the ships are heading?"

"The Anartas. Dvarka." Amara Simha passed a weary hand over his face.

"Exactly the way our friend who is under lock and key in the city garrison told you," said Vikramaditya. "That's why I summoned this emergency meeting of the council. We have to quickly decide on a course of action."

"We waited one entire night to meet?" Amara Simha looked incredulous. "We knew about this yesterday evening..."

"The Mother Oracle knew about this yesterday evening," Kalidasa interrupted, speaking for the first time. "Unfortunately, she took ill before she could share this with any of us. Late last night she told Shanku about it, who informed the samrat *this* morning."

"Oh, I see." The grammarian flexed his brawny forearms and frowned at the patterns formed by the coral and lapis lazuli that lined the sun-crest emblazoned on the council table. "What have we decided?"

"A message is being dispatched to Chief Yugandhara's court, notifying him of what we have learnt from the Mother Oracle," the samrat said. "I presume Ghatakarpara has already shared what you gleaned from the scout with the chieftain."

"He should have," Amara Simha nodded.

"Our responsibility doesn't end with that, though," Vikramaditya looked at his council. "The Anarta Federation has sent fifteen thousand of its soldiers to Avanti and Matsya to help guard the frontier. So they are fifteen thousand men short when it comes to defending Dvarka and the Anarta coastline. We must equip them with at least the same number, if not more."

"More, I would say," Vetala Bhatta offered. A nod of heads all around backed him.

"How many men could a thousand ships accommodate?" Amara Simha wondered aloud.

"It depends on the size of the ships," answered Varahamihira. "They are plying on a river, so they can't be very large. At the same time, from what we have heard, the Dark River is very broad – many times broader than the holy Kshipra, broader than even the mighty Yamuna. So... maybe a hundred per ship, maybe more."

As the number was extrapolated in a quick exercise of mental math, there was an audible intake of breath around the table.

"We must realize that a thousand ships could just be a figure of speech," said Kshapanaka. "The actual number may be much less."

"Or, by that logic, far more," Dhanavantri gave Kshapanaka a sidelong glance, making the latter pull a face.

"We must send back as many soldiers who're from the Anartas as possible," said Vararuchi. "The federation's soldiers know the lay of their land, which is always an asset in battle."

The samrat nodded. "How many soldiers from the Anartas can we muster quickly?"

"Unfortunately, I dispatched the bulk of them to Matsya," Vararuchi replied. "Of the few left in Avanti, most have been deployed along the frontier, some as far north as Gosringa. I don't think we can rally more than two or three thousand of them at short notice."

"Let us send those three thousand back to the Anartas immediately," Vikramaditya instructed. "Also, get a message out to the garrison of Lava to dispatch five thousand of our men to Dvarka right away. Get our troops from Sarmista and Sristhali to move into the Anartas, and order Atulyateja to send replacements for those troops from Udaypuri. The city garrison will also have to prepare to send five thousand men west by this evening. I want the soldiers from the city garrison marching quickly – and make sure there's a good mix of infantry, cavalry and archer platoons."

"What about the soldiers we have from Heheya and Vatsa?" Kshapanaka butted in. "Some of them can go as well, can't they?"

"They definitely can," the samrat was emphatic. "Anyone who is readily available at hand can and *must* be drafted in. Every spare sword and spear, every additional pair of fighting hands will make a difference."

As the king paused, Vararuchi made to stand up, but Vikramaditya wasn't done speaking.

"The Anarta chiefs stood by us in all our troubles, even when the Anartas were relatively safe from the invaders. We have a debt to repay, and now is the time. I want one of us to go to Yugandhara's court and fight alongside his men to defend Dvarka."

"I will go," Amara Simha sprang forward in his seat. "Come on, I went to the frontier to fight a few battles, but the only time I got to use my axe was to behead what was already a dead body. You people owe it to me."

"But it has only been hours since you returned from the frontier, councilor," Vikramaditya fixed a concerned gaze on Amara Simha. "You've already had one long, tiring ride back, and Dvarka lies even further to the west. Whoever goes has to leave right now – while you... I think you need some rest."

"I'm fine," Amara Simha insisted. "I can always get some rest..."

The loud scarping of a chair being pushed back muffled Amara Simha's protest. The king and the councilors turned to see Vararuchi get to his feet.

"No, *I* will go," the samrat's half-brother said in a tone that overruled all other possibilities.

Seeing a look of exasperation creep over Amara Simha's face, Vararuchi raised a hand. "Bear with me, my friend. I said earlier that knowledge of the terrain is a critical factor in battle. I have no doubt that you will fight like a lion, but the fact is you know little about the Anartas and Dvarka. You have never been there, whereas I have. I spent more than a month in and around Dvarka during my travels to the Southern Kingdoms. That experience will come in handy in this battle."

"Vararuchi is right," the Acharya nodded, giving Amara Simha an understanding pat on his arm.

"Then let us both go," Amara Simha argued. "Two can fight the Hunas better than one."

"I can understand your disappointment, councilor," said the king. "But there is a reason we decided to call you back from the frontier. We need as many hands as possible to defend Ujjayini whenever the devas or the asuras arrive next."

"Okay, fine." Amara Simha slumped back in his chair. "As long as they come."

"I think the councilor has a point when he says two can fight better than one," Kalidasa leaned his elbows on the table and looked at Vararuchi. "I can spare you a good *samsaptaka* with detailed knowledge of the Anartas."

"Who is this?" asked Vararuchi.

"Udayasanga."

"He knows the Anartas?"

"Very well. Udayasanga spent much of his early life visiting Dvarka and Bhrigukaksha. His father, an ivory merchant, had hoped the son would pick up the trade." The giant paused to chuckle. "All the son ever learnt was to pick fights with the other ivory merchants whom his father competed with."

"I would love to have Udayasanga come with me," Vararuchi smiled.

"He would be honoured to accompany you. I will also pick a dozen other *samsaptakas* to travel with you. I'll make sure they're ready for departure in a couple of hours."

Once the council had disassembled, the Acharya left the chamber with Amara Simha, who looked tired and dispirited. As the two walked down a gallery, the raj-guru put a friendly arm around his companion's shoulder.

"Cheer up, my friend," said Vetala Bhatta. "All is not lost."

"At the rate things are going, I will have to retire to the farmlands and reserve my axe to till the soil," Amara Simha didn't bother concealing his grumpiness.

The Acharya heaved a sigh and gripped the muscular shoulder hard. "You've seen what this city has been through, haven't you? Well, let me tell you, Ujjayini hasn't seen the last of it. There will be abundant opportunity for you to wield that axe of yours. That much I can vouch for."

* * *

The first vyala to emerge from the bank of black rainclouds was Amarka's mount.

Shaking off the raindrops that clung to its scales, the beast soared into the chilly heights far above Devaloka, rising steeply until the droplets of moisture on its wings froze and turned into a thin encrustation of ice. Still it kept up its climb, its five snaking heads stretched upward, the five beaks pointing straight at the sky that was quickly changing colour from blue to deep purple and then black. The higher it went, the colder it got, and Amarka could feel his fingers going numb on the cold metal of his battle-axe.

The ascent continued and Amarka had to clench his jaw to stop his teeth from chattering. Casting a backward glance, he saw the rest of the asura army breaking through the clouds below, their vyalas tearing after him in a fearsome display of competitiveness. Blinking away the ice that was forming on his eyelashes, he observed Chandasura in the lead, his vyala streaking ahead of the others in a bid to catch up with Amarka's mount.

Soon, breathing became hard, and Amarka's vision swam each time he moved his head. He noticed that his vyala was growing lethargic too, its wing beats faltering as it slipped a few notches every now and then. Drawing on the reins, Amarka was surprised to see the vyala slow down willingly, offering none of its customary belligerence. Realizing the cause behind the beast's sudden pliability – vyalas functioned best in torrid conditions – he concluded that they had reached the limits of their skyward journey.

It took a while for Chandasura and the rest of the asuras to catch up, their vyalas straining to breathe and keep their heavy bodies airborne in the thin atmosphere. When Chandasura drew level with him, Amarka saw that his brother's lips had turned blue from the cold, as had his, he guessed. The two coasted side by side for a while, allowing their fatigued mounts a spot of rest.

"I don't know if we can risk going any higher, brother." When he spoke, clouds of vapour rolled out of Amarka's mouth into the frigid air, hanging there for a second like visual symbols of his indecision, before dissipating and blowing away.

"I don't either," Chandasura replied. His broad chest heaved as he scanned the dome of purple-black overhead, before surveying the vyalas and their mounts gliding gently a little below them. The beasts appeared uncharacteristically subdued.

"The question is whether we are within range of the garudas," Amarka pondered. "Or are they still too far above us?"

Chandasura only shrugged. His breathing was laboured, and he was trying to conserve as much energy as possible. "Only one way of finding out," he said at last with some effort.

"We let the knots slip?" Amarka brushed off some of the ice that had formed on the tips of his black moustache.

His brother nodded.

Looking down, Amarka caught the eye of an asura hovering close by and signaled with his hand. The asura immediately turned to his fellow asuras and signaled, and thus, slowly, in ever-widening circles, like ripples in a pond, the message spread to the furthermost members of the army.

Moments later, Amarka and Chandasura mumbled a mantra, and the bonds around their vyalas' beaks snapped and fell away. The two vyalas opened their ten beaks in a combination of relief and anger, and their fierce, energized cries rose in an earth-shattering crescendo of discord, mauling through the stillness. The other vyalas quickly joined in, all screaming and crowing together, a clamour that made the very air quiver, and forced the clouds far down below to tear apart and scatter.

Slowly, Shukracharya's sons guided their wailing, lamenting

and cursing mounts into a wide, circular flight path. The asura army followed suit, and soon the vyalas and their masters had formed a huge, wheeling formation of four concentric circles high in the sky – a sky resonating with the incessant shrieks of the monstrous, five-headed beasts from Patala.

So began the hunt for the garudas.

Amaravati

The Acharya went through the contents of the scroll for a second time, before carefully rolling the fabric up and retying it with a string. Placing the knotted scroll back on the marble side table by his elbow, the raj-guru glanced across at Kalidasa, Kshapanaka and Amara Simha, who sat looking at him intently, waiting for a reaction. The samrat was standing by a full-length window, gazing out over the palace lake.

"Queen Sumayanti sent this through an official rider?" Vetala Bhatta's bushy eyebrows rose with curiosity.

"Through a personal messenger of hers," the king shook his head, still staring out of the window. "The good queen couldn't have risked using one of Heheya's official riders."

"Quite a relief knowing at least *someone* in Heheya still wears a sane head," Amara Simha scowled.

The king and the four councilors were in a small anteroom adjoining the council chamber, often used for informal meetings and consultations. Vararuchi had already departed for Dvarka, Varahamihira was at his workshop at the other end of the city, Dhanavantri was attending to the oracle, while

Shanku was busy welcoming the first of her relations from the Wandering Tribe who had arrived to see their ailing matriarch.

"What do you make of it, raj-guru?" Vikramaditya asked, crossing his arms, his head cocked to one side.

"It's fairly obvious that Harihara has taken leave of his sanity," Amara Simha answered in place of the Acharya, gesticulating and rapping his fingers on his temple. "This is... *sheer lunacy*!"

"This is how he chooses to repay us for having rescued Princess Rukma from Kulabheda's filthy grasp – he promptly hands her over as a prize to another pair of filthy hands." Kalidasa leaned across and looked at Vikramaditya. "You see what I meant when I said Harihara isn't deserving of our friendship?"

The samrat walked over to a low-slung divan and sat down.

"I see a bit of spite in this as well," he said.

"Spite?" The chief councilor's head snapped up in surprise. "How's that?"

The king nodded, chewing his upper lip as he meditated the matter. "When King Harihara was here for the *rajasuya yajna*, he brought a proposal to the Queen Mother."

"What kind of proposal?" Kalidasa asked.

"He suggested that Rukma come to this palace as a bride."

"A bride to whom?"

Vikramaditya looked at the faces in front of him. "Me."

As the Acharya, Kalidasa and Amara Simha exchanged astonished glances, Kshapanaka's face flushed with anger.

"What gall!" she exploded. "He was... he asked me how Vishakha was, how she was doing... He sounded so nice and caring." She paused and stared at her hands in bitterness. "It was just a sham – all the while, his heart was full of plans to get Rukma to take Vishakha's place."

Amara Simha instinctively put a comforting arm around

Kshapanaka and patted her. Vetala Bhatta looked at the king.

"I presume you turned down Harihara's proposal, and that's what you mean by spite?"

The samrat nodded. Leaning forward, elbows on knees, he addressed the councilors.

"I understand King Harihara's predicament," he said, keeping his voice even. "Rukma is of marriageable age, and a daughter is a father's responsibility. The king knows he isn't going to be around forever, so it is natural of him to want to have the princess married off."

"But to Shoorasena?" Kshapanaka shook her head in bafflement, her voice still ringing with newborn resentment for Harihara. "After knowing the prince killed his own father?"

"Siddhasena was his *friend*," Amara Simha rose from his seat in agitation and began pacing the room. "How can Harihara even entertain the idea of giving his daughter to his friend's killer?"

Vetala Bhatta raised his eyes to meet the king's gaze. "We cannot allow this, Vikrama."

"I agree with all of you," the samrat replied. "This alliance cannot happen."

"Someone needs to knock sense into Harihara," said Kalidasa. "He needs to be reminded about things like friendship and loyalty – and basic decency."

"Kalidasa is right," Amara Simha smacked his palm with his fist. "I would love to teach him a lesson that he won't forget easily."

"There is a reason behind Queen Sumayanti's message," Vikramaditya raised a hand, calling for attention. "She clearly doesn't approve of what King Harihara has in mind. At great personal risk, she has reached out to us – not because she thinks we can teach the king a lesson, but because she believes we can help him see the light. The task before us is to solve this problem amicably. We owe that to Queen Sumayanti – and to an ally who has let himself be misled."

"What are you proposing, Vikrama?" the raj-guru asked.

Conscious of the four pairs of eyes on him, the samrat paused to collect his thoughts.

"King Harihara's primary concern is Princess Rukma's marriage. If that concern is suitably addressed, we have a solution." Vikramaditya's eyes settled on Vetala Bhatta. "You know King Harihara from father's time, raj-guru, so if you would be kind enough to go, I would like you to make a trip to Mahishmati. The earlier you leave, the better."

"I shall embark at daybreak tomorrow. But what is the proposal that you want placed before Harihara?"

The councilors leaned forward as the samrat explained what he had in mind.

* * *

The balconies and terraces overlooking the southern drawbridge of the palace were lined with apsaras and devas, jostling for room, leaning over one another and craning their necks to catch a glimpse of the garuda that had smashed down onto the bridge.

The garuda lay in an untidy heap of red, brown and white feathers and ochre fur, its bones twisted at unnatural angles, its large kite's head lolling, white beak half-open in death. One broken wing dangled loose over the edge of the bridge, suspended over the abyss like bait for some fearsome moat monster, its feathers riffling in the wind.

The sight filled the devas and apsaras with foreboding, yet they couldn't take their eyes off the crumpled form. For though reports of garudas dropping out of the sky had been coming in from all over Amaravati all morning – a dozen garudas had already plummeted past the palace windows and balconies into the abyss below – to many in the palace, the inert body on the bridge was the first dead garuda they had ever set eyes on.

From every possible vantage point they gawked, shocked and fascinated, as four devas ran onto the bridge to retrieve the body and carry it back to the broad palace courtyard, which was crammed with commanders and officers of various deva divisions, many of them already bearing arms. So dense was the gathering that devas spilled onto the twenty-odd steps that led up to the raised platform at the head of the courtyard. It was with some difficulty that the dead scout was borne through this throng, and a square of space cleared at the foot of the steps for the four devas to set their burden down.

"Is it dead?" a horrified voice whispered, making Narada glance up at an adjacent balcony. The speaker was an apsara, disbelief shining in her eyes.

"How is that possible? It is a garuda – *an immortal*," a deva by the apsara's side wondered. "Nothing can kill a garuda."

"This one is dead," insisted a third deva. "Like all the others that have fallen."

"It must be an illusion," the apsara began arguing, but Narada was distracted by Brihaspati's voice at his shoulder.

"What do you make of the situation?"

"What amazes me is the asuras' move to pluck straight at Amaravati – very bold," Narada replied, peering at the sky from behind the curtained window where he and the chamberlain stood. "And taking the garudas out before attacking anything else – very clever of them."

"I was speaking of the morale down there," Brihaspati thrust his chin in the direction of the courtyard. "There is fear and uncertainty – and your words aren't exactly inspiring confidence."

Narada turned his attention to the courtyard below, filled with restive devas, and to the platform where the golden-haired, sleepy-eyed Ashvin twins stood in the company of another brawny, bearded deva. He understood what the chamberlain was referring to – the crisis that loomed was unprecedented, and the devas were sorely missing the reassuring leadership of Indra. It showed in their cloudy eyes, the shuffle of their feet and in the listless hunch of their shoulders. The Ashvins and the Maruts could have filled that vacuum, but the upsets they had suffered in Sindhuvarta were still uppermost in every deva's memory.

"I am simply stating facts, gurudev," the diplomat shrugged.

"If the asuras are behind this, Amaravati and the palace need to be defended, Narada. Someone has to get that crowd to square shoulders and fight," Brihaspati's voice rose to a frantic pitch. Perspiration shone on his smooth forehead and ran down his chubby, ageless cheeks.

"Then let us see what we can do, gurudev," the diplomat looked down his sharp nose at the much shorter chamberlain.

Narada turned to leave the privacy of the room, but Brihaspati hung back. Glancing out of the window, he remarked, "I don't see Jayanta. Weren't summons sent to him as well?"

"To lead the defence of Amaravati?" the diplomat's eyebrows rose in faint surprise.

"The boy may still be young to lead in battle, but he should be standing with everyone else when the fighting begins. That is the minimum to expect from one who will preside over Devaloka one day."

Narada studied his fingers for a moment before answering. "I would summon him if I knew where he was, gurudev. Unfortunately, I have not seen him in nearly two days. Besides, his own father doesn't trust him with a sword – so why would we? He would probably do more harm than good being around."

The inchoate murmur that rippled through the courtyard died once Narada and Brihaspati stepped onto the platform.

Pushing past the Ashvins and the giant, Narada took two steps in the direction of the garuda, as if with the intention of inspecting it from closer, but seeing the beast spread out on the cold stones, broken in body and spirit, dead beyond hope, he changed his mind. Instead, he let his gaze skim over the faces assembled in the courtyard.

Pointing at the garuda, he said, "This should lay all doubts to rest. We have to presume we are under attack."

"What have we gathered about the attack so far?" asked one deva.

"Nothing at all, other than the fact that whatever is causing the garudas to die like this is somewhere above us," Narada replied.

The diplomat's words instinctively made the devas look upward in apprehension.

"Did we send any of the palace garudas up to investigate what is happening?"

"All ten of them were dispatched, but none of them returned." With a wry grimace, Narada clarified, "Or rather, none of them returned *alive*."

"What about the garudas that are still up there?" piped in another voice. "Have we tried summoning any of them back?"

Narada exchanged a glance with Brihaspati, who waddled forward on bowlegs.

"We did try, but not a single garuda has answered our summons. Perhaps there are no garudas left over Amaravati to hear us calling." The chamberlain licked his lips and ran a palm over his damp forehead. Eyeing the garuda stretched out at the bottom of the steps, he said, "Perhaps they are all dead. Perhaps this one was the last of them."

"Garudas never die, gurudev." All eyes turned in the direction of the speaker, an old, wrinkled deva standing on the sidelines. "Other than our summons, nothing can get to the heights the garudas fly at. No spear or arrow has been crafted that can soar as high as a garuda can. No spell can reach those limits of the sky; no curse can climb to where the garudas circle."

"Yet they are falling faster than ripened berries," said Narada.

"Could it be a plague that has afflicted them?" This time, it was a young deva from the far end of the courtyard.

"Plague or pestilence, we cannot rule out the hand of the asuras," the diplomat replied. "Neither can we rule out their intent."

A glum silence, lacquered with fear, fell over the courtyard. The gigantic deva on the platform stepped forward. Built like an ox, he rose treelike into the air, his muscularity all gnarled and massive and solid. A light brown beard reached halfway down his torso, and brown hair fell to his waist in two heavy plaits. He bore a large iron shield and a thick iron mace, its weighted, bulbous head moulded to resemble a horned demon skull.

Holding the shield to his chest, the deva twirled the mace over his head and brought it down hard across the face of his shield. The impact of the blow made him rock back on his heels, the thunderclap of metal on metal so loud that its echo crashed and bounced off the surrounding cliffs, and even appeared to erupt out of the very depths of the abyss.

"Hear me, brothers," he roared, his voice drowning out the last of the echoes. "It matters not how the garudas are dying or what is killing them. Whatever it is, it is bound to come down and reveal itself to us. When it comes, we have to be ready to give it death. I, Manyu, Keeper of the Palace, Slayer of Foes, am ready for it. Are you?"

A murmur broke through the courtyard. The giant swung his mace again and banged it on his shield.

"I am ready to give it death, brothers," he hollered. "Are you?"

Picking up strength and momentum, the murmur rapidly turned into a rumble, a swell of voices and raised swords and fists, everything yelling back the willingness to take on the hidden threat to Devaloka. Narada's spirits lifted, and looking across, he saw respite on the chamberlain's face as well.

The diplomat waited for the frenzy to settle. Raising his voice, he said, "Return to your divisions and prepare them for battle. By sunset, I want fires lit all around Amaravati, and on the cliffs around the palace. I want all eyes scanning the sky for the first glimpse of threat – that is where the attack is bound to come from. I also want word..."

Narada paused as a flutter of excitement washed over the assembly. The devas were looking behind him, toward the entry into the palace, and he caught the word 'fireborn' uttered in awed whispers. He turned to find a graceful, exotic figure attired in loose orange robes emerging from the doorway. The figure's head was shorn of hair, but from the softness and angularity of the face – the colour of ebony, with a plain silver nose ring on one nostril – it was plainly an apsara. Small flames licked the hem of her robes, and as she walked onto the platform, she left a fine trail of white ashy footprints in her wake that quickly blew away in the wind.

"Agneyi, my greetings," the diplomat's eyes sparkled with relief and delight as he bowed. "Thank you for answering my summons and joining us."

"I couldn't decline a brother's request," the apsara replied, returning the bow. Transferring her gaze to the chamberlain, the twins and Manyu, she added, "My greetings to Guru Brihaspati, the Ashvins and to the Keeper of the Palace. May I know what is wanted of me?"

"Amaravati is under an attack of some sort. We don't yet know what to expect, but we know it is coming for us. From above."

"You want me to weave a web of fire over Amaravati,

brother?" Agneyi looked at Narada for confirmation. "It will be done."

"Thank you. Devaloka will remember to repay this debt."

Agneyi withdrew and the diplomat addressed the gathering once again. "By the fireborn's grace, we will have both light and fire in the sky overhead. But I still want fires on the cliffs and all eyes on the sky. Also, ask the Maruts to come into battle. Now make haste – the sun is already dipping to the west."

The courtyard emptied rapidly. As palace hands came out to clear the yard of the dead garuda, Narada turned to those on the platform.

"I trust you will see to the defence of the palace and the drawbridges, Manyu," he said, looking up at the towering figure of the keeper.

The giant nodded and lumbered off, mace hoisted over one shoulder.

The diplomat addressed Nasatya and Dasra. "The Ashvin brotherhood will assume charge of protecting the cliffs. Your arrows will take down everything that comes out of the sky. Don't let anything get past you and alight on the palace."

The twins turned to depart, but Narada placed a restraining hand on Nasatya's shoulder. "And whatever happens, don't let fear take control the way it did in Sindhuvarta."

"We won't," Dasra replied. Appraising the diplomat shrewdly, he said, "You have summoned the fireborn and asked for fires to be prepared everywhere. What if what is up there isn't willing to wait until sundown?"

"It had all day; it would have showed itself by now if it wanted to." Narada gazed skyward, his face grim. "Whatever is up there is waiting to surprise us at the right moment – when the darkness is absolute and blinding."

* * *

Bathed in an even, luxuriant blue light, Amaravati rushed up from the surrounding darkness to meet Chandasura.

Glimpsed even from this height, the sight awed him. The city spread below him for miles in every direction, and twinkled in every conceivable corner like a superbly cut gem. Countless shapely spires rose a mile high from the ground, and geometrical boulevards crisscrossed the city, creating deceptive, illusory patterns in the eye. Buildings, statues, parks, bridges – wherever he turned, Chandasura could see exquisite examples of art and architecture. Though the black crystal palace, which housed the Court of the Golden Triad, was a marvel of corresponding eminence, Chandasura surmised that nothing in Patala quite matched Amaravati in the extent of its grandeur and beauty. Seated the way it was in the night, the capital of Devaloka reminded him of a turquoise diadem set against black satin.

This was their father's city, he thought as he speared down on the back of his screeching vyala. Then, correcting himself, he thought, *this was the city where their father had been born and raised*.

This was no longer their father's city.

He and Amarka had grown up hearing Shukracharya tell of how Amaravati had come into being, planned and built painstakingly over many years under the watchful eye of the master architect Vishwakarma, when the ancient town of Devaprastha had become too small to accommodate a growing population. Those were the days of concord, when the devas and asuras had lived together as one big family. Their father, the noble Sage Kashyapa, had envisioned Amaravati as a place where devas, asuras, kinnaras, yakshas, apsaras, kimpurushas, nagas and all other beings could live in harmony, which was why the city had been built on such a scale.

As always, fate, however, had other plans. The rivalry between the cousins flared even before Amaravati was fully constructed, and both devas and asuras were soon locked in an intransigent tussle to rule the city and Devaloka. The details of what transpired thereafter varied according to which side was telling the story – the devas blamed the sorceress Diti, Kashyapa's second wife and mother of the asuras, for trying to stoke a rebellion; the asuras accused her sister and the sage's first wife Aditi of trying to engineer a coup on behalf of her children, the devas.

In an effort to settle this bitter quarrel, a heartbroken Kashyapa proposed the division of Amaravati and Devaloka among his feuding wives and children, but fortunately for Amaravati, the thought of partitioning the city appealed to neither the devas nor the asuras. So the sage came up with a new formula for peace: one side would inherit Amaravati and Devaloka, while the other would have to leave and find new lands to claim as their own – the catch being that Kashyapa himself would join the side that chose to leave Devaloka. The devas picked Amaravati without a moment's hesitation, while the asuras, seeing value in being guided and mentored by their father, opted to depart. Thus had Kashyapa, Diti and their brood left Amaravati's gates and eventually gone on to rule Patala.

Yet, the allure of Amaravati had neither dulled nor diminished with time, and as he descended through the inky blackness over the charmed city, Chandasura could see why the asuras still coveted it. But the fascination with Amaravati was not limited to the asuras, Shukracharya had often reminded him and Amarka.

"Amaravati is everything to the devas," he remembered his father saying. "They allowed their own father to walk away with the asuras so they could keep Amaravati. Kashyapa wanted Amaravati for everyone, but the devas wanted it entirely for themselves. Look at it – the asuras are now in Patala, the yakshas have been exiled to Alaka, and the kinnaras and nagas have been slowly pushed into the mountains along Devaloka's borders. Only the kimpurushas still remain in Amaravati, but their status is no better than that of slaves. The devas have ensured they are the only ones left to enjoy the pleasures of Amaravati. Destroy the city, and you destroy all that the devas hold dear."

Chandasura was in no doubt that Shukracharya despised Amaravati. The city had rejected his father, made him into an outcast, and forced him to make Patala his home. It embodied deva arrogance and pride in Shukracharya's mind, and for that, his father craved its destruction.

Looking at Amaravati anew through his father's eyes, Chandasura found the city a lot less attractive. The ostentation of the city's structures was suddenly rude and offensive, the comforts they offered, crude and amateurish. This was a place that his mother's people had a right to, but instead they had had to roam the wilderness before lowering their roots in Patala. The thought filled him with rage, and he flicked the vyala's reins with renewed vigour.

Chandasura had figured that the blue light over the city was a spell, and as he drew closer, he observed a fine, shimmering web stretched across his path, suspended all the way across the city like a protective dome. Recognizing it to be the handiwork of a fire-wraith, he noted that the web's purpose was not just to cast a light but also serve as a fiery shield against intruders.

Chandasura smiled to himself. If the devas were thinking of mounting a defence with a mesh of fire, they were in for a very rude shock.

All around him, vyalas were dropping like stones, and the first one to make contact with the web was a little to Chandasura's right. He watched with interest as the web sparked and blazed briefly at the spot where the vyala struck it, the vyala's wings seemingly catching fire as it entangled in the mesh. However, the next moment, the beast had torn through the web's constricting filaments and continued its plunge, leaving a charred, tattered hole in its wake.

In hardly any time, the rest of the vyalas had also ripped past the fire-wraith's web, coming out unscathed, stronger and more cacophonous as they descended on Amaravati. Emerging from the mesh, his vyala's wings sucking in and absorbing the flames from the web as they slipped through, Chandasura glanced down at the city they were about to invade – and gasped in disbelief at the spectacle that met his eyes.

He then broke into a laugh, marveling at their good fortune.

Looking at it from far above in the web's blue light, the city had appeared to be twinkling with a multitude of lights, far too many even for a city the size of Amaravati. Chandasura had put it down to his eyes playing tricks in the dark – or another of the city's numerous eye-pleasing illusions that he had heard spoken of – but now he saw that the lights were real, and were coming from hundreds of fires that had been lit all over Amaravati.

The devas had been right in assuming that the attack would come under cover of darkness. In order to see the approaching enemy better, not only had they got the fire-wraith to cast its web, they had also lit fires everywhere. The strategy could not be faulted, Chandasura conceded. It might even have worked in the devas' favour, except for a minor detail which the city's defenders couldn't have factored in. *The vyalas.*

Bred and nurtured in great secrecy in the lava pits of Patala, the vyalas drew their sustenance, their aggression – their very nature – from heat and fire. Fire and heat was their essence, and that was what Amaravati had served up so richly that night, a veritable feast for the grisly beasts. He and Amarka couldn't have planned the assault better.

A shower of arrows sailed into the air to greet the diving vyalas.

The long shafts whizzed past the asuras and their mounts.

Quite a few arrows found their marks – out of the corner of his eye, Chandasura saw one ill-prepared asura tumble off his perch and fall, limbs cartwheeling as he crashed out of sight. But the arrows that struck the vyalas just glanced off their hard, scaly bodies.

The beasts, of course, didn't take kindly to the arrows. They counterattacked by opening their beaks and shrieking and squawking with even greater vehemence, each vyala setting off the other, raising a din that struck fear in the deva archers' hearts, making them drop their weapons and cover their ears in alarm. Then, in response to some invisible signal, the vyalas unfurled their tongues and spat balls of fire at the cringing, cowering archers. The fireballs sped in a flat trajectory and hit the devas square, each ball setting groups of devas on fire. While the victims screamed in agony and fell, their mates scattered and ran, abandoning position in a bid to seek cover. The vyalas' heads, however, sought out the fleeing figures and set them aflame with the next torrent of fireballs.

They were now skimming low over the city, and Chandasura noticed its defenders lining up with javelins and swords in hand, expecting the asuras to make a landing. The vyalas stayed airborne, though, just out of reach of the javelins, screeching and directing fire at buildings now. There was so much fire all around, Chandasura wasn't certain which ones had been started by the vyalas, but he saw a mansion and three watchtowers go up in flames.

"Their heads, their heads," he heard a voice shout over confusion. "Shoot at the creatures' heads."

Chandasura turned to see a group of deva archers clustered on a broad terrace. The group was looking the other way at four vyalas, the speaker in their midst, pointing and shouting out instructions. Chandasura instantly wheeled his vyala around and made for the terrace. The speaker was making sense, issuing the right instructions. He had to be silenced.

Flying low, he came up from behind the archers as they braced themselves and took aim at their targets. Balancing himself carefully and taking a firm grip on his mace, he swung the heavy weapon at the deva as the vyala swooshed over his head. The mace's flanges smashed into the back of the deva's helmet and dug into the metal, shattering his skull. The deva pitched forward, struck the terrace's low stone railing and keeled over it, dead before his body hit the ground many floors below. Meanwhile, the vyala's razor-sharp talons caught one of the archers in the back, hooking him under the shoulders, squeezing him in a vice-like grip and lifting him up into the air.

Startled and disoriented by the unexpected attack, the archers on the terrace loosed off their arrows at Chandasura. The arrows had been shot in a hurry and were poorly aimed, so they missed Chandasura as he pulled away and soared into the air. Only one arrow hit something – their fellow archer, whom the vyala had plucked off the terrace. The deva, already in agony over the talons biting into his back and shoulders, screamed even louder in pain as the arrow buried into his fleshy thigh. The scream choked and died suddenly, as the vyala's claws pierced the deva's armour and punctured his heart. The beast then let go of him in mid-air, and he fell without a sound.

The opening assault had been spectacular in its intensity and impact, but Chandasura could see that the surprise had worn off and the devas had begun rallying. More and more arrows were being shot at the vyalas' heads, and even though they were difficult targets to fire at, the move was meeting with some success. One arrow thwacked into one of his mount's necks, skewering it and making the head droop and loll. However, an asura passing by instantly moved in and severed the head and the embedded arrow free, allowing a new head to replace the old one.

Chandasura acknowledged the asura's assistance with a nod of thanks. "Where is Amarka?" he shouted through his visor. It was time to make their next move.

The asura pointed. Chandasura looked over his shoulder to see his brother directing his vyala over a forested park where deva archers sat concealed in trees. Amarka's vyala spouted a stream of fire, setting the forest and park aflame, incinerating the hidden archers.

Chandasura maneuvered his mount and approached as Amarka completed his attack and began an upward climb. Seeing his brother, Amarka reined his vyala into an easy glide.

"We must move toward the palace," Chandasura hollered, jerking his arm in the direction of the towering pinnacles that rose in the distance.

Amarka nodded and banked his vyala, deftly changing course to head for the pinnacles. Chandasura cast one sweeping glance around him, taking in the circling vyalas as they vomited fire over Amaravati. With a satisfied flick of the reins, he swung around in a wide arc and followed his brother's path, summoning more asuras to join him as he flew, making straight for Indra's palace, the seat of deva power.

* * *

Pallavan could not help noticing that the three pairs of eyes evaluating him in the light of the lamps were remarkably alike in one aspect – they were grey in colour, a tone otherwise quite rare in Sindhuvarta. That was where the similarity ended.

Asmabindu, the legal adviser, was a tall man with a heavy, salt-and-pepper beard that flared in all directions and seemed to weigh his head down, imparting him a permanent stoop. Diganta, an expert at trade relations, was also tall, but had just a thin moustache on his lean, narrow face. Bhaskara – whom Uttama had introduced as 'recently retired from the palace' –

was a dark, thickset individual with a square, manicured beard the colour of snow.

"This Gajaketu..." Asmabindu coughed and cleared his throat apologetically. "Where is he right now?"

"In Sravasti, safe in our custody," said Pallavan.

"Right, right," Asmabindu coughed again delicately. "And how do we know he is not making the whole thing up?"

"As I just explained, he has nothing whatsoever to gain from cooking up such a story. Moreover, he has recounted what he saw many times over, on many different occasions. Not once does his version change, even in the little details. If he were making it up, there would naturally have been minor embellishments in every subsequent narration – it is the way we humans behave when we lie."

"Let us, for the moment, assume he is telling the truth," Bhaskara butted in, his voice gruff and gravelly. "The question is whose word are people more likely to believe – a travelling musician's or that of the king of Magadha?"

"You have a point," the diplomat from Kosala conceded, shooting a quick look at Uttama, who sat to one side. "But the fact is that the three of you have chosen to come all this way in the middle of the night to listen to me, when you could have rubbished it as a musician's ramblings. Doesn't this show there is enough merit in Gajaketu's account for people to want to give him a patient hearing?"

"We came because the account came to us from Uttama, who heard it from a respected diplomat such as yourself," said Bhaskara dryly. "I know what you mean, but there's a difference between hearing you say it and hearing some lowly musician say the same thing. And I don't foresee either you or Uttama walking around Girivraja saying all that you have told us without being charged for treason."

Pallavan inclined his head. He knew the retired palace official was right in his assessment of the situation. Letting the subjects of Magadha know exactly what had transpired between Siddhasena, Shoorasena and the Kikata bodyguard that morning was not an easy challenge to surmount.

"Also, making an accusation of this nature is one thing," Asmabindu spoke into his beard. "With no other witnesses to back the musician's claim, how do we begin proving what really happened, short of Shoorasena admitting to having killed the old king?"

"We could make a start by sowing doubt and suspicion in the people's minds," offered Pallavan.

The Magadhan officials shuffled in their seats and exchanged dubious looks. Bhaskara rose and walked to the window to stare into the pitch dark. Had there been light outside, he would have seen a dense orchard stretching half a mile around the small mansion, handed down to Uttama by his ancestors, a picturesque and private retreat nestled in the hills a few miles north of Girivraja.

"What do *you* propose we do?" Diganta, who was not given to many words, locked eyes with the diplomat as he ran a finger along the line of his moustache. "You must have some plan in mind."

Conscious of the close scrutiny, Pallavan gestured toward Bhaskara. "I agree with our friend that none of us can air the musician's accusations in public without attracting censure. So, the only option we are left with is to get the word out to the public through the rumour mill."

"Meaning?" Bhaskara narrowed his eyes in confusion.

"Meaning… we can let select people in Kosala know that a musician has sought asylum in Sravasti because of what he saw happen here in Girivraja. And who are the people who shall be told about Gajaketu's existence? Merchants, traders and craftsmen – men of commerce who deal regularly with Magadha, who are in touch with bargemen and caravan owners. If the news lands in the right ears, it is bound to catch and spread, and in no time, the citizens of Girivraja will hear of it. Imagine a cartman sitting in one of Girivraja's taverns and telling the story; now imagine ten cartmen telling the same story."

"What good would that serve?" asked Asmabindu.

"People in Magadha will talk about Gajaketu's version, and it will only be a matter of time before the story finds its way to the palace. We would have set the cat among the pigeons. It will be interesting to see how Shoorasena reacts to the news."

"The king would immediately rubbish the theory and probably pass a decree to the effect that those found indulging in such rumourmongering are liable to be punished," Diganta remarked.

"That is where the four of you will have roles to play," said Pallavan, his eyes glittering in triumph. "Rumours like this one can't be suppressed, and the four of you can allow it to float around the palace. You can assess how the story affects your esteemed colleagues and members of the royal council, who dismisses it as nonsense and who is open to the possibility of its being true. Each of you can gauge public opinion *and* influence it in subtle ways. Why, you might even be able to find out if anyone else in the palace had knowledge of the plan to assassinate King Siddhasena – that might be all the evidence we need."

"And then?" asked Asmabindu, rising from his seat and pacing the room in small, measured steps.

"Honestly, I don't know. If we are able to plant doubt in enough minds and influence public sentiment, Shoorasena will be compelled to act in some way. Ignoring this problem won't make it go away for him. Then who knows... maybe he will demand an explanation from Kosala. He might even insist that my king clarify that no such musician exists in Sravasti. Our task is to force his hand. Whatever Shoorasena does will determine our subsequent course of action, but we will not rest until justice has been delivered to the old king."

Asmabindu nodded. Looking at his companions in turn, he raised his tufty eyebrows in enquiry. "What do you say?"

"It is not the best plan I have heard, but in the absence of a better one, I shall go with it," said Bhaskara. "If for nothing else, at least for our beloved King Siddhasena – he was a man of peace and didn't deserve the death he got."

"I agree," said Diganta, looking at Uttama, who was also nodding in support.

"That's settled then," Asmabindu resumed his pacing and reached Bhaskara's side. Scratching his beard vigorously, he stared out of the window for a moment before turning his eyes on Pallavan. "If things go according to your plan, and *if* the need arises, can you and King Bhoomipala produce Gajaketu at short notice?"

"Of course," Pallavan assured. "If you can set up a tribunal and bring charges on Shoorasena and anyone else involved in the old king's assassination, we can have the musician escorted to Girivraja so Magadha's citizens can see and hear him."

"Very well. And when can you start planting his story among Kosala's trading community?"

"As soon as I get back to Sravasti. It is a question of picking..."

A sudden commotion somewhere outside interrupted the diplomat; a rush of feet, a shout, followed by the banging of a door.

"What's happening, Uttama?" Bhaskara asked in mild alarm.

"I don't know," the tax administrator replied, rising from his chair. "We have had robbers raiding the orchard for mangoes... maybe a couple of them have been sighted or caught. Let me check."

Uttama had covered less than half the distance to the

shut door when footsteps sounded outside. The door was thrown open inward, and Pallavan and the four Magadhan officials saw a captain of the Magadhan army step over the threshold and swagger into the room, brandishing a long sword. Immediately behind him came a posse of five soldiers, all bearing swords and spears.

"What is the meaning of such behaviour, captain?" Bhaskara demanded angrily, though Pallavan could sense it amounted to little more than bluster. "Is this how you show your respect for members of the palace?"

"The mansion is surrounded by soldiers; do not attempt to run or resist," the captain spoke mechanically, not bothering to acknowledge Bhaskara's outrage. "I have orders to take you alive, but given sufficient provocation, I am at liberty to kill you as well."

"What is this all about?" asked Diganta.

To Pallavan's mind, the question was unnecessary. It crossed his mind that he had a dagger concealed on his body, but seeing the futility of the situation, he junked the idea. There would be bloodshed, but no escape, that much was plain.

"I am here to place all of you under arrest for conspiring against the throne," the captain's monotone took an ominous edge. "You are accused of high treason against King Shoorasena and the kingdom of Magadha."

Brothers

"The Asuras have been training vyalas all along."

Brihaspati's voice was hushed, rustling with astonishment and disquiet in equal proportions. "I had thought the last of the vyalas had become extinct a thousand years ago."

"They very clearly hadn't," said Narada, following the downward swoop of one of the beasts with grim eyes. "A few must have somehow stuck around, and the asuras have done a tidy job of keeping their survival a secret."

The diplomat and chamberlain were in the company of a few other devas, all standing under the protection of a large, covered portico that overlooked the northern drawbridge, keeping a close watch on the battle's course.

Not that it was much of a battle; not with the asuras toying with the city's hapless defence, setting fire to anything that caught their fancy, while the devas sheltered where they could and did their best not to get scorched.

The vyalas had been the attackers' biggest asset, totally blindsiding the devas. Not only had the devas been woefully unprepared to deal with something on this scale, Narada realized that they had only strengthened the asuras' hand by setting up all those fires around Amaravati. As if that wasn't bad enough, when the vyalas arrived over the palace, the Ashvin cavalry had attacked them with their flaming arrows, the Maruts with their hot energy bolts.

Getting the Ashvins and the Maruts to cease attacking with heat and fire, calling off the fire-wraith, and dousing the fires they had lit – none of these measures had served any purpose as far too many fires were burning in the city, many kindled by the vyalas themselves. With so many energy sources to draw from, the gruesome beasts were virtually unstoppable.

To make matters worse, the asuras stayed airborne – beyond the reach of the Maruts' spine-swords, Manyu's iron mace and the Ashvins' lances – using the vyalas to set the deva infantry and cavalry divisions on fire. Narada knew that the only way the devas could even the odds was by engaging the asuras in close combat, but that wasn't possible unless the asuras chose to get off their mounts and meet Amaravati's defenders on firm ground.

"It was indeed a well-guarded secret if even the most alert garuda knew nothing about the vyalas' existence," Brihaspati agreed. Displaying a sudden burst of resentment toward the scouts, he added, "It serves the garudas right that they were they first to suffer at the hands of these beasts."

"Was it the vyalas that killed the garudas, gurudev?" one of the devas enquired.

"It was."

"But can vyalas soar as high as that, gurudev?" asked another young, incredulous deva.

"They can't," replied Brihaspati.

"Then how did they succeed in killing..."

"The garudas died because the vyalas' screams carried up to the cold heights," Narada interrupted, carefully scanning the cliff wall directly opposite.

Seeing the devas' befuddlement, Brihaspati offered an explanation. "The first garuda and the first vyala were twins born to Ayanemi, the immortal Mother Bird. Ayanemi first gave birth to the vyala, and the agony of birthing made her scream. The scream became a part of the vyala, deforming it, making it ugly. But when the garuda was born, she felt no pain and her joy made the garuda beautiful. Ayanemi despised the sight of the vyala and grew partial toward the garuda, so when the time came for her to pass on the gift of immortality, she chose to give all of it to the garuda, ignoring the vyala entirely. Then, fearing that the vyala would steal her blessing from the garuda, she sent the garuda into the skies and cast the vyala into the fires of Naraka. Filled with rage and hatred, the accursed vyala swore that it would have its revenge on its sibling whenever their mother's scream fell on a garuda's ears. That is why the vyalas are always screaming, and that is why the garudas, who had never heard such a fearsome sound before, died of fright."

"So the vyalas' screams were the only things that could harm the garudas," a deva whispered in awe. "And the asuras used this knowledge to their advantage."

A vyala chose that moment to make a low lunge over the palace, a terrifying screech issuing from the bottom of its lungs. The devas covered their ears and cringed, flinching as a bolt of fire shot from the beast's mouth and set alight a group of three Ashvins who had foolishly stepped out of cover. Two of the horsemen crashed to the stones of the courtyard, the fire catching as they writhed in pain. Meanwhile, the third Ashvin's horse reared on its hind legs before making a blind, fiery dash across the courtyard and disappearing over the edge of the moat, mount and rider falling headlong into the abyss and twinkling out of sight.

As the vyala lifted back up into the sky, two Ashvins rode into the courtyard and shot two arrows each at the heads of their fallen brothers. Both figures ceased wriggling and slumped in death, the flames charring their bodies black.

"What matters now is figuring out a way of getting the asuras to face us at close quarters," Narada urged. Pausing to give it a thought, he addressed one of the junior devas. "Summon the Maruts as fast as you can."

To the young deva's credit, he was able to round up Diti's seven demon sons in no time. The diplomat quickly sketched the problem facing the city's defenders, and the Maruts listened to him in silence, waiting for him to finish before speaking.

"I can't see how we can tackle the asuras in close combat when they are up in the air," one of the giants appraised Narada with his cold, moonlight-white eyes.

"We can do what you say only if they alight on the ground," another Marut seconded.

"Which, from what we can see, they have no immediate intentions of doing," replied Narada, lifting his face up to the four-horned rakshasas towering over the knot of devas. "So, if they won't come down to fight us here, the only option left is for us to go to them."

"How do you propose we do that, Narada?" asked Brihaspati.

"By way of those cliffs," the diplomat's finger pointed across the chasm. He looked at the Maruts. "If you were able to get halfway up the cliffs, do you think you could leap onto the backs of any of the vyalas passing over the abyss?"

The Marut right in front placed his hands on his hips and stared at Narada, flexing his thick neck muscles by tipping his head from side to side. The downward curving horns swayed dangerously close to Narada, but the diplomat neither blinked nor backed away. At last, the Marut looked back at his brothers, who all nodded impassively.

A short while later, a group of Ashvins emerged into the open and shot volleys of flaming arrows into the sky. The arrows went nowhere close to the vyalas – their only purpose was to distract the asuras long enough for the Maruts to sprint across the northern bridge undetected.

Narada watched the arrows ascend before shifting his sights to the far end of the bridge, anchored to the rocky cliff and the road that led through it into the city. He sighed with relief as the barely-distinguishable rakshasas slipped past the bridge and melted into the cliff's shadows.

***

Amarka almost missed the blur of movement coming at him out of the darkness.

A moment ago, there had been nothing in his line of vision except Indra's palace, the abyss surrounding it and the rocky cliff to one side. The next instant, out of the corner of his eye, he sensed something large and heavy, but surprisingly agile, materialize from the black cliff face, hurtling toward him as his vyala swooped low over the abyss, hunting for targets to set on fire.

Amarka whipped his head around just in time to see an enormous figure leaping straight at him. There was just enough light to make out the huge, jagged sword that the figure wielded, and the four sweeping horns on its head. While still in mid-leap, his assailant swung the sword at one of the vyala's five heads, severing it in one clean stroke. Without missing a beat, the figure completed its leap, crashing into the vyala with such force that the beast pitched alarmingly before correcting its course.

The figure hooked an arm around one of the vyala's necks and began hoisting itself onto the beast's back. It was a bit of a struggle, and seizing the opportunity, Amarka brought his axe down hard on the heavy forearm wrapped around the vyala's neck. To his amazement, the axe-head bounced and juddered as if it had struck stone, the impact sending hot barbs of pain up his arm. The figure managed pulling itself halfway up, so Amarka aimed his next blow at its shoulder, but again the axe ricocheted away. The figure turned, and as he stared into its face in astonishment, Amarka noticed the moonlight-white eyes looking back at him.

It was one of the Maruts! Even as the realization dawned, in his peripheral vision Amarka saw two more of Diti's seven abominations detach themselves from the cliff's side and throw themselves onto passing vyalas.

Amarka raised his axe a third time, this time targeting the head, unprotected by the shell-like exoskeleton. But before he could land the blow, the Marut took a broad, vicious swipe at his chest with its sword. The strike came in fast and carried such power that his armour buckled under its pressure, and Amarka felt as if a hot iron had been run through his torso. The breath went out of him in a rush, and as he lost his balance, he was unseated from the vyala's back.

The next moment, Amarka was spinning and tumbling through the air.

Down and down he went, gravity tugging him relentlessly into the bottomless depths of the chasm. The vyalas' shrieks receded until he could hear nothing but the rush of air in his ears, and the light of the fires dwindled as the hungry darkness of the pit sprang up to claim him. Fear erased all thoughts from his mind, supplanting them with one single idea – the knowledge that this fall could last forever. No one in all three worlds knew if this abyss had a floor, and if it did, how far below it actually was. No one had ever found the bottom of this chasm and come back to speak of the feat.

All of a sudden, something took a vice-like grip on Amarka's wrist, breaking his fall.

The abrupt shift in momentum jolted his hand, and as he dangled over emptiness, a searing, tearing pain erupted at his shoulder. Blind and disoriented, he had just begun fearing his arm would come apart at the joint when he sensed a change in the flow of air currents and realized he was being drawn upward.

"Take my hand and pull yourself up, brother."

Chandasura's voice came to him as if from far away, but looking up, Amarka saw his brother leaning over his vyala's shoulder, peering down at him. He grabbed Chandasura's muscular forearm, which was supporting all his weight.

"Are you hurt?"

"No."

Reaching out with his free hand, Amarka hauled himself up inch by painful inch, until with one final, powerful heave Chandasura yanked him up so he could climb onto the vyala's back. The beast soared back toward the light, and Amarka held his brother's shoulders with trembling hands.

"That was close," he said into Chandasura's ear. "Thank you for coming after me, brother."

"I had to," Chandasura threw a backward glance. The visor muffled Chandasura's voice, but Amarka could tell he was smiling. "No way would I have gone back to father without you."

"It is the Maruts," Amarka spoke as the palace came back into view, a sparkling encrustation on the spur of rock rising out of the abyss. High above the palace, four vyalas were engaged in mortal combat. "They are taking control of the vyalas."

"I know," Chandasura grunted, urging his mount toward the four vyalas fighting overhead. "The mother sorceress should have strangled those seven at birth instead of leaving them in the cold for Indra to find and adopt as his own. But they are just seven – we can easily take them on."

Two of the four vyalas had been taken over by the Maruts, who were now clashing with the asuras riding the other two.

Even as Shukracharya's sons approached the group, one of the asuras fell off his vyala, his body cut in two by a Marut's sword. Uttering an angry oath, Chandasura swooped over the Marut's vyala, swinging his mace at the four-horned head. The Marut, however, saw the descent of the weapon just in time and dodged, but the mace still cut its cheek, making the demon's silver blood run. The rakshasa responded swiftly, its sword arcing toward Chandasura's head, but the asura parried the assault.

Attack met with counterattack. The encounter was ferocious, bloody and closely contested. Though outnumbered, the Maruts fought with all their demonic strength, leaping from one vyala to the next, throwing the asura riders down to the ground one after another. The notion of the tables finally turning on their tormentors brought a ragged cheer out of Amaravati's defenders. Emboldened devas rushed out to the fallen asuras, hacking at those who were unfortunate enough to survive the drop. Chandasura estimated that they had lost a dozen asuras, and more were going down with every passing moment.

Knowing that stopping the Maruts was imperative, he pressed more and more asuras into the fray, and the advantage slowly tilted back in the attackers' favour, as Diti's unwanted seven began tiring. Moreover, notwithstanding their dauntlessness, the rakshasas were handicapped by their lack of skill in handling the quick-tempered vyalas. One by one, the frustrated Maruts dropped back to the ground in the hope that the attackers would follow them so the deva army could join the battle. But the asuras and their vyala mounts stayed firmly out of reach.

The sky gradually turned grey to the east, and before long, the first light of a new day touched the tips of the vyalas' wings.

"We have wreaked plenty of havoc, as was demanded of us by father," Chandasura said to Amarka, getting his vyala to turn around. "Let us depart."

Sweeping over the palace in a wide circle, the brothers signaled to the asura army. Slowly, the vyalas rose into the air, higher and higher, still rasping and screeching as they started heading south.

Chandasura looked back at Amaravati one last time as he crested the summit of Mount Meru, but all he could make out was a pall of smoke stretching for miles, with the pinnacles of Indra's palace poking through its dirty grey layers.

A sight that would have pleased his father no end, he thought with satisfaction.

Kubera

Ghatakarpara peered at the prisoner through the grille set high in the door. The man sat hunched in one corner of the tiny cell, his back pressed against the wall, hands dangling between his knees. Eyes closed and head lolling to one side, he appeared to be asleep, but Ghatakarpara could hear him crooning softly to himself. He swayed forward occasionally, only to rock back on his dirty, cracked heels.

"Has he said anything since I left?" the prince asked one of the three soldiers of the Frontier Guard who stood guard by the door.

"No, your honour," the soldier replied. "Not one word that any human can understand."

"Hmmm," Ghatakarpara pursed his lips and turned back to the prisoner, who had also just realized there were people on the other side of the door. The man stared at Ghatakarpara with beseeching, fear-filled eyes, and instinctively covered his cheek with one hand, as if to guard himself from being slapped. Hugging his knees with his other hand, he rolled himself tighter into a ball, trying to make himself disappear into the shadows of the cell.

He had been found wandering near the outpost of Balipura around mid-morning, just as Ghatakarpara was preparing to leave the outpost to survey the border positions nearby. When accosted, the man had been unable to explain who he was and what he was doing in the area, so the soldiers had brought him in for further questioning. Ghatakarpara had joined in the interrogation briefly, but not only did the man not seem to understand them, his entire vocabulary consisted of monosyllabic *aai*s and *aau*s and *uuh*s. When even a few tight slaps failed to loosen his tongue, he was put in confinement, his fate to be decided once Ghatakarpara returned from his inspection of the border.

"What should we do with him, your honour?" one of the soldiers asked.

"We can't just let him go," the prince answered, squinting into the bright, noonday sunlight that emptied into the outpost's courtyard. "For all we know, he could be a Huna scout."

"He doesn't look like much of a scout, your honour," remarked the third soldier, a veteran with a big, grey moustache. "He seems a little soft in the head to me."

"It could just be an act. Even his speech disability could be put on." Ghatakarpara vaguely wondered whether the outpost would have a convenient dead body around so he could try Amara Simha's trick on the prisoner. He promptly dismissed the idea, unsure if he could even pull off the stunt without losing the morning's breakfast. "Are we certain he is a stranger to these parts?"

"We checked, your honour. None of the soldiers have seen him hereabouts before. The men who caught him also asked a couple of local goatherds if they recognized him. None of them did."

"He has to be a scout then," said the prince. "Unlock the door."

Entering the cell, Ghatakarpara took three strides and stood before the prisoner. The prince guessed the man to be in his mid-twenties.

"Okay, enough of this nonsense. Who are you and what are you doing here? C'mon, *speak up*."

The man jerked his head back as Ghatakarpara barked the last words out. "Aaaaau... uuuuh."

"That is not going to get you very far," the prince snapped.

"Aaaai... uuh... aaaaaa..."

"Perhaps all he needs is a sound beating," suggested one of the younger soldiers.

"You heard him," Ghatakarpara pointed at the soldier, bending and bringing his face close to the prisoner's. "You will be beaten, you will be starved, you will be tortured until we get the truth out of you. Do you want all that done to you?"

The man flinched. "Aau... aaaaaa..."

The prince straightened. His military training told him that he needed to carry out some of his threats for his words to be taken seriously. Yet, the absence of guile in the prisoner's eyes made him think twice. Perhaps the man was harmless. Then again, perhaps the man was an exceptional actor. It was all so exasperating. None of his training had prepared him to handle such situations.

"Shall I take him out and tie him to the stake for a whipping, your honour?"

Still unable to make up his mind about the man – and acutely aware that the soldiers were sizing him up and would judge him against the decision he took – Ghatakarpara was saved from offering a half-baked reply by the crunching of heavy wheels on gravel. Craning his neck around the open door, he observed a one-horse carriage roll to a stop outside the stockade that ran along the periphery of the outpost. A bright, colourful canopy at the back sheltered the passengers from the sun's glare, and as the prince watched, the curtains parted and two women stepped hurriedly off the carriage. At the same time, three men – local villagers, by their looks – trotted up to the outpost's gate.

As the soldiers gawked at the arrivals in open curiosity, three guards approached the carriage with caution, their spears tilted and ready for any eventuality. One of the women – the younger of the two, Ghatakarpara noted – took a few steps in the direction of the advancing soldiers.

Stopping just inside the gate, one hand on her hip, she demanded, "Who is in charge here?" Her voice was sharp and brimming with indignation.

The soldiers were still exchanging uncertain glances when the prince stepped onto the verandah of the building that housed the cell.

"I am," he said in a tone lazy with authority. "What do you want?"

The woman entered the compound, fixing Ghatakarpara with a cold and belligerent stare. Seeing her from closer, the prince realized she was young, probably just out of her teens. She was short and built on the slightly heavier side. Her face was round and chubby, light brown in complexion. A small gold ring adorned her nose, and her lips were full as they pouted at Ghatakarpara in anger.

"Soldier, your men have captured and forcefully brought a man here this morning," she said. "Is that right?"

"Maybe," Ghatakarpara shrugged and brushed a few strands of hair back from his eyes. "What of it?"

"I want you to set him free immediately."

"Who are *you*? And what is this man to you?"

"I am Aparupa, and the man is my maid's son," the girl pointed in the direction of the older woman, who still stood by the carriage. The woman, who was probably around forty-five, bowed her head and raised her clasped hands at Ghatakarpara.

The prince looked at the ring of soldiers around the courtyard. "Does anyone here recognize the maid? Or her, for that matter?" He gestured at the girl standing before him.

The soldiers had just begun shaking their heads when the girl snapped at Ghatakarpara. "Obviously none of them will. We are not from these parts. We are from Udaypuri. I am here visiting my grandparents, who have their home in the village of Balipura." She turned and threw her arm at the three men who had followed the carriage on foot. "Ask them, if you don't believe me."

One of the villagers came forward. "I am the local cobbler, sir. I have often mended the sandals, belts and harnesses of your men." Ghatakarpara saw a handful of soldiers nod in agreement.

"What the lady says is true, sir," the cobbler continued. "Her grandparents have been living in Balipura for ages, and her grandfather is a well-known incense maker in this region. The lady and her maid come to the village at least once every year, and I know them both well, sir. I have even seen the boy a couple of times over the years."

"Satisfied?" Aparupa tilted her chin at Ghatakarpara in challenge.

The prince couldn't help thinking that the big, black eyes flashing at him were immensely attractive. "Bring him out," he said to one of the soldiers.

Cowering and shaking with fright, the man was escorted out of his cell. As he blinked in the harsh light, a hollow gasp escaped the elderly maid's lips.

"My son," she uttered in a trembling voice, taking a couple of steps forward.

The moment his eyes adjusted to the light and he saw his mother, the man rushed into the courtyard with open arms. "Aaaaai... aaaaa... aaaau," he moaned in despair and threw himself into the woman's embrace, the grief of separation and the relief of reunion weaving an unmistakable symphony in Ghatakarpara's ears. Watching mother and son weep, Aparupa turned back to the prince.

"How can you just take someone captive like that?"

"He was moving around the outpost suspiciously, and when the men questioned him, he couldn't provide any satisfactory answers," Ghatakarpara replied.

"Can't you see he can't talk and is mentally backward?" the girl shot back. "And you arrested him without even bothering to find out who he was?"

"We asked some goatherds, but they didn't recognize him," the prince suddenly felt irritated at being pushed into the defensive.

"Goatherds!" Aparupa literally stamped her foot in anger. Flinging an arm out, she shouted, "The village is less than two miles away. You could have asked *there*."

"Right. From now on, that's what the Frontier Guard and Imperial Army will do every time they make arrests – parade suspects from village to village for proper identification. A circus of convicts touring the kingdom!" Ghatakarpara snorted in derision. "What a marvelous idea – somebody must suggest it to the king!"

Spots of red heat blossomed and spread across the girl's cheeks. "I didn't say village to village. Balipura is just *here*."

"And what if he had been from two or three villages further away? Then it would have been fine to arrest him, beat him up and even kill him, I suppose?"

Before the girl could stitch together a fitting retort, Ghatakarpara pressed his advantage. "And what are you standing here and ranting about? You *know* the fellow can't talk and is mentally backward. Why did you let him roam wherever he pleased when one of you should have been keeping an eye on him? He is your responsibility, not mine. If you care so much about him, you should keep him in Udaypuri under lock and key."

"How dare you! Is that how you would treat a backward member of your own family?" Aparupa clenched her fists, frustration and rage shimmering in her eyes. "That's it!" she blazed, wagging a finger at Ghatakarpara's face. "You have no idea of what I can do. My father is a well-connected man, soldier. You will regret this day dearly. I shall make you stand before me and apologize for everything you have said and done."

The girl whirled around – her long plait of hair spinning with her – and stomped out of the courtyard. Watching her and her maid and the recently captive son climb back into the carriage, the prince wondered why she had kept addressing him as 'soldier'. Then it dawned on him. He was attired in the common uniform of a Frontier Guardsman, and not the formal clothes and decorations that he habitually wore in the garrison of Udaypuri.

"How stupid of her to be threatening you, your honour," the old soldier with the big, grey moustache gave a wide, broken-toothed grin. "You should have told her who you were. But I think you still shut her up nicely."

With a feeble smile at the heads nodding around him, Ghatakarpara trailed the departing carriage with an inward sigh, feeling strangely empty and forlorn. He wished the girl would carry through her threat once she returned to Udaypuri. That was probably the only way he would see her again.

* * *

"Can I offer you another helping of rice?"

"No, I am done," Vikramaditya replied. "I can't eat an ounce more."

"But I have..." Vishakha glanced at the samrat uncertainly.

"You have...?" Vikramaditya gave the queen an encouraging nod.

They were seated in a little alcove by the king's bedchamber, surrounded by potted ferns and flowering vines. A small fountain gushed nearby, with three placid white fish swimming in the sparkling pool that formed its basin.

"I made something for you."

The samrat watched Vishakha reach under the table and bring out a small plate covered with a square piece of light muslin. Setting the plate in front of him, Vishakha removed the cloth to reveal six conical dumplings made of rice flour.

"Aha, *modaka*!" Vikramaditya's face lit up. "These are my favourites."

"I know," Vishakha smiled back at him shyly.

The king had picked one *modaka* and was about to bite into it, but hearing Vishakha's words, he paused.

"You remembered that I like these?" His voice quivered with hope.

The queen dropped her eyes. "The Queen Mother told me you liked them," she answered in a small voice.

"I see."

Doing his best to keep the disappointment from showing, Vikramaditya bit into the warm dumpling, savouring the grated coconut and jaggery filling. It tasted exactly the way they had always tasted whenever Vishakha had prepared the delicacies in the past.

"Delicious," he said, reaching for a second one.

"I heard someone say he couldn't eat an ounce more," Vishakha gave the king a mischievous glance.

"I didn't hear someone say *modaka* before I said that," the samrat shot back playfully. "This is *so* good."

"Still not as good as the way *badi-maa* makes them," Vishakha said. Seeing the king look at her in surprise, she added, "She is the one who taught me how to make these. Always so kind and generous and helpful she is."

Vikramaditya pushed his plate away and rose from the table. He couldn't believe the queen had managed recalling even *badi-maa* – Vararuchi's mother had never lived in the palace, and Vishakha wouldn't have visited her on more than five occasions in all the time she had spent in Ujjayini. Yet she remembered *badi-maa*... but not him.

"Wouldn't you have one more?" Vishakha looked up at him, her eyes wide with doubt. "Aren't they nice?"

"Of course they are," the samrat gave her a reassuring smile. "I am only saving them for later. Now come... it is my turn to give you something."

Vikramaditya entered his bedchamber and went over to a wooden chest sitting in one corner. Opening it, he rummaged inside before pulling out a small box made of ironwood.

"This is for you," he said, taking Vishakha's hand and placing the box on her open palm.

The queen pried the lid open carefully and peeked inside.

"This..." she whispered, her eyes shining in awe, "...this is my mother's gift to me."

With delicate fingers, she extracted a ring fashioned out of polished jade, forest green in colour, and flecked with white. Vishakha's name, inscribed by a master artisan, ran all the way round the ring's outer surface.

"I believe it was made when you turned three," said the samrat.

"Yes, mother gave it to me when Kshapanaka and I left Nishada... it was her parting gift to me. I was to wear it the day I turned fourteen." Her brows knitted in distress. "I... I remember losing this once. Yes, it was in the palace bath, the one to the northeast with the big peepal growing by its side. I was heartbroken that day, I remember. I never thought I would get this ring back. But by some miracle, it was found. I swore never to wear it on my finger again, but to keep it safe somewhere."

Wiping the tears that had sprung up in her eyes, the queen looked at Vikramaditya in gratitude. "Thank you for giving me this."

"I had kept it safe for you – for the day when you would come back."

Vishakha studied the ring in silence, twirling it between thumb and forefinger. At last, she slipped it onto a finger on her right hand. "Then, for you, I shall wear it again," she said.

After a short pause, she raised her head to the king. "Kshapanaka tells me that you were a wonderful husband. I am beginning to think she is right."

They stood there for a moment, looking at one another in hope and despair. Then Vishakha took a step forward and put her arms around Vikramaditya. The samrat responded by putting a protective hand around his wife's shoulder, but their embrace was stiff and awkward – there was a stranger between them that neither could ignore.

"I should go," Vishakha said, pulling away gently. "You said you have a meeting with the council and the courtiers. I will send someone to clear the table."

Once the maids had cleaned up and left, Vikramaditya lay down on the bed and covered his eyes with an arm, resisting the urge to cry out in anguish.

Vishakha remembered the ring. She remembered losing it in the palace bath. She remembered it having been found later. But she didn't remember the one who had spent half the day in the dark depths of the bath, searching for the lost ring. She didn't remember him sitting beside her that evening at dinner, quietly slipping the ring into her palm.

She remembered everything but him. Maybe that was how it would always be.

The thought of such a possibility was tearing him apart, ravaging him from within.

* * *

"It has come for the deva."

The voice was so sudden and unexpected, tearing through the stillness of the lake house, that it startled Indra.

The lord of the devas looked around and behind him, then let his gaze return to the path that led to the water's edge. He noticed that Menaka had also stopped halfway down the path, and was glancing back at the lake house, trying to place the source of the voice. Her eyes finally locked with his, and Indra realized the apsara was as mystified as he was.

"Not you, apsara," the voice rang out again, shrill and irritated. "The boat has come for the deva."

This time, Indra was certain the voice had come from somewhere right behind him.

"The parrot. It's the parrot," Menaka exclaimed in surprise.

"What? This thing can talk?" Indra muttered half to himself, approaching the cage, peering through the wickerwork to catch a better glimpse of the bird. He stopped a foot away from the cage and glared at the parrot. "Never heard you talk before – full of tricks, aren't you? How about me showing you a trick by crushing your head in my hand?" Indra clenched his fist at the cage, his knuckles popping loud under the pressure.

"Let the bird be, my lord," said Menaka, stepping onto the terrace. "The message from the yaksha king has been delivered. The boat is waiting for you. Go!"

Wading into the lake, Indra closed in on the boat gingerly, afraid that the vessel might slip away at the last moment, revealing this to be just another of the games that Kubera loved playing. The boat, however, didn't budge until Indra was seated on board, whereupon it pushed away from the shore, propelled by unseen hands. As the boat eased through the whispering veils of mist, Indra looked back to see Menaka leaning against the terrace parapet and sobbing, her cheeks wet with tears of respite.

Shortly after his departure, the king of the devas started losing all sense of time and space. There were moments when the mist thinned and, through its shreds, he saw the night sky above him, decked up in stars like a bride, a half moon hanging low like an exquisite bridal pendant. The mists drew together again, and the next time they parted, Indra caught sight of a violent sunset, the sun bleeding red into a sky bruised purple. At times, the water beneath the boat appeared so clear he could see into the lake's bottom, where he fancied he saw palaces with moats around them, and farmlands stretching away on all sides. But at other times, the water underneath was dark and oily and impenetrable, yet he could sense ghastly forms with hollowed eyes and sinewy tentacles rippling and roiling and waiting in ancient hunger... Then, suddenly, there was no water under the vessel. Just empty air and cold mountains down, down below.

For all he detested Kubera, Indra couldn't help marveling at the city that the yaksha and his followers had built for themselves from the dreary, inhospitable glacier that Lake Alaka once had been. The golden spires that broke through the mist and caught the sun; the giant mermaid statues that lay sprawled on rocks, their lips parted in lustful invitation; the waterfalls that spilled out of the mouths of humungous lion and elephant heads cut from black granite... every sight made the deva draw his breath in admiration.

Eventually, the ceaseless glide of the boat, the cool scented breeze and the drifting mists lulled Indra to sleep. He had no idea how long he had dozed, but when the deva opened his eyes with a start, he saw that the boat was at a standstill, docked against a narrow wooden pier. White mist hid the other end of the pier from view, but Indra was certain there was a diffused glow of yellow lights dancing within its folds.

Stepping off the boat, Indra walked down the pier, the soggy, rotting planks creaking under his weight. He made his way into the mist, expecting it to fall back naturally, but instead it swarmed and eddied around him like smoke, growing thicker, whiter and more opaque. Alarmed at what the smothering mist might be hiding, the deva stopped.

"Anyone here?" he called out, conscious that the mist was muffling his voice. "I am Indra, lord of the devas, here to see Kubera."

"Welcome to Alaka, friend, welcome," whispered a sly voice that conjured a reptilian image in Indra's mind.

Instantly, the mist slipped away, as if repelled by a sudden magnetic force. It rolled back down the pier, retreating until it obscured the other end of the pier with the boat at its tip. Watching the mist withdraw, Indra was struck by the transformation that the pier underwent – the old, waterlogged wood changed into hard, white marble, flecked with gold.

Pivoting on his heel, the deva looked around, his jaw dropping as he took in the spectacle. He was standing in a large hallway, its walls, pillars and balconies plated in gold. Yet, it wasn't so much the hall's width as its height that was impressive. The ceiling rose steep into the air in a series of arches and domes, and from these, suspended at various heights, were elaborately cut crystal chandeliers and plates of shining gold. At the very apex of the structure burned one single lamp, and Indra realized that the light from that solitary lamp, reflecting off the gold plates and refracting through the carved crystal, lit the entire hall.

Then he spied Kubera, standing on a high balcony, beckoning him with a wave of a hand.

"Come. Let the mist guide you," the yaksha's voice whispered in his ear.

Again, for a matter of moments, a swirl of mist wrapped itself around Indra, spinning sideways and upward with him trapped in its vortex. In the blink of an eye, the mist was gone – and the deva drew his breath at the sight before him.

He was in a small marble gazebo, erected in the middle of a sedate pool filled with blooming water lilies and lotuses. A ridge encircled the pool, and a waterfall gushed over the lip of the ridge and cascaded into the pool from all directions, forming a white curtain of fast flowing water all around the gazebo. Yet, there was no sound of falling water, and the waterfall didn't trigger even a single ripple across the pool.

"Would you admit that we have created a city more beautiful that Amaravati?"

Indra turned to survey Kubera, lounging on a divan. The yaksha was fat beyond words and hairy to boot, an atrocity of flab and fur. Except for his dhoti, he was unclothed, but thick, matted hair covered most of the exposed skin. Bedecked in an array of gold ornaments that clinked whenever he moved, Kubera sported a thick black beard that covered his fleshy face, but failed to hide his thick, puffed lips. His eyes were the colour of charcoal and filled with guile.

"I would admit you have done well for yourself, Kubera," Indra replied casually as he lowered himself onto a vacant divan placed opposite the one the yaksha occupied.

"Do I detect faint praise there?" Kubera made a show of cupping his ear. Seeing there was nothing more coming from Indra, he clapped his hands together. "Well, what can I offer you? Nothing less than soma for the lord of the devas, isn't it?"

Indra sensed a movement near his shoulder, but before his eyes could focus properly, the mist-wraith was gone. Glancing down at the table by his side, he saw a goblet filled with soma waiting for him. Kubera watched Indra take a long sip of the refreshing wine.

"So what brings the lord of the devas to the humble abode

of the yakshas?" Indra caught the mocking tone in Kubera's voice. "It must be something terribly important for him to wait patiently for so many days."

Indra heaved a deep sigh. "I need your assistance to put a human king in place."

"A human king?" The yaksha stared at Indra in disbelief before bursting into laughter. "Why would the lord of the devas want my help in dealing with a *human* king?"

"This king has been the cause of much agony," Indra's reply was cold.

"If he has been such a pain, why not just use your vajrayudha to..." Kubera stopped, a wicked gleam forming in his eye. "I see. You can't use the vajrayudha because this king you speak of has done you and Devaloka no harm. Use the vajra on him and you lose the right to wield it forever. How interesting!"

Indra switched his attention to the goblet to avoid the yaksha's gaze.

"Exactly what sort of agony has the king been giving you?"

"How does that matter?"

"I would like to know," Kubera shrugged adamantly. Seeing Indra hesitate, he added, "If you are afraid I will judge you poorly, let me assure you that I have already judged you for what you are. If you remember, there are few secrets between us, and I don't think you can fall any lower in my esteem."

The deva's face went red with anger at Kubera's impudence, but the yaksha didn't appear to notice.

"And if you worry that what you will tell me will arouse my greed and make me want to covet it..." The yaksha spread a hand out, pointing around him, the rings on his finger glinting in the sunlight. "I have everything I want here in Alaka. There is nothing anyone can give me that I don't already have."

"Alaka doesn't have the apsaras you lust after, yaksha

lord," Indra's smile was rich with malice. He knew he had found a sensitive spot at last, and drawn level with Kubera.

The yakshas and devas had shared a troubled relationship even before the former were forced out of Devaloka. The yakshas had always fancied themselves as being equal to the devas, and it was no secret that Kubera had nursed ambitions of sitting on the throne at Amaravati. However, for all their talk of matching the devas, the yakshas lagged miserably when it came to attracting apsaras – the nymphs of Devaloka were invariably reluctant to consort with the yakshas. And although the yakshas were hermaphroditic, the apsaras held a special charm, making the yakshas covet them even more.

Things came to a head when three yakshas were charged with abducting an apsara with the intention of ravishing her. The three accused pleaded innocent at the trial, but even when the evidence was inconclusive, the tribunal adjudged them guilty.

Drubbing the whole affair as a conspiracy to malign his kind, Kubera demanded that the yakshas be exonerated. When Indra declined to overturn the tribunal's ruling, Kubera accused the deva himself of bias, insinuating that Indra was not fit for the throne if he couldn't dispense proper justice. The slur was too severe to overlook. Indra instantly decreed that the yakshas were to go into exile, terming them a blot on the beauty of Amaravati. Kubera and his followers had left Devaloka under a solemn oath – that they would construct a city of their own that surpassed Amaravati in its beauty. Over the years, Alaka was built to rival Amaravati, and the yakshas slowly gained mastery over the black arts. Yet, for all the magical powers they had acquired, Kubera did not dare move against Devaloka – he continued to fear the vajrayudha that Indra wielded to protect his realm.

The other aspect that did not change for the yakshas was

their enduring passion for the apsaras, who were now strictly out of bounds.

"What do you want from me, Indra?" Kubera asked, his face darkening at the deva's words.

"I told you. I want you to bring misery on the human king."

"And why would I do this for you?"

"I brought you the apsara."

Leaning back on his divan, the yaksha lord gave a scornful laugh. "You think you can walk in here with that plaything of yours, have her entertain me for a few days, and expect me to do whatever you wish? That might have worked in the past, but no... not any longer."

"If you do what I want, you can have Menaka in Alaka. For keeps."

Toying with one of the rings on his fingers, Kubera scrutinized Indra from under furrowed brows. The silence was so profound that the deva thought he heard the slightest gurgle of water falling into the pool.

"I can also send two dozen apsaras to Alaka for your followers," Indra extended the bait.

"You would do that?" Finally, there was greed on the yaksha's face.

Indra tossed back the contents of the goblet and nodded, stroking his rich golden beard in satisfaction.

Kubera swung his legs off the divan and perched himself on the edge of the seat. "Tell me what you want done to the human king," he said. "Tell me how much harm you want me to cause him."

Proposal

An amorphous haze of red dust, drifting slow and listless across the open field, was all that remained in the wake of the eight horses that had just thundered past Kalidasa, Shanku and half a dozen keepers and officials of the Imperial Stables. No breeze disturbed the flaps of the pavilion where the councilors and the horsekeepers stood, and the heat was unbearable even in the shade. Far to their right, at the other end of the field, close to fifty horses stood in an enclosure, snorting and swishing their tails to keep the flies away.

"What do you make of the lot we just saw, Warden?" Kalidasa asked of the small, wiry man sporting the badge of the Warden of the Stables. Keeri.

"I would definitely pick the dappled mare and the brown stallion with the white hind leg, your honour," the Warden said, running his fingers through his mop of silvery hair. "And maybe the white mare too, the one with the short tail."

"Each one of mine is a fine specimen, your honour, just ideal for the Imperial Army," a portly man butted in. From his general manner, it was plain he was a merchant. "I vouch none of the eight will ever give Avanti's cavalry grief."

"What's your opinion?" the giant mopped the sweat off his brow and looked down at Shanku.

"I would agree with the Warden, particularly about the mare with the short tail," the girl said, giving Keeri an appreciative smile. "She may not be the fastest among the lot, but she is all heart. But let us first look at what the other merchants have brought us."

The stockade opened and another set of horses cantered onto the field for inspection.

It was another three hours before Kalidasa and Shanku finally rode away from the pavilion, heading back for Ujjayini. The afternoon had been long and tiring, the procedure of drawing a shortlist and then inspecting each mount carefully before selection, a time-consuming one. Avanti was badly in need of horses. Over seventy steeds had died in the course of the battle against the pishacha army at Trehi, and half that number had been killed during the attack by the rakshasas. Those needed to be replaced. Moreover, the threat of a Huna-Saka invasion had led to a spike in demand for horses at all horse stations and garrisons. Of the sixty-odd animals that had come up for sale that day, only a third was deemed worthy of the Imperial Stables, a number that didn't even begin covering the shortfall.

"Still not a bad number," Kalidasa offered, squinting up at the sun, which was halfway to the western horizon. A breeze had struck up an hour earlier, helping the day cool.

"Not at all," Shanku agreed, looking back over her shoulder at the field, where the Warden and his staff were still negotiating rates with the merchants. "In fact, seven or eight of them are very good buys."

"The short-tailed mare being one of them?" Kalidasa smiled gently at the girl.

"I like her," Shanku smiled back.

They rode in silence for a while, both horses on a gentle trot.

"There is something I have been meaning to ask you," Kalidasa said at last.

"What is it?"

"I don't know if... this is going to make any sense to you..." the giant fumbled, his heavy square jaw clenching in inner turmoil. "It... could seem stupid..."

"What is it?" Shanku asked again, this time gentler and more encouraging.

Taking a deep breath and sitting up on his saddle, Kalidasa blinked and looked straight down the path they were following.

"I am... I have been seeing things in my head for some time now. Images... *visions*. I see them all the time."

Shanku knew what the giant was referring to.

"It's like... they are like dreams, but I see them in my head even when I am awake," he continued. "Even right now..." He broke off and glanced at Shanku. "I know it doesn't make sense. I must sound like a fool. I'm... sorry I brought this up."

For the briefest of moments, Shanku was tempted to tell the giant that she understood every word of what he was saying, but doing so would mean having to explain how she had ended up at the *samsaptaka* training ground that morning. That was a secret she wasn't yet prepared to share with anyone.

"No, it's fine," the girl reined her horse to a slow walk. "Tell me what you see."

Feeling reassured, Kalidasa recounted everything that the girl had already heard while hiding in the mulberry thicket.

"I keep hoping these visions will go away, but every day they grow stronger," the giant bit his lips in nervousness. "Dhanavantri prescribed me an unction to help me sleep better, but it is not helping. I am afraid... I am going insane."

Glimpsing the helplessness in Kalidasa's eyes, Shanku felt rattled. She had always seen the giant as a pillar of strength and self-possession. She had grown up believing nothing could shake his composure, so the sight of him, shoulders slumped, looking drawn and anxious, was disconcerting. She was overcome with a sudden rush to hold him tight and assure him that he was just fine.

"No, you are *not*," she said, instead. "Let us talk to Dhanavantri once we get to..."

"I don't think Dhanavantri can help. But *you* might be able to."

"Me? How?"

"Perhaps we can ask the Mother Oracle if she can find out what's happening to me." Kalidasa looked at Shanku hopefully. "I don't know... she might not be able to..."

"There is only one way of knowing whether she can or cannot."

Spurring her horse with a flick of the reins, Shanku began pulling away from Kalidasa. Up ahead, the watchtowers of Ujjayini were poking into the air amidst the treetops. As she rode, she threw a glance over her shoulder at the giant.

"What are you waiting for, councilor?" She tossed her head in the direction of Ujjayini. "Let us go ask the oracle."

* * *

Shukracharya couldn't make up his mind whether it was himself or the *mandala* that vexed him more.

It wasn't just vexation. There was also anxiety.

He had consulted the bones over and over since the time they had revealed that Kubera had finally granted Indra an audience. But each time he had wanted to learn the outcome of the meeting in Alaka, the bones had been at their enigmatic best.

A yaksha is being sent to claim that which the human king has promised to protect.

The bones could only mean Veeshada's dagger, but the high priest struggled to make sense of this. He understood that Kubera had been tempted with the promise of apsaras, ever the fail-safe bet when it came to the stupid yakshas. But why would Indra trust the yakshas – whose intentions the devas had always been suspicious of – to claim the Halahala for him? And what purpose would sending *one* yaksha to Ujjayini serve? They were powerful and wily beings, well versed in the black arts, of that Shukracharya had no doubt. Still, what could a lone yaksha achieve where the Ashvin cavalry and the Maruts had failed?

Therefore, he had repeatedly gone back to the *mandala* in search for answers, but all he got from the bones was what they had already told him.

A yaksha was coming to Ujjayini to spirit away the Halahala that Vikramaditya had somehow concealed in the tree in the cremation ground. No matter how inconceivable this seemed, the revelation bothered Shukracharya, robbing the pleasure he had been deriving from observing Vishakha selectively regain her memory – and watching the samrat sink lower into despair. Even the joy of the destruction of Amaravati was quickly paling in the face of the threat from the unknown yaksha.

He had to do something to foil this yaksha.

Sighing in annoyance, the high priest lay on his mat and stared up at the ceiling, counting the minutes to dusk, when he could make the trip to the cremation ground and do what needed doing under cover of darkness.

* * *

"You know what hurts the most, Harihara?"

Vetala Bhatta's choice of address was intentional – dropping the honorific title of 'king' and calling Harihara by name showed he was in no mood to adhere to protocols and niceties in this conversation. It was a calculated move. Not only was he senior in age to the king of Heheya, as an ambassador of Avanti, he had played a crucial role in brokering the alliance between the young Harihara and the more powerful King Mahendraditya. The Acharya was now leveraging age and shared history.

"You know what hurts most?" he asked again. "It is the sneakiness with which you have conducted this whole affair. If you remember, old king Mahendraditya used to say that he would rather die from a sword buried in his chest in broad daylight than an arrow shot under cover of darkness. That you chose to go behind our backs saddens me."

Sitting across the chief councilor with drooped shoulders, his feet shuffling in discomfort, King Harihara looked every inch the man whose life was coming apart around him. The single lamp set on the table between the two men threw the king's shadow on the wall behind, looming like a past sin over him, ready to dig its claws in and devour him.

"I did what I think is right for my daughter," he mumbled, knotting and unknotting his hands.

"Like every father should," said the Acharya. "Yet, you don't have the courage to look me in the eye. Could that be because deep in your heart, you know that this is not in your daughter's best interests? Or are you ashamed at not having taken Avanti and its king into confidence?"

"I would have told you," Harihara protested. "I would have told each one of Sindhuvarta's kingdoms when the time was right."

"You would have told us when it would have been too late," the raj-guru said levelly. "Too late to stop you."

"How does any of this matter to anyone?" Harihara

threw up his hands angrily, resorting to blunt defiance. "Vikramaditya is free to choose whether or not to accept my daughter's hand in marriage. But he doesn't have a right to decide whom I should get her married to."

Vetala Bhatta scrutinized the king. Vikramaditya had been correct. There was resentment here at being passed over as a prospective father-in-law of the Samrat of Sindhuvarta.

"The samrat's objection is limited to Shoorasena." The Acharya paused for a moment, his tone changing and becoming acidic. "It hasn't been more than a few months since King Siddhasena left us, murdered by the very one you want to make your son-in-law. The dead king must be very proud of the friendship he shared with you."

Harihara squirmed under the councilor's severe gaze. A *tchik-tchik-tchik* chirp, repeated in quick succession, broke somewhere nearby. Glancing up, the raj-guru spied two house lizards scrambling up a wall, one in hot pursuit of the other.

"Okay, Siddhasena is dead anyway, and the dead perhaps don't matter," Vetala Bhatta waved a dismissive hand. "What about Princess Rukma? Is she pleased with this match?"

"Why wouldn't she be? My daughter has been raised to find happiness in the happiness of others."

"Is that so? I would like to hear this from her. If she says she has no objections to marrying Shoorasena, this topic ends here and I shall take your leave. Go on, call her."

Harihara remained seated miserably in his chair. Vetala Bhatta sighed inwardly in relief. He knew he had taken a gamble there, and his bluff could have been called.

"Now let me tell you something, Harihara." The Acharya leaned in and dropped his voice. "The Samrat also cares greatly for your daughter's happiness – that is why he is against this proposed alliance. The kingdoms of Sindhuvarta – at least Avanti, Kosala, Vatsa and Matsya – have decided that Shoorasena has to answer for what he has done. Punishment *will* come to him, one way or the other. Now, if Princess Rukma marries him, she will suffer for his sins too. Vikramaditya doesn't want that happening to her. The question is, do you?"

Harihara stared at the raj-guru, eyes round with anxiety and indecision.

"You won't knowingly send your daughter into trouble and uncertainty, would you?"

The king shook his head slowly, the first clear indication of surrender.

"Now, the Samrat understands a father's concerns," Vetala Bhatta's voice was soft and mollifying. "He knows you acted as any father would, and he bears no grudge against you. In fact, he has even sent a proposal for your consideration."

"Which is?" Harihara's face lifted with hope.

"You need a suitable match for Princess Rukma. Why not consider Prince Shashivardhan?"

The king was silent for a while as he considered the possibility.

"Shashivardhan is not a king yet," he said slowly.

The Acharya was taken aback for a moment. Then he got it.

"But he will be. King Chandravardhan..." the councilor stopped to pick his words carefully. "I don't know if you are aware of all the reports, but King Chandravardhan is not doing too well. There is a possibility that he may never recover enough to dispense the duties of a king. And Shashivardhan is already taking charge of those responsibilities."

"But... will he become king of Vatsa?"

"Of course," the Acharya said in surprise. "Why should we assume otherwise?"

"I don't know," Harihara shrugged. "The prince is known to have a problem with drinking and gambling. It has often been said that he is a full-fledged drunkard."

"That is a gross exaggeration. Anyway, matrimony has a way of mellowing men down. A wife like the princess is perhaps all the anchor he needs. You can take it from me that Shashivardhan has his heart in the right place."

Harihara still looked unhappy.

"And if the choice is between a drunkard who can be reformed and a murderer who will definitely face retribution, which would it be?"

The old councilor's voice was calm and reasoning. There was even a disarming smile on his face. But the eyes that shone back at Harihara in the lamplight were hard and pitiless, pinning him in a pincer-like grip.

"What assurance can Avanti provide that Shashivardhan will be king of Vatsa?"

The two men assessed one another like combatants across the table.

"A coronation might not be possible just now, but if you want, we can have it formally announced that Shashivardhan would succeed Chandravardhan to Vatsa's throne," said the councilor. "That should satisfy your lingering doubts. We will even take this proposal to Kausambi on your behalf, if you wish. Now what do you say?"

The king nodded slowly, but he still sat hunched on his chair.

"There is only one problem, Acharya," Harihara sighed. "Messengers bearing my proposal to Shoorasena have already left for Girivraja. There is no way I can call them back, which means Shoorasena will inevitably receive my letter."

He paused and swallowed hard. "What if he accepts Rukma's hand?"

"Then I'm afraid you will have to tell him the princess's hand has already been taken."

* * *

The taverns by the riverfront were emptying the last of the

day's patrons as Shanku stepped off the boat and onto the steps of the *ghat*. Revelers hugged and clapped each other on the backs before breaking into smaller knots, some stumbling up the steps and back into the city, others teetering down to the boats that were waiting to ferry them home. The night was full of bonhomie and song, and Shanku couldn't help feeling buoyed by the cheer of the moment.

It helped that she herself had spent a few good hours in the company of her clansmen of the Wandering Tribe. When word of the oracle's desire to see them had reached the tribe, the clansmen had come to Ujjayini in good numbers – far more than had been expected, and many times more than the palace could accommodate. A potential embarrassment had been averted, however, when the chief of the clan – Shanku's granduncle – had announced that the tribe did not wish to impose upon either the palace or the city; they were happy to camp outside Ujjayini, since they preferred the vast, open countryside anyway.

The tribe had set up their tents at the base of a hill a mile to the west of Ujjayini, from where the clansmen visited the Mother Oracle in small, manageable groups. That evening, they had invited Shanku to dine with them, and on her grandmother's pressing, she had agreed. In retrospect, it had been a good idea.

The girl now picked her way up the darkened *ghat*, heading for the City Watch picket just inside the western gate, where she had tethered her horse.

Shanku was still some distance from the gate when she turned and cast an idle glance over the river. There was no particular reason to do so – she had simply felt like it. But, owing to that pause, she happened to spot the small boat gliding up to the *ghat*. Again, it wasn't anything specific that made her stop and observe its lone passenger, a dark smudge of a figure hunched against the night. It could have been anyone returning to a city of thousands. The boat docked, the passenger disembarked, paid off the boatman and started mounting the steps.

Dwelling on what the oracle had had to say to Kalidasa earlier in the evening, Shanku was about to resume her trudge to the city gate when a wayward finger of light from one of the tavern windows fell across the approaching figure. The beam lit the figure's face for only a fraction of a second, yet Shanku discerned a beard – and an eye-patch over the left eye!

Instinct made the girl step behind a nearby tavern's wall. She poked a cautious eye out and looked down the *ghat*. The Healer kept climbing, head down, eye on the steps.

Sticking to the shadows, Shanku watched the Healer draw level with her, and then move on toward the city gate. Slipping out of cover, she raced down the steps on her toes, hoping the ringing of her anklets wouldn't carry. She looked back now and then, checking if the Healer had detected her, but he had disappeared from sight, through the gate, into Ujjayini.

"*Aiy*, *aiy*," she shouted, waving her hand to attract the boatman's attention. "Stop there!"

The boatman had already rowed a few metres into the Kshipra, but he slowed and looked toward the *ghat* and the silhouette at its lowest step. "I am going home," he said. "It is late."

"Come here," Shanku motioned with her hand, frantic.

"I have to go home," the boatman grumbled, staying in his place in the water. "Please get another boat."

"I don't want to cross," the councilor pleaded. "I want to speak to you, that's all."

"About what, girl?"

"There's a coin in it for you."

It worked. The boatman drew the boat in. As it nudged the *ghat*, he asked, "What do you want to know?"

"That man you just dropped off..." Shanku thumbed in the direction of the city gate.

"Yes, the Healer..." The boatman paused. "What about him?"

"The Healer... yes." It struck her that the Healer was one of the most well-known faces in Ujjayini these days. "Where did you bring him from?"

"The other bank," the boatman said matter-of-factly.

"Do you know where he was coming from?"

"Why do you want to know, girl?"

Shanku turned her face such that light from one of the taverns fell across her features.

"Councilor... it is you," the boatman's voice echoed with fear and embarrassment as he recognized his interlocutor. "I am... stupid of me... I didn't know..."

"Do you know where the Healer was coming from?"

"I... No, your honour. I don't... I am a poor boatman, your honour. I don't dare ask my passengers where they come from and where they go, your honour. Pardon me..."

"Were you the one who took him across as well?"

"I was, your honour."

"When was this? I mean how long ago?"

"After sunset, your honour. Same as usual."

Same as usual.

"Are you saying you have ferried the Healer before as well?"

"A few times, your honour. He always departs after dark and returns around the time the taverns shut. Only once did I take him across late in the afternoon. It was the first time, if I recall correctly."

"And he asks you to wait for him?"

The boatman nodded. "He pays well."

"You just take him across the holy Kshipra and back?"

The boatman nodded.

"You know nothing about where he goes?"

The boatman shook his head.

"But he makes this trip often, and almost always after nightfall."

The boatman nodded.

"Here is the coin I promised." Shanku dropped a copper ring into the man's hand. "But remember, mention nothing of this conversation to the Healer, clear?"

"Yes, your honour."

The girl had turned to climb the steps when the boatman spoke again. "There is one thing I can tell you, councilor. Whenever the Healer returns, his clothes and feet are covered in layers of fine ash."

Visions

The clang of metal as swords clashed against one another; the heavy drum of hooves on hard, sun-baked earth; the roar of voices, hooting and screaming as they hurled shrill war cries at the sky. All these merged into one deafening din as he charged across the plain.

Gripping the horse under him with his knees, his arms thrown tight around the steed's thick, sweaty neck, he bent low in his saddle, offering as little resistance to the wind as possible. The horse's mane whipped across his face, the coarse hairs stinging his flesh and getting into his eyes, making him blink, but he kept his head down, peering at the line of trees that marked the edge of the plain. As another wave of cries and hoots broke from behind him, he turned in panic and threw a glance over his shoulder.

The man was still behind him, driving his horse hard, rapidly narrowing the distance between the two horses.

He swung his head wildly to look at the fast approaching tree line, beyond which the forest grew, dense and green. Then back at the man pursuing him.

The man was now standing on his stirrups, balancing himself skillfully on his mount as he handled the bow and arrow. Nocking the arrow in place, the man raised the bow and drew the bowstring back.

Caught between the prongs of fear and fascination, he watched the bow bend and quiver under the strain as the man took aim, the arrowhead pointing straight at him… He saw the man's sunburned face behind the bow, his curly black beard turning grey at the temples.

He saw the man open his mouth and shout at him…

"Commander, stop. Please stop."

Kalidasa blinked and turned to see Angamitra jogging across the mud pit toward him. The captain of the *samsaptakas* had his sword drawn, the shield in his left hand positioned as if ready for combat, and judging by the alertness of his posture and the anxiety in his eyes, he appeared to be under a bit of stress.

"What is it, captain?" Kalidasa asked, suddenly aware that the sound of clashing swords had died all around him. Everything had fallen dead silent.

As Angamitra came to an uncertain halt, the giant turned to survey the mud pit that the *samsaptakas* used for their training. All around him, Kalidasa saw *samsaptakas* standing and gawking at him, the swords in their hands hanging limp by their sides. In their faces, he saw awe, amazement and fear – the last most pronounced when they switched their gazes toward his feet.

Following their line of sight, Kalidasa looked down to see the *samsaptaka* he had been training with lying on the sand on his back. A relatively new recruit, the *samsaptaka* was a sincere and enthusiastic cadet, one of those of whom Angamitra had high hopes. The young warrior now lay quiet, with his left hand thrown over his eyes. The sword that he had wielded lay in the mud a few feet away from his outstretched right hand –

and a deep, red gash extended from under his right collarbone all the way to the extremity of his right shoulder.

Blood oozed from the wound, matting the hair on his chest and spilling down past his armpit into the sand.

Still, it wasn't until he noticed the smear of blood on the tip of his scimitar that realization fully dawned on Kalidasa. His eyes growing wide in horror, he was about to bend down to check on the fallen form when the boy stirred. Moving his hand away from his eyes, the warrior pushed himself painfully up on his elbows, squinting up at his commander against the glare of the early morning sun.

"You're okay?" Kalidasa was conscious of the tremor in his voice.

The *samsaptaka* nodded and smiled, the smile turning to a wince as the movement of a muscle snagged and stretched at the wound. "I am, commander," he replied weakly.

"This is what happens when you lose your sword in battle," said Kalidasa as he went down on one knee and placed an arm around the boy's shoulder with the intention of helping him up. "You get cut down by the enemy. So never ever lose your grip on your sword. It's all that keeps you alive."

"I understand, commander."

Three other *samsaptakas* immediately rushed over to assist, and within moments, the warrior was on his wobbly feet, propped up by his comrades. Coming over to the group, Angamitra inspected the wound.

"It's deep but not serious," he observed with relief. "Just needs some stitches and perhaps a poultice. Take him to the physicians."

As the soldier was escorted out of the pit, Kalidasa looked around at the remaining *samsaptakas*, who were still standing in a daze.

"Let that be a lesson for all of you as well," the giant said. "Hold on to your swords." He smiled at the heads nodding at him in agreement, but deep inside, he felt chilled and scared with what had just happened.

"You heard the commander," Angamitra barked at the *samsaptakas*. "Now hold on to your swords and get back to your training. C'mon, *move*!"

With the metallic ring of swords striking one another rising around them, Kalidasa and Angamitra made their way toward an outhouse that served to store weapons and other equipment for the *samsaptakas*. Once they were sufficiently out of earshot, the captain raised an enquiring eyebrow at Kalidasa.

"Is everything alright, commander?"

"Yes, of course," the giant looked down at his deputy's face, noting the concern plastered all over it. "Why do you ask?"

Angamitra jerked his thumb over his shoulder. "What happened there – for a moment I thought you were going to kill the boy."

"Not at all," Kalidasa threw his head back and laughed, his voice harsh and artificial to his own ears. Breaking out in cold sweat, he shivered mildly and wiped his palm surreptitiously across his thigh. "It was just *training*. I wanted... to push the boy a bit."

"It's been just over a year since he took the Death Oath, commander. He is still fresh and raw." Angamitra waited to see how his words were being absorbed before continuing. "Seasoned *samsaptakas* would have struggled to fend off the moves and strikes you made against him. If he wasn't half the fighter that he is, he wouldn't have got out of here alive."

"I didn't realize I was driving the kid so hard," the giant said after a long pause. "I suppose I owe him an apology for causing him that wound."

"Oh, fear not, he will wear that like a badge for the rest of his life," Angamitra answered with a smile. "How many *samsaptakas* can boast of a scar given to them by Kalidasa?"

After a slight pause, he added, "I am not worried

about him. He will heal. It is *you* I am more concerned about, commander."

"Me? I am alright." Noticing the brotherly affection in his deputy's eyes, Kalidasa smiled and clapped him on his shoulder. "Really, I'm fine."

However, walking out of the training ground a little while later, heading for the stable to find his horse, the councilor suffered no illusions about things being fine with him. His face was tense, his fists rolled into tight balls, and he could feel fear and frustration mounting inside him.

Allow the visions to come to you and embrace them. Let what is yours come back to you, so you can become whole again.

The trouble was he was not becoming whole. He was going to pieces. And moments before, he had nearly taken an innocent *samsaptaka*'s life in the bargain.

Striding toward his horse, Kalidasa thought back to what the Mother Oracle had told him the other evening.

The oracle had been categorical that she would not be able to help in deciphering his visions. "I am a sign-reader and future-teller, not an interpreter of dreams," she had explained. Then, when he had admitted to being afraid he was losing his mind, the old woman had shocked him with her words.

"I think the opposite might be true," the oracle's old eyes had held his in a steady gaze. "I am no expert at this, but you might actually be *recovering* your mind – or rather, your memory."

The possibility had unnerved him. He had accepted that he would never learn about his past – that everything that had happened to him before he had been discovered hiding in that Kali temple by Avanti's soldiers would forever remain shrouded in mystery. He had come to terms with the void in his life and made his peace with it, secure in the knowledge that what he did remember – his childhood in the palace, building a bond of friendship with Vikramaditya – brightened his days.

He had been happy not knowing the part of his life before the Kali temple. But now, if what the Mother Oracle had said was right, that life was pushing its way in through a crack in the door. A crack whose existence he had not even known.

"Learn not to resist what you see, councilor," the oracle had called after him as he had taken her leave. "Allow the visions to come to you and embrace them. Let what is yours come back to you, so you can become whole again."

Since that night, he had done as the old woman had advised, not fighting, not resisting, allowing the visions to play through his mind repeatedly, an infinite, tantalizing loop that concealed more than it revealed. Kalidasa realized there was more behind that closed door. More visions, more information, more past – pushing hard, trying to burst through the crack, trying to bust the door open. He had been prepared to wait it out, but not after what had just occurred in the training ground.

What was already on this side of the door was driving him mad. The desire to know what was on that side was driving him blind. Blind to everything that was happening around him, blind to the hurt he might be causing others.

That was something he would not accept.

Tightening the straps and buckles around his horse's chest and shoulders, the giant decided he had to act. If Dhanavantri and the Mother Oracle could not sort the visions out for him, he would have to seek assistance elsewhere.

Fortunately, he knew just the person to turn to for help – someone who had proved to be an expert at unlocking lost memories.

* * *

The town of Raivata had not changed in all these years,

Vararuchi concluded as the road to Dvarka dipped into the valley. It still looked the same, serene in the valley's floor amidst lush green fields of paddy and millet, protected on three sides by a high wall and backed up on the fourth against the Raivata Mountain, from which the town drew its name. The town had always appeared to him to be in gentle slumber, and even now, the sight of the town's banner, flapping in the cool morning breeze atop Chief Manidhara's residence a quarter of the way up the mountainside, lulled him into a welcome calm.

"The place has remained the same for as long as I can remember, your honour," a gruff voice spoke at Vararuchi's shoulder, surprising him.

Turning around, the councilor saw Udayasanga looking in the direction of Raivata. Strongly built and perhaps not much shorter than Kalidasa himself, the *samsaptaka* had a large face to accommodate the huge moustache that curled all the way up to his cheekbones. He also sported a finely combed beard that ended in a chiseled point under his chin.

"The only addition is the wall," Udayasanga added. "I often get the impression time comes to a standstill at Raivata."

The tranquility about the town dispelled quickly, however. Even as Vararuchi and the small band of *samsaptakas* were descending to the valley's floor, Raivata's main gate opened to disgorge over three hundred armoured riders. The horsemen, bearing the town's banner, assembled quickly before taking the road west toward Dvarka.

The town's guards matched the urgency displayed by the riders when Vararuchi's party announced itself at the gate. The gate was thrown open without preamble, and while the rest of the *samsaptakas* were shown to the barracks for bath and breakfast, Vararuchi and Udayasanga were escorted directly to Manidhara.

"Vararuchi my friend, welcome, welcome," Manidhara threw his arms wide to embrace the councilor. "Good to have you visiting us after so many years. I just wish we didn't have other pressing matters at hand – we could have sat and discussed music way into the night over cups of soma."

"You have my word I shall make time for that as well once we have peace, chief," Vararuchi replied with warmth as he disengaged from the hug.

"And you – I remember you," Manidhara wagged a stern finger at Udayasanga. "You are the fellow who almost murdered the five men who tried to break into that ivory caravan the night it was camped in town, isn't it? I remember the mess you created. So what's this – Avanti rewards you for that by making you a soldier?"

Despite the severity of his words, there was an undercurrent of levity in his voice.

"I realized that as long as I wore a uniform, I wouldn't get punished for getting into fights and breaking people's heads, chief," the *samsaptaka* grinned. "But you have my deepest apologies for what happened that night."

Manidhara waved a hand, dismissing the matter and inviting his visitors to breakfast. As they settled down around a table filled with fresh fruits, pancakes and jars of fresh, frothing milk, Vararuchi eyed Udayasanga.

"I guess you were the reason the wall was put up around the town."

Accepting a cup of cooling coconut water from Manidhara, the *samsaptaka* grinned again. But at the mention of the wall, the chief's broad, fair face grew grave under the traditional multicoloured turban of the Anartas.

Vararuchi observed the change in the chief's expression. "We noticed riders leave for Dvarka as we were approaching. Is there something we need to know?"

"We received a message from cousin Yugandhara just before daybreak," Manidhara replied. "The Huna ships have been sighted."

Vararuchi stared at the chief, the cup in his hand frozen halfway to his lips. Exchanging an alert glance with the *samsaptaka*, he asked, "Where? How far from Dvarka?"

"A couple of our ships espied their black sails moored a few miles to the north of the salt marshes of Kachcha."

"That means they are still some distance away," observed Udayasanga.

"Yes, but this news was from yesterday afternoon," Manidhara eyed his guests. "If the ships have set sail, the Hunas won't be far from Dvarka... in fact, they might already *be* in Dvarka. That's why the rush."

"We must leave immediately," Vararuchi exclaimed, emptying the cup. Dvarka was almost a full day's ride from Raivata. Grabbing a pancake, he tore it in two and thrust one of the halves into his mouth. "Why didn't you tell us earlier, chief? We could have dispensed with breakfast and simply carried on."

"Battles are not fought and won on empty stomachs, my friend," said Manidhara, helping himself to another pancake while placing one each on his visitors' plates. "Eat well, for if the Hunas are at Dvarka by the time we reach, there is no saying when we will sit in front of a meal next."

The three men were quiet for a while as they made their repast.

"How many ships are the Hunas using to make the crossing?" Vararuchi asked.

"Our ships didn't stop to count, but the guess is about thirty or thirty-five of them."

"That's all?" The councilor sighed with obvious relief.

"First of all, that is a *guess*," Manidhara replied. "And even if the guess is right, we have no idea how many more Huna ships are lined up all the way up to the mouth of the Dark River, ready to sail south. Your oracle spoke of a thousand, didn't she?"

"She did, though that may have been just a way of saying many," Vararuchi said.

"Even so, if there are just thirty ships, those thirty are longboats." There was an inflection in the chief's voice, a grimness that forced the councilor and the *samsaptaka* to look at him. "A longboat can easily carry up to two hundred and fifty men."

Manidhara's fingers took a tight grip along the edge of the table.

"Which means there are at least seven thousand five hundred ruthless barbarians from the Marusthali out there, all set to attack and destroy Dvarka."

* * *

"The way I see it, we don't have a choice, Vikrama. King Harihara has come around to our point of view. It is our turn – and in our interest – to make a concession."

Vikramaditya nodded, but his eyes were troubled as he stared down into the leafy atrium two floors below. The samrat and the raj-guru were in a private terrace, soaking in the early morning sun as they sipped freshly crushed sugarcane juice spiced with cinnamon.

"His wish to marry the princess to a king is understandable. What I don't get is why he is insistent on a formal announcement." Vikramaditya looked over his shoulder at the chief councilor. "Does he think there's a possibility that Shashivardhan would *not* become king?"

"It appeared so to me," the Acharya shrugged.

"How do we take this to King Chandravardhan? We cannot possibly go to him saying it is time Shashivardhan was made king of Vatsa." The samrat's tone made it plain that he found the whole affair quite distasteful.

"It will need tact," Vetala Bhatta conceded. "I don't even

know if King Chandravardhan is well enough for the matter to be broached with him. Perhaps the people who first need to be convinced and won over are Councilor Yashobhavi and the rest of the council of ministers."

The samrat said nothing as he leaned on the parapet and frowned unhappily into the atrium.

"I know this makes you very uncomfortable, Vikrama," the raj-guru stepped forward and placed an understanding hand on the king's shoulder. "But I have told Harihara that we will assist in this matter. For us to get something from him, I had to give him something in exchange."

"I appreciate that, raj-guru. You did what the occasion demanded. As always, you only have Avanti's interests in mind." Vikramaditya paused. "By when would we need to send someone to Vatsa?"

"As early as possible. The thing is, even before I reached Mahishmati, Harihara had already dispatched Rukma's proposal to Shoorasena's court." Vetala Bhatta eyed the samrat meaningfully. "If Shoorasena accepts – and I see no reason for him not to – and his reply reaches Harihara before we can confirm Shashivardhan's coronation to him... well, both of us know what Harihara would do."

"In that case, someone should leave for Kausambi without delay."

"I shall prepare for departure right away."

"No raj-guru, not you."

"Who then, Vikrama? Vararuchi isn't here. And for all his experience, Amara Simha is not one to be trusted in dealing with tact."

Vikramaditya was quiet for a while, stroking his moustache in thought.

"Dhanavantri," he said. "We all agree he's a master of wit and words. In addition, he has a very good reason to make a visit to Chandravardhan's court – the king's illness. The visit will look natural enough, and he can use the opportunity to get everyone in Vatsa around to declaring Shashivardhan as Vatsa's next king."

"A clever idea, but what if we are suddenly in need of the physician's services?" Vetala Bhatta warned. "Ujjayini can no longer take that chance – not with the devas and the asuras still in the hunt for the Halahala."

"We have the Healer, raj-guru," the king exclaimed.

The chief councilor frowned. "I still think it would be good to have Dhanavantri around."

"He will be gone for what – a week? We can manage, I'm sure. And Kunjala and the other court physicians can always assist the Healer if the need arises."

Grudgingly, the Acharya inclined his head. "Very well, I shall send word to Dhanavantri. It would be good if he left today itself."

Dvarka

What do you mean we shouldn't start a war?" the lord of the devas stared at Narada, his rage barely contained in his cold, blue eyes.

"Look at this beautiful city of ours," Indra flung an arm over the railing of the balcony where he and the diplomat stood. The balcony was set high on one of the spires of the palace, and commanded a magnificent view of Amaravati, still wreathed in great skeins of sooty-grey smoke. "Look at it, defiled and laid to waste by the asuras. Look at it, Narada. The war has already started. And *I* wasn't the one to start it – though I have every intention of finishing it."

"I urge you to reconsider, my lord. In my…"

"There is nothing to reconsider," Indra overruled, his voice quivering with outrage. "What do the asuras take us to be – deer in the forest that they can come and hunt as they please? Does Hiranyaksha think his army can invade Devaloka and we will do nothing in retaliation? Inform the Ashvins, the Maruts and the fire-wraiths to prepare the deva divisions for battle. Have a message sent to the kinnara lord Tribhanu – he is to spare us as many divisions of kinnaras as he can. And summon Takshaka. Tell him Devaloka is in need of the assistance of the nagas. Make haste. The sooner we are ready, the sooner we can set forth for Patala."

"If we leave for Patala, we will be playing straight into Shukracharya's hands, my lord. It is exactly what he wants from us."

The lord of the devas peered at the diplomat dubiously. "Shukracharya *wants* us to attack Patala?"

"Not exactly, but his intention is to keep us distracted from the Halahala," Narada replied. "That was the only purpose behind the attack on Amaravati."

Seeing the incomprehension on Indra's countenance, the diplomat nodded. "The attack was brutal, and we were fighting with our backs to the wall, my lord. Yet, the battle lasted less than half the night, and the asuras left as unexpectedly as they came. They had us cornered, but instead of pressing home the advantage, they made no bid to claim territory, here or elsewhere in Devaloka. Why relinquish a position of strength after such an elaborate and effective assault, my lord? What purpose would such an attack serve?"

"It would keep our minds engaged on things other than Veeshada's dagger," the light slowly dawned on Indra.

"Precisely. We would spend our time worrying about the vyalas, or we would plot retaliation and retribution." Narada shook his head. "We can't afford to dwell on those things, my lord. The dagger is our primary concern – we can have all the revenge we want once we have secured it. But if we shift our attention to waging war on Patala now, we dilute our efforts at claiming the Halahala, and Shukracharya would achieve what he wants."

"We do nothing then – after all the havoc that the asuras have caused?" The idea clearly affronted Indra.

"I suggest we strike a truce with the asuras, my lord."

"A *what*?" Indra's eyes bulged as he glared at Narada, scarcely believing his ears. "What absurdity is this!" he exploded, throwing his hands into the air. "They invade my city and burn it to the ground, and you expect me to negotiate a *truce* with them? Have you gone insane?"

"It is a way of making sure we aren't distracted by any more asura attacks, my lord," Narada kept his tone calm and even.

"Since when have the devas become so weak to be incapable of defending themselves from asura attacks? You speak as if we live in mortal fear of them. Have you forgotten I wield the mighty vajra?" Indra turned contemptuously away to face the city, crossing his hands behind him. He shook his head, his mouth slanting at the corners in disdain. "You disappoint me, Narada. Cowardice has caught up with you in your old age and..."

"A truce with the asuras is not a sign of fear or weakness, my lord. It is an instrument to buy us time. And a way to keep a close watch on the asuras so we know what they are up to."

"And why would Hiranyaksha and Shukracharya even entertain the idea of a truce?" Indra's lips twisted with scorn. "Are they fools not to see through our motives?"

"Both devas and asuras share a common enemy in the defiant human king, and a common objective – the king's defeat. Vikramaditya has thwarted us both. Instead of fighting one another, it is in the interests of both sides to join forces against him."

"Surely you are not saying there is no other way of defeating the human king?" Indra blinked at Narada narrowly.

"I think both sides realize the Omniscient One has chosen well, and that the human king will not yield to anyone readily," the diplomat shrugged. "Under the circumstances, I'm inclined to believe Hiranyaksha would see sense in the devas and asuras uniting."

A light drizzle had begun, rendering the already grey afternoon over Amaravati even greyer. Indra watched the needle-like drops fall as he weighed the diplomat's argument.

"Even if Hiranyaksha agrees to a treaty, I refuse to give up our efforts at finding and taking Veeshada's dagger," the lord of the devas was firm.

"Oh absolutely, my lord. And we can be sure neither will the asuras. The treaty's only purpose is to keep off each other's toes while we bring about the human king's downfall."

* * *

"Set me free of these ropes, deva. I have done as you bid me. Show an old kinnara some mercy, *please*."

Jayanta gave no sign of having heard the piteous words, turning his back on them as he surveyed Ujjayini with a cold and detached expression. The city's lights were blinking and multiplying as twilight swept the plain, and though the hill on which he stood was well beyond Ujjayini's walls, the prince could make out the palace even from this distance, a bloom of radiance in the middle of the shimmering lake. To most observers, such a pleasing sight would have held more than a bit of charm, but the beauty of the moment was lost on Jayanta's dark and brooding mind.

The prince knew that the task he was about to accomplish was risky, and would consume every ounce of his energy. Yet, he drew satisfaction from the fact that at the end of it, he would have put everyone who had laughed at him and dismissed him in their proper place. Ahi was his revenge on everyone around him – and it mattered little if that revenge meant the destruction of the city that now lay across the plain from him. One miserable human city was nothing in front of the eternal admiration and gratitude Jayanta hoped to earn from his father.

"What have I done to deserve such treatment, son of Indra?" the plaintive voice persisted. "Have I not kept my word? Have I not delivered you to the land of the humans as promised? Is this how you reward me for having risked bringing you this far?"

With a sigh of vexation, Jayanta turned to assess the speaker, a centaur with the head and torso of a man and the hindquarters of a horse. The kinnara had a mop of unruly grey hair, while a scraggly grey beard sprouted on its chin. Its body and arms were scrawny, the ribcage sticking out through its shriveled, yellowing chest, and its face was haggard, the eyes old, colourless and weary. Yet, its four equine legs were long and strong, and the tan coat covering its back, belly and flanks shone with youth and vigour. The kinnara's wrists and forelegs were bound with stout ropes, tightly knotted over, and a rope passed around its neck as well, tethering the beast to the trunk of a nearby tree.

"This may not look like a reward to you, kinnara, and rightly so," Jayanta replied irritably. "But believe me when I say it is no punishment either. It's a simple precaution I am taking so you don't run off by yourself when the fancy strikes you."

"Why would I do that, deva?" the centaur protested. "I have given you my word that I shall take you back to Devaloka, and you know very well that a kinnara holds his word dear."

"I doubt neither your word nor your intentions. What I do mistrust is your instincts when faced with fear." Noticing the puzzlement on the kinnara's face at the mention of the word fear, the prince added, "But let me assure you that no matter what you see or hear, you have nothing to be scared of. As long as you are here with me, you are safe."

"Safe from *what*?"

"I myself don't know," Jayanta shrugged and looked over

to Ujjayini, which was now nothing more than pinpricks of lights in the darkness below. "But we shall find out soon enough."

"You... you don't mean to harm that city, do you?" The kinnara's voice rose in alarm as it caught the subtext in the prince's words. When Jayanta didn't reply, the centaur became even more agitated. "You told me that you had to come here to deliver a secret message on behalf of the lord of the devas. That is why I agreed to bring you here."

"Don't expect me to fall for that one," the prince scoffed, fixing the exotic beast with a harsh glare. "You brought me here because I promised you a mansion of your own in Amaravati and privileges at the royal court. Don't take me for a fool, kinnara. Now stop making a fuss and think about what you should do to earn that mansion and those privileges. It'll help keep your mind off other things."

Jayanta spun on his heel and strode toward a flickering rectangle of light that defined the entry to the old, abandoned woodcutter's hut that he and the kinnara had chanced upon earlier that afternoon. The hut was a ramshackle affair, but it was ideally suited for the prince's purpose. It was secluded, hidden from view among brambly trees, yet it offered a panoramic scene of Ujjayini – a perfect location to oversee and orchestrate Ahi's destruction of the city.

Inside the square, windowless hut, on a bare spot on the mud brick floor, a large *mandala* was drawn using charcoal, flour and vermillion. Seven lamps arranged in a pattern along the floor illuminated the hut, their light falling on the contours of the *mandala*, revealing a crude outline of a snake consuming its own tail. Stacked in the middle of the *mandala* was a small pile of palm leaves, next to which sat a heavy, wide-brimmed copper bowl topped with water.

The prince approached the *mandala*, stepping cautiously over it so as not to smudge its lines. Squatting by the palm leaves, he drew a small knife and a lemon from a satchel. Muttering incantations, he first sliced the lemon in half and squeezed seven drops of its juice into the bowl of water. Then, using the knife, he made an incision on his right thumb, causing the blood to well up.

Holding his thumb over the copper bowl, Jayanta let seven drops of his blood flow and dissolve into the water. Stirring the lime, blood and water into a solution, he poured a few drops of the concoction into each of the seven lamps. As the solution mixed with the oil and caught, the light of the lamps changed colour – from golden-yellow to a fiery red – and burned with greater intensity.

Jayanta returned to the centre of the *mandala* and sat down, crossing his legs under him. He set the bowl in front of him and reached for the palm leaves, permitting himself a deep conspiratorial smile, one that was full of hatred, anger and vindictiveness toward a callous, unforgiving world.

* * *

Dvarka was burning.

Yet, the city's defenders could only stand and watch, horrified and helpless, as the Huna ships ceaselessly rained balls of fire down on them.

Vararuchi and Manidhara, riding at the head of a hundred horsemen who included the fourteen *samsaptakas*, had sighted the blush on the western horizon around nightfall, but both men had initially ascribed it to a prolonged afterglow of sunset. Only when the glow persisted – pulsing and becoming more pronounced, leeching higher and higher into the night sky – did the warriors riding from Raivata see it for what it really was.

By the time Dvarka came into view an hour's ride later, flames had engulfed large sections of the city's waterfront, and thick stacks of smoke were rising above its rooftops. On nearing the eastern gate, which connected the port to the rest of Sindhuvarta, the incoming riders saw the citizenry streaming out and taking to the neighbouring countryside in panic.

"We are too late," Manidhara had screamed with understandable angst, digging his heels into his horse and picking up speed. "Faster, men... faster. Dvarka needs us."

Their charge into the city had, however, been slowed down by the evacuation underway, and though it caused Manidhara to curse and fret, in hindsight, the delay had its advantages. For one, a hundred-odd riders suddenly pouring through the city's gates could have confused Dvarka's defenders into assuming the newcomers were Huna horsemen – an avoidable misunderstanding with potentially catastrophic consequences. The second outcome of the delay was that Vararuchi and Manidhara were able to learn from a city guard that while Dvarka was under attack, the Huna army was still out at sea and had not yet laid foot on land – so while there was need for hurry, they had time to meet Yugandhara for counsel.

The third and possibly biggest benefit was that in their rush, they might well have blundered into a wrong smoke-filled street and died of asphyxiation.

"The smoke clouds are causing as much harm and havoc as the fire," said Yugandhara, his anxious eyes darting across the waterfront and the bay beyond before returning to Vararuchi. "Eighteen already dead, by the last count. Heaven knows how many more are trapped, dead and dying, in the smoke."

The war council had gathered on a small hillock a little to the north of the wharfs and docks of Dvarka, much of which was already on fire. The spot was upwind and far enough from the waterfront not to let the heat and smoke affect them, yet adequately close for Yugandhara and his commanders to oversee the action and issue quick instructions to Dvarka's soldiers.

"What is in those infernal fireballs?" asked Manidhara, scrunching up his nose at the thought of the searing, pungent smell that had hit them as they had made their way through Dvarka. Even now, as the breeze shifted, it floated up to their nostrils, foul in form and intent.

"I have no idea, but whatever they are filled with is doing a great job of setting my city on fire and smoking it dead," Yugandhara's handsome face was pale as he took in the sight of small groups of soldiers and townsfolk struggling to contain the flames.

In every street, it was a futile, unequal battle, as a sustained barrage of fireballs crossed the bay and landed in the city, setting something new on fire and forcing the defenders to scatter and retreat. Shouts of pain and fear rose with alarming frequency, the city slowly falling back on itself under the onslaught.

"I smell oil and sulphur," said Udayasanga, lifting his head to sniff the air. "And something else that I can't quite place."

"Mustard," Vararuchi pointed out. "Anyone who's been in a kitchen knows the smoke from burning mustard seeds can be irritating. If used in appropriately large quantities, the same smoke can be extremely toxic. It is sometimes known as the soul-hunting fog in the Southern Kingdoms."

"I'm amazed they are using an *agnikantaka* from the deck of a ship," said Manidhara, peering at the lights clustered in the darkness of the sea, which, according to Yugandhara, marked one set of Huna ships. "Who taught these savages such tricks? I thought they couldn't even row a boat."

"We believe there are two *agnikantakas* on those ships, not one," said one of Yugandhara's commanders with a dark frown.

"What countermoves have we made so far?" Vararuchi looked from Yugandhara to his commanders. "You must have tried to engage the Huna ships and get to the *agnikantakas*?"

"We did, but with little success, councilor," the Anarta chief admitted. Pointing to the sea, he explained, "A tight ring of ships protects the vessels that have the *agnikantakas* on board, and we have failed to breach that protective ring three times. To compound matters, there are rows of Huna ships in the flanks to the north and south. When our ships move out toward the ring, they close in from the flanks like pincers, attacking us from three sides, forcing us to back down. Two ships we sent out haven't even returned."

Vararuchi let out a low whistle that was part amazement and part admiration for the Hunas' tactics. "How many ships do they have out there?"

"Probably twenty-five or thirty," a commander answered. "They moved in after dark, so it is hard to say."

"And how many do *you* have?" the councilor asked.

"Around thirty, here in Dvarka. There are a few more along the coast, and another ten-twelve on their way from Bhrigukaksha, but those won't be here until tomorrow mid-morning."

"You have thirty ships here?" Udayasanga gaped at the Anarta commanders. "We are evenly matched, so what prevents us from launching a full-fledged counterattack?"

"That," said Yugandhara, pointing at the flaming waterfront.

"Pardon me, but I don't get it," Vararuchi was blank-faced.

"More than half of our ships are moored out in the bay," the chief said. "To reach them, our soldiers need to be rowed out in smaller boats... which are either already on fire in the wharfs, or inaccessible because of all the smoke down there."

Vararuchi followed a flaming ball lobbed up by one of the flamethrowers in the Huna ships. It traced a loopy arc over the intervening stretch of water, a burning orb with a flaming tail, before descending into the waterfront and hitting the edge of a stone embankment. It broke into two pieces, one falling into the water beneath with a hiss, the other rolling onto a pathway, spewing sparks and tentacles of noxious fumes that licked the air, as if seeking out prey.

"See what I mean?" said Yugandhara. "Even if it burns nothing, it spreads its slow poison. As long as those fireballs are hurled our way, our men won't be able to step into any of the streets that lead to the wharfs and the boats."

"And Dvarka will keep burning," Manidhara added on an ominous note.

"What if the *agnikantakas* or the ships that bear them can be demolished?" asked Udayasanga.

"If that happens in time, we might be able to douse the fires, save some boats and make a bid at storming the Huna navy," replied Yugandhara, his eyes on another projectile making its way to Dvarka. This one landed on a fisherman's hutment, setting it instantly on fire. "But I don't see how we can even begin achieving that."

"I can see a boat beached in that corner that might be accessible from the other side of the docks," said the *samsaptaka*, pointing at a small barge docked on a spit of sand.

"My friend, do you have any idea how long it would take *one* boat of that size to ferry an army of soldiers across the bay?" The commander who posed the question smirked.

"How long would it take a boat that size to ferry a dozen men close enough to the ships guarding the *agnikantakas*?" Udayasanga twirled his large moustache and grinned as he saw confusion descend over the Anarta commanders. Turning around, he saw Vararuchi staring at him thoughtfully.

"What do you propose?" asked Yugandhara.

"I propose that we *samsaptakas* row over to those ships, kill a few dozen Hunas, destroy the *agnikantakas*, and return to port."

Manidhara and the Anarta commanders were shaking

their heads at the foolhardiness of the enterprise when Vararuchi spoke.

"Will you do it?" Before the *samsaptaka* could answer, he said, "If you will, I shall come with you, Udayasanga."

"The *samsaptakas* will be honoured, Councilor Vararuchi," Udayasanga said. "But no, let this be a treat for us and us alone. There will be many more challenges coming your way here."

"So be it," Vararuchi nodded, interpreting the *samsaptaka* correctly. The mission called for a level of precision and coordination that the *samsaptakas* were trained for – his presence in the group would handicap that natural coordination. The mission was also potentially suicidal, and Udayasanga was right in pointing out that the councilor's role in helping defend Dvarka went beyond throwing himself into a risky gamble.

"This is not going to work, young man," Manidhara insisted, even though he and the Anarta commanders were looking at Udayasanga in awe and newfound respect.

"It is either this or nothing, chief," the *samsaptaka* grinned back. "Look at it as repayment for having raised hell in Raivata that night many years ago."

Yugandhara came forward and clasped Udayasanga's hand. "I would be lying if I said I don't want you to do this," he said. "So instead, you have my thanks, friend of the Anartas."

The *samsaptaka* turned to Vararuchi with the intention of bowing, but the councilor took him in a warm embrace. Clapping the warrior gently on the shoulder, he said, "Fight well and make Avanti proud tonight."

"We will, your honour."

With that, he was gone, a shadow in the night.

* * *

The knock on the door was so soft that Vetala Bhatta first thought he had imagined it. Then it came again, a quick muffled rap of knuckles on wood.

"Yes, yes," the councilor addressed the door, easing himself out of bed. "Give me a moment."

Opening the door and squinting into the torch-lit gallery, his eyebrows rose in surprise at the sight of the diminutive figure standing outside.

"What brings you here at such an unearthly hour, girl?" Vetala Bhatta craned his neck to peek into the gallery. The girl was alone. With a twitch of concern, he asked, "Is everything alright?"

"My apologies for bothering you, raj-guru," Shanku replied in an undertone that still managed conveying urgency. "But there is something I needed to speak to you about."

The Acharya saw that the girl's large, black eyes were troubled. "No bother at all," he said, stepping back to let Shanku enter. "I hadn't quite fallen asleep. Let me just light a lamp."

"Okay, what did you want to talk about?" The old councilor looked expectantly at his visitor once they were seated on a simple straw mat.

"It is about the Healer, raj-guru."

"The Healer?" Vetala Bhatta's interest was whetted. "What about him?"

"The Mother Oracle doesn't trust him, raj-guru."

"Doesn't trust him... in what sense?"

"You know, when she fell ill a few days ago...?" Shanku waited for the Acharya to get the context right. "Well, grandmother was adamant she did not want the Healer to treat her."

"Oh! Did she tell you her reasons?" Vetala Bhatta felt the anticipation kindle in his stomach.

"In her own cryptic way, yes." The girl gathered her

thoughts before continuing. "Later that night, I asked her what put her off so much about the Healer. She said she thought there was something sinister about him."

"*Sinister.*" The Acharya let the word roll on his tongue. "Just sinister? Nothing else, nothing specific?"

"She also said she didn't want the Healer's shadow over her, ever."

"Finding the Healer sinister can be reason enough for *her* not to trust him, but it isn't a reasonable ground for suspicion. It is just her opinion of the man. It proves nothing."

"I know, raj-guru, but there was another conversation that the oracle and I had shared with regard to the Healer quite a few days back. What grandmother said about him that day refuses to leave me alone."

"Go on." Vetala Bhatta shifted forward on his seat to listen better.

"It was after the last attack on the city, and I had taken her out to the park on the hill. I happened to mention how much we citizens of Ujjayini owe the Healer for all his help. To that, the Mother Oracle said something strange. She said she feared that when the time comes, the price the Healer will exact from Ujjayini will be severe."

"Why didn't you bring this to the samrat and the council's notice earlier, girl?" The Acharya kept his voice down, but his tone was sharp, reprimanding. "Of all people, *you* know the Mother Oracle never utters words like these without reason."

"What could I have told the royal council, raj-guru?" Shanku didn't flinch under the senior councilor's firm gaze. "It was something she mentioned in passing, an insinuation which she would not care to clarify. Without a good explanation to back what she had said, her statement would only translate as prejudice toward the Healer. As you just pointed out, her words prove nothing."

The girl paused to draw a breath. When she resumed

speaking, her tone remained calm and matter-of-fact. "There are very few families in Ujjayini who have *not* benefitted from the Healer being here, raj-guru. Nearly everyone in this city is in complete awe of the man. Especially after his role in the queen's incredible recovery, how many people in this palace would be inclined to listen to, much less tolerate, anything that casts aspersions on the Healer?"

Vetala Bhatta nodded slowly. He remembered the stable warden's daughter being remarkably perceptive even as a child, and he was glad youth and its brashness had dimmed none of her intelligence. Shanku was right. Confronted with unsubstantiated accusations, the Healer could easily rely on the king, the Queen Mother and Kshapanaka to back him. Furthermore, having brought Ushantha relief from her nagging arthritis, the man had won over Vararuchi as well. For the time being at least, the Healer had admirers in excess, and any critics or detractors of his were unlikely to find much favour in Ujjayini.

"The oracle never hinted *why* she thought that way about the Healer? Or what the nature of this severe price could be?"

"She evaded the question. You know how she is, raj-guru. Always speaking in riddles, leaving it to her listeners to decipher her words."

The Acharya had to admit to the girl's shrewdness. Realizing that approaching the king and the council was untenable, she had paid him this visit, volunteering information and setting him on the path, knowing it was within his ability to investigate the Healer's agenda discreetly. He saw the merit in her approach, but one thing still needed clearing.

"You knew all this before, so why did you delay in coming to me? Why come now?"

"I wasn't sure about the Healer's motives then; I had nothing to go on. But now I do."

"Meaning?"

"I saw something the other night, when you were away in Mahishmati, Acharya." In a few succinct strokes, the girl narrated what she had seen and learnt from the boatman about the Healer's mysterious nocturnal visits across the Kshipra.

"Very suspicious indeed," the raj-guru muttered into his beard once Shanku had finished.

"Something else also occurred to me this afternoon," the girl's voice dropped even lower. "Something the oracle had said that had completely slipped my mind."

"Which is?" Vetala Bhatta prompted.

"The same evening we spoke about the Healer in the park, I asked grandmother if she could help us find the traitor who had killed the Huna scout in Sristhali. She said she couldn't, but she added that the enemy was… that the enemy *is* indeed near. At the time, I assumed she was referring to the Hunas at the frontier, but this afternoon, it struck me that perhaps she wasn't speaking about the Hunas *in general*. Could she have been referring to the Healer as the enemy, and could he be some sort of a spy working for the Hunas? Are his trips across the river part of some undercover job? Could his treachery be the price that Ujjayini would have to bear?"

"The way you put it, the probability cannot be overruled," Vetala Bhatta's expression was grave. "You have acted wisely, girl. We will have to find out more about our very talented guest very quickly."

Once Shanku had left, the Acharya snuffed the lamp out and lay back in his bed, mulling over what the Mother Oracle had told her granddaughter. His instincts about the Healer had been right all along, he realized. Something had drawn the man to Ujjayini and the palace, and it definitely wasn't his charitable streak.

Sleep having deserted him for the moment, the councilor got up and went over to one of the open windows to catch a breath of fresh air. Leaning out, he peered in the direction of the palace's southern wing, which housed the rooms and quarters of the royal guests. In one of the windows on the third floor, he noticed a light burning. The window was too far away – and its angle too acute – for him to make out any other details, yet Vetala Bhatta's eyebrows immediately knitted with suspicion. He knew to whom that particular room had been allotted, and he wondered what was keeping its occupant up this late.

As if suddenly conscious of his scrutiny, the lamp was extinguished. The councilor blinked and turned away, pondering his next move. By the time he left the window and returned to his bed, he had determined what his course of action would be.

Had Vetala Bhatta stayed at the window a few moments longer, he might have observed a tall, strapping figure step onto the terrace that led out from the Healer's third-floor chamber. He might even have followed the figure with interest as it crossed the terrace and climbed down a stairway to a gallery on the second floor, before entering the palace through an open doorway.

As luck would have it, Vetala Bhatta missed sighting the figure – whom he would otherwise have easily identified as Kalidasa.

Udayasanga

The bulky hulls of the Huna ships slipped over Udayasanga's head as he sneaked under the dark, icy depths of the bay. Occasionally, the water above him lit up when the barbarians launched a fireball at Dvarka, and in those brief flares of light, Udayasanga caught fleeting glimpses of his fellow *samsaptakas* swimming alongside.

Progress was slow and hard. The *samsaptakas* struggled against the cold and strong sea currents that kept tugging at them, throwing them off course. The darkness was disorienting too. Besides, every now and then they had to surface for air – and to establish their bearings – huddling in the ships' shadows to avoid detection. Stealth marked their every move, and it came at the price of speed.

The *samsaptakas* had little more than a foggy idea of the *agnikantakas*' exact position; they knew even less about the defences that the Hunas had mounted around the catapults. But time being short for a proper reconnaissance, the warriors had decided to head straight into a strike, hoping their resourcefulness and luck would see them through.

It was a big gamble, Udayasanga thought to himself as he hugged the hull of one ship and rose to the top. He didn't emerge from the water immediately, though. Holding his breath, he waited until the next fireball left an *agnikantaka*, its light refracting through the water. Making a note of the ball's trajectory, he followed its fiery course, aware that the eyes on the decks above were likely to be on the destructive fireball, and not on the waters below. The eyes above would also be dazzled by the flame's glare. He broke the sea's surface softly.

Udayasanga discovered he had surfaced between two rings of vessels forming protective circles around the flamethrowers – an outer ring and an inner ring. The smell of oil, sulphur and burned mustard was overpowering, clinging about the ships' masts and sails, and creeping around corners like a cancerous fog. He caught the murmur of voices from the decks, and though the words were incomprehensible, from the tone he gathered that instructions were being relayed. There was no urgency or vigilance in the voices – he even fancied discerning a spot of boredom, the sort that is born out of complacency.

He liked that. The Hunas had their guard down.

Around him, the heads of the other *samsaptakas* popped out from under the water, one by one. Udayasanga counted all thirteen before he motioned with his fingers, drawing his men's attention to a wedge between two ships that bobbed and swayed in front of them.

A vessel lay beyond the narrow gap, a hulking skeletal contraption made of wood rigged crudely onto its deck. Three men were operating a winch, which was attached to a levered arm of the contraption. The ladle-shaped arm dropped progressively lower with the tightening of the winch, until it was at an almost horizontal position, a foot off the deck. One of the men quickly slipped a knot under the arm, securing it tight.

The *samsaptakas* exchanged sharp, furtive glances. They

were looking at one of the Huna catapults. The second couldn't be very far away.

Udayasanga gestured once again, and the *samsaptakas* began submerging. He glanced at the ship one last time to see two figures stagger into view bearing a squat, heavy object between them. They placed the load in the bowl-like depression at one end of the levered arm, and immediately one of the Hunas put a torch to the object, which sizzled and started belching smoke. The men on the vessel waited until the fire had caught fully before one of them freed the rope holding the levered arm in place.

As Udayasanga sank back into the bay, the spring-loaded arm slung yet another blazing missile at Dvarka.

* * *

The yaksha was an incandescent blur high up in the black sky, a meteor hurtling through the stratosphere, a shining white streak of earthbound light.

Down he came in free fall, lower and still lower, a burning block of rock and mineral, heading straight for Sindhuvarta.

Eventually, the yaksha dipped into a stack of cumulonimbus clouds, but instead of emerging and continuing his downward path, he tucked himself into its soft folds and switched form. From meteorite, he changed into a water crystal, allowing himself to cool and fuse with the moisture already packed in the cloud. Hidden in the lap of the cloud, he caught his breath as he coasted along in the wind blowing from the east.

The clouds bore gently over the western tip of the Vindhya Mountains, but soon they ran into a cross current blowing from the south. The cool, eddying winds made the clouds droop over the mountain's rolling ridges, and the yaksha felt drops of rain forming around him. He let himself melt and fall as a raindrop for a short distance, but moments before he emerged from the cloud, the yaksha's form underwent yet another change.

When he came out of the cloud, the yaksha was a falcon, its black and red-brown plumage wet with rain.

The falcon circled over the dark, forested valley, stretching its wing muscles and getting the blood flowing. Then, as the rain intensified and poured over the hills, the bird straightened its course, its beak pointing due west in the direction of Ujjayini.

* * *

The *agnikantaka* was rigged to the centre of the ship, a few yards from the main mast, and was held in place by thick ropes attached to the ship's sides. Other than the three Hunas operating the winch and the two who loaded the sling, Udayasanga counted a little over a dozen other warriors who, he guessed, were entrusted with the task of guarding the ship. The guards seemed to be taking their responsibility very lightly, though. They stood in lazy clusters around the catapult, weapons slack in their hands, staring out over the ship's nose at Dvarka.

Crouching where the shadows were deepest near the ship's stern, Udayasanga could see why the Huna sentries appeared so lax. Dvarka was a bonfire. Fanned by a stiffening sea breeze, the blaze had spread beyond the waterfront to consume localities in the inner city, and a heavy phalanx of smoke was rapidly rolling inland. Udayasanga briefly wondered if disabling the flamethrowers would serve a purpose any longer, but he pushed the thought aside. They were here to take the catapults out; they would do that if it was the last thing they did.

Udayasanga looked over his shoulder as the seventh and last *samsaptaka* in his group hauled himself over the ship's raked stern and dropped noiselessly onto the deck. He then sneaked a quick glance toward the ship with the second flamethrower on board, moored a little distance away. He hoped all seven *samsaptakas* charged with dismantling *that* catapult were also in position. The two groups were to operate independently, interpreting challenges and responding to situations the way they deemed fit, but Udayasanga wished they could stage a synchronized assault. It was their best chance at success.

At a signal from him, the *samsaptakas* behind him began stealing forward on soft feet, bending low as they scuttled between the shadows of the ship's rigging. Their plan, chalked out in haste as they had rowed away from the burning docks, was primitive in its simplicity. It hinged on the element of surprise, and involved five *samsaptakas* tackling the Huna guards and taking down as many of them as was possible. With the guards engaged and diverted from the *agnikantakas*, the remaining two *samsaptakas* would move in from the flanks and destroy the catapults.

Sword in one hand and a short dagger in the other, Udayasanga crept along the deck, his eyes on a knot of four Hunas who stood to the left of the deck, their backs to him. Beside him, spread out in a ragged line, were his six mates, each focused on his chosen target. They had covered under half the distance to their prey when, all of a sudden, the deck illuminated as a missile was ignited on the other ship. One of the guards in Udayasanga's sights turned idly to observe the missile's launch. The light caught the guard's face square, the dark *hriiz* carved on his forehead stark against his oily brown skin.

In an instant, the guard's expression switched from passive interest to alarm.

"*Urug ha'kyi, ayo!*" The guard shouted, flinging his arm and pointing over the water in the direction of the second ship.

Udayasanga didn't understand a word, but the panicked

pitch told him an alert had been raised. Ducking low, he darted a glance at the other ship. As the catapult's arm jerked and arced, lifting the fireball into the air, Udayasanga saw two bare-bodied *samsaptakas*, swords in their hands, etched clearly in its light. In despair, he noted that the two warriors were nowhere close to the fifteen-odd Hunas grouped around the *agnikantaka*. Worse, the shrillness of the guard's voice had carried across the water, and all the Huna warriors on the other deck were swinging around to look at the interlopers.

With a sinking feeling, Udayasanga realized that not a single *samsaptaka* was within striking distance of either flamethrower, and their cover was already blown.

"*Da'aro meke.*"

Udayasanga turned back to the Hunas in front of him to see that one of them – a lean and hardened warrior wielding a heavy, long-handled axe – was taking charge of the situation.

"*Da'aro meke,*" he snapped once again, louder, his eyes flashing in anger. "*Ozheb yan'tah.*"

One of the guards unhooked a ram horn that hung at his hip. As he raised the horn to his lips to sound an alarm and summon help, Udayasanga heard a roar of voices from the other ship's deck, followed by the stamping of feet and the clash of metal.

The horn's hollow, mournful echo resonated across the deck, drowning out all other noises. Taking advantage of the din, Udayasanga and his *samsaptakas* broke cover and rushed at the Hunas, swords and daggers flashing in the firelight.

The speed of their attack was frightening. They narrowed the distance to the guards in a matter of seconds, shadows brandishing swords, bearing down upon the Hunas before they could realize that their ship too was under attack. Udayasanga's sword sliced through the midriff of the guard closest to him, almost cutting him open in half. Even as the guard grabbed the side of his stomach and sank to his knees, his scream lost in the blare of the horn, Udayasanga leaped at a second warrior, a well-placed slash at the wrist making the Huna lose his sword in agony. Coming in close and cramping him so the warrior had limited room to maneuver, the *samsaptaka* buried his dagger deep in the guard's neck, giving the blade a vicious twist so it severed several arteries. At the same time, Udayasanga lashed out with his sword at the guard blowing the horn, but being constrained for space, he only managed inflicting a painful gash along the man's shoulder and upper arm.

The guard let the horn drop from his lips with a yelp. The same instant, a sword of another *samsaptaka* ran through the guard. The horn's moan fell away into the waters of the bay, quickly replaced by the harsher grunts and screams of the battle raging on the two decks.

Out of the corner of his eye, Udayasanga saw the lean Huna heave his axe over his right shoulder. In the split second it took the Huna to balance himself to deal the blow, Udayasanga judged that the man was aiming for his broad, exposed back. Instead of making a move, the *samsaptaka* held still, clutching the guard whom he had stabbed in the neck close to his chest, gouts of the dead man's blood spraying over him.

Uttering a ferocious curse, the Huna swung his axe at Udayasanga. The *samsaptaka* waited just long enough for the man to commit himself to the strike – so he couldn't check or correct himself – before he spun on his heel, hoisting and swinging the dead Huna around so the dead body was between him and the scything head of the axe. The axe buried itself into the Huna's back with a crunch of bones, the force of the blow and the weight of the dead body propelling Udayasanga back two steps.

Recovering quickly – and giving his attacker no time to think – Udayasanga shoved the body that had shielded him to one side. The axe was buried so deep that the sudden movement yanked the Huna axeman forward, throwing him a bit off balance. The *samsaptaka* instantly stepped up and drove the dagger hard into the Huna's face, ramming the point of the blade between the man's eyes, right under the clumsy mark of the *hriiz*. As the Huna's head rocked back and his mouth opened in a bloodcurdling howl, Udayasanga kicked him on the chest and pulled the dagger free. While the axeman pawed at his face, which was drenching in blood, Udayasanga stepped in once again and stabbed him right under the sternum.

Letting the Huna fall back on the deck, the *samsaptaka* took stock of the assault. All around him, the fight was in full swing. His mates had fared almost as well as he had – he could see five of them cutting and thrusting at the Hunas in wild melee, bodies sprawled at their feet. Looking around, he saw a familiar figure lying to one side, a red blossom of blood at the throat – one of the *samsaptakas* charged with destroying the *agnikantaka*.

The sight of his fallen comrade brought an angry flush to Udayasanga's face, but the thought of the flamethrower sobered him. That was what they were here for, he reminded himself.

Seeing the *agnikantaka* perched on the deck unprotected, Udayasanga reached for the handle of the axe that was sticking out of the dead Huna's back. With a savage twist, he prised the weapon free and headed for the catapult.

That was when the first arrow struck him on his chest, just under his right shoulder.

Bands of pain shot across his chest and shoulder and ran down his arm, making him tighten his grip on the axe. In surprise, he looked at the feathered shaft impaled right in front of his face. Then, as another arrow thudded into the wooden deck, inches from his feet, Udayasanga realized what was happening. It was the Huna archers from the surrounding ships.

Wrenching the arrow's shaft out with a snap, the *samsaptaka* made a dash for the *agnikantaka*. Arrows zinged past him, one grazing him high on the forehead, making the blood run, but he stayed his course. From behind, he could hear choked screams as men were cut and skewered by sword and arrow. Still he ran, thinking of nothing but the catapult.

Reaching the contraption, Udayasanga swung the axe at one of its four supporting legs. The wood was old and hard, and though the beam splintered near the surface, the impact wasn't deep enough. The *samsaptaka* took another swing at the leg, and this time the axe went a little deeper. As he raised his hands high for the next swipe, an arrow drilled into his stomach. His breath left him in a rush, and he doubled over in agony.

They could have donned their armours and helmets, but the armour would have weighed them down in the water. Wincing and gulping air as he leaned on the axe, Udayasanga knew they had made the right decision. They would never have made it this far wearing armour.

A third arrow found him, this time piercing his right thigh, immediately above the knee.

Gritting his teeth, Udayasanga straightened. Breaking both arrows off and casting them aside, he raised the axe and brought it down hard on the beam. The violence of the blow sent jolts of stinging pain up his arms, but with a loud crack, the beam buckled and broke. Without pausing for a moment, Udayasanga turned his attention to the catapult's second leg.

He hacked and chopped without cease, and arrows hit him without respite. By the time he had cleaved the flamethrower's third leg, he had stopped removing the arrows. Blood from two wounds on his head mixed with sweat and flowed down his face in rivulets, catching and clotting on his flamboyant beard and moustache.

When the fourth and final leg gave way, the *agnikantaka*

toppled with a crash that made the ship shimmy uncertainly in the water. Letting the axe slip from his grasp, Udayasanga dropped to the deck on all fours, his head hanging while he caught his ragged breath. One eye had gummed over with clotting blood, and the spittle on his lips had flecks of blood in it as well.

He lifted his head and peered along the deck where the *samsaptakas* and the ship's guards were still locked in combat. A flurry of arrows from the other Huna ships rained down on the fighters, and every now and then, an arrow struck someone – sometimes a *samsaptaka*, sometimes a Huna.

The ruthlessness of the Huna strategy made Udayasanga's blood run cold.

The distance between the ships was too much – and the night too dark – for their archers to be able to distinguish Huna from *samsaptaka*. Yet the archers shot their arrows, not caring whether they hit friend or foe. What mattered to the savages was clearing their ships of enemies and protecting the flamethrowers. Killing off a few dozens of their own warriors to meet that objective was clearly not too heavy a burden for the Huna conscience to bear.

These people had no mercy. And these people now wanted to take Sindhuvarta. If they succeeded, Udayasanga understood how it would end. He threw his head back and bared his teeth to the sky in a guttural yell that was rage, fear and helplessness. Then, staggering to his feet, he broke into a hobbling run.

Destroying the *agnikantakas* wasn't good enough. The Hunas deserved much worse.

Udayasanga ran past the few fighters still left standing, his eyes on the small torch that the Hunas had used to light the fireballs. The torch lay guttering on the deck, emitting weak blue flames. Ignoring the arrows that missed him by mere inches, he traversed the length of the ship and went down painfully on one knee to retrieve the torch.

He blew hard on the embers, coaxing life into them until three tongues of orange flame erupted. Taking the rescued torch, he made for the pile of unlit fireballs placed in one corner of the deck. Oil, sulphur and mustard. That was all it had taken the Hunas to set Dvarka ablaze. It was time to return the favour.

An arrow pierced Udayasanga from behind, striking him below the left shoulder blade. It went deep, smashing through flesh and bone before perforating a lung. The *samsaptaka* coughed and teetered, blood spilling from his lips. Still he persevered, swaying and stumbling toward the stack of fireballs. His legs gave under him, but he crawled and clawed forward until he reached the pile.

Stretching his hand out, he touched the torch to the nearest ball. Nothing happened for a moment. Then the incendiary mix in the fireball sparked and caught. The fire spread quickly from one ball to the next, flames leaping and soaring in eagerness. The wooden deck began smouldering underneath, while the masts and the sails started combusting overhead. The deck lit up, first yellow, then bright orange.

The glow from the fire shone on Udayasanga's face, streaked with grime, sweat and blood. It flared in his dark eyes as he lay still on the deck, his gaze frozen, staring into eternity.

* * *

The splash in the water was so loud in the stillness of the hut that it startled Jayanta out of his meditative trance, forcing his eyes open.

The sudden exposure to the brightness of the lamps made him wince and blink, even as the brassy echo of water ringing on metal zinged and dwindled in his ears. As his vision adjusted to the light, the prince looked down at the copper bowl. The water in the bowl rocked and swayed in a gentle motion – it was already on its way to regaining calm – but whatever had caused the disturbance had sent a shower of droplets over the bowl's lip onto the mud-baked floor.

Jayanta edged closer and peeked into the bowl.

At first, he saw nothing but his own shadowy face, stretching and distorting in rhythm with the water's movement, reflected in the shallow depths. Then his heart skipped a beat.

A ripple. Not on the water's surface, where ripples are generally observed, but at the very bottom of the vessel.

Not even a ripple, really. More a *slither*.

An extended, elongated slither along the curvature of the bowl, like the dart of an eel, except there was no eel. There was no body or form or substance either. Just a vague, sinuous current – shaped out of water, slipping away and disappearing into the water it had sprung from.

The prince's breath caught in his throat and his cheeks flushed with excitement. He was on the right track.

Sitting back, he resumed chanting under his breath, but he kept an eye on the bowl. Within moments, tiny bubbles started forming at the bottom of the bowl, rising to the surface in thin jets as the water's temperature changed. Unexpectedly, there was another violent upheaval, a churning, as three slithering crosscurrents nipped and chased one another, tails lashing in anger. The turbulence yielded another splash, this one louder than the one before, and water drizzled around the bowl, a few drops scalding Jayanta's exposed legs and feet.

The prince, however, was too far gone to notice, his lips chanting furiously, eyes glittering and crazed with the lust for revenge. He could sense that Ahi was finally within hailing distance. Any moment now, he would gain control of the terror.

Any moment now, his fortunes – and the fortunes of the human king and his city – were set to change.

Fleet

The atmosphere along the ship's deck was turning rancid with sweat and fear. In every breath he took, Vararuchi could smell the panic, base and pungent, radiating feverishly off the bodies pressed around him. It mingled in the briny air, mixing with the drifts of toxic smoke that hung over their heads, curdling in the humidity, a miasmic concoction of foulness that made the stomach churn. And when he chanced to look into the eyes of the men, all staring rigidly at the silhouettes of the Huna ships that were steadily drawing closer, the councilor glimpsed the dread lurking in their souls.

Give this lot enough time and they would kill themselves with fear, Vararuchi sighed unhappily to himself, bracing his legs against the deck as he gazed over the choppy waters at the nearest Huna ship, tossing less than half a mile away. He then glanced backward, over the heads of the hundred-odd perspiring men crammed on the deck, at the straggling line of boats ferrying more soldiers from Dvarka to the Anarta ships waiting in the bay.

"Watch out! The arrows are coming again!"

The warning came from one of the lookouts posted near the prow, and this time, almost as one, the men on the deck went down in a crouch, raising their shields above their heads to guard themselves from the lethal shafts shot from the Huna ship. Vararuchi did likewise, not bothering to check if their ship was, indeed, the target of the Huna archers. If they were, they would know soon enough. Instead, folding himself as tightly as possible, he huddled under his shield, waiting for the arrows to come down around him again, anticipating cries of pain as the barbs inevitably found some unprotected, fleshy target. The first volley aimed at the ship had already claimed three soldiers and gravely injured four others.

The screams did come, but not from close. This time they were from much further away, from somewhere beyond the ship's deck.

"They've gone back to attacking the boats," someone announced in a frenzied voice.

Cursing under his breath, the councilor rose and looked back in the direction of the boats. The five boats were too far for him to tell which ones had been on the Huna archers' sights, though he sensed that all five had been. He thought he saw a figure in one of the boats slouch forward and fall.

"We need to move faster," Vararuchi shouted. Looking around, he caught Manidhara's eye. "Can we speed up the ship, good chief? We must stop their archers quickly."

"The oarsmen are rowing as hard as they can, councilor," the chieftain from Raivata replied dismally. "It's the best they can do in such rough waters."

"We should have got archers of our own along," Vararuchi gave a rueful sigh.

His gaze drifted from Manidhara to the burning wreckage of the two Huna ships with the flamethrowers on board. The protective formation around them had long scattered, and both ships sat exposed in the bay, derelict and abandoned, two small islands of tarry fumes and fire that were imploding and going underwater in bits and pieces. The sight of the first ship erupting in flames in the darkness was fresh in the councilor's mind, and when, moments later, the second ship caught fire, the cheer that had broken out and spread through Dvarka had been deafening. The rain of fireballs had ceased forthwith, prompting Yugandhara and Vararuchi to marshal the defenders for a swift offensive.

Their counterattack, however, started coming apart almost before it began, taking much of the euphoria with it. Just as the first few boatloads of soldiers rowed out to the Anarta ships anchored offshore, the sea unexpectedly turned turbulent, forcing the first change in plans. Despite being well-trained, efficient and hardy fighters, the troops from Avanti were poor sailors; with the sea heaving around violently, they would be hopeless in open waters. So, with the exception of Vararuchi and a handful of others who had some sailing experience, the rest of Avanti's troops had stayed back in Dvarka, leaving the challenge of meeting the Hunas at sea squarely on Anartas' soldiers.

Overwhelmed as they were by this, there was worse in store for the Federation's troops. The blaze in Dvarka had lit up the wharfs, and the boats heading out to the Anarta ships were plainly visible to the Hunas in the bay. The Hunas had quickly pressed their archers into service, attacking the outgoing boats and inflicting severe casualties on the defenders. Less than half the soldiers in each boat made it to the Anarta ships alive, and even these were often too grievously wounded to carry on a fight.

Struck by the absurdity and futility of running this gauntlet, Vararuchi had put forth an audacious proposal. He and Manidhara were already on board two of the ships, with a little over two hundred men for company. Instead of waiting endlessly for the entire fleet to be ready – and putting boatloads of men at the mercy of the Huna archers – the councilor had proposed storming the vessels carrying the archers, giving the Federation's troops a better chance at crossing over to the remaining ships.

"Do you really think this is going to work, my friend?"

Vararuchi turned to see that Manidhara had elbowed his way through the crowd to join him.

"If we fight like lions, yes."

Manidhara was silent for a moment. As the ships pitched over a deep swell, he grabbed a rope for support and spoke into Vararuchi's ear. "The men are of the opinion that this is an omen."

"What is?" Vararuchi turned to the chieftain.

"The sea," Manidhara indicated the surging mass of water around them.

"It must be an approaching storm," the councilor shrugged. "I would think your men should be fairly used to this."

"If it's a storm, where are the storm clouds and the wind?"

Vararuchi examined the sky through the smudges of smoke. He saw a heavy sprinkling of stars, the Milky Way a rich vein of silver to the southwest. There were no clouds, no wind, the sails overhead hanging limp from the masts and the crosspieces. The air scarcely stirred, the breeze that had blown inland and fanned the fires in Dvarka all evening only a memory.

"The men are right," said Manidhara with a doleful shake of his head. "It is an omen."

"If it is one, it must be a good omen," the councilor had to raise his voice over the creaking of the ship's timbers. "Your men have sea legs, whereas the Hunas don't. Your men are far more adept at dealing with such tricky conditions than the enemy is. The rougher the sea, the more the odds tilt in our favour."

"You may have a point there, my friend." The councilor's

logic didn't seem to cheer the chieftain much. "Except there are a hundred of us here and a hundred more there..." He jerked his thumb at the second Anarta ship following them. "...while the Hunas have many, *many* times that number. Such odds can't be easily evened."

"In battle, it is not the strongest or the bravest or those with the greater numbers who win," said Vararuchi. "Victory belongs to the side that best understands the price of defeat."

"You might want to tell the men that," Manidhara looked at the councilor hopefully.

Vararuchi cast a quick glance at the Huna ships. They still had some distance to cover, so he climbed onto a chest meant to store mooring ropes.

"Warriors of Anarta," he faced the soldiers, modulating his voice so it would carry to the last man on the deck. "The task we have set ourselves might seem impossible, and in all honesty, I don't know if we will succeed in overcoming the Huna archers."

The men on the deck shuffled nervously. Manidhara shot Vararuchi an apprehensive glance, not sure where the councilor was going with this.

"But remember that it took just *fourteen* men to put an end to the *agnikantakas*," the councilor's arm went out toward the sinking Huna ships. "Those fourteen did what they did not because they are brave and skillful fighters, but because they once had everything taken from them – their lands, their families, their self-respect. It took years and countless lives to win all that back. Those men know the cost of giving in to the invaders. They and I will challenge fate to keep the Hunas' shadows from darkening our lands again. You have been more fortunate, but the barbarians are now at your doorstep. Will you stand by and watch them take what is yours by right? *Your* sea, *your* land, *your* freedom? *Your* wives, *your* pride and *your* dignity?"

Manidhara could sense the mood shift along the deck. Shoulders were squaring, heads were holding up with greater firmness, and there was more steel in the men's eyes.

"The outcome of battle is never in a warrior's control. What *is* in his control is how he chooses to fight and what he chooses to fight for." Vararuchi raised his hand high so his coiled *urumi* was visible to all. "Today, I choose to fight to keep the Anartas and Sindhuvarta free of the invaders – and I choose to fight such that the enemy will speak of me in their legends for generations to come. What will *you* do, brave warriors of Anarta?"

"We will fight likewise, your honour," a soldier shouted back. Heads around him nodded in vigorous agreement.

"We will fight for the Anartas, for Sindhuvarta and our *freedom*," screamed another, raising his spear skyward and shaking it. Spears, swords and axes lifted into the air in response, the soldier's mates picking up his words and relaying them in an impassioned battle cry.

"For the Anartas and Sindhuvarta and *freedom*," shouted Manidhara, locking grateful eyes with Vararuchi.

Acknowledging the chieftain's appreciation, Vararuchi returned his attention to the Huna fleet. The ships with the archers were less than hundred yards away, and the councilor noticed that a couple more were moving in from the sides to intercept the Anarta ships. The sea, however, had turned even rockier, waves rising almost up to the rails and sending water sluicing across the deck. The Huna oarsmen were struggling to keep their ships on course, and the sight of the enemy vessels lurching and fishtailing in the pale half-light of dawn relieved Vararuchi. The Hunas outnumbered them by a huge margin, but for now, there probably was greater disarray in their ranks. He couldn't count on it, but the thought offered hope.

As they drew closer, the Huna archers unleashed another volley of arrows. Owing to the uneven movement of their ships, the shots were poorly aimed, and not more than two dozen arrows even hit the Anarta ship. Still, Manidhara saw the threat clearly.

"Draw your shields together and get behind them," he issued instructions to his men, pointing and shouting. "Once we are close enough, they won't miss. Keep your shields closer, cover every point... quick. You there... get down on your knee. And you... cover the shoulder of your mate in front."

Vararuchi slipped into line, raising his shield and placing it square next to the shield of one soldier. All around him, soldiers assembled, their shields knitting together and forming a single shell of metal behind which they crouched or stood, heads lowered, hands gripped tight on their weapons. The archers launched another volley, better aimed this time, but the formation withstood the attack, the arrows glancing harmlessly off the shields.

Slowly, ploughing through the turgid and resistant water, the Anarta ship hove toward the Huna vessels. Arrows flew thick over the narrowing stretch of sea, but the Anarta formation held fast. Nearer and nearer their ship edged, maneuvering around until its side bumped hard against one of the ships with the archers.

"Attack!" Manidhara hollered at the top of his lungs.

The warriors from the Anartas broke cover, shields parting to reveal heavy battle-axes, curving swords and long lances, all pointing and thrusting toward the Huna ship, an avalanche of keen blades, thirsting for blood. The warriors burst into a run, feet pounding across the deck, weapons waving in the air, their shouts drowning out the crash and fall of the waves. They hurled themselves over the ship's side at the Huna archers, just as the first light of dawn touched the sky behind Dvarka.

* * *

The second-floor window overlooking the bath opened so softly, even the parakeets nesting in the jamun tree growing by the window barely stirred in their sleep. It was still dark outside, though a faint brushstroke of light low in the east signaled the birth of a new day.

It was even darker within the room, and the Acharya was nothing but a shadow as he leaned out of the window and peered down at the bath and the path that led to it from the palace. He searched, in particular, for the black rectangle of the pool, but when his eyes failed to discern clear shapes, he strained his ears to catch the distinctive swish-splash of water being displaced by a bather. No sound came from the direction of the bath, though, and apart from the deep *coop-coop-coop* of a coucal calling from across the lake, the morning was steeped in silence.

Pinching his eyelids together, the raj-guru wished the Healer would put in his appearance only once there was sufficient daylight. He had been awake practically all night, going over everything that Shanku had told him, playing every little incident connected to the Healer back in his mind, and now he felt the fatigue pulling at him, a leaden weight, slowing his faculties, dulling his mind. The councilor feared he wouldn't be able to bring himself to focus on the Healer's mind if it was too dark to see properly.

The room was situated diagonally above the palace's northeastern bath, hidden from below by the spread of the jamun. Reserved as a studio for visiting court artists who wished to sketch or paint in privacy, it was rarely in use, and suited Vetala Bhatta's purpose nicely; he did not want anyone getting an inkling of what he was up to, at least not for the time being.

Dawn crept in on a grey sky smeared with clouds. An easterly wind herded more clouds over Ujjayini, but near the ground, the air was warm and stuffy. As time passed and there was no sign of the Healer, Vetala Bhatta began wondering if he had misjudged the man's routine. He knew the Healer favoured this bath, but perhaps he had chosen one of the others in the palace that morning.

Nearly half an hour passed, and the raj-guru was on the verge of calling off his vigil when he heard the clacking of wooden *padukas* on stone. He edged forward and peeked to find the Healer approaching. Sighing with relief, the councilor waited for the bearded figure to descend the bath's steps, take off his *padukas* and enter the pool. He then stretched for his spear, propped against the wall nearby.

Keeping the spear carefully concealed from view, Vetala Bhatta clenched a fist to his chest while his gaze fixed on the back of the Healer's head, bobbing half-submerged in the water. As the Healer immersed himself in the pool, the councilor closed his eyes and began reciting a silent mantra.

The two skulls hanging from the Acharya's spear glowed and smouldered at their cavities.

Then, in a breathless rush, two images flooded the raj-guru's mind, one after the other – a complex *mandala*; and a vast, sunlit ground with a single banyan tree at its centre.

* * *

The dawn that broke over Dvarka was rich and glorious, the colour of molten gold, but it went sadly unnoticed. Those who had fled the city and sheltered in the countryside were too scared and broken to look beyond their misery and misfortune, while those who had stayed behind were too busy trying to beat the fire back – or salvage what they could from the encroaching flames. And those out in the bay had other thoughts to occupy themselves with. Thoughts like how to make every swing of the axe, every cut of the sword and every thrust of the spear count, and how to make it out of the bloody battle alive.

For the battle that was underway that morning was the bloodiest that had been fought, at least in the collective imagination of Anartas' soldiers.

The Hunas were wild and brutal warriors, and displayed an incapacity for fear – and a disregard for death – that was unnerving. They came at Dvarka's troops with swinging axes and cleaving swords, screaming curses, their eyes crazed with bloodlust. They came in groups, mowing into their adversaries, their swords plunging into chests and stomachs, their axes burying into heads and shoulders; and they came in ones and twos, throwing themselves at knots of Anartas' soldiers only to be impaled and torn apart in a matter of seconds. Strong and majestic, they fought like lions; savage and ruthless, they brawled like rabid dogs.

Yet, the troops from the Anartas did not quail. They stood firm and fought, matching blow for blow, giving as good as they got. If fear did lay a finger on any among them, the soldier only had to look at Vararuchi to draw courage and face the Hunas anew. For the councilor from Avanti was seemingly everywhere, from one end of the ship to the other, in the thick of every fight.

One moment his *urumi* was flaying a Huna who was about to behead a fallen Anarta soldier; the next, he was fending off a withering blow from a battle-axe before ducking under his attacker's arm to slit his throat with a *katari*. Suddenly he was leaping and scrambling up the ship's rigging to escape half a dozen Hunas coming after him; a moment later, he was swinging over the deck on a rope, ambushing the same six men with the skill of a predator. Vararuchi moved along the deck like a spectre, weaving away from lunging blades and sidestepping lethal lances, leaving those Hunas who crossed his path hopelessly crippled and mutilated. Or lifeless.

At some moment during the course of the battle, a couple of the other Huna ships moved in to disgorge reinforcements, and the scales began tipping rapidly in favour of the invaders. Outnumbered four to one and pressed on the back foot, the soldiers from the Anartas began falling, one among them being Manidhara, who was brought down by a spear driven into his left thigh, just above his knee. With a yell of pain, the chieftain buckled and went down, his good leg slipping and giving way on the deck slick with blood.

As Manidhara teetered on one knee, his injured leg trailing behind him, a Huna raised his axe with the intention of splitting his head in two. The Anartas' soldiers were too busy battling for their own survival to notice the fate that was about to befall their chief. However, with fractions to go before the Huna brought his axe down, a form leaped at him from over the heads of the men fighting all around. The figure rammed into the Huna warrior, throwing him off balance and sending him crashing to the deck.

By the time the Huna's shoulder hit the deck, he was dead from the *katari* buried in his chest, its blade driven through his ribs into his heart.

A stunned Manidhara looked at Vararuchi climbing off the fallen Huna, wresting the *katari* from the dead man's torso as he spun around to meet an attack from the other Hunas nearby. However, neither the councilor nor the chieftain was in anyone's sights at that moment, so Vararuchi threw a quick backward glance at Manidhara.

"Can you use your sword?" he asked tersely. Seeing Manidhara nod, the councilor quickly bent and lent him a hand so he could rise and prop himself against a mast. "I shall be close by, but I won't be able to watch over you all the while, chief. So hold the sword well – we need every strong hand we can get."

The councilor had just turned back to take on the Hunas when the ship lurched viciously, sending soldiers on both sides spinning in all directions. Waves crashed onto the deck, and for a moment, the ship's bow pointed at the sky while its stern gazed into the depths of a dark trough. The next instant, the vessel righted itself and was fully back in the water, and Manidhara looked at the volatile sea and the ships tossing about with a mixture of bewilderment and fear.

Overhead, the sky was clear of clouds, the sun was a hot blaze in the east, and there was still no sign of a wind. The sea's roughness defied every law of nature.

The turbulence had brought the battle to a brief, stunning halt, and as attackers and defenders alike struggled to their feet, the first of the ships from Dvarka arrived, bringing more of Anartas' troops to help their beleaguered brothers. The fighting resumed in small skirmishes, but the pluck seemed to have finally left the Hunas. As more and more vessels from Dvarka joined the fray, the invaders were slowly pushed back, their warriors jumping over the ships' sides into the bay.

"They are fleeing," Manidhara heard someone shout, and looking over his shoulder, he saw the Huna ships disengaging. A hoarse cheer went up along the deck as Vararuchi appeared by his side.

"We drove them back," the chieftain clapped a hand on Vararuchi's sweaty shoulder, grinning and grimacing with pain at the same time. "Our resistance paid off."

"It did," the councilor agreed as he examined a cut on his upper arm. Letting his eye rove over the deck filled with dead and maimed men, he said, "Your men fought exceptionally, though the sea played a role as well."

"The important thing is the barbarians are on the run." Eyeing the retreating sails, the chief asked, "Shouldn't we be going after them? Teach them all a lesson?"

"We must confer with Yugandhara first," answered Vararuchi, scouting the other Anarta ships for a sign of the chief. "If we must go in pursuit..."

The councilor stopped, conscious of a change that had

suddenly overcome the ship. The men had ceased talking and shouting, and they stood in small groups, their weapons limp in their hands, gazing wide-eyed in the direction of the Huna ships.

"Sails!" said a soldier in hushed voice.

Exchanging a puzzled look with Manidhara, Vararuchi took a few steps forward to see what was in the soldiers' sight, behind the bulk of the fleeing ships. At first, except for the tumultuous waves rising and falling, their crests frosted with surf, there was nothing for him to see.

Then, as one wave fell and stabilized, he saw the first sail. Then another, followed by a third. In no time, the northwestern segment of the horizon was crammed with black sails, all growing larger and more clearly defined as they drew closer to Dvarka.

"Heaven help us." Vararuchi heard Manidhara, who had hobbled forward to join him, whisper in his ear. "That's probably the entire Huna army."

"How many ships by your estimate, my friend?"

"At least fifty," the chieftain's face was pale, his eyes haunted. "We cannot tackle so many of them. We have to withdraw."

Facing the approaching Huna fleet, Vararuchi felt hopelessness settle on his shoulders and root his feet to the deck. The assault on the *agnikantakas*, the storming of the Huna ships, the fury of the battle and all those lives sacrificed – everything they had done to save Dvarka had been useless. The city was still going to fall to the Hunas.

* * *

The pool scarcely rippled under the broad, leaden sky. Submerged below its surface, Shukracharya didn't move a muscle as he held his breath, trying to calm his nerves. But his mind was in relentless churn, thoughts chasing and dislodging one another, frantic and refusing to settle. They harassed him like wayside dogs, tenacious and discordant, tailing him wherever he went, closing in on him when his back was to them, but pulling away the moment he turned his attention on them. They had left him sleepless and drained, inducing a fever that the high priest could sense building in his tired bones.

There was plenty to worry about, Shukracharya conceded, slowly rising to the water's surface to draw breath.

There was the yaksha, who, according to the bones, was making speedy progress toward Ujjayini. Over his last few visits to the cremation ground, the high priest had cast many potent spells around the banyan, yet he couldn't be certain any of them would be strong enough to ward off a resourceful and determined yaksha. To know what would stop the yaksha, he needed to see it in person, but try as he might, Shukracharya had failed to deduce a way of sneaking out of the palace and journeying to the cremation ground in broad daylight.

As if the yaksha was not doing enough to keep him on tenterhooks, the bones had made another startling and perplexing disclosure late the previous night. The high priest had wanted to check on what was happening in Devaloka in the wake of the attack on Amaravati – he suspected Indra would be rallying a counterattack. However, to his astonishment, the bones had revealed that Narada was travelling to Patala. *Alone*.

Shukracharya was still attempting to work out the purpose of the diplomat's mission as he resurfaced from the pool for the third and final time and joined his palms in obeisance to the sun, concealed behind the clouds. What scheme were Indra, Brihaspati and Narada hatching this time around? He had already dispatched a message to Patala, forewarning Hiranyaksha of the visit; he hoped the message would get through before Narada's arrival.

Then there was the councilor Kalidasa's nocturnal visit to his chamber, and his strange request to help him recover his memory from the mists of time.

– when the time comes, the price the Healer will exact from Ujjayini will be severe.

Mounting the bath's steps, Shukracharya stopped and blinked in confusion. What were these words that had just flashed through his mind, and where had they come from?

– could his treachery be the price that Ujjayini would have to bear?

This time, the words were accompanied by an image. A young girl's face, lit by a lamp. The girl was speaking, and high priest recognized her as one of the king's councilors. The one they called Shanku, the one who had miraculously escaped from under the Marut's foot.

The image vanished.

Bewildered, Shukracharya gazed ahead of him, staring at nothing as he tried to make sense of what was happening. Then, a split second later, he saw another image – an elderly man with a tired, downcast expression, whom he had never seen before. *Shoorasena will inevitably receive my letter* – the man was saying – *what if he accepts Rukma's hand?*

The next instant, that image disappeared too. In its place, he saw Vikramaditya. The human king was standing and stroking his moustache as he spoke. *Dhanavantri. He has a very good reason to make a visit to Chandravardhan's court – the king's illness.*

Vikramaditya faded, and a series of images came and went in rapid succession. A view of a part of Ujjayini's outer wall under construction; the king and his councilors in the council chamber, listening to Narada speak – *you will benefit greatly by befriending us*; the king lying on a bed, eyes closed and looking deathly pale; a curtain of white fog with something vague, large and shadowy concealed in its shifting folds...

Then the girl's face again – *the boatman says he has ferried the Healer many times, raj-guru.*

In a flash, the young councilor disappeared and a fresh image implanted in the high priest's mind. A great, rectangular bath in the shadow of a towering peepal tree, a solitary figure standing on the bath's steep steps. The figure wore *padukas*, a wet dhoti and an eye-patch over the left eye. The high priest drew his breath in sharply, jerking his head in surprise and disbelief – and the man on the bath's steps did likewise.

That is when the significance of what was happening struck Shukracharya like a bolt from the sky.

He was experiencing someone else's thoughts, he realized with a shock, seeing and hearing things that were registering and playing on the other person's mind. The doors between their minds had opened, allowing thoughts to flow unhindered.

The high priest could think of only one good reason why those doors were open all of a sudden. Someone had unlocked them with the intention of reading his mind.

Ahi

Someone is trying to read my mind.

Feeling the words wash over him, the Acharya hurriedly pulled away from the window, hugging the shadows and thrusting his spear deeper into the gloom. A faint tremor gripped his body, causing his legs to tremble, and a sense of unease coursed through him, making sweat break out on his forehead and trickle down his temples.

Someone in the palace is trying to read my mind... someone who is familiar with the human king and his council, someone who enjoys their trust.

Sick with fear, the raj-guru listened in on the Healer's thoughts. He could almost feel the weight of the Healer's eyes on him, prying into his mind, probing into the dark corners and recesses in an effort to get him to reveal his identity.

Who are you? Where are you?

With a supreme effort of will, the Acharya loosened the hold that the Healer's mind had over his. Even as the Healer's thoughts tried to reassert themselves, seeking him out, the raj-guru blinked the sweat from his eyes. Wetting his lips, he uttered a few hasty mantras…

– it is not the physician or Vararuchi –

…struggling to break the links that he had forged with the Healer's mind…

– the person is trying to escape. Can it be? –

…and suddenly, like the drawing of a curtain, the Healer and his thoughts were gone!

In their place, there was silence, and the panicked and relieved hammering of his heart, accompanied by the voices of his own mind, out of breath and clamouring and irrational, urging him to flee the room so he couldn't be found out.

Stepping forward gingerly, Vetala Bhatta poked his head around the jamb of the window. The Healer was still on the bath's steps, erect and alert, head swiveling slowly as he scanned the palace. Seeing the Healer turn in his direction, the raj-guru again ducked out of sight, holding his breath and counting the seconds. He had just begun wondering whether it was safe to risk another peek when the clack of the *padukas* rose to his ears, briskly receding into the distance. The Acharya stuck his head out in time to see the Healer disappear behind the parijata shrubs that lined the closest entrance to the palace.

The Acharya let his breath out in a long, quivering sigh and relaxed his grip on the shaft of his spear, slick under his sweaty palm. The light had left the skulls, black sockets and cavities now staring and grinning at nothing in macabre mirth.

The Healer had been conscious of what was happening! The Healer had nearly caught him.

The realization alarmed the raj-guru. As a rule, he never attempted reading minds without consent, but in the few rare instances when he *had* read people in secret, his subjects had never guessed that their thoughts were being laid bare. What had given him away to the Healer? What had he done that had almost exposed him? Even as he searched for answers, the Acharya's thoughts turned to what he had gleaned from the Healer's mind.

The *mandala*. He had seen the Healer use tantric *mandalas* while working on Vishakha's cure, but the *mandala* itself was very different from the one he had observed drawn on the floor of the queen's bedchamber. The one in the Healer's mind was much more elaborate, a network of maze-like grids and circles that had felt vaguely ominous. In addition, he thought he had seen pieces of what resembled bones scattered over the *mandala*, imparting a sinister aspect to the drawing.

Then there was the solitary banyan that had kept flitting in and out of the Healer's mind. It had taken the Acharya no time to place the tree – it was the one in the cremation ground outside the city. The tree explained what the ferryman had said to Shanku about the Healer's clothes and feet being covered in ash on his trips across the Kshipra. But what fascination did the banyan – *or was it the cremation ground itself?* – hold for the Healer?

Yet, what confused and perturbed the Acharya more than the *mandala* and the mystery of the banyan tree was an image that had fleetingly imposed itself in the Healer's mind. It was a face, barely a flicker, but the raj-guru was inclined to believe it had been Narada's; the same intelligent eyes, sharp nose and broad forehead he had first seen the day the deva had come to trade Indra's friendship for the Halahala.

If the face was Narada's, his and Shanku's assumption of the Healer being a Huna agent was way off the mark. If the face was Narada's, the palace was hosting someone infinitely more dangerous and devious than the Hunas, Vetala Bhatta realized.

The councilor opened the door to the room a crack and surveyed the corridor outside, making sure the coast was clear. Stepping out, he shut the door behind him, his mind briefly on Kalidasa.

You have helped the queen remember – will you help me too?

Kalidasa had also come under the Healer's sway. Shanku had been right. The more popular the Healer became, the more fans and followers he acquired, the more he lived up to his reputation, the harder it would become to shake people's faith in him and get them to see his darker side, the Acharya mused bitterly.

He had to unearth the Healer's true identity, and do it soon. Unfortunately, he no longer trusted his ability to spy on the Healer without revealing himself. That left him with just one alternative.

Quickening his pace, the raj-guru went in search of the Mother Oracle.

* * *

The steam rising out of the copper bowl was dense, oppressive and mildly viscous. It hung in the air of the hut, clinging to itself, as if reluctant to escape out of the hut's narrow door. Dank and mopey, it dripped back over Jayanta, mingling with his sweat and running down his head and shoulders as he sat mouthing the esoteric incantations listed on the palm leaves. It cast ghostly auras around the seven lamps that lit the room; it beaded the hut's cracked, mud-brick walls in pustules that quivered with suppressed malice.

The steam rising from the bowl was grim and alive and ripe with possibilities.

The prince's legs had gone to sleep under him, the small of his back hurt from hunching for so long, and the sweat kept getting into his eyes, making them smart, but he didn't appear to notice the discomfort. His faculties were all pinpointed at summoning Ahi.

So deeply engrossed was Jayanta in the task that it took

a while for his mind to register the subtle changes occurring around him.

As the water in the bowl bubbled and roiled, breaking apart and coalescing into shadowy, reptilian currents, the steam escaping from its depths changed to a murky shade of grey. The wisps began rising over the bowl in distinct flows and patterns, a slow dance that harvested more and more steam, fusing air currents to air currents. At first, the forms that emerged out of this lacked substance and shifted around aimlessly, but as the vapours banded together and engorged, a rudimentary serpent took shape, an apparition rearing out of the water and shimmering over the bowl, its plumed head swaying slowly to some primeval rhythm.

Darkness dipped in all around Jayanta as the lamps shrank and guttered in fright, and even the grey rectangle of morning light at the door seemed to withdraw with a gasp. The air within the hut turned chill, causing the cloak of steam to dissipate, and making the moisture accumulated on surfaces turn to frost. A void of silence took possession of the room, a noiselessness as old as time, and in its heart was the hollow, hateful echo of a hiss – not so much a sound audible to the ear as a whisper sensed deep in the marrow.

Shivering with cold and excitement, the prince held his breath and stared at the nebulous form before him. His eyes shone with delight and disbelief at what he had achieved; he had awakened Ahi and brought it into the light, exactly the way it had been said in the ancient texts.

Now to command the fearsome beast to do as he willed.

Uttering mantras all the while, Jayanta nicked his thumb once again with the knife, letting the blood flow so the serpentine form could pick up its scent. The apparition perked its head up, opening its mouth wide to allow a forked tendril of vapour to flicker into sight, seeking out the blood. The musty smell of the ocean floor spilled out of the yawning cavity, and lingering under it, the prince caught the rotten whiff of death. Choking down the bile that was forcing its way up his gullet, the prince extended his hand to the apparition.

"Follow the trail of your blood and mine, follow the hand that guides you," the prince whispered the memorized lines. "Obey the blood that has given you life, mighty Ahi. Obey, and come to where your blood awaits you."

The ghost-serpent responded by craning its neck and lunging at his bloodied fingers, its forked tongue in a slavering frenzy. It bent over the rim of the bowl, its moist head coiling around Jayanta's hand, smearing itself in the prince's blood. At last, pulling away with a great deal of reluctance, the apparition's head turned this way and that, its tongue flicking the air furiously, as if searching for something.

Without warning, the form unraveled and came apart, individual strands of vapour springing free and disappearing into the cold currents eddying about the cramped little hut. In a matter of moments, there was nothing left of the ghost-serpent.

* * *

Voices raised in alarm. Men, women and children, shouting and screaming as they abandoned their homes and joined the last, desperate evacuation of Dvarka; the shrill and rushed flow of commands as soldiers were deployed to defend one quarter of the city or the other; the thudding of soldiers' feet, rushing down lanes and alleyways. And over all this, the plaintive yet ominous lowing of the Huna war-horns, rolling in across the bay in tides, like harbingers of doom.

The din was a deafening swirl around Vararuchi as he strode along the smouldering waterfront, heading for the hillock where the city's war council had gathered just hours earlier. By his side were three *samsaptakas*, the only surviving members of the party of fourteen that had raided and destroyed the *agnikantakas*.

"Are you certain none of the others got away?" Vararuchi looked from one to the other of the men accompanying him.

"It is very unlikely any of them did, your honour," one of the *samsaptakas* replied. Pointing at one of his mates, he added, "The two of us were the only ones to get off the ship we had picked."

"And you...?" the councilor eyed the third *samsaptaka*, who had a bloodied cloth wrapped around his left fist.

"Everyone else on my ship fell to the Hunas, your honour." The man's eyes were haunted with grief and anger at the fate his comrades had met.

"So Udayasanga is also dead." Vararuchi shifted his gaze briefly toward the bay in memory of the *samsaptaka*. They had struck up a good friendship during their ride from Avanti, and the councilor had developed a healthy respect and liking for the large, quick-witted warrior.

"I saw him go down, your honour," said the soldier with the bandaged hand. "I tried my best to help him, but by the time I got to his side... There were half a dozen arrows sticking out of him – but he still demolished the *agnikantaka* and set the ship on fire, your honour. It was my good fortune to have fought alongside such a valiant warrior."

The councilor nodded, taking note of the pride and the anguish in the *samsaptaka*'s voice. Glancing at the man's hand, he asked, "Is it bad?"

"Two fingers that I never had much use of anyway," the soldier replied, inspecting the soiled rag. "Also, I am right-handed. Fortunately, the barbarians were too stupid to notice that."

A faint smile played on Vararuchi's lips. These were men who wouldn't break easily, and he was glad to have them with him when the Huna army eventually alighted on Dvarka's shores.

They reached the hillock, where Yugandhara and two other Anarta chieftains stood in consultation with half a dozen Anarta commanders. Once the fresh fleet of ships had been sighted and its strength assessed, the city's defenders had ditched the pursuit of the older Huna vessels and returned to the shore in haste. Engaging the much larger Huna fleet was out of the question – even though no one quite knew what purpose could be served by seeking refuge on land, where the Huna army was decidedly more at ease.

Noticing Vararuchi and the *samsaptakas* approach, the three chieftains inclined their heads in a silent salutation. Vararuchi reciprocated, casting another glimpse at the bay, amassed with the Huna ships. The strange disturbance in the bay's waters had abated a bit since the battle, and though the sea was still rough and undulant, the sting had clearly gone out of it.

"How is Chief Manidhara?" he asked, raising his voice over the war-horns.

"He has been evacuated," Yugandhara replied, training his gentle, brown eyes on the councilor. "The wound is deep, and the physicians fear the spear's impact may have broken a bone. Of course, he wanted to stay on and fight."

"Manidhara said you saved his life, brave councilor," said one of the other chiefs. "For that you have our gratitude."

"When we save other's lives, we salvage a little bit of our own," Vararuchi replied with a short bow. He turned to survey the bay. "What do you make of the situation?"

"Bleak," Yugandhara waved an arm in the direction of the ships. "Their numbers are worrying."

"How many ships do they have?" From what Vararuchi could tell, there were over two dozen vessels in the bay, plus the ones that had arrived the previous evening. He also observed that a handful of Huna ships had sailed further south, instead of closing in on Dvarka.

"Forty to forty-five, your honour," one the commanders replied. He pointed further to the north, where more sails had just started showing above the horizon. "With another dozen or so still to join this lot."

Vararuchi felt his spirits sag. The strategy that the savages were employing was painfully obvious. While their main fleet was stationed in the bay, within striking distance of Dvarka, the Huna commanders were sending vessels south along the Anarta coast, so their warriors could come ashore outside the city. Vararuchi suspected that the ships on the horizon would head for a point north of Dvarka – the whole idea being to spread Dvarka's line of defence thin, so the city could be taken with minimal effort.

"When are the ships with reinforcements from Bhrigukaksha expected?" the councilor asked. If those ships were nearing Dvarka, they might be able to intercept the Huna vessels heading south, he hoped.

"Our estimation was between mid-morning and noon," Yugandhara replied. "If the winds are favourable, that is."

That was almost two to four hours away, Vararuchi thought without cheer, remembering there were, at the most, a dozen ships coming from Bhrigukaksha. He had no idea how well or how poorly manned each of those vessels were, so pinning hopes on those ships was unreasonable. They had to think of some other way of stopping the Hunas.

The councilor was about to address his thoughts to Yugandhara when someone let out a sudden shout.

"*What's that?*"

Almost simultaneously, Vararuchi heard one of the *samsaptakas* standing at his elbow draw his breath in sharply. "What are they *doing*?"

Realizing that the war-horns had fallen silent, Vararuchi

glanced at the Huna ships. At first, he saw nothing that warranted a fuss. Then, his eyes trailed further out into the bay – where a broad column of steam was rearing up from the sea's surface into the air. The councilor guessed the column was many yards in diameter, a thick, spiraling stack of vapour, nearly cloud-like in density, sprouting vertically from the water.

"It has to be sorcery," whispered one of the chieftains in awe and fear. "Look at the sea."

All of a sudden, the bay's waters had turned violent again, and waves rose and fell, crashing blindly into one another. Great rollers came rushing at Dvarka's wharfs, roaring and frothing as they smashed and spilled onto the waterfront, sending showers of spray and mist into the air. Boats were tossed here and there with disdain, and even the bigger barges creaked and corkscrewed in their moorings.

At the same time, Vararuchi sensed a change in the light. It was not as if the sun had gone behind a cloud – the sky was still without blemish. The light itself had changed, growing darker, thicker and somehow more beastly and ravenous. It was as if the sunlight had been touched by a curse.

The waves were now rising to worrisome heights, and the swells coming in splashed across the charred and gutted buildings that dotted the city's shoreline. The spray rose as high as the hillock, drenching the men standing there in fine, salty droplets.

"This is indeed sorcery," whimpered one of the Anarta commanders. "The barbarians intend flooding and drowning Dvarka."

"Whatever is happening is not the barbarians' doing," said the councilor. "Look at their ships. Why would they do that to themselves?"

The Huna fleet in the bay was in a state of utter disorder. Caught in the vortex of the bizarre upheaval, the ships were being spun and thrown against each other. Even at this distance, the city's defenders could see the ships' timbers cracking as they collided, holes opening in their hulls, sails entangling hopelessly. Giant waves battered and washed over the ships' decks, sweeping Huna warriors into the sea, and a dozen vessels started listing precariously, while at least three turned turtle and began their long journey to the floor of the bay.

The fate of the Anartas' own ships moored at sea wasn't very different – but the fact that there was hardly a soldier or sailor on board was a big consolation. So while the sight of their ships floundering about brought despair to the faces of the Anarta chieftains and commanders, it was overshadowed by the elation they felt at seeing the Huna navy falling apart. A slow cheer started building along the city, growing in volume –

– but it stilled into an awed silence in a matter of seconds as a serpent's head, monstrously large, black and hideous, began forming at the top of the swirling column of steam.

Vararuchi watched the scaly, sinuous head and neck take shape and rise over the Huna fleet. The serpent had a crown of black and brown feathers running from its crest down its back, and its eyes were slits the colour of amber, volcanic and shining with truculence. A forked tongue protruded from its mouth, black as coal. More and more of the monster materialized out of the steam – and then, with a ferocious spin, the column suddenly collapsed and disappeared to reveal the serpent in all its glory and viciousness, shiny black in colour and a league in length.

"What *is* this thing?" Yugandhara gasped. "Is there no end..."

A bone-chilling hiss drowned out the last of the chieftain's words. It emerged from a place deep within the serpent's being, raw and full of wickedness, and it dispersed like poison through the air over Dvarka, seeking out fear in the hearts of men. It made the men recoil in horror, shriveling their souls and choking their senses. It was only a sound, barely audible, but it made the men quake with fright.

The hiss died as abruptly as it had been born, and in the silence, the cries of terror from the Huna ships carried across the bay. The screams appeared to incite the serpent, which turned its head in the direction of the ships, its tongue darting out of its mouth. The next instant, it opened its jaws wide and spewed a jet of greyish-white liquid over the ships.

The vessels started disintegrating and going up in smoke. Ships broke into two as the timbers that held them together crumbled and turned to sawdust and ash. Sails caught fire, and the flesh of Huna warriors sizzled and melted off their bones as their agonized screams rent the dark sunlight that was rippling with unseen shadows. The men on the hillock watched in fear and fascination as, between them, the serpent and the rough sea decimated the Huna fleet.

The carnage was not restricted to the bay. The ships that were approaching the coast from the north had drawn to a halt out at sea, but with a swish of its tail that sent a mighty wave at Dvarka, the sea-monster turned on them as well, hissing and discharging its acidic venom. Meanwhile, waves kept assaulting the port, flooding its streets and alleys with seawater.

Suddenly, for no apparent reason, the creature spun around to survey Dvarka. With a mighty plunge, it disappeared underwater – only to resurface well inside the bay moments later. Water sluicing off its back, its plumes ruffling in the light breeze, the serpent reared up high and glared down at the port, before turning its cold, amber eyes on the hillock, where the war council stood rooted, too stupefied to move.

"We are finished," one of the chieftains croaked in a dry, hopeless rattle.

The next moment, the serpent glimmered and became

translucent, its body losing density and substance. Then, with a sudden, noiseless burst that sent a shower of rain all over the waterfront, the beast once again turned to vapour and vanished into the sunlight, which grew bright and cheery almost immediately.

"On the contrary, I think we are saved." Letting out a long breath of relief, Vararuchi pointed to the sea.

The bay was still very disturbed, but the waves had already begun falling into one another and subsiding. Stranded in the middle of the churning waters were the carcasses of the Huna ships – torn, broken and devastated.

Yaksha

A fine, powdery spray fell on Vishakha's upturned face, making her crinkle her eyes in delight. She stuck her tongue out playfully, trying to taste the teensy drops, but catching herself with a self-conscious giggle, she shot a glance at Vikramaditya, who was riding by her side.

"This is so much better than riding in a carriage or a palanquin," she said, stretching her palm out to feel the spray.

The samrat smiled and lifted his own chin to let the droplets fall on his face, wondering when he had last felt the rain – truly felt it, *sensed it emotionally* – on his skin this way. Not in almost two years, he was certain. Weightier cares and concerns had left little scope for those kinds of feelings.

"Thank you for agreeing to this outing. And for her," Vishakha gently patted the neck of the white mare she was riding.

"I am not the one to be thanked for her," Vikramaditya nodded at the mare. "The one deserving of that is the soldier of the City Watch who gifted her away when he heard that you liked her."

"I will, once we are back in the palace," said the queen. "Do you think I should give him something... as a token of my thanks? She was *his* horse, after all."

"The Warden of the Stables has already given the soldier an excellent replacement, but yes... something from you would be greatly appreciated."

King and queen lapsed into silence, allowing the stillness of the morning to take them in its soft embrace. The only sounds were the muted thud of their horses' hooves on the grassy pathway, and the periodic jangle of harness from behind, where a dozen soldiers of the Palace Guard followed them at a respectful distance. The pathway led through countryside just south of Ujjayini, a small diversion off the main road connecting Ujjayini to Mahishmati. Small, rural farms and paddy fields dotted both sides of the path, and the party occasionally chanced upon herds of buffaloes dawdling in muddy ponds.

"Aren't we almost there?" Vishakha enquired, even as the path traversed a narrow bamboo bridge and worked its way up a steep, forested embankment. She looked around her, as if seeking her bearings. "This bridge... and yes, that stone well down there... Isn't the meadow just over that ridge?"

The samrat looked keenly at the queen. It amazed him to see her unexpectedly – *effortlessly* – recall so many things, as if lit pathways had opened magically at her feet, guiding her from memory to memory. Yet, there were places where it was still too dark for her mind to venture...

"Yes, we are nearly there," he replied. Leaning a little forward, he asked, "Are you certain you want to go there?"

"I do," Vishakha nodded.

Two nights ago, Vishakha had broached the subject over dinner. Her desire to visit the meadow had surprised the samrat, but Vishakha had persisted. "A visit there is probably all that is needed for me to heal," she had argued. "Maybe I can end this where it all began."

They rode up the gradient in silence, but anticipation – and the nibbling fear of crashing disappointment – leaped and fluttered between them like a heartbeat. Even the two mounts seemed to sense the nervousness and excitement, twitching their ears and tossing their heads as they climbed the steep path.

Cresting the ridge, Vikramaditya and Vishakha reined in their horses and stared across the shallow valley that separated them from the next ridge, a mile away. The valley was full of wild, fruit-bearing trees, and through their branches, the king and queen saw the flat, grassy floor of the meadow far to the left.

"There it is," the samrat pointed.

Vishakha nodded and looked at him. For a moment, their eyes held, as if afraid to let go, afraid of what the next moment might bring. Then, with another small nod at one another, they disentangled their gaze to survey the meadow once more, before urging their horses down the path into the valley.

* * *

– when the time comes, the price the Healer will exact from Ujjayini will be severe.

Deep in thought, his grey eyebrows knitted together, Shukracharya paced the breadth of his chamber in restlessness.

The young councilor had mentioned him by name – *the Healer*. Somehow, she seemed to know – or seemed to have guessed – that he was up to something, that he had a hidden agenda of his own. But how much did the girl really know, and more importantly, who was the mind reader with whom she had been sharing her fears?

The high priest knew it couldn't have been Dhanavantri

or Vararuchi… or Shanku, for that matter. The physician was in the court of Vatsa, while the king's half-brother was somewhere in the Anartas. It couldn't have been Vikramaditya himself – he had seen the king in the mind reader's thoughts.

– the boatman says he has ferried the Healer many times, raj-guru.

He had it. The Acharya!

The high priest cursed himself for his stupidity. It shouldn't have taken him this long to guess the mind reader's identity – the old councilor had always been hostile, and if there was one person capable of secretly probing his thoughts, it was the raj-guru.

Shukracharya sat down before the *mandala*. Something had caused the girl to take her suspicions to the Acharya. Who else had they spoken to? Was Kalidasa's visit last night linked to this? He didn't suppose so. The giant had come across as being sincere in his plea for help.

He also didn't know how much of his thoughts the raj-guru had managed reading. He had sensed the panic in the Acharya's mind, the fear of having been found out, which meant the councilor had gone deep enough to see and hear his thoughts. The question was whether the raj-guru had learnt enough to incriminate him. And if he had, what he would do with the information.

Deciding it was best to stay on his guard and wait for the Acharya to reveal his hand first, the high priest turned his attention to the pressing matter of the yaksha. Cradling the bones in his palms, he whispered mantras over them and cast them on the *mandala*.

The yaksha has reached the end of its journey.

Shukracharya sat bolt upright, staring at the bones, checking and crosschecking the answer. Sweeping the pieces up, he chanted on them again and threw them down a second time.

The yaksha is in a forest to the south of the human kingdom's capital.

Again, the bones were picked up and cast down.

The yaksha lies in wait for that which the human king has promised to protect.

For one last time, the high priest scattered the bones over the *mandala* and sought the whereabouts of Veeshada's dagger.

It is in the banyan that holds up the field of endless pyres.

Shukracharya sat back and stared out of the window at the clouds drifting by, grey and miserable. He was confounded. If the Halahala was still somewhere in the tree in Ujjayini's cremation ground, why wasn't the yaksha coming to claim it?

Why, instead, was the yaksha waiting in a forest located to the south of the city – and what was it lying in wait for?

* * *

The quick shuffle of approaching footsteps alerted Vetala Bhatta even before he heard the knock on the door. The chief councilor stopped the nervous drumming of his fingers on the arms of the chair and opened his eyes, just as the muted rap of knuckles on wood fell on his ears.

"Enter," he said, clearing his throat and rising to his feet in impatience.

The door opened to reveal a palace attendant standing in the gallery outside. The Acharya stepped toward him with one eyebrow cocked in enquiry. "Is the Mother Oracle back from her bath and ready to see visitors?"

"I am... your honour, no... I don't know," the attendant mumbled in confusion.

"You don't know what, young man?" the councilor frowned in irritation. "Aren't you here to tell me... what are you here for?

"Councilor Shankubala has urgently requested your presence in the council chamber, your honour."

"Why?" Vetala Bhatta's eyebrows rose in alarm. "What's happened?"

"The Mother Oracle has warned of something strange happening in the hills to the north, your honour."

When the raj-guru stalked into the council chamber, he found Kalidasa, Kshapanaka, Amara Simha and Shanku already seated at the table. As he nodded his greetings and sat down, Varahamihira hobbled in as well.

"Has the Samrat been notified to join us?" the Acharya enquired.

"A message was sent to the Samrat, but it couldn't be delivered as he is not in the palace, raj-guru," Shanku replied.

Seeing the surprise on Vetala Bhatta's face, Kshapanaka spoke. "The Samrat and Vishakha have ridden to the *meadow*." She stressed the last word to make herself clear. "The queen wished to see the place."

"I didn't know if I should send a messenger after them, raj-guru," Shanku said.

"We will decide once we hear exactly what the oracle had to say."

Seeing all heads turn to her in unison, the girl clasped her hands over the table self-consciously. "The Mother Oracle summoned me to her chamber a little while ago. It seems she was having her bath when she observed a flock of birds in the sky. From their twittering and the beat of their wings, she discerned the birds were in morbid terror of some occurrence in the hills to the north of the city."

"What kind of occurrence?" Varahamihira asked.

"The oracle couldn't be sure, but she thinks the birds spoke of something cold and evil being awakened in the hills. She said the birds carried frost and darkness under their wings, so they must have been touched by whatever it was that had frightened them."

"There are just two hills to the north of Ujjayini..." The Acharya looked at the faces around the table. "Finding this occurrence shouldn't pose a huge problem."

"I will go," Amara Simha jumped to his feet with a glare that brooked no arguments. "I know the hills, I know the lay of the land, I know *everything*. This time *I* will go."

"I don't think any of us need to go, my friend," the raj-guru's tone was sombre. "If something evil is being awakened, its purpose is not to stay in the hills but to come here."

As the brawny councilor nodded and subsided in his seat, Kshapanaka said, "Mustn't we also try and stop those who are awakening whatever this evil is?"

"I agree." The Acharya looked across the table at Kalidasa. "Will you ask Angamitra to lead five hundred men of the City Watch to search the hills?"

Kalidasa nodded. His face was drawn, and it was plain to the raj-guru that the giant had had a poor night's sleep. *You have helped the queen remember – will you help me too?* The thought of the Healer made the raj-guru wonder if *he* had something to do with whatever was coming their way next. Did this too have something to do with all those mysterious nocturnal journeys the Healer had been making?

"We will need to prepare to defend the city," he rose to his feet, his manner instilling urgency among his fellow councilors. "Get the City Watch to start patrolling the walls and set up watches on all the towers. Ask the Imperial Army and the *samsaptakas* to keep their divisions on standby. Alert the Scouts Master, get the gates..." Vetala Bhatta waved a hand. "You all know the routine."

"We should send a message to the Samrat alerting him and Vishakha," Shanku reminded.

"Immediately," the raj-guru gave a vigorous nod. "And see

to it that the Palace Guards are prepared to move the royal household to the Labyrinth at short notice."

Discussing the city's defence, the six councilors exited the council chamber and walked to the end of the gallery, where it branched into three. Kshapanaka and Amara Simha hurried off in one direction, while Varahamihira limped down a flight of stairs. Shanku went off to put the Palace Guards on alert and have a messenger dispatched to Vikramaditya, leaving only Kalidasa in Vetala Bhatta's company. The giant was about to turn away to dispense his duties, when the raj-guru laid a hand on his shoulder.

"The visions are still bothering you, I presume." Vetala Bhatta's voice was gentle and full of sympathy, but his eyes were sharp as they searched Kalidasa's face.

The giant nodded. "In the Mother Oracle's opinion, they are from my lost childhood."

The Acharya waited to see if Kalidasa would mention the Healer, but he didn't. With a nod of his own, the raj-guru let his hand slip back to his side. The Council of Nine had never kept secrets from one another before, and the giant was almost like a son to him. "You should go and get Angamitra's search party organized," he said, trying to conceal his disenchantment.

As the Acharya turned to go and seek out the Mother Oracle, Kalidasa spoke again. "If they are visions from childhood, I know at least one thing now – my childhood had something horrible to do with the Hunas."

Vetala Bhatta stared. "How do you know that?"

"Instead of fighting them, I have been trying to let the visions reveal themselves to me. The Mother Oracle suggested that might help. Early this morning, for the first time, I saw something new in one of the visions. The one where the man with the drawn bow is chasing me on horseback, remember?"

The Acharya nodded. "You thought the man looked familiar."

"I still don't know who he is, but the man is a Huna. I am certain because he is marked with the *hriiz* – a big, black scorpion carved in the middle of his forehead."

Turning his broad back on the Acharya, Kalidasa descended the stairs. The chief councilor stood for a few moments watching the giant depart, afraid of the horrors that lay hidden in that mind, waiting to creep out. If the savages from the Marusthali had had anything to do with the giant's childhood, it was no surprise that the trauma had wiped the boy's memory clean. If there were Hunas in Kalidasa's childhood, it would have been best had they remained forgotten.

Vetala Bhatta had begun tracing his way to the Mother Oracle's chamber when the hiss broke over Ujjayini. It seeped through the air, through the palace walls and through the silence, cold and predatory, taking an icy grip on the Acharya's heart. It came from the time before time, a sound like no sound, stifling everything in its path in spreading waves of terror.

Man-Lion

Fear coiled itself tightly around Shukracharya the moment the chilling hiss came to his ears.

The bones were wrong about the yaksha, he thought to himself, leaping to his feet with a curse and hastening to the window. The mystical being from Kubera's court was not lying in wait in some forest after all – it was here in Ujjayini, seeking out Veeshada's dagger. And he wasn't prepared for it because the bones had it all wrong.

Thrusting his head out of the window, the high priest looked in all directions to try and locate the source of the diabolical sound, but the hiss seemed to come from everywhere – seemed to *be* everywhere. The ragged shouts of palace guards rose from somewhere down below, followed by the panicked rush of feet, and across the length of the courtyard, Shukracharya thought he glimpsed Shanku and three guards dart across a far gallery.

"There, in the sky," a voice rang out from far away, carried to him by wonder and fear. Even as the high priest raised his head, he heard the voice again. "Up there… to the west."

The windows of his chamber opened to the northeast, however, and commanded a view of a different section of the sky. Whirling around, Shukracharya hurried out of the room, following the gallery to an open terrace that overlooked the palace causeway. He stepped onto the terrace, his eyes on the western sky, but all the high priest initially saw were the clouds, heavy and moping.

A moment later, his vision was drawn to one patch of cloud. It was darker than the ones around it, and its shape shifted quicker as well, as if it was subject to a unique set of natural laws. From light grey to slate to black, it changed colour in a matter of seconds, twisting and weaving across the sky in eerie patterns, until the high priest began making out the contours of something enormous and menacing concealed in its folds and shadows.

This was no yaksha, he realized. Yet, the relief he should have felt was missing.

All of a sudden, the cloud composed itself into a dense mass, and in the twinkling of the eye, it transformed into the head and neck of a mammoth serpent, the rest of its body still obscured by the clouds. Shukracharya could almost hear a collective gasp escape from Ujjayini as he stared at the black head with its plume of black and brown feathers, and its harsh, amber eyes.

He could scarcely believe what he was seeing.

"What misery might this be?" whispered a voice from somewhere close. The high priest turned to see a clutch of courtiers and palace attendants gaping at the grotesque creature from a neighbouring terrace.

It is a misery like few others in all three worlds, Shukracharya was tempted to remark. But nothing he said could convey the horror of the thing in the sky better than the beast itself – and he was certain the beast would very shortly put up a grand display of what it was capable of.

As if taking a cue from the high priest's thoughts, the serpent unhinged its jaws and squirted a viscous, grey liquid down at Ujjayini. From where he stood, Shukracharya had no way of knowing where the venomous discharge had landed, but he saw a cloud of dust kick up from somewhere across the lake. At the same time, he felt a tremor under his feet as the ground shook for a fraction of a second. Then, as the cloud of dust slowly mushroomed into the air, the wind bore the echoes of screams.

The screams galvanized the palace into action. The cries and commands of palace guards rose up from the courtyard below, growing louder as the hissing suddenly ceased and the serpent vanished from sight in a smoky swirl. Hooves thundered on the causeway, and Shukracharya saw Amara Simha and Kshapanaka ride out at the head of a dozen soldiers. Vetala Bhatta emerged into the courtyard, issuing instructions to the palace guards.

The high priest did not wait to see more. He needed to know what – and *who* – had brought the primordial serpent-dragon Ahi to Ujjayini.

Shukracharya retraced his steps to his chamber at a fast clip. However, on turning a sharp corner, he nearly cannoned into a figure coming from the opposite direction. Drawing up short, he noticed that the pockmarked face inches away from his own was that of the lame councilor Varahamihira.

"Where were you?" the councilor's eyebrows rose in surprise. "I've been looking for you all over the palace."

"Looking for *me*?" Shukracharya's tone was guarded. "Why?"

"I want you to come with me. Dhanavantri is not in Ujjayini, and the city needs a physician of your talent and experience."

"Where do you want me to come?"

"Wherever that monster creates havoc, I suppose. The only

way of knowing where you might be wanted is by stepping out of the palace. Come."

The councilor hopped around on his crutch to lead the way, but the high priest hung back. "I... I don't think I can go..." Seeing the councilor's dark face turn back at him sharply, he added, "I... need to see the queen... shortly."

"You heard the screams from across the lake. The need of Ujjayini's citizens is far greater right now," Varahamihira spoke evenly, his eyes searching Shukracharya's face. At just that moment, the discordant notes of alarm bells struck up around Ujjayini. The councilor cocked an ear at them before looking back at the high priest with a light shrug and a told-you-so expression. "Don't worry about the queen – you can't see her for a while anyway. Let's go."

At a loss for excuses, the high priest allowed himself to be led into the courtyard, which was in a state of ferment. Palace guards ran about securing doors and gates, and setting up defences along the causeway, even though their manner showed precisely what they thought of the precautions they were taking against the beast overhead. Every now and then, they cast apprehensive glances skyward, but the demon itself had not reappeared – though, in a strange way, its absence only heightened the fear already instilled in the men. The pealing of the alarm bells had risen to a deafening roar, and Shukracharya had to lean into the councilor's ear to make himself heard.

"I don't have a horse," he shouted, trying not to sound hopeful. "And no one here is exactly in a position to spare me theirs."

Acting almost as if he hadn't registered a word, Varahamihira motioned with his fingers, urging the high priest to keep up with him. Frustrated but helpless, Shukracharya tagged along, and they traversed the length of a covered portico and rounded a corner. In front of them stood an open, two-horse chariot under a thorny babul tree.

"You have a chariot?" the high priest feigned surprise to keep his disappointment from showing.

"How else do you think I move around with this leg of mine?" Varahamihira hoisted himself aboard the chariot and made room for the high priest. "Come, Ujjayini needs your services."

* * *

Kshapanaka and Amara Simha watched the man emerge, ghost-like, out of the cloak of dust. He broke into a staggering run, wilting under the weight of the young girl he was carrying in his arms, his mouth moving in a silent wail of distress. Tears flowed down his cheeks, leaving wet trails across the layer of chalky dust that coated his face and lay in heavy sprinkles over his head and shoulders. Dust covered the girl as well, imparting vividness to the red splotch of blood clotting on her left temple. The girl was limp in the man's arms, one hand dangling loose in a way that inspired neither confidence nor hope.

The man approached the councilors and the small company of soldiers, but instead of slowing down and appealing for aid, he carried past them as if they were invisible to him. He made no sign of noticing the tattered ring of onlookers either, curious but fearful townsfolk who hung back and watched the pall of dust, ready to bolt at the first sign of threat.

"Somebody, help him," Kshapanaka hailed over the pealing of the alarm bells, waving her hand at the nearest clump of onlookers.

Two people from the crowd stepped forward, jittery and tentative, but the man brushed past them blindly, a high-pitched moan breaking from his lips. Kshapanaka followed the man's anguished and delirious run with sympathy until he disappeared around a bend in the street. When she turned back to the dust-obscured locality that was home to Ujjayini's ironmongers and metalworkers, her face was flushed with anger.

She urged her horse forward and the others followed. They picked their way through the stone-paved street, strewn with rubble and pocked with craters, slowly pushing inward through the blinding dust, which was wracked by the screams of the maimed and the bereaved. People ran helter-skelter across the councilors' path, and where the dust thinned, the visitors from the palace could see collapsed houses and caved-in roofs.

"Salutations, your honour," said a captain of the City Watch, materializing out of the dust. "There are many buried under the debris. They will die if they're not pulled out soon. We need help."

Amara Simha nodded and addressed one of the soldiers in the group. "Get a message out to the five closest City Watch posts. Tell them to send as many people for rescue work as possible. Enlist labourers working on the city walls, get volunteers from the public... Ask that lot outside not to just stand around but to pitch in... Quick!"

As the soldier turned his mount around to carry out the instructions, a man and a woman blundered out of the dust. The woman was supporting the man, who was bleeding from a crushing wound to his shoulder. Seeing them limp out of sight, Amara Simha waved the dust from his face and looked at the captain. "How bad is it really?"

"Hard to say, your honour," the captain replied. "Several houses further down the street have been flattened, that much I know. Many are trapped, and many have..." he paused, struggling to find the right word, "...many have melted."

"Melted?" Kshapanaka asked sharply.

"Like wax," the captain shivered. "The spittle from the creature's mouth melts the flesh and bone into pulp. I saw three people die that way – it is horrible."

"Did the venom also destroy the houses?"

"Yes, your honour. Everything that comes in contact with it breaks or melts."

"Any idea how many..." Kshapanaka began, when a sudden wave of frenetic cries sprang up from all sides, cutting her short.

The horses instinctively reared and sidled, snorting in fear. Fighting to control their mounts, the councilors and soldiers shot nervous glances at one another, but before a word could be exchanged, the ground beneath them trembled under the impact of something heavy. Cracks instantly appeared underfoot, and the street listed alarmingly to one side, causing the horses to slip and slide and struggle to find a firm footing. More shouts and screams rent the air, followed by the panicked rush of feet.

"It is the creature again," yelled Kshapanaka, wheeling her horse around and making for the break in the curtain of dust. "Archers, come with me."

The councilor burst into the open street with her bow in hand, an arrow nocked in place. Behind her came three horse archers of the City Watch, bows and arrows at the ready. Balancing herself on the stirrups, Kshapanaka searched the sky overhead, but except for the dreary grey clouds, it appeared vacant. Then her eyes alighted on two young women cowering under a doorway and pointing high over her shoulder. Reining her horse in, Kshapanaka turned to see the serpent hovering low over the rooftops of a neighbouring locality, from where a fresh cloud of dust had started rising into the air. Executing another about turn, the councilor spurred her horse in the opposite direction.

Amara Simha and the rest of the company of soldiers emerged from the dust just in time to see Kshapanaka and the horse archers disappear down the end of the street. Without wasting a second, the burly councilor went in pursuit, throwing an order at the men to follow him. Their charge took them down winding lanes and back alleys packed with houses, but through the breaks between buildings, the men were able to catch occasional glimpses of the black, wet body of the serpent. With every turn, the men drew closer to the creature, until finally they spilled into a broad street that led to the marketplace.

Pulling up, Amara Simha looked first one way then the other for Kshapanaka. Then he froze.

Kshapanaka and the three archers had had a head start, and the quartet now stood in the middle of the deserted street with their bows drawn taut, taking aim at the plumed head of the monster swaying menacingly over the rooftops. The serpent, for its part, was assessing the councilor and the bowmen with its narrow, malevolent eyes, its eager black tongue flicking in and out of its mouth. Time stood still in the street, and even the pealing of the alarm bells seemed to fade into a void of suspense.

Using her knees, Kshapanaka slowly urged her mount forward and closer to the serpent; the horse archers did likewise, only with a lot less resolve. As Amara Simha watched, scarcely daring to breathe, Kshapanaka pulled the bowstring back one last inch before letting the arrow fly. A split-second later, the three horse archers also shot their arrows, the four twangs sounding like one as they resonated in the stillness of the avenue.

The four arrows lifted toward the serpent in perfect synchrony. The monster, however, barely blinked as it followed the ascent of the barbs, and when the arrows struck its head and snout, Amara Simha saw splashes of muddy water spurt into the air at the points where the shafts had made contact. The next moment, the four arrows disappeared into the serpent's body, as if swallowed whole, and all that remained were minute ripples on the creature's shiny, wet skin.

It was as if the arrows had been shot into a pool of water, Amara Simha thought as the serpent, unharmed and now filled with spite, raised its head high and opened its mouth in retaliation.

"Watch out!" The warning tore its way out of Amara Simha's throat, but it was too late.

Ensnared in the monster's hypnotic gaze, Kshapanaka and the bowmen stood rooted as the dreadful hiss unfolded from the serpent's throat. A chill draught rustled up the street, bringing with it the whispering odour of old battlefields and dungeons, and Amara Simha had to fight to keep fear from entering his heart. Then, with a sudden hacking cough, the creature spat a stream of its deadly venom at its assailants.

His eyes widening in horror, Amara Simha saw Kshapanaka bear the brunt of the attack. The spray hit the councilor and her mount square, its force unseating her from the saddle and hurling her backward into the street. While her horse gave a piteous neigh and distorted into a mangled, squishy pulp, Kshapanaka herself went rolling until she came to a stop against a wall. Meanwhile, the three horse archers and their mounts dissolved into shapeless pools of bubbling, blistering flesh, while steaming cracks surfaced on the street where the venom spattered.

The serpent paused to survey the damage it had wrought before swooping and stretching along the length of the street, its eyes on Kshapanaka – dead still, disheveled, her clothes in tatters, but otherwise miraculously unscathed by the venom. The monster weaved through the air until it hovered over the councilor, its tongue flicking the air suspiciously. Suddenly, its eyes turned a hateful shade of yellow. Arching its neck once again, the creature opened its mouth to eject venom over the councilor.

The sight of Kshapanaka lying defenceless on the road as the obscene black cavity opened above her filled Amara

Simha with a red, boiling rage. The girl had grown up in front of his eyes, a wisp of a child who had never understood the complexities of Sanskrit grammar, but who could outshoot Ujjayini's best archers before she turned twelve. He still remembered the first time he had put a bow in the girl's hands, she had very nearly buried an arrow into his small toe. He had been convinced she would never shoot straight, and now she lay at the monster's mercy because she had learnt to wield a bow as few others had.

Taking a firm grip on his battle-axe, Amara Simha leaped off his horse. His feet had barely touched the ground before he took off across the street, hurtling toward Kshapanaka, a low bestial growl building at the very pit of his being.

As he ran, the councilor started undergoing a rapid and remarkable transformation.

Amara Simha grew in size. He gained both height and bulk, a proportionate enlargement in body mass and muscle that made a giant out of him. His thick mop of red hair turned a shade darker, as did his beard, both growing to form a dense mane around his neck and shoulders. Simultaneously, the councilor's human features changed and became distinctly lion-like, while a fine layer of tawny fur replaced his fair skin. Sharp, retractable claws sprouted from the tips of his fingers, and long canines were visible under the snarl of his lips.

In five powerful bounds, Amara Simha narrowed the gap to the serpent. Even as the creature turned its head toward this new threat, the councilor reached its side, his transformation from human to part-lion complete. The serpent lashed its tongue out at him and stretched its jaws even wider to disgorge its venom, but Amara Simha moved in with dazzling speed. Raising his battle-axe, he propelled himself into a leap and brought the flashing blade down hard over the serpentine head.

The moment the axe sunk into its head, the monster

exploded into a million drops of water. The shower drenched the street and the buildings adjacent to it, and drops sizzled and rained over the entire neighbourhood for nearly a minute. Caught off balance by the sudden disappearance of the serpent, Amara Simha stumbled and sprawled on the road. Recovering quickly, he got to his feet and spun in all four directions, searching for the monster.

There was no sign of the serpent.

A sudden fit of coughing made Amara Simha turn to see Kshapanaka stirring and propping herself up. Taking a couple of strides to her side, he looked down at her.

"Are you alright?"

Kshapanaka blinked, looked up – and instinctively drew back with a gasp. But her expression changed from alarm to wonder as she stared at the strange man-lion towering over her.

"Councilor Amara Simha?" Seeing the figure nod, she asked in a hushed voice, "What happened to you?"

Amara Simha shrugged, studying his arms and hands, baring and retracting the claws of his left hand. He raised his head to see the company of City Watch soldiers looking at him in amazement and apprehension. He thrust a hand out to Kshapanaka so she could hoist herself up. "Something bizarre is happening to us. Whatever it is, it protected you from the monster's venom."

The skies opened up and it began raining in heavy, wind-driven sheets. Taking the proffered hand gingerly, Kshapanaka pulled herself to her feet. She looked down at herself in disbelief.

"Nothing happened to me? And the others? The archers?"

"All gone, turned to pulp," Amara Simha pointed to the four piles of gooey mass swirling in the rainwater. "Your horse too. Though, funnily, your bow is still in one piece."

The soldiers had crossed the street and were approaching

them in ones and twos. Around them, windows and doors unfastened, and heads craned out, eyeing the councilors in awe.

Kshapanaka limped to her fallen bow and picked it up. "Is the creature dead?"

"It's gone. That's all I can say for certain."

"I think you killed it, your honour," one of the soldiers began speaking, not being able to take his eyes off Amara Simha. "I saw it shatter into..."

The hiss came again, shredding through the curtains of rain. It came from the opposite end of the street that gave into the market, and as the councilors and soldiers spun that way, they saw a thick black tail slip past the market and vanish.

"It is very much alive," said Amara Simha, hefting his battle-axe to his shoulders. Turning to Kshapanaka, he added, "You seem to be immune to its venom, so you are probably the only one who can get close enough to kill it – *if it can be killed at all.*"

* * *

The chariot jounced over Ujjayini's uneven back roads made wet and slippery with rain, and careened round sharp corners as Varahamihira pushed the horses into a punishing gallop. The heavy rumble of wheels from underneath met the roar of the rain and the sharp, acidic pealing of the alarm bells in a jarring storm of noise, making Shukracharya wince as he gripped the chariot's sideboards tight and watched the city roll by, scared and dispirited.

Questions plagued the high priest. Millennia had passed since Ahi had been banished and the art of summoning the beast lost for good. At least that was what everyone had come to believe. Yet, the mantra had somehow been secretly preserved. And the son born of Shachi to Indra – Shukracharya was reasonably sure of this as only half-bloods could master the demon, and there was only one half-blood in Devaloka – had now used it to invoke the serpent. Instinct told him Jayanta had summoned the beast at his father's wishes, but the fact that the bones had *not once* warned of Ahi made him wonder. Furthermore, Indra had already enlisted the yaksha to claim the Halahala, so sending Ahi to Ujjayini did not serve any purpose to Shukracharya's mind. But if Indra hadn't called for the demon, who had?

"Where are we going?" the high priest demanded of the councilor. From what he had been able to make out before the rain came pouring down, there were dust clouds rising from three different locations in the city – two side by side, and one from what he guessed was the direction of Ujjayini's main market.

"The neighbourhood closest to us is the one where the metalworkers dwell," Varahamihira shouted above the clang of the bells and the rattle of the chariot. "Let us see what..."

The hiss came suddenly, filling the air, drowning out everything else. The same instant, a flock of over a dozen terror-stricken townsfolk swarmed into view from a side street, muddling straight into the chariot's path. Screeching with fright, a few leaped out of harm's way, but the majority stood gawking at the onrushing chariot, too paralyzed to move. Varahamihira yanked at the reins, pulling the horses back with all his might, and the beasts reared in pain and surprise. Still the chariot rolled inexorably forward, bearing down upon the hapless citizens under the sheer force of momentum. Just when it looked as if some of the townsfolk would inevitably come under the trampling hooves, the horses dug their heels in, and the chariot came to a grinding halt inches away from the crowd.

Shukracharya had barely heaved a sigh of respite when the enormous head of Ahi squirmed out of the street the townsfolk had just exited. The sight of the menace sent the crowd scattering; in no time, all that remained in the street were the chariot and the serpent, facing one another.

The high priest watched Ahi appraise the chariot as it drew out of the side street. The horses whinnied and perked up their ears, shuffling sideways in an effort to break free of the harness, but Varahamihira held the reins tight as he scanned the surroundings for a way out. The lanes branching right and left were all too narrow to accommodate the chariot, while the street wasn't broad enough to facilitate a quick about-turn.

"I think you should leave when you have the chance to," the councilor muttered, jerking his head sideways to make himself clear.

"And you?" Shukracharya assessed his companion.

His eyes still on Ahi, Varahamihira gave a wry smile. "A lame man cannot hope to outrun that thing," he said. "Right now the city needs a Healer more than a councilor. Please go."

The high priest was about to reply when, out of the corner of his eye, he saw the beast open its mouth. He caught the smell of rot – the smell of bloated corpses bursting open under a torrid sun. The next instant, the serpent squirted venom at the chariot.

Shukracharya was partially protected by a mantra that he had secretly invoked just as they had left the palace; the venom would hurt him, but leave no lasting damage. The human would be annihilated, though – which was just as well, the high priest thought to himself. Rid of the councilor, he would be free to pursue his enquiries into Ahi, the yaksha and the dagger. Steeling himself, the high priest watched the spray of venom arc toward the chariot.

Acting on impulse and reflex, Varahamihira flinched and flung one arm up to shield himself from the venom – and Shukracharya observed the strangest thing.

Out of nowhere, a thin glistening curtain of energy, sheer

and barely perceptible to the eye, sprang up between the serpent and its target. Ahi's venom splashed across the flimsy barrier – and both venom and curtain disintegrated and disappeared into thin air, leaving the chariot intact.

Shukracharya blinked at Varahamihira in surprise. The councilor darted a stunned gaze at the high priest. They turned back to see the serpent cough up more venom. The councilor stretched his hand out, dubious and tentative, and the curtain flickered into existence, frayed, patchy and insubstantial. However, as the venom shot through the sizzling rain, Varahamihira thrust his arm up with more surety. The curtain instantly stabilized, enclosing the chariot in a quivering, dome-shaped bubble. The venom struck the curtain, but this time the curtain held, even as the venom nebulized and dissipated.

As the energy curtain thinned out, the councilor took a firm hold of the reins. Twitching them lightly, he urged the horses down the street, slowly narrowing the gap between them and the serpent. The demon instantly reared and hissed in fury at this open act of defiance. The next moment, it unraveled into vapour and was lost in the mist of rain.

"That was close!" Varahamihira relaxed his grip on the reins. He craned his neck in all directions, making sure the monster wasn't sneaking back on them. "Whatever this thing is, we have to find a way of stopping it."

The high priest sized up the councilor with something that approached respect and a morsel of sympathy. He knew destroying Ahi was next to impossible – even the ancient gods and sages of old had only managed to exile it. The serpent was an elemental demon, conjured out of water and controlled by its master's mind, so nothing could really kill it. For all of Varahamihira's deft tricks, the only way of overcoming the beast was by weakening Jayanta's control over it – a tricky job that involved the casting of spells, with no assurance of success. Yet, nothing else would spare the humans from Ahi's mindless wrath.

Shukracharya was undecided over whether he should step in to assist the humans – or leave them to their sad fate and use the opportunity to find the Halahala.

"Where did you learn to do what you just did?"

"I didn't even know I could do something like that," Varahamihira shucked his shoulders and turned to the high priest. "It just... happened."

"*Twice?*"

"Okay, the second time I made an effort. But I still don't know where it came from."

Shukracharya turned away as the secret to Varahamihira's newly discovered talent suddenly dawned on him. Like the parting of a veil, suddenly *everything* was clear and obvious.

Varahamihira's energy shield; Shanku's disappearing act from under the Marut's foot; Vararuchi's incredible leap over the market square; Kshapanaka's demolition of the Marut's armour; Kalidasa's barehanded fight against the third Marut... Everything was connected and everything made sense.

"– fight it with the Hellfires."

"What?" The high priest blinked at Varahamihira. He had been too preoccupied to follow the thread of the councilor's words.

"I was saying it would be good if the Samrat returned soon. Perhaps we can combat this creature with the Hellfires."

"Where is the king? Isn't he in Ujjayini?"

Varahamihira shook his head. "The Samrat and the queen rode out to the meadow where the queen had her fall." He gestured with his hand in a southerly direction. "It is a few miles out of the city."

Shukracharya went rigid. The rain had eased a little, and the metalworkers' neighbourhood was coming into view at the far end of the street. Soldiers and townsfolk rushed about as rescue efforts went on in full swing.

"Stop the chariot."

"What?" The councilor raised his eyebrows at the high priest in surprise. "Why?"

"I said *stop*. The queen's life is in grave danger."

The sharpness and authority in Shukracharya's tone made Varahamihira draw on the reins. "What sort of danger?" he asked in alarm.

Instead of replying, the high priest leaped off the chariot even before it came to a standstill. He looked around wildly for a moment before heading to a blacksmith's workshop nearby. As Varahamihira watched in bewilderment, the high priest bent over the cold, open furnace and scooped up a handful of ash. Clutching the ash, Shukracharya stepped back onto the road and closed his eyes.

Of all the emotions, sorrow was the most overpowering and debilitating. More than fear, sorrow distracted the mind, weighing it down, sapping its resolve. So sorrow it would be, the high priest decided, whispering the Spell of Sorrows into the small mound of ash. Unclenching his fist, he blew on the ash, sending the fine particles into the moisture-laden air.

"I must go," he said, dusting the ash off his palm. He flagged down two passing cavalrymen of the City Watch. Looking from one to the other, he asked, "Do you know the way to the meadow where your queen had her accident?"

One of the soldiers nodded slowly, unsure of where this was going.

"Good. You can lead me there." The high priest turned to the second soldier. "I need your horse, soldier. Right now."

Perplexed, the soldier looked from the high priest to Varahamihira, but ultimately, the briskness of Shukracharya's tone – and the respect he had for the Healer – overrode any doubts and he slipped off the horse's back. The high priest immediately got onto the saddle.

"You can't just leave like that. You are needed here – *they* need you," the councilor protested, pointing to the tumble of houses down the street. "Tell us about the threat to the queen and we shall have soldiers sent to protect her..."

"The dead here are beyond help, and the injured can wait," Shukracharya interrupted, looking Varahamihira in the eye. "But you can take my word that no amount of soldiers Ujjayini can spare will be enough to protect the queen. I am the only one who can do that – provided I reach her before it is too late."

The high priest turned to leave, but checked himself and addressed the councilor again. "I have done what I can to weaken the serpent. Apply yourselves to stopping it, else the dead and injured will only gain in numbers." With a nod at the soldier who was to be his guide, he spurred the horse and departed in a thunder of hooves and a shower of spray.

The yaksha is in a forest to the south of the human kingdom's capital. The yaksha lies in wait for that which the human king has promised to protect.

The bones were never wrong, Shukracharya thought ruefully as his escort took the road that led to Ujjayini's southern gate. *He* was the one who hadn't understood their intent. Indra had not sent the yaksha for Veeshada's dagger, but to take what was dearest to the human king; the one Vikramaditya had promised to protect while taking his marriage vows.

Vishakha.

Her death was the revenge that Indra had plotted on Vikramaditya.

Meadow

The rain was a steady rush echoing in Vikramaditya's ears, a wet, hollow sound interspersed with the heavier patter of drops striking and ricocheting off the leaves and branches of the spreading suvarnaka that he and Vishakha sheltered under. The samrat and the queen were both soaked to the skin, their hair clinging to their foreheads and napes in wet, cumbersome curls.

"You still think riding here was a better idea than bringing the palanquin along?" the king leaned close to Vishakha to make himself heard.

Blinking rainwater off her eyelids, Vishakha turned and smiled, but the rigidity in her jaw made the effort seem laboured. "Had we brought the palanquin along, we would be on our way back to Ujjayini instead of being here together," she said. "I... I much prefer this."

Vikramaditya gave a small, crushed smile of his own and looked across the grassy meadow at Vishakha's white mare tethered next to his own brown charger. The small knot of Palace Guards sat astride their own mounts a few paces away, taking what cover they could as they waited for their king and queen.

"Are you disappointed?" Vishakha asked abruptly, glancing up at the samrat with wide eyes.

"Are *you*?" One question to parry another.

Vishakha's gaze dropped to the jade ring on her finger. She ran a thumb over the finely etched letters of her name, feeling their edges on the ring's smooth green surface. "I was hoping coming here would somehow help..." She let the words trail off, her sad eyes wandering over the rain-drenched clearing, seeking that one elusive thread that would lead her all the way back to the man who stood faithfully beside her.

"I am glad we came," the samrat took her hand and gave it a reassuring squeeze. "Had we not taken the chance, we would have been in Ujjayini right now instead of being here together. For that alone, the trip was worth it."

Exchanging smiles that healed and wounded them at the same time, they stood holding hands, leaning gently into one another, listening to the rain.

"Will it be alright if I never remember?" Vishakha looked up at Vikramaditya searchingly. "Or will it all then come to a hopeless, grinding halt?"

The king gave the question careful thought before shaking his head. "The road begins when we start walking and ends where we stop. The road is not at our feet; it is in our minds." He paused to smile at the queen. "As long as we care to walk, we shall find roads to walk upon. If not old ones, then new. When neither of us is willing to halt, what have we to fear?"

The words brought comfort, and the king and queen settled back into silence, waiting for the rain to abate.

As if in deference, the rain dropped in intensity, softening to a heavy drizzle. Casting a glance across the meadow, Vikramaditya saw the Palace Guards go into a huddle. Then, in an uncharacteristic breach of etiquette, one of the guards spurred his horse across the clearing and approached the king and queen.

"My deepest apologies, Samrat," the guard drew to a halt the moment he was within hailing distance. He fidgeted on his horse, his manner tentative but tense. "I… the captain of the Guard asked me…"

"What is the matter, soldier?" The samrat demanded as he stepped out from under the suvarnaka. "Speak up."

"Your honour, the bells."

"What bells?" Vikramaditya frowned, and then his face cleared. Cocking his head, he listened. At first, he heard nothing but the drizzle, but with a shift in the wind, he thought he caught the clang of Ujjayini's bells, indistinct and elusive.

"We aren't sure of it ourselves, your honour," said the soldier. "We might be mistaken…"

"We can't take chances. Get the horses ready."

The guard left to do as commanded. Vikramaditya spun around and stretched one hand out to Vishakha. "We must go. Ujjayini is probably under attack."

"Is it demons like the last time?" the queen asked as they hastened across the meadow to their horses. "Kshapanaka told me they were almost inside the palace."

"It could be rakshasas, or even something sent from Devaloka," the samrat spoke without breaking his stride. "We'll know only once we get to Ujjayini. But first, we have to get you to the safety of the Labyrinth."

"That's easily done, especially from here," said Vishakha. "We only have to take the underground passage back through the stone well that we passed while coming here."

"You remember the secret escape route from the Labyrinth to the stone well?" the samrat stared at his queen in amazement.

"Yes. It was shown to us by Vik…" Vishakha stopped. Her eyes widened, and her voice almost dropped to a whisper. "… by *you*."

The samrat held his breath, hardly believing his ears. "What do you remember of that day?"

"We were young, Kshapanaka and I. Vikrama and Kalidasa showed us the way out of the Labyrinth. We were told to use the route if ever we needed to get away from the palace and the city." Vishakha looked through the king, into the past. "I was so scared in the dark passageway. I thought we would all get lost. Then Kalidasa slipped on a ledge and nearly fell into a chasm, but Vikra... *you* caught him. You saved him just in time." She blinked and refocused on her husband. As she stretched her hands out toward him, her voice quivered. "You... didn't have a moustache then."

Vikramaditya held Vishakha by the tips of her fingers, too choked for words, feeling the relief well up in his eyes as tears. The last obstinate lock had finally turned when he had least expected it. It was now a question of time before she remembered –

The samrat spotted something in the periphery of his vision. *He froze.*

An arrow. Skimming across the meadow, coming straight at Vishakha!

It was just a blur of motion, a whisper in the drizzle, slipping deceptively through the rain and the light and shadow of the trees around the clearing. It came in fast, nosing through the air with murderous intent, its vicious barbed head pointing directly at the soft curve of Vishakha's exposed neck. As it approached, it keened and sang with bloodlust.

Alerted to the unseen threat by some sixth sense, Vishakha's pupils dilated and her mouth opened in fear. However, before she could say a word, Vikramaditya grabbed the queen's wrist with one hand and pulled her toward him and out of harm's way. In the same fluid motion, he spun on his heel and drew his sword. Pivoting all the way round, he slashed at the arrow with his sword, timing the stroke to perfection so the shaft snapped into two at the middle.

The broken halves of the missile fell to the ground, but even as they touched the grass, both bits transformed into writhing parts of a snake – the barbed head turning into the pointed, triangular head of a viper, the feathered shaft changing into a lashing tail. Even as the tail squirmed and flailed in the grass, the part with the head went straight for Vishakha's ankle.

The queen uttered a small shriek and hopped, but she was always going to be too slow for a viper in the grass. The reptile was just a foot away from her when the tip of Vikramaditya's sword skewered its head, splitting it, impaling it to the ground. There it thrashed about for a moment – and then the snake lost form and became its own shadow, a black ripple that freed itself of the sword and slipped into the tall grass, toward a clump of thorny bushes.

"Guards, protect the queen," the samrat shouted, bringing his foot down hard on the tail that was still flopping about, trampling it into a gory pulp. At the same time, he drew Vishakha back, putting himself between her and the bushes where the viper's shadow had disappeared.

In a thunderous gallop of hooves, the Palace Guards came rushing over and formed a tight, protective circle around their king and queen. Four guards dismounted and moved in close, helping Vikramaditya shield Vishakha from all sides.

"What are we guarding against, your honour?" asked the captain of the Guards, scanning the nearby forest for danger.

"Sorcery," Vikramaditya said brusquely. "An arrow was shot at your queen from the forest. I cut the arrow into two, but the arrow turned into a snake. I tried killing the snake, but it became a shadow and went into the bushes there."

A crested bulbul lifted out of the bushes and rose into the trees on the other side of the clearing. The samrat watched the bird closely as it flitted from branch to branch before vanishing amidst the thick foliage.

"We need to get the queen out of here," said Vikramaditya, switching his sight from the bushes to the tree where the bulbul had disappeared. "Move toward the horses."

With small shuffling steps, the group inched across the meadow. The guards were watchful, their swords drawn and shields up, the three cavalry archers ready to unleash their arrows at the first glimpse of an assailant. Yet, for all their alertness, none of the soldiers noticed the javelin come plunging out of the sky – until it was too late. The javelin struck one of the cavalry archers in his chest, burying in deep and barreling through his body until its pointed tip emerged out of his lower back, streaked with blood.

Two shrill screams rent the damp air over the forest. One was the archer's, choking and thrumming with agony; the other belonged to Vishakha, horrified at the sight of the impaled soldier reeling on his saddle. The others were still recovering from the shock when the archer's scream died abruptly, and his bow slipped from his lifeless fingers. He toppled sideways off his mount, but before his body hit the ground, the javelin protruding from his back transformed into a tongue of orange flame. Within seconds, the entire shaft was a burning spoke of fire – and then the fire went out, leaving no trace of itself or the javelin. All that remained was a lazy tendril of black, oily smoke spiraling and lifting over the clearing.

"Move, move, move," Vikramaditya shouted, snapping the men out of their stupefaction, instilling urgency in them.

The soldiers broke into an awkward, stumbling run, struggling to stay together to cover the queen even as each of them fought the urge to break free and flee from a threat that none of them could comprehend. The horses that bore no riders had no such conflicts to deal with – surrendering to fear, they charged off in all directions, taking to the forest. As the king crossed the dead archer, he bent over to grab the man's bow and quiver, slinging both over his shoulders.

Behind and above the fleeing party, the wisp of smoke stretched, elongated and looped in the air. In the twinkling of an eye, it turned into a thick, sinewy vine sprouting large, brambly thorns. It whipped around and reached after two of the mounted guards, coiling its ends tightly around their necks and unseating them both with a ferocious tug. Both soldiers crashed heavily to the ground, croaking and gasping as the vine constricted, its thorns digging into the soft flesh of their necks.

Seeing the guards writhing and kicking on the grass, the samrat turned and sprinted back. He attacked the vine with all his might, hacking away until the tough fibres split and began giving way. Still the vine held the guards in an ever-tightening grasp. The soldiers clawed desperately at the coils around their throats, fingers lacerating against the hooked thorns, panicked eyes bulging out of their sockets. Vikramaditya swung his sword at the vine until it finally severed, but by then, it was too late for the guards. The thorns had sunk deep into their necks, bursting arteries. Blood spilled from under the vine's coils as both men spasmed to slow, painful deaths.

"We are ready, your honour," yelled the Guards captain.

With a frustrated cry, the samrat whirled and made a dash toward the group waiting by the edge of the clearing. Vishakha was astride her mare, her face white and bloodless against the darkness of the forest. Her eyes met his, frightened and looking to him for help and protection. Reaching his horse, the king swung himself onto the saddle.

"Stay as close to the queen as possible," he ordered, unslinging the bow and nocking an arrow into place. "Let's go."

The clearing echoed with the beat of hooves as the group spurred into action and headed for the path to Ujjayini.

Throwing one final glance over his shoulder at the clearing, Vikramaditya saw the vine relax its hold over the two dead guards. Uncoiling, it quickly dissipated into thin air. The samrat raised the bow and pulled its string back, his eyes searching the forest.

The threat had not passed, he knew. Whatever it was, it didn't like being thwarted. It would come at them with renewed fury, more vengeful and vicious than before.

* * *

The heady smell of burned cannabis. And the stale fragrance of *aguru* and sandalwood oil.

Jayanta looked around the narrow confines of the hut with a start, wondering where the smells had come from. The seven lamps had burned low, and the room had grown dark as the rainclouds gathered and shed their misery over the plain. Outside, the kinnara was moaning again. Jayanta sniffed the air delicately, then inhaled deeper, but all he could smell was damp, mouldy wood.

Yet, the prince was certain that layered somewhere beneath was the discernable whiff of cannabis and sandalwood oil.

The scents stirred something old and melancholic inside him. He associated the scent of cannabis and sandalwood with his mother – not the one who had existed before Puloman's death, but the one *after*. The one obsessed with the paintings of the cliffs; the relic who haunted a wretched, abandoned corner of Amaravati's palace.

The prince gave his head a vigorous shake to expel thoughts of Shachi, but the trapdoor had been unlatched long enough for the memories to come pushing through. In a rush of sadness, he remembered Shachi clutching him to her breast and weeping at the death of Puloman. Indra, in an exceptional act of vindictiveness, had forbade Shachi from even seeing her father's dead body, and Jayanta could still feel his mother's anguish as she begged her husband to grant her one last sight of Puloman. Indra had stoutly refused, and Shachi had spent two whole nights crying into Jayanta's shoulders.

It was on the third morning that Shachi painted the cliffs for the first time.

Jayanta felt a wetness on his cheeks and tasted salt at the corners of his mouth. Sniffling and wiping the tears away, he stared down at the simmering bowl in front of him, trying hard to keep his thoughts from straying. Ahi was in Ujjayini and there was work to be done...

Shachi's laughter was the oldest memory the prince had of his mother. It was a clear laugh, like tiny brass bells, full of joy every time she threw him in the air and caught him, or spun him round and round as she held him by his plump little baby fingers. He heard his own gurgling laughter mingling with hers, his world a riotous twirl of light and colour with Shachi at its centre. She laughed when he chased butterflies in Amaravati's gardens, and she laughed when he spoke to her in a baby language that none but the two of them understood. Jayanta had never quite observed the gradual fraying and fading in Shachi's laughter – and then one day it was gone, eclipsed forever by a stillness far deeper than pain.

The thought of that forgotten laughter brought fresh tears to Jayanta's eyes and his chest tightened with sorrow. Somewhere, a small voice inside him kept reminding him that Ahi had to be controlled, that he should stay focused on retrieving the Halahala...

Urvashi was another one with a delightful laugh.

He remembered the apsara in his father's court when Puloman was alive, but it was only after Puloman's death – and Shachi's exile into her private world – that he had begun seeing more of her as he wandered, aimless and uncared for, around the palace. For a long time, he had wanted nothing to do with her, and Urvashi too had stayed out of his way. But all that had changed the morning they crossed paths near the palace bath.

The prince had been sauntering along the landscaped garden that lined the bath when he chanced upon Urvashi plucking orchids from a bough that overhung a channel of gently flowing water. The apsara was standing on a wooden bridge, and as she stretched to reach a far bunch of flowers, she lost her balance. She made an instant grab at the bridge's railings, and although she saved herself from falling, her flower basket slipped from her hand. The basket struck the railing and went over, tumbling toward the water.

Jayanta had instinctively reached for the basket and caught it – but his lunge was poorly timed, causing him to tip over and splash headlong into the stream. He surfaced, coughing and spluttering, to hear Urvashi's laughter. Not a heartless, derisive laugh at his plight, but one brimming with mirth and sympathy and innocence. When he had hauled himself out of the water and handed her the basket, half-full of dripping flowers, the apsara had picked out a sprig of violet orchids and given it to him with the sweetest of smiles.

That was the moment when Urvashi's beauty had first blinded Jayanta. When, in those deep and enchanting eyes, he had seen the love and passion that the apsara was capable of harbouring. That day, on the bridge by the bath, desire for Urvashi had kindled in his heart.

He loved the apsara over everything else and was willing to go to any lengths to please her. Yet, she toyed with him. She flirted with every other deva in the court, and she preened and pouted at Narada, laughing at his silly jokes – that innocent, youthful laugh of hers that she ought to have reserved exclusively for him, but instead shared wantonly with everyone.

Urvashi and Shachi, the two women he cared most about. One had struck him with love, the other had showered him with affection. Yet, both had grown distant with the passage of time. Both, in their own ways, had left him hopeless and pining for their love.

The scent of dew-fresh orchids and stale sandalwood washed over the prince once again, smothering him in inconsolable grief. He didn't know why he felt such overwhelming sorrow, but he surrendered to its softness, sinking deeper and deeper into its folds as memories overtook him.

Jayanta hardly noticed when the first barbs of hot pain shot through his body.

* * *

As Kshapanaka crouched on the rooftop and bent her bow at the monster, Shanku's words, spoken just minutes ago, flashed through her mind.

"There is something special in you, something rare and unique that protects you from the serpent's venom. It also helped you destroy the armour of the rakshasa that attacked the palace. The oracle says these things are gifts, that we are blessed to have them. But she says we have to learn to use these gifts – otherwise they are useless and we are better off without them. Believe in your gift, Kshapanaka. Believe that you can harm the serpent."

Summoning all the anger she had felt at seeing the devastation in the ironworkers' quarters, Kshapanaka let the arrow slip from between her fingers. She watched the shaft shoot across the grey sky and bury itself in the monster's head. She saw the splash of water where the arrow struck, the same dirty brown splash that had appeared every time she had shot at the beast. However, this time she saw something else as well.

A current, dense and jet-black in colour, that forked and rippled across the serpent's skin, causing it to flinch as if in pain.

Kshapanaka fitted another arrow into her bow. Pulling

back the strings, she brought to her mind the image of Sadguna, the dead chief of the Palace Guards, lying headless at the foot of the stairway. The old man had given his life to protect the palace household from the rakshasa; death was an unjust reward for his loyalty to the crown. The thought filled her with rage and she shot the arrow at the serpent.

The creature almost staggered back, and as it raised itself, Kshapanaka noticed that it was waning in places and losing substance. Its malevolence had far from dimmed, though, and as it surveyed the councilor, it opened its mouth wide to spit venom.

"What's happening? Any luck?"

Kshapanaka darted a glance at the street below, where Amara Simha and Shanku huddled behind a wall for protection. Amara Simha had returned to his human form, and was staring at her from under his furry red eyebrows.

Before Kshapanaka could reply, a blast of venom hit her hard, and even though she had braced herself for it, she lost her footing and had to grab the tiled roof to steady herself. The venom, which smelled of juiced lemons and rancid water, drenched her completely, but left her otherwise unharmed, and the councilor swiftly nocked an arrow and bent her bow. However, before she could shoot, the monster burst and scattered into the pouring rain.

Cursing under her breath, Kshapanaka returned the arrow to the quiver. Slinging her bow over her shoulders, she quickly slithered down the roof and descended to the street. "It's gone again," she said in a resigned tone, wiping rainwater from her forehead with one arm.

"Wonder where it will show up next," Amara Simha growled in vexation. "I even wonder if what we are doing is helping at all."

"It is helping," said Kshapanaka. "Shanku was right. I have been able to inflict pain on the monster and weaken it."

"You have?" Shanku's face shone in excitement.

"I saw it jerk in pain," Kshapanaka nodded as she mounted the horse lent to her by the City Watch.

"That hasn't stopped it from spitting venom," said Amara Simha, getting onto his saddle.

"The venom has weakened." Kshapanaka pointed up to the spot where she had been crouching. "The venom hit the roof, but only left a few cracks."

The three councilors spurred their horses down the street, keeping their eyes on the sky for signs of the beast.

"If I understood correctly, you can... go wherever you want, be anywhere you want to be. That's *your* gift..." Amara Simha looked at Shanku, who nodded. "Can't you go and find out where this creature might be?"

"I haven't fully mastered the art yet. Even if I had, the creature could be *anywhere*. I could go only where I know the creature *is*, not where it *will be next*." Shanku shot Kshapanaka a dimpled smile, eyes sparkling with mischief. "My grandmother is the clairvoyant, not me."

Halfway down the avenue, a cavalryman of the City Watch informed the councilors that the serpent had been sighted to the east, near the palace, but it had promptly disappeared into the clouds. The councilors turned toward the palace, but soon they saw the monster in the sky to their left, closer to the city's north gate. By the time they arrived at the northern quarter, soldiers of the City Watch informed them that the beast had once again vanished from sight.

"Is it playing a game with us?" Amara Simha growled.

"Either that, or it is fleeing from us," shrugged Kshapanaka.

"It appears to have lost strength, your honour," one of the soldiers ventured. Pointing to a line of buildings adjacent a public bath, he said, "It spat venom over the row of shops over there, but all the houses and shops are intact."

Kshapanaka gave Amara Simha a look of vindication. The

brawny councilor nodded and said, "Let us find the vile thing and finish it off then."

After almost half an hour of chasing and dodging, the councilors and soldiers were finally able to corner the beast in a market that sold earthenware. The serpent hovered tentatively over the market, pulsing in and out of the rain as it hissed angrily at its assailants. The soldiers were still wary of the creature and hung back, but the three councilors approached it, Kshapanaka leading the way with her bow drawn taut.

The monster's jaws unhinged as it prepared to assault the attackers with venom, and Kshapanaka quickly fired three arrows into the black, foul-smelling cavity. With each shot, the serpent wavered in the air, coming slowly apart at the edges as water sluiced down its plumed back in ragged, unruly torrents. With one final heave, it ejected a thin stream of venom, but the jet evaporated before it reached the councilors.

As Kshapanaka slipped a fourth arrow into place, she thought she heard a whimpering sigh of sadness escape from the serpent's mouth. At the same time, the beast's eyes changed colour from amber to a light touch of gold, and it raised itself skyward as if breaking free of shackles. Then, thinning out rapidly like mist, it was lost in the falling rain.

* * *

The branches of the trees on both sides of the crude path interlaced over the riders' heads, forming a canopy that shielded the falcon from Vikramaditya's sight. The samrat occasionally glimpsed the bird in the interstices between branches, skimming across the grey sky as it chased the small group pounding along the forest floor.

The king twisted his neck around and squinted up to see if he could get an arrow through the knotty branches, but he doubted it. They were moving fast across scarred and uneven ground, and the falcon was moving even faster, a tight, compact streak overhead. Moreover, he knew he didn't share Kshapanaka's talent for marksmanship – *she* would have been able to take the bird down.

Not that Vikramaditya laboured under the illusion that shooting the bird would solve the problem in any permanent way. The thing – whatever it was – was spectacularly resilient, and had thrice resuscitated itself after being cut by his sword. There was no reason to believe an arrow would work where the sword had failed. The thought made the samrat nudge his steed closer to Vishakha's in anxiety.

What did the thing want with Vishakha? She had done no one any harm, so what did anyone gain by attacking her? What also worried him was the single-mindedness with which the thing had killed the three guards in their escort. Its coldblooded intent was clear – it would remove every obstacle in its way to Vishakha. It would take any form to...

The samrat's jaw clenched as he darted a quick glance overhead. There was no sign of the falcon. He swung his head to both sides, craning to peer through the branches, searching frantically for the bird, but it was gone.

"Watch out around you," he hollered at the guards. "Keep your eyes open."

Vishakha looked back at Vikramaditya, scared and bewildered. The samrat gave a tight nod, hoping it would reassure her, even though he himself was on edge. He then went back to scanning the forest, looking up now and then for the falcon.

The trail curved away to the left and rose up a small embankment. Once they were over the embankment, they would be out of the forest and back in the open, on the road to Ujjayini. The samrat was hoping they could get to the road as quickly as possible – it would be harder for the thing to attack with no cover around.

From the corner of his eye, Vikramaditya saw the black dot come arcing out of the undergrowth. It took the king a second to realize it was a big bumblebee, buzzing as it sped toward the riders on the path. Without sparing a moment's thought, Vikramaditya raised the bow and aimed at the bee. He could be wrong, but he wasn't taking any chances. Drawing the arrow all the way back, he tracked the bee's swerve carefully, waiting for it to come close. Just as the insect straightened and came at the group in a low dive, the samrat let the arrow fly.

The arrow hit the bee square, its barbed head smashing the insect so hard that it exploded into tiny bits, body parts flying in all directions. For a fraction of a second, Vikramaditya was certain he had killed a harmless bee, but before remorse could set in, the insect's shattered pieces drew back together like iron filings responding to a magnet. The bee sizzled and turned into a small, blazing ball of light that shot into the sky through the mesh of branches.

"Faster, men. Hurry," the samrat exhorted, taking Vishakha's mare by the bridle, urging it to greater speed.

The group topped the embankment in a melee of hooves and emerged out of the trees onto the road to Ujjayini just as a fresh burst of rain came down. Not pausing for even a second, they charged down the road, putting distance between themselves and the tree line.

"Stay on your guard and watch for the *thing*," Vikramaditya's voice was now hoarse. "We only have to get as far as the well."

They had travelled only a hundred paces when the guards leading the pack dropped speed, forcing those coming behind to slow down. "What's the matter?" the samrat snapped as the escort drew to an inexplicable halt. Ploughing through the crowd, he commanded, "Keep going, men. The threat has not passed."

"Your honour," one of the soldiers in the vanguard pointed,

drawing the king's attention to the road ahead, where two riders were approaching.

Rain made visibility poor, and Vikramaditya instinctively urged his horse in front of Vishakha, shielding her while he nocked a fresh arrow and raised the bow. The guards followed suit, taking up defensive stances and forming a tight knot around their queen. As the two riders neared, the samrat's eyebrows rose on identifying the eye-patch one of them was wearing.

"What you are doing here?" Vikramaditya asked as Shukracharya and his guide pulled up in front of the king's party. The bells of Ujjayini were clearly audible now, and the king turned a troubled face in the direction of the city, a smudge on the northern horizon. "Why are the bells ringing? What is the matter?"

"I am here to protect the queen," the asura high priest chose to answer the first question as he got off his horse. Going down on one knee, he scooped up two big dollops of the wet, churned mud, which he then slathered over his palms. Looking up at the samrat, who was staring at him in bafflement, he said, "You were attacked, I take it. What was it?"

"How did you..." Puzzlement made way for a grimmer expression on Vikramaditya's face as the gravity of the threat reasserted itself. "We don't know what it is, but it takes many forms. An arrow, a snake, a spear... a bee. The last it changed into a ball of light. And nothing seems to be able to kill it."

"It has already taken three men's lives, respected Healer," the captain butted in.

Shukracharya nodded, observing the Palace Guards blink water out of their uneasy eyes and look warily into the surrounding plain. "The men died because they were impediments," he said. "It only wants the queen."

"We must get her to the protection of the Labyrinth quickly then," said the samrat in alarm. "We are too few here..."

"This will keep her from harm for a while," said Shukracharya, striding toward Vishakha. The guards parted way, and the high priest stepped up to the mare. "It would have been good if I had sandalwood paste and honey, but this will have to do for now. Bring your face close, child."

Vishakha bowed her head as Shukracharya muttered mantras into his palms. Keeping up the incantations, he smeared the queen's cheeks, forehead and hair with the slime until dirt caked her face and ran down her chin and neck in muddy rivulets.

"That should help," the high priest said, stepping back to survey his efforts. With a satisfied nod, he swerved back toward his horse. "We can go."

"What about the men?" Vikramaditya asked. "They are being attacked as well."

"There are nine of them. It would take much too long to perform the spell on all of them, and the effects of the spell on the queen would begin wearing off. What good would that serve?"

"They are protecting the queen with their lives," the samrat looked down at the high priest with a stubborn set of the jaw. "They deserve all the help you can give them. If the delay is a concern, I shall ride ahead with the queen."

One hand on the saddle of his horse, Shukracharya assessed the king for a moment. "That won't be necessary. I will do what I can, but we will have to hurry."

Filling his hands with mud, the high priest began the process of anointing the Palace Guards with spells. While the king and the soldiers kept a lookout for danger, no one – not even Vishakha herself – noticed the ten discoloured drops of rain that splattered over her shoulders and back. Defying gravity, the ten grey drops wriggled and ran across her back in a haphazard manner, crisscrossing back and forth, searching for ways to get at her. But Shukracharya's spell held true. Losing their drive, the drops slid simultaneously downward, past her waist, over her hip and onto the saddle – where, one by one, they transformed into black scorpions.

Neither the guards nor Vikramaditya saw the creatures scuttle into the folds of the saddle or crawl into the white mare's underbelly, their vicious stingers hooked and ready to strike. When the mare whinnied and stamped a foot in fright, Vishakha merely stroked its neck and spoke a few soothing words into its ear.

The asura priest had just completed casting his spell over the guide from the City Watch when Vishakha's mount bucked and reared, belting out a neigh that shivered with agony. Jolted by the sound, everyone turned to see the mare kick up its hind legs and let out another shrill neigh as Vishakha hung onto the saddle for dear life. Then, before anyone could react, the horse spun around wildly and bolted down the road, kicking up mud and spray as it went.

"Get the horse," the samrat screamed, staring into Vishakha's terror-stricken eyes as she turned around to look at him in helplessness. The king pushed his mount into a run, and as one, the guards responded, charging after the mare. Behind them, Shukracharya ran and leaped onto his horse, turning the beast around so he too could give chase.

The mare bucked and neighed every few seconds, and though the motion tossed Vishakha around mercilessly, it slowed the beast's progress, allowing the pursuers to close in on the queen. Vikramaditya and the Palace Guards were not more than a dozen paces behind the mare when it swerved off the road and plunged into the countryside.

The samrat and his men followed through the driving rain, and the chase crossed over to the wet grassland. The land rose into tiny hillocks, the grass gave way to scrubby bushes and coarsely pebbled earth, and the horses began to tire. Yet,

Vishakha's mount pushed on, driven insane with the pain inflicted by the scorpions.

The mare crested a hillock and disappeared over it – and when Vikramaditya reached the top of the rise seconds later, his eyes flew open in horror.

Below was an unexpectedly sharp depression, one that neither Vishakha nor her mount had anticipated. The mare had lost its footing and taken a nasty tumble, flinging Vishakha off the saddle. As his own steed reared precariously at the lip of the ravine, the king watched the mare and Vishakha skid and roll down the precipitous incline, taking an avalanche of mud and loose stones with them to the bottom. The mare was somehow able to stop its slide and get back on its shaky legs, but Vishakha flopped and bounced until she came to rest by the tattered little rivulet that trickled past the ravine.

"*Vishakha!*"

The queen's name left Vikramaditya's lips in a shriek. The next moment, the samrat was slipping and sliding down the side of the depression, mindless of the thorny bushes that left painful scratches across his face and forearms. He reached the floor in a stumbling sprawl, but picking himself up, he tripped over to the queen's side and went down on his knees. He turned her gently onto her back and bent over her mud-stained face.

"Vishakha," he whispered, patting her cheek anxiously. "Open your eyes, Vishakha. *Vishakha...*"

The queen stirred. Her eyelashes fluttered open and she looked up at the samrat.

"Thank heavens you are fine," Vikramaditya breathed with relief.

There was no response from the queen.

"Vishakha?" A terrible sense of dread and despair settled over the king. "*Vishakha!*"

The queen said nothing. She stared resolutely *through* him.

The familiarity of that gaze – blank, vacant, unseeing – was shocking. The gaze that had ignored him – mocked him – from Vishakha's pillows for two years. Vikramaditya saw his world spinning out of control.

"Vishakha, no... *no*. Don't do this to me." Vikramaditya grabbed her wrist to feel her pulse under his fingers, strong and regular. Her chest rose and fell rhythmically to her breathing. Only her eyes stayed immobile, remote and uncaring.

The samrat crushed the queen's hand to his chest in desperation. "Don't go away again, my love. *Please*... please don't," the words came out in a tormented sob. But she had already left, withdrawing into the void where nothing would reach her.

Vikramaditya hung his head and squeezed his eyes shut, holding back the tidal wave of grief surging inside him, fighting to burst out of his ribs, threatening to rip his universe into a million shards of hopelessness.

Aparupa

Deva... We should be gone from here, deva.

Jayanta stirred and surfaced from the fog of misery that cocooned him. Wiping the tears and snot from his face, he blinked in the half-light. The lamps had all gone out, taking the cheer with them and allowing the dampness back in, which seeped through his body like poison. The water in the copper bowl was cold and still. The only evidence of what had transpired in that meagre space was the loose stack of palm leaves and the dull outline of the *mandala*.

With a tremendous effort of will, the prince got to his feet. His body was riddled with aches and his throat felt hoarse and torn, as if it had been stabbed with a dozen quills. Angry, red welts ran along his arms and shoulders, terminating in ugly purple bruises that made his skin pucker. His head hurt the most; Jayanta was certain it would tip over and fall at the mildest jerk.

"The humans are near, son of Indra. Please... we have to go *now*." There was panic in the kinnara's voice, accompanied by a fretful and anxious stamping of hooves.

The prince stuffed the palm leaves crudely into his satchel and stumbled out of the hut. He fell on his hands and knees, and stayed there a while, staring at the wet earth.

"The humans bear swords and spears, deva," the kinnara hissed urgently. "They will kill us if they find us."

Jayanta winced and glared at the centaur, which was hopping and straining at its bonds. Then, cocking his head, he listened. A murmur of voices came from not very far away. Someone was issuing orders. Twigs cracked and the undergrowth scrunched under trampling feet.

Hurrying as best as he could, the prince limped over and began sawing at the kinnara's ropes. By the time the centaur was free, the voices were dangerously close to the hut. Slipping his knife back into his satchel, Jayanta heaved himself painfully onto the kinnara's back, clutching the beast tight with his knees. The kinnara needed no prompting – whipping around, it bolted away in the direction opposite to the one the men were coming from. As the beast slipped past the tree line, Jayanta glanced back at Ujjayini, which lay quiet under the murky sky, a dark wound on the face of the plain.

There was no sign of Ahi. Freed from his control, the demon had vanished.

The city was still standing, while he was fleeing. The city had won and he had lost. Yet again. There would be no triumphal return to Amaravati, no feasts in his honour. Instead, there would be derision and laughter.

Hurt swelled in his chest, overriding all other pains. But Jayanta didn't care as the memories of Shachi and Urvashi crept up on him again. He slumped on the kinnara's back, wrapped his arms around the beast and let the torrent of hot tears flow.

* * *

Without anyone noticing, morning gave way to afternoon. Not that anyone could tell the difference from the slant of the light. The same dull grey clouds piled one upon another, the same erratic spurts of rain, the same morose semi-darkness; everything just carried over into the second half of the day.

Not that anyone in Ujjayini even cared what time of day it was. Far more pressing matters commanded people's attention.

In all, the monster had reduced six localities to rubble, and the damages and loss of life suffered in four of these were considerable. Entire neighbourhoods had come out to assist the councilors and the soldiers of the City Watch in rescue efforts, and Ujjayini's hospices were overflowing with the dead and the injured who had been trapped under falling debris. Of those killed by the serpent's venom, there was nothing to show. What little had remained of the victims had dissolved in the rainwater and had been swept into the city's gutters without a trace. Misery slowly laid its cold hand on Ujjayini, and there were few streets in the city where women could not be seen beating their chests in sorrow, or men sitting on their haunches, clutching their heads in dejection.

Inside the palace, the atmosphere was frenetic and tense. Vishakha had been brought into the Labyrinth through the secret route that led down from the well – a perilous passage that Vikramaditya and the Palace Guards had negotiated with both care and urgency. By the time of their arrival, the threat from the serpent-monster had passed, and Vishakha was taken up to her bedchamber so the court physicians could attend to her.

The physicians consulted amongst themselves and called for a variety of treatments as they awaited Kunjala, who was out tending to the city's wounded. Palace hands rushed back and forth fetching ingredients for the prescribed unctions, liniments and *kashayams*. A good-sized assembly of courtiers, junior palace officials and servants hung about the gallery and stairway outside the queen's chamber, and it was through this throng that Kunjala – a senior physician of the palace, second only to Dhanavantri in skill and experience – was finally ushered to Vishakha's side.

Bowing stiffly to the samrat, the Acharya and Queen Upashruti, Kunjala shuffled up to the bed. "What has the queen been administered so far?" he demanded of his assistants once he had checked Vishakha's pulse, peered into her blank, open eyes and otherwise taken stock of the situation. He listened patiently as the junior physicians rattled off the measures they had already taken to treat the queen. At last, with a huge sigh, he turned to face the samrat. But before he could say a word, Kshapanaka pushed past the crowd at the door and entered the chamber, her face streaked with sweat, grime and alarm.

"Is she alright?" Kshapanaka blurted, her head swinging wildly from face to face. Her eyes finally settled on Vishakha, and she slowly tiptoed into the room to stand by the foot of the bed, staring into her sister's vacant gaze. The chamber appeared to hold its breath, the eight lamps illuminating the room throwing more shadows than light as cobwebs reattached themselves to the lives of the palace household.

Kshapanaka tore her eyes away from Vishakha and looked at Vikramaditya. "They said she fell... again."

Drawing his breath in, the king gave a small, stiff nod. He then turned to Kunjala. "What do you make of it?" he asked in a tone that suggested that he already knew the answer.

"It would..." The senior physician stopped to pick his words carefully. "Her injuries are neither nasty nor too deep. I think she needs rest. Everything that has happened to her this morning has been very stressful..."

"Do you think you could treat her?" Vetala Bhatta asked bluntly. "Will she recover?"

"I can treat her," Kunjala answered cautiously, looking

down at his gnarled, cadaverous hands. "I will use the same remedies that Councilor Dhanavantri had used earlier. Once he is back, he can..."

"Dhanavantri will not be back for a while," Kshapanaka exclaimed. She turned to the samrat. "We need the Healer to look at her. Where is he?"

"Yes, son," Queen Upashruti trained her eyes on the king as well. "The Healer has already treated her, cured her. He was the one to come and save her from whatever was attacking her. He will know what to do. Send word out for him."

No one observed the shadow that clouded the raj-guru's face at the mention of the Healer, or the way the Acharya narrowed his eyes as he appraised Vikramaditya.

The samrat took a moment to consider the Queen Mother's words. Finally, with a nod, he addressed one of the courtiers. "Send riders out to look for the Healer. We last saw him a little distance from the well that leads into the Labyrinth, but he could be anywhere."

The courtier hastened to carry out the order, but before he reached the door, the king's voice stopped him. "When he is found, he is to be presented at the council chamber."

"Why the council chamber?" Queen Upashruti said in surprise, an ounce of annoyance in her tone as well. "Vishakha is here. What good will it do..."

"I know what I am doing, mother," Vikramaditya raised a firm hand, quelling all argument. The Queen Mother fell silent. The samrat turned back to the courtier. "The Healer is to be taken straight to the council chamber. I will see him there."

* * *

Ghatakarpara's spirits buoyed as he sauntered along Udaypuri's main street, soaking in the air of festivity. The previous afternoon, a travelling carnival had made the garrison town its next stop, and once it opened its grand tent to visitors, the townsfolk had responded with fervour. The gaiety that the carnival had stoked was infectious, prompting Udaypuri's own shopkeepers to bedeck their stores in colourful silks and satins to catch the eye. Makeshift stalls selling an assortment of goods from carved lacquer lamps to dainty lace hand fans to buttermilk seasoned with rare herbs sprang up in every street corner, as travelling merchants of all denominations made a beeline for the town.

The streets were abuzz with people, many dressed in finery reserved for special occasions, and Ghatakarpara thought he even recognized a couple of faces from the garrison offices. There was a smattering of soldiers of the Imperial Army and the Frontier Guard as well, men who were off their shifts, enjoying a deserving break from the tedium of patrolling the frontier. Yet, children outnumbered adults by far. They were everywhere, scampering between stalls and threading between shoppers, jabbering and screeching excitably as they shot out of view round corners. The scene was reminiscent of his own childhood in Ujjayini during the spring festival, and the prince felt a pang of nostalgia.

Then he stopped, arrested by a face diagonally across the street, a face that he had seen before. *Once.*

Tucking his gold, sun-crest medallion out of sight, Ghatakarpara squeezed and elbowed through the crowd, which was staring in admiration at a man juggling with knives as he balanced himself on stilts. However, when he made it to the opposite footpath, there was no sign of the face he had come in quest of.

The prince stood on his toes and craned his neck, his eyes darting everywhere, but to no avail. Turning back with a disappointed slump of his shoulders, he had taken no further than four paces when he saw her step out from behind a stall selling fresh garlands a little way down the street. His heart lifted at the sight, and squaring his shoulders, he set off in her direction.

By the time Ghatakarpara neared her, she had moved to a shop displaying bangles. As she stood inspecting the merchandise, trying on a pair or two, the prince sidled up to her from behind.

"The last I heard, I was going to be reported to my seniors and pulled up for my behaviour," he said in an undertone, almost leaning into her ear.

Aparupa turned sharply and drew her head back so she could get a better look at the speaker. Her eyes widened in recognition, and a mild blush came over her cheeks. She opened her mouth to say something, but thought the better of it as the prince's eyes smiled and locked with hers.

"What happened to that?" he asked, raising one eyebrow in enquiry.

"I just thought it was too much effort to expend on a common soldier," Aparupa answered with a saucy toss of her head. Slipping a brass bangle over her hand, she turned her wrist this way and that, inspecting the ornament. She took it off and placed it back in its tray.

As the girl began moving away, Ghatakarpara said, "The next time you threaten to take someone to task by reporting them, at least ask them their name. Else how do you expect that person to take your threat seriously?"

Aparupa blushed again and looked at the prince out of the corner of her eye. With a quick, disarming smile, Ghatakarpara reached for a shell bracelet that glowed iridescent with nacre. "I think you should try this one on."

"I don't wear shells," the girl shrugged.

"You don't?" The prince's eyes twinkled at Aparupa before they strayed to her ear, adorned with a small stud made of shell.

"I meant shell bangles," the girl's cheeks turned red for a third time, and the blush lasted much longer.

Ghatakarpara held the bracelet to his ear for a moment, as if listening to something. Then, shaking his head, he put it back in its place. Aparupa gave the prince a dubious stare. "What did you just do?"

"You rejected the bangle, so I wanted to check if it was alright." The prince looked at the girl earnestly before giving a sad shrug. "You broke its heart. Here, see for yourself." Picking up the bracelet, he brought it close to Aparupa's ear and gave it a mild shake. The tiny beads inside the bracelet's hollow casing rattled and rolled, making a small pattering noise. "See?" He gave her a cheeky grin.

Aparupa turned to hide her smile in the shadow of her hair, which fell in loose locks over her face and shoulders. "You are fairly impudent for a common soldier," she said. Injecting a critical note in her voice, she added, "And judging by the way you dress, you have aspirations to nobility."

Turning her back to the prince, she began drifting toward the next shop in the street, and Ghatakarpara fell in step beside her. Aparupa glanced at him, but gave no indication of not wanting him around. Emboldened, Ghatakarpara looked casually around as he spoke. "I can't say about aspirations to nobility, but I do have an eye for beauty and refinement."

Aparupa didn't answer, and for a while, the two ambled along. They paused briefly to marvel at a little gypsy girl of about six walking a tightrope as she balanced a long-necked pitcher on her head. Then, as they moved away from the crowd, Ghatakarpara broke the silence.

"How is..." his brow furrowed as he tried to recollect something. "...your maid's son? I don't remember his name."

The girl stared at the prince in surprise and her face softened. "Dveeja. Though I don't think I mentioned him by name that day," she said. "He's okay."

"Has he... always been like this? Since childhood?"

Aparupa nodded.

"Look, I'm sorry about that whole affair the other day. But what choice did we have? The frontier is thick with Huna spies, and no one can be trusted."

"Does Dveeja look like a Huna scout to you?" The girl squinted at him skeptically.

"Huna scouts don't walk around wearing the *hriiz* on their foreheads, if that's what you think," the prince threw up his hands in exasperation. "They disguise themselves to look like us. You wouldn't be able to tell a Huna spy if he were standing *right... next... to... you*." Ghatakarpara spaced out the words for emphasis, chopping the air with his palm to punctuate each word.

Aparupa shucked her shoulders and looked away. The space between them was again turning frosty. Discussing Dveeja was proving to be counterproductive, the prince realized, so he began rummaging furiously for something else to talk about.

"That day... at the frontier... you said that your father is well connected." Seeing Aparupa incline her head, he continued, half in jest, "How well-connected is he? I mean, does he know the governor? Does he know the Samrat?"

"Yes, he knows the governor. And yes, he knows the Samrat as well." Seeing Ghatakarpara turn to her with interest, the girl added, "Even *I* know the Samrat."

As the prince's mouth fell open in astonishment, Aparupa said, "It's another matter that the Samrat knows neither my father nor me." A spark of mischief flared in the girl's eyes and the next moment she burst into laughter.

Ghatakarpara gave a goofy grin and ruffled his hair in embarrassment.

They had walked a little way further when it was Aparupa's turn to pose a question. "What is your name – so I know the next time I need to complain against you?"

"Ghata... Ghataraja," the prince dredged the name up in a stab of inspiration.

"A pompous name for a soldier," Aparupa said. Her voice was not unkind, though, and her tone was teasing.

"You said I have aspirations to nobility. I must have got them from my parents, who named me so grandly," Ghatakarpara said with an elaborate shrug and a cheeky smile.

Aparupa laughed again, a warmer, richer laugh that melted and dissolved the distance and unfamiliarity between them. They chatted as they walked, neither noticing the diminutive figure observing them intently from the corner of an alley across the street. The man's eyes tailed them all the way to the point where the street bifurcated, and Ghatakarpara and Aparupa were finally lost from his sight.

Chewing his lip thoughtfully, the man turned and traced his steps back toward the garrison. The man was Chirayu, flunkey to Governor Satyaveda.

Alliances

I am Shukracharya, mahaguru of the noble asuras."

The high priest threw the words down like a challenge for Vikramaditya and his councilors, who stood in a grim ring around the far end of the gigantic council table. The words resonated off the walls, magnifying in volume and causing the four lamps that illuminated the darkening chamber to gutter in their recesses. Outside, the rain came down in sheets, bringing evening to Ujjayini well before sunset.

"And the thing that attacked the queen this morning was a shape-shifting yaksha, hired by Indra to kill her."

There was a quick, incensed draw of breath from Kshapanaka. "Why Vishakha? What has *she* done to Indra?"

"Indra's idea of a fair fight, I suppose?" the samrat gripped the back of his chair at the head of the table as he held the high priest in a steady gaze.

"The thirst for vengeance is invariably bereft of perspective and morals," Shukracharya's good eye burned in the lamplight as it switched between Kshapanaka and the king. "By defeating the Ashvins and the Maruts, you stoked a rage in Indra that wasn't easily appeased. I presume he wanted to cut you where it hurt the deepest."

The samrat's jaw hardened. *A yaksha hired by Indra.* Even as he and the Palace Guards had ridden away from the ravine with Vishakha slumped against his shoulder, he had turned one last time to see the Healer struggling to contain a black, writhing form, part light, part shadow, by the lip of the ravine.

"What has become of the yaksha?" he asked.

"It is gone. I tried capturing it, but it slipped away. It won't come back, though."

If Vikramaditya felt any relief at this, it failed to register on his face. A momentary silence hovered over the chamber, broken by Varahamihira. "You spoke of us defeating the Ashvins… and *the Maruts*." He shifted his crutch so he could lean better against the table. "Who are these Maruts whom we have supposedly defeated?"

"The four-horned rakshasas who came down the other night in bolts of lightning."

"Those were rakshasas, which means they were of asura extract," Varahamihira countered. "How could the lord of the devas have commanded asuras…"

"It is a long story," the high priest interrupted. "But take my word when I say the asuras had nothing to do with the Maruts coming here."

"*Your* word." Vikramaditya rested an elbow on the back of his chair. "All these days we believed you were a nameless healer from the banks of the Lauhitya, only to be told otherwise now. And you want us to take your word?"

"I can't make you believe me, yet it is the truth," the high priest gave a small shrug. "The Maruts were Indra's doing. As were the Ashvins, the yaksha and Ahi."

"Ahi being… the monster that attacked Ujjayini today?" Amara Simha glowered from under his thick eyebrows.

"The serpent-dragon, yes. Invoked by Indra's son Jayanta,

undoubtedly at his father's behest. It is this city's good fortune that Jayanta has a feeble mind, so my spells were able to break his hold over Ahi. Otherwise..." Shukracharya let the unspoken fill the samrat and the council's mind.

After the shortest of pauses, the high priest half-turned toward the council chamber's door. "I would like to see the queen now," he said in a brisk tone that implied the discussion was over.

"So you admit that the blind ogre and the pishacha army that attacked Avanti came at your command," the samrat spoke as if he had not heard the high priest.

"I admit to a lapse in judgment on my part," said Shukracharya. "Which is why I came to Ujjayini to help and make amends."

"If the intention was to make amends, why the disguise of the Healer, why the subterfuge?" Vikramaditya pressed.

"I feared you would refuse my offer of assistance if I revealed my true identity, Samrat. Ujjayini needed my help; the queen needed my help. Therefore, I chose to win your trust first."

Vetala Bhatta, who had been quietly stroking his beard all the while, leaned forward. "And this desire to... *make amends*, as you put it... is all that brought you to Avanti?"

Shukracharya took a moment to answer – a moment that betrayed him. "I realized we can be friends," he said stiffly. "My help is a token of the value the asuras place on this friendship."

"Everyone wants to be friends, yet ironically, ever since we've had that word thrust at us, all we've had to deal with is enmity, hatred and bloodshed," remarked Varahamihira.

"What is your obsession with the cremation ground?" the raj-guru changed the drift of the conversation without warning.

"What?" Shukracharya almost staggered back in surprise.

Regaining his composure, he managed to sound dumbfounded and indignant at the same time. "What cremation ground?"

"And why do you move secretly around Ujjayini at night?" It was the Acharya's turn to ignore the high priest's defence. "You routinely take a boat across the holy Kshipra – Councilor Shanku has spoken to people who have seen you."

"I seek rare herbs for the potions I brew to cure the queen. Herbs that can only be picked by night." Shukracharya's gaze flitted from one councilor's face to another, assessing the impact of his improvisation. The light outside had faded even more, and the chamber was steeped in shadows, making it hard for the high priest to read their expressions. Even so, the rigid postures facing him told their own story.

"What is the price you will extract for your help and friendship toward Avanti?" the samrat peered at Shukracharya. "Wait, don't tell us. Could it be Veeshada's dagger? That's where all this begins and ends, doesn't it?"

The high priest inhaled deeply and drew himself up to his full height. "You have seen the lengths the devas will go to, Samrat," he said. "And the depths to which they can plunge. Look at your city – what haven't they done to Ujjayini to get hold of the dagger? You need our assistance if they are to be stopped. What is the dagger to you but a burden? Give it to the asuras and we will protect you. *I* will protect you. I have already saved Ujjayini twice from destruction. I will happily do it again."

"You saved Ujjayini?" Amara Simha's voice rang with skepticism. "*Twice?*"

"How do you think the Maruts were defeated, councilor? I cast a Regeneration Spell over the city – *over all of you* – so you could fight the Maruts better. Today, it took my Spell of Sorrows to loosen Jayanta's grip on Ahi. Without my spells, Ujjayini would have ceased to exist."

"Ujjayini and its defenders are not made of clay that we will cease to exist because some serpent comes hissing out of the clouds," Amara Simha's shoulders bunched in anger. "Where is the evidence of the spells that you speak of? Or do we simply have to take your *word* for it?"

"There is no evidence, and I can't prove it," the high priest admitted with unexpected candour. "But the samrat and the Palace Guards are testimony that I saved the queen's life today. If I hadn't reached her in time, the queen would be dead by now."

A fidgety silence descended over the table. When no one spoke, Shukracharya petitioned Vikramaditya.

"You need me here in the palace, Samrat. I hear the queen has had... a relapse. I brought her back the last time, and I can bring her back again. I will cure her. Not just the queen. There are others like Councilor Vararuchi's mother and..." the high priest glanced in the direction of Kalidasa, standing mute to the right of the king, but the giant's face was inscrutable. "... and so many of Ujjayini's citizens in need of aid."

The samrat approached Shukracharya in slow, measured steps. He stopped when they were just three paces away from one another.

"I thank you for all that you have done for me and this beloved city of mine, mahaguru," he said. "None of what you did was of my asking, still I would like to give you something in return. Unfortunately, I cannot give you what you seek – for I cannot part with what is not mine. If there is anything else you want that is mine and mine alone, name it and it shall be yours."

Shukracharya remained silent.

"If there is nothing else I can offer you, let me offer you this – a safe passage from Avanti. You may leave as you came, with no one to accost or harass you."

"Don't act in haste, Samrat," the high priest raised a hand

in one last, desperate gamble. "Spare a thought for the queen. Allow me to look at her once..."

"The queen's destiny has already been forged," the king nipped into Shukracharya's speech. "So has mine, and so has yours. The palace cannot entertain you any longer. You may take your leave."

The high priest considered the samrat's hand, which was motioning him toward the door. "I will return," he said in a tone heavy with menace.

"My offer of safe passage holds only for your departure," the samrat said, unruffled. "You have until morning to leave Ujjayini, and two days to put Avanti's borders behind you. Thereafter, you will cease to be welcome anywhere inside my kingdom. Should we cross paths again, our meeting won't be so amicable."

The door shut on Shukracharya's back with a heavy finality, a hard, irreversible thump that sent aftershocks through the council chamber's walls. Vikramaditya considered the closed door briefly before turning to his council. "I wish to be left alone for a while," he said.

Once the six councilors had departed, the king sank into a chair. Folding his hands on the council table, he rested his weary head on his forearms and closed his eyes. He had no notion of how long he sat there, letting helplessness and despair ebb and flow out of him. It was the sound of the door opening and closing that finally stirred him. Propping his head up, he saw Queen Upashruti come in with a lamp.

"How are you, son?" she asked, running her fingers through his hair as she stroked his head.

"Tired." It was all he could muster. He put his head back down on the council table.

Setting the lamp down, the Queen Mother drew one of the chairs closer and sat down. For a while, she was silent. The rain had ceased, but the drops continued to fall from the eaves. Somewhere, crickets and frogs vied for supremacy in a fearsome medley of sharps and flats.

"I heard that you sent away the Heal... the high priest?" she asked softly, unable to contain herself any longer. Seeing Vikramaditya nod without raising his head, she said, "You could have let him take one look at Vishakha."

The samrat lifted his head and appraised his mother. "Despite knowing who he is and what he wants from me? Never." Shaking his head, he sat up erect.

"What was the harm, son? I am told he offered to see her..."

"Had I allowed him to see her this time, I would be in his debt, mother. I will not knowingly incur a debt that I cannot repay." Rising abruptly, Vikramaditya left the chamber so that the Queen Mother would not see the tears that burned in his eyes like sparks.

* * *

It was only in the light of the following day that Ujjayini took full stock of itself. Of the six neighbourhoods that had crumbled under Ahi's senseless rage, the two worst affected were the ones that housed the ironworkers' colony, and another, which was a residential district for the wealthier merchants and traders of the city.

With close to a hundred-and-fifty dead and nearly the same number injured, it was no surprise to see a renewal in the flow of refugees from Ujjayini. Bullock carts and horse carriages trickled past the city's gates at the first light of dawn, and by the time the sun was a quarter of the way up the sky, the outbound traffic was dense enough to create snarls at the gates, where they met incoming caravans bearing commodities for the markets. Yet, not everyone had somewhere to go to – the poorer artisans and tradesmen were forced to pitch tents in one or the other of the city's grounds, and some families even erected makeshift shelters in the half-burned ruins outside Ujjayini's northern wall.

The lack of the Healer's familiar and comforting presence only compounded the people's trauma. But as the news of the Healer's identity – and what had transpired in the council chamber – filtered out of the palace, a sense of despondency gripped the public. There were dark mutterings in some quarters over the wisdom of banishing the Healer in such times of dire need, and there was at least one instance where supporters of the samrat's decision and those who questioned it came to blows. When Shanku and Varahamihira visited one locality, a grief-stricken old carpenter had railed against Vikramaditya, saying all the king cared about was his promise to the Omniscient One, and nothing for his people's misery. It took a gentle but firm reminder from Varahamihira about Vishakha's state for the man to simmer down with an apology.

If there was despair on the one hand, there was also wonder and passionate pride at the manner in which the councilors had combated the monster. Amara Simha's spectacular transformation into man-lion, in particular, caught the public's frenzy, and even though the transition had been fleetingly short – and less than twenty people had been witness to it – word of it spread quickly. Kshapanaka's immunity to the serpent's venom was almost as big a talking point, as was Shanku's talent at being able to transport herself anywhere at will. Only Varahamihira's skill remained a secret – the councilor had spoken of it to none but the king and his fellow-councilors.

Vikramaditya himself spent the morning visiting the worst-hit neighbourhoods, listening to his people's travails and offering condolences, support and hope where he could. Strangely, people's woes were not limited to the losses they had suffered directly at the hands of Ahi. The merchant community was worried at the large-scale exodus of citizens from Ujjayini; they feared that a sudden slump in demand for goods would take a toll on trade. Similarly, the ironmongers and metalworkers were concerned with the hike in duties on iron and bronze. They insisted that the demand for their wares was dropping due to the high duties on raw materials, and now with homes and smithies in need of rebuilding, their livelihoods were at risk.

"The metalworkers are right about the slip in demand for their products," said the raj-guru. "After all, we were the ones to impose higher duties on iron, bronze and lumber to cut demand, so that our armouries wouldn't have to deal with a scarcity of weapons."

The king and the councilors were back in the council chamber to exchange notes and decide upon the next course of action.

"If we reduced the duties a little... would it help?" the samrat enquired.

"It's not just they who need iron," Vetala Bhatta pointed out. "Six neighbourhoods now need to be rebuilt, four almost from scratch. And, of course, our own forges and armouries also need metal."

"We must strengthen our reserves promptly, buy more iron," observed Amara Simha.

"One small problem, though," Varahamihira scratched his pockmarked cheek. "There is no iron available in the market."

"What do you mean, no iron?" Amara Simha stared in surprise.

"I was speaking to an overseer of the Royal Engineers last night. It seems the flow of iron has virtually dried up. There are no fresh supplies coming out of Dandakabhukti."

"Shoorasena," said the Acharya to no one in particular.

"What we had feared has come to pass," growled Amara Simha. "We can't let Shoorasena choke the supply of iron like this. This shortage will impact all our allies across Sindhuvarta."

"Short of marching an army against Magadha, I can't see what we can do about it," replied Vetala Bhatta.

"That is out of the question at this moment," the samrat's tone was firm. "We need our army at the frontier. And any men we can spare from the frontier are needed here in Ujjayini."

Amara Simha inclined his head. "How do we get around this iron crisis then?"

"We have to find another source to replenish our iron reserves," the samrat replied.

"Other than the mines of Dandakabhukti, there is only one more known source of iron in Sindhuvarta," Vetala Bhatta said slowly. "The deposits found along the treacherous slopes of the Riksha Mountains, bordering the Ghost Marsh."

Vikramaditya nodded. "The deposits are relatively smaller, but a few samples have shown that the ore is even richer than what Dandakabhukti produces."

The air above the council table hummed with fresh possibilities.

"Will Queen Abhirami and King Veerayanka even entertain a request of this nature?" the raj-guru pondered. "The deposits aren't large, possibly just enough to meet Odra and Kalinga's demand."

"And even if they could trade, the question is *would* they?" said Varahamihira. "Odra and Kalinga have never reciprocated to our overtures in the past. I can't think of a more distrustful and standoffish pair of rulers than Abhirami and Veerayanka."

"There's no harm in asking. If Shoorasena takes Vanga, he will definitely levy higher taxes on all goods that come through Tamralipti. It would be advisable to look for another port that trades with the kingdoms of Sribhoja and Srivijaya – and that port could be Tosali or Uttara Tosali."

"There's merit in what you suggest," said the Acharya, chewing his lip. "Perhaps it is time we once again sent feelers out to Odra and Kalinga."

"Do we speak to the iron traders to open a dialogue with their counterparts in Odra?" asked Kshapanaka.

"No, this conversation has to be taken up at the highest level – with Queen Abhirami. We are not simply looking for trade partners. We are working toward building alliances." The samrat gazed deeply into each councilor's eye until his vision rested on Vetala Bhatta.

"I hate to do this to you, raj-guru, especially at your age. However, I cannot think of anyone better suited to pay Queen Abhirami a visit and impress upon her the need to collaborate with us. I know the journey to Uttara Tosali will be long and exhausting. So forgive me for asking, but would you agree to go nevertheless?"

"What is there to forgive, Vikrama?" the Acharya replied with a kind smile. "It is in Avanti's interests; I will proceed at the earliest."

* * *

The light from the two flickering torches struggled to penetrate the darkness beyond the stout iron bars that held Pallavan in his cramped and musty cell. Still, it was sufficiently bright for the envoy to make out his three visitors, who stood appraising him critically as he sat on the rough, stone floor of the dungeon, his hands shackled behind him, one foot chained to a heavy bracket on the wall.

"Never in my wildest dreams would I have imagined us meeting under such strange circumstances, dear sir," said Shoorasena, an amused smile playing on his thin lips. The new king of Magadha had his arms crossed in front of him, his head tilted to one side, his beard and moustache immaculate in the torchlight. "You and your king truly amaze me."

Pallavan made no attempt to speak, partly because he could think of nothing appropriate to say, and partly because his bruised and puffed lips made speech painful.

"Living out of a commonplace caravanserai, sneaking about Girivraja in disguises, planting stories in my courtiers' ears, stoking a mutiny in my absence..." Shoorasena shook his head theatrically in mock wonder, but his green eyes were cold and hard in the torchlight. "Very resourceful, but also very unbefitting a person of your noble stature. You know how much it pained me to discover all this as I rode into Girivraja? I wanted to celebrate the fall of Vanga with my people, but instead I am in this stinking dungeon talking to vermin like you. I'm quite tempted to have you killed right away – and I might just do that, you know?"

"No matter what you do, you will pay for everything," Pallavan mumbled, wincing as a crack on his lip stretched and opened. "There is no getting away from any of this."

"Is that so?"

Shoorasena raised his eyebrows in an exaggerated display of surprise and looked at the two men who flanked him. The one with the broad face, curling moustache and big, *tambulam*-stained teeth Pallavan recognized as General Daipayana; the other was a dark, square-jawed man wearing the medallion of the Magadhan council, whom he had never seen before. The general and the councilor grinned at Shoorasena, who turned his eyes back on the envoy.

"You sit at my feet in chains and you tell me there is no getting away from any of this? Your time would be better spent thinking how *you* can get away from *this*," Shoorasena drew a circle with his finger at the surrounding blackness of the dungeon.

Daipayana leaned forward and smiled, as if making a friendly suggestion. "The king is right. But let me tell you, even *that* would be a waste of time – because there is no getting away from here either." The general's eyes glinted in manic delight as he threw his head back and let out a laugh that was all teeth and spittle.

"I'm not concerned about what happens to me," said Pallavan, trying to muster as much dignity as he could while shifting around to find a more comfortable position on the filthy floor of the cell.

"I would love to hear you say that when we put a rope around your neck and string you up in the city market along with your co-conspirators," said Shoorasena with an acidic smile. With that, he turned on his heel to leave the cell.

"If anything happens to me, you are assured of earning the displeasure of my king," the envoy addressed Shoorasena's back.

The new king of Magadha was stooping to exit the cell's door, but he stopped to consider Pallavan. "In which case, we shall save a place in the market to string Bhoomipala up as well." Turning to the councilor at his elbow, he added, "Make sure the dungeon keepers feed him just enough so he doesn't die of starvation."

Shoorasena, Daipayana and the councilor were climbing the winding stairway leading out of the dungeons when the councilor spoke. "When are we executing him, your honour?"

"Executing who?"

"The envoy, your honour. You said he would hang in the market."

"We are not executing him," Shoorasena gave the councilor a withering look. "Those were just threats to keep him from sleeping too soundly."

The councilor and the general sneaked confused glances at one another. "May I know the reason behind keeping him alive, your honour?" Daipayana enquired.

"We'll use him as a hostage to demand a ransom from Bhoomipala," Shoorasena replied.

"I'm not sure I understand, your honour," said the general.

"We'll tell Bhoomipala he can have his envoy back, alive and in one piece, if he agrees to give us what we want in return."

"And that is...?"

"The musician." Seeing the look of surprise on his companions' faces, Shoorasena explained, "Remember what Pallavan told Uttama, Asmabindu, Diganta and Bhaskara? Even in Sravasti, very few know the musician even exists. So we trade Pallavan for him. Once we lay hands on him, we kill him, and with his death, all proof of what happened disappears."

"That might be true, your honour," Daipayana said thoughtfully. "But Bhoomipala, Pallavan and a few others in the court of Sravasti still know what happened. They can start spreading the news..."

"What would they say?" the king butted in. "That there is a musician who saw something nasty happen in Girivraja? If they do say that, people would want to know where this musician is. What would Bhoomipala and Pallavan say to that? That they traded the musician with Magadha to save their envoy's life? I doubt that would show Kosala in a very favourable light. No, I am certain Bhoomipala and his court will keep their mouths shut."

"And if Bhoomipala refuses to barter?"

Shoorasena shrugged. "It'll be a good test of what Kosala holds dear."

"What if we did execute Pallavan instead of letting him go scot-free, your honour?" asked the councilor.

"What do we achieve by doing that? It puts Bhoomipala and his court against us, and we blow all chances of getting hold of that musician."

"We could attack Kosala and demand they hand over the musician, your honour. Kosala sent Pallavan to Girivraja to act against you and the throne. Isn't that provocation enough?"

The king came to a halt and turned to face the councilor. "Okay, we attack Kosala. What happens next? Vatsa, Matsya and Avanti will come to Kosala's assistance. We cannot fight their combined force and win, not at this point. Even if we do choose to fight, the musician could still slip away to spread his story. And his story is bound to reach Magadha eventually. Pallavan is correct. If the truth reaches enough people, the seeds of doubt would have been sown. Our problem is the musician. As long as he is alive, we cannot rest easy. We have to find him and silence him, quickly and quietly."

"I see your point, your honour," said Daipayana. "It is wisest to negotiate over Pallavan and the musician. Let us send a messenger to Bhoomipala."

"What about the others, your honour?" The councilor saw the confusion in Shoorasena's face. "I mean the courtiers Diganta, Uttama and Bhaskara?"

"They must die," replied Shoorasena, his brow furrowing darkly. "They must be punished for daring to scheme against me, thankless dogs. Charge them for plotting to help the Kikatas and have them hanged in the market at dawn tomorrow."

"Yes, your honour. Which reminds me..." the councilor paused. "Courtier Asmabindu has sent in a formal request to be considered for the post of governor of Vanga. That was the... *arrangement* that we had worked out."

"Yes, of course. His pound of flesh. And I always thought him to be one of father's staunchest loyalists." Shoorasena smiled wryly. "Let the courtier know that his request will be considered in all earnestness."

"I will, your honour."

Gaining the top of the stairs, the king and his men entered a gallery where three palace guards stood waiting. With the guards were two men who looked travel-worn, even though their attire was fresh and presentable.

"Salutations, your honour," one of the guards bowed deeply. He pointed to the two men. "These are messengers from Heheya, from the court of King Harihara, your honour."

Shoorasena arched one eyebrow at the strangers. "Your purpose here?"

"Your honour," said one of the men, extracting a sealed canvas scroll. "We bring a message from our king. We shall await your reply, should you have one."

Shoorasena waited for the men to withdraw. He then broke open the seal and unfurled the scroll. Reading its contents, a smile hovered on his lips, slowly spreading its light across his face.

"Good news, your honour?" Daipayana peered expectantly at Shoorasena.

"Very good," the king replied, rolling the scroll back and gloating at the general. "Harihara proposes that I take his daughter Princess Rukma's hand in marriage. Heheya has always been a slave to Avanti. Harihara could never see beyond King Mahendraditya, Vararuchi and Vikramaditya. But this..." he waved the scroll about like a wand. "This is Harihara's first sign of respect to anyone outside Avanti. It is an indication of Magadha's rise to glory, general."

"Without doubt, your honour. Will you be accepting Harihara's offer of Rukma's hand?"

"Why wouldn't I?" Shoorasena stood tall and erect, his face smug and handsome. "What better way to start breaking Avanti's hegemony over Sindhuvarta?"

* * *

Vikramaditya was on the verge of turning away from the Mother Oracle's doorsill when he heard a dry croak emerge from the darkness.

"Why is the wise and clever king going back? You *had* come to see me, hadn't you?"

The samrat turned, wondering if he had imagined the note of sarcasm in the voice. "I didn't know you were here, mother," he said, peering into the pitch-black interior of the oracle's room. "Why don't you have a light on in there?"

"My eyes have seen a lot of this world, my king." The old woman's voice was weary. "At times, it is a relief to not see. But why are you still standing outside? Come in."

"I can't find my way without a light, mother."

"Embrace the darkness, my king. Sometimes, it is important to let the darkness guide you."

Feeling around for obstacles, the king took a few steps into the room before deciding he had come far enough. He lowered himself to the floor and crossed his legs under him, orienting himself so he faced the direction of the voice.

"You finally found the time to come." The sardonic undertone was unmistakable this time.

"I have had a lot on my hands and on my mind, mother." Vikramaditya paused and took a deep breath. "But you are right. I have neglected coming to see you. I apologize. I should have come earlier to thank you for warning us about the serpent."

"I should be the one to apologize, wise king." The samrat's eyes had got accustomed to the dark, and he discerned the oracle's outline from the shake of her head. "I was vague about the threat, and I didn't alert Shanku early enough; so many lives that could have been saved were lost."

"You did your best, mother. It is not as if you failed."

The woman was quiet for a moment. "I am also sorry I couldn't warn you of the yaksha," she said. "Had I learnt about it in time, things might have turned out differently."

"Things turn out the way they are meant to turn out. And anyway, *I* was the one who didn't heed your warnings about the Healer." Vikramaditya hung his head in shame. "So how can I hold what you *didn't know* against you?"

"You must love her dearly to have taken such a risk." The oracle's voice was gentle and sympathetic.

"And all that for nothing," the samrat stared down at his hands. Raising his chin, he looked at the Mother Oracle. "She remembered me, mother. Moments before the yaksha's attack… she finally recalled a memory of me. Now it has gone again. Everything's gone."

"It is probably a test, my king."

"A test… or maybe a punishment. Veeshada's dagger has descended on me like a curse, taking everything that I hold dear. I couldn't protect the woman I love; I can't protect my people. What do I tell them when they ask why the dagger is more important to me than their lives, mother? What do I say to those fleeing their homes out of fear?" Bitterness filled Vikramaditya's voice. "I have let the people of Ujjayini down badly."

"Still you know you have done the right thing."

"At what cost, mother? The lives of innocents who have nothing to do with the dagger or the promise I made to the Omniscient One? And all in the knowledge that more lives will be sacrificed the next time the devas or asuras send a monster after the Halahala? The odds were always against us, but they are only going to get stiffer in the days to come."

"Then it is time you evened the odds a little by finding yourself some new allies."

"There are hardly any new allies around, mother." Again, the samrat's tone grew acidic. "And even some of the old ones have begun turning their backs on us."

"I am not referring to the human kingdoms of Sindhuvarta, my king. The best way to counter one demon is with another."

Vikramaditya stared at the oracle's face, trying to read her features in the dark. "I am not sure I follow you."

"What do you know of the danavas?"

"The danavas!" The king's voice rang with surprise. "I... well... they are a long lost race of demons who are believed to dwell in the deepest reaches of the Forest of the Exiles. But that is just a story meant to scare naughty children into behaving themselves..."

"The danavas are not a myth," the Mother Oracle spoke with sudden sharpness. "I have heard the breeze that blows from the Dandaka speak of them as living beings."

"The danavas are for real?" Vikramaditya spoke in a hushed, childlike whisper.

"Do you know how they came to inhabit the Dandaka?" Seeing the king shake his head, the oracle said, "The danavas were the original inhabitants of Patala. Back then, Patala was a dense forest – you know the danavas are forest spirits, don't you? Well, the danavas lived in a magical city made out of a charmed wood stronger than iron. They were a peaceable and hospitable race, and welcomed anyone who ventured into Patala. That is how the asuras, who had been compelled to leave Devaloka, came to settle in Patala."

"How do you know all this, mother?"

"Nature is forever brimming with stories and tidings, wise king. What do you think happens when the wind rustles the leaves, birds chirp, brooks babble and the surf roars against the seashore? Stories are being shared." The Mother Oracle paused to resume her narrative. "Anyway, once the asuras arrived in Patala, they started remodelling the land to suit their tastes. They cut down a great many acres of trees to clear space for their own city, and began sinking mines for iron, bronze and other metals. They built dykes along the Patala Ganga to irrigate their farmlands... The asuras did everything to desecrate and destroy nature's flow, which was dearest to their hosts, the danavas. Being the rightful owners of the land, the danavas objected to what the asuras were doing, and soon guests and hosts were in conflict. To cut a long story short, with the blessings of Sage Kashyapa and the sorcery of Diti, the asuras ultimately prevailed, and the danavas were ejected from Patala."

"That's how they came to the Forest of the Exiles?"

"And to this day, the danavas harbour a deep animosity toward the asuras," the old woman nodded. "If you can convince the danavas that the asuras are using the Dandaka to attack Avanti, and that you need their assistance, you would have won yourself a powerful and magical ally."

The samrat sat in silence for a long while, assimilating everything he had just heard. At last, he addressed the oracle, "The danavas are so reclusive – how does one even begin a conversation with them?"

"You must have heard of the town of Janasthana, deep in the forest. That is the seat of the danavas."

"No one even knows *where* Janasthana is within the Dandaka," Vikramaditya pinched his lip in bewilderment. "How are we ever going to find it in the midst of such a thick and vast jungle that none of us have been inside before?"

"It is the Forest of the Exiles, my king," the oracle spoke as if to a particularly slow child. "Rumour has it that there are half-a-dozen condemned men who actually escaped from the Dandaka and returned to Sindhuvarta. These men are obviously familiar with the jungle and the trails that wind through it. You only have to find one who is willing to lead you to Janasthana."

"That might prove even harder than finding Janasthana, mother. But yes, it is worth a try." The samrat sounded distinctly brighter and more upbeat.

"Remember one thing, though," a shadow of caution crept into the hoarse, gravelly voice. "Because of their history, the danavas are a suspicious race, deeply untrusting and hostile to strangers and anyone they see as intruders. They are not the easiest of folk to befriend."

"You give hope and take it away in the same breath, mother," the king remarked wryly.

"All I'm saying is if you want the danavas as your ally, you will have to work hard for it."

Truce

How do we know it is not a ploy, mahaguru?" The Witch Queen's icy blue eyes clouded over with mistrust. "It might even be a trap, sprung in retaliation to the attack your brave sons led on Amaravati."

"I would tend to agree with Holika, mahaguru. The devas are not to be trusted after the way they tricked Puloman into going to Meru, and then killing him when he was defenceless. No, mahaguru, in my humble opinion, Narada's talk of truce reeks of deviousness."

From behind him, restive mutterings came to Shukracharya's ears. The high priest knew what the asura generals gathered in the Court of the Golden Triad were thinking – their misgivings were obvious from the manner in which they shuffled their feet and whispered to one another. Many of them had shown up in court upon hearing of his return from Sindhuvarta, most believing he had brought the Halahala back with him. Once that misconception had been dispelled, their disappointment had found an outlet through the guarded grumblings over his suggestion that Hiranyaksha take up Narada's offer to make peace with Indra.

"Oh, it *is* a ploy, no doubt about that," replied Shukracharya, considering Hiranyaksha and Holika from the foot of the steps that rose up to the black crystal throne of Patala. "When a truce is offered, it is born either out of fear or cunning. We can definitely rule out fear in this instance."

"Yet you believe it is in our interest to accept Indra's invitation to Devaloka?" Holika looked in bewilderment from the high priest to her brother-consort seated by her side.

"It is a ploy, but it is *not* a trap." Shukracharya heaved a weary sigh and lowered himself onto a low, cushioned stool by the lowest step. "Narada is smart enough to have interpreted the real purpose behind our attack on Amaravati. He realizes the futility of battling us when he would rather turn his attention to taking the Halahala from the human king. The truce is just a way to get us off Indra's back."

"If your plan is achieving its desired results, why ease the pressure on the devas, mahaguru?" The frown on Hiranyaksha's brow deepened the lines in his dark face and cast brooding shadows over his features.

"Because, for once I agree with Narada when he says the devas and the asuras have a common enemy in the human king, and that both sides must set aside their differences and unite against the king." The high priest paused to let the sibling-consorts absorb his words. "Of course, when Narada said that to you, they were just empty words – he probably didn't believe a word of what he was saying. Yet, in his falsehood, he unwittingly touched upon the truth."

"You ask the asuras to shed our pride over an ordinary human being, mahaguru?" Fire from the lamps lit along the steps to the throne caught and burned in the asura lord's golden eyes. His voice cracked in disbelief. "What would I tell Hiranyakashipu when he returns from his penance – that we struck a truce with the treacherous devas on account of a *human* king?"

Again, a tide of murmurs – dismayed, incredulous, circumspect – washed back and forth across the wide hall. Chandasura and Amarka's triumphant return from Amaravati had boosted asura morale, and the high priest was sensitive to the asuras' reluctance to surrender a hard-won initiative. Yet, he couldn't let this show of dissent get out of hand...

"You forget much, lords of Patala," Shukracharya chose to ignore the court by addressing only the sibling-consorts, but the pitch of his voice was clearly meant to quell the generals. "You forget that Vikramaditya wields the Hellfires, and that his councilors are the bearers of the Nine Pearls. I have seen and heard much during my stay in the human kingdom. I have witnessed the king's resolve, and the bravery of his council."

Pausing to draw his breath, the high priest got to his feet and climbed four steps so his eye could sweep over the gathering of Hiranyaksha's generals. "Haven't I just told you about how the humans fought off the Maruts and Ahi? Didn't I tell you how the king refused my help when I offered to heal his queen? What would you make of a man who sacrifices his deepest hopes and yearnings for the sake of his duty?"

Shukracharya turned back to fix a severe gaze on Holika and Hiranyaksha. "Ever since he demanded that I leave his palace, I have spent my time learning everything I can about the king and his council. The conclusion I have arrived at is simple – we devas and asuras can fight and trick each other all we want for ownership of Veeshada's dagger. But neither of us is going to win the dagger until the human king is overcome. And neither of us can do that by ourselves – definitely not if we are at one another's throats at the same time. However, if you still insist, you are welcome to try."

The high priest's challenge mounted the steps to the crystal throne and lifted into the arched ceiling, crashing off the walls before subsiding in the muted roar of the cataracts that scarred the Patala Ganga's progress past the palace. Holika rose from the throne, the silks she wore swishing softly against her golden skin as she descended a few steps in Shukracharya's direction. When she spoke, her tone was subdued and conciliatory.

"It was never our intention to question your wisdom, mahaguru. If we gave that impression, we regret it. We will do as you say..." she gave a slight pause, "...but if I may ask, what happens to Veeshada's dagger once we defeat the king?"

"Fear not for the Halahala." Shukracharya's face had softened at Holika's apology, and he even allowed a devilish gleam to light his eye. "The bones have hinted at where the king has concealed the dagger. Once his little kingdom begins falling apart, I shall devise a way of retrieving the Halahala before the devas can."

* * *

Two amorous black-and-yellow butterflies chased one another in brisk courtship across Dhanavantri's line of vision, forcing him to blink and follow their loopy, manic flight over the proliferation of hibiscus bushes in the garden. Yet, for all the distraction the colourful insects provided, the physician's thoughts were elsewhere as he sat soaking in Kausambi's bright, early morning sunshine and mulled over the next course of action.

The journey from Ujjayini had taken much longer than expected, his progress plagued by incessant rain, which had caused most of the Yamuna's tributaries to spill over and flood large tracts of the river plain. It was only two days since Prince Shashivardhan and Councilor Yashobhavi had finally welcomed the physician into Vatsa's royal palace.

Yet, Dhanavantri had still not broached the matter that

had brought him this far. The reason for that was King Chandravardhan.

Within an hour of his arrival, the physician was escorted to Chandravardhan's chamber. In so many days, there had been little improvement in the king's condition, and Dhanavantri was honest enough to admit to himself there wasn't much he could do to remedy the situation. Still, partly out of habit, and partly to leave a favourable impression on Yashobhavi and the rest of the council, Dhanavantri concocted a salve, which he then judiciously massaged into Chandravardhan's paralyzed limbs. When he left the king's side that night, it was with the resolve to talk to Yashobhavi the very next morning about Shashivardhan's succession to the throne.

But when the next day dawned, bright and sunny, it brought with it a surprise for the people of Kausambi. Chandravardhan had woken to discover that he could wiggle his fingers and toes, and even slur a few words out. Dhanavantri was sent for, and the physician observed that the king looked less ashen and listless – he was even able to hold Dhanavantri's eye and mumble a few words of gratitude. Dhanavantri prescribed a fresh set of salves to augment the treatment, and once again applied the medication himself. By the afternoon, Chandravardhan was able to shift on his bed without much assistance as the strength slowly flowed back into his limbs. When Dhanavantri went to see him at night, the king was able to construct an entire sentence in slow, laboured steps.

"God... bless Vikrama for... sending... you here for... treat... me," he had said with a small nod of thanks.

Chandravardhan's words had left the physician ashamed and confused. The king's treatment was just an excuse, a sleight to conceal the real motive behind his visit. But with Chandravardhan now showing active signs of recovery – Dhanavantri had no idea what had brought about such a remarkable change almost overnight – he was at a loss over how to take his agenda forward.

"Your honour, King Chandravardhan is awake and awaits you in his chamber."

The physician gave a start and looked around. A servant of the palace stood a little to his left, bent at the waist in a deep bow. Dhanavantri was conscious of a renewed kindling of respect for him in Kausambi; everyone naturally assumed that his role had been vital in the king's recovery, even though he himself had no reason to believe so.

Dhanavantri allowed himself to be led through a series of narrow passageways, open courtyards and winding staircases. Vatsa's royal palace was a modest affair in comparison to the lake palace in Ujjayini, yet it took many minutes before the physician was ushered into Chandravardhan's presence.

"Greetings, my king," said Dhanavantri, taking in Yashobhavi, Shashivardhan and the quartet of Vatsa's physicians who hovered around Chandravardhan. The king sat propped up against pillows, and he joined his hands in a *pranaam* in response to Dhanavantri's salutation. "How are you feeling this morning?" the physician asked cheerfully, taking note of the colour that had returned to the king's cheeks.

"The king is much better, vaidyanath," the head physician of the palace replied, looking at Dhanavantri in awe and reverence. "As you can see, the king is able to sit up. He says he is even feeling strong enough to stand. You have indeed worked a miracle, vaidyanath."

"It is the king's will, and the care and attention that all of you have bestowed that has worked. Your dedication is the miracle cure," Dhanavantri replied graciously, approaching the bed. Addressing Chandravardhan with a small shake of his head, he added, "And about getting to your feet... a little patience, my king. Perhaps we can try it tomorrow?"

"I am... feel... fine," Chandravardhan offered a token protest, but let Dhanavantri have his way. All five physicians applied themselves to the task of preparing and administering oils and salves, and it was close to an hour before the four palace physicians withdrew, leaving Dhanavantri alone in the company of their king, the prince and Councilor Yashobhavi.

"What news... Dvarka?" Chandravardhan enquired of Dhanavantri.

Seeing the physician's puzzled expression, Shashivardhan said, "We heard of the Huna plan to attack Dvarka. Do you have any updates on that, councilor?"

"Ah, that." Dhanavantri nodded in comprehension, then immediately shook his head. "I left Ujjayini at almost the same time as Vararuchi left for the Anartas to help protect Dvarka. We did turn many of Anartas' troops back to defend their lands, and we diverted a good number of Avanti's own troops to Dvarka as well. Beyond that, I know nothing."

"You do know that the Sakas have begun conducting frequent raids along Matsya's borders, don't you?" Yashobhavi squinted at a point over Dhanavantri's shoulder.

"Yes, King Baanahasta brought it to our notice at the Samrat's *rajasuya*..."

"No, councilor," Yashobhavi interrupted. "These raids are more recent and more serious in nature. Numerous watchtowers along Matsya's border have been systematically burned down and destroyed, and there have been instances of patrols being ambushed. Slowly but surely, the Sakas are moving in."

"I didn't know of this," Dhanavantri said with an unhappy sigh.

For a little while, no one spoke. "It was very generous of Samrat Vikramaditya to spare you to attend to father," Shashivardhan finally said. "Especially at a time when the citizens of Ujjayini themselves are in great need of your talents.

We understand that the attacks by the devas and asuras have crippled Ujjayini."

"Yes, the people of Ujjayini have suffered much," Dhanavantri admitted slowly, struggling to make up his mind. "Actually, there is..." he paused, then decided to take the bull by the horns. "There is one more reason to my visit. It pertains to a proposal from King Harihara."

Chandravardhan's eyebrows rose quietly, the one on the paralyzed side of his face drooping a little below the other. Feeling the weight of three pairs of eyes on him, Dhanavantri plunged headlong into the account of Harihara's proposal to Shoorasena, Queen Sumayanti's message to Vikramaditya sent in secret, and the Acharya's subsequent trip to Heheya to talk Harihara out of his foolishness. All three men listened without interruption, and it was only when Dhanavantri finished that Yashobhavi spoke.

"If I understand correctly, King Harihara has come around to discarding Shoorasena as a prospective son-in-law if Prince Shashivardhan accepts Princess Rukma's hand."

"Yes. It was something that was suggested to Harihara by the Samrat." Dhanavantri fidgeted and looked at Chandravardhan in appeal. "It would help keep the alliance of the kingdoms of Sindhuvarta intact."

"Stupid... man," Chandravardhan chewed and spat the words out. If there was any doubt about who he meant, his next few words cleared it. "A murderer... for a son-in-law!"

An uncertain silence laid hold over the small group, but it didn't last long.

"Samrat... is right," Chandravardhan nodded and looked at Shashivardhan. "Kingdoms must... stay... united... against Hunas. Will you marry... her?"

"If that will keep Sindhuvarta bonded together and strong, I will, father," the prince answered without batting an eyelid.

"Good." Chandravardhan settled lower into the pillows.

"There is... Harihara has one condition, though." Dhanavantri's discomfort was plain as daylight. "He wants Rukma to marry a king." When no one said anything and he realized that he hadn't been properly understood, the physician added, "Shoorasena is a king. But Shashivardhan isn't one – as yet."

"So?" Chandravardhan propped himself up again.

"Harihara is adamant that he will marry Rukma only to a king."

"He wants Shashivardhan to be crowned king of Vatsa? Is *that* his condition?" Yashobhavi finally pounced on what Dhanavantri had been getting at. His face contorting with outrage, the councilor almost shouted. "How dare he? King Chandravardhan is still very much here..."

"Harihara does not insist on a coronation," Dhanavantri held up a soothing hand. "He only wants the king to make a formal declaration that proclaims the prince as his successor to the throne of Vatsa."

"Who is Harihara to tell our king what he should or should not do? Our king will do..."

"I will... make... the declaration."

Chandravardhan's words sliced through his minister's fevered rant like a sword, bearing a stunned silence in its wake. Dhanavantri and Shashivardhan stared at the king in surprise as the king passed a weary hand over his eyes; none of them observed Yashobhavi stiffen and pass a narrow, rigid glance from father to son.

"I will... do it for Sindhuvarta," Chandravardhan repeated. "Harihara can be... informed... of decision. We shall send... message to him... also. We accept Rukma as... future queen."

With a tired sigh, the king sank into his bed and turned on his side, signaling the desire for peace and quiet. As Shashivardhan unfolded a thin cotton shawl to spread over his father's feet, Dhanavantri rose from the stool by the foot of the bed.

"I shall take your leave, my king," he said. "I will be back to check on you in the evening." Bowing to Shashivardhan and Yashobhavi, he left the room.

The relief of having accomplished his mission lifted the physician's spirits, and there was a jauntiness in his stride as he retraced the way to the chamber allotted to him. So, when he exited a door into one of the passages, it was plain good fortune that averted a collision between him and a figure coming down the passage from the opposite direction.

"Oh, Pralupi!"

"You, councilor?" Pralupi was surprised to see him, but whether she was pleased or not, Dhanavantri couldn't be sure. With the princess, it had always been hard to tell. "What brings *you* here?"

"I came to have a look at the king… see if I could help with his ailment," the physician answered vaguely. "I heard you and Prince Himavardhan had gone to Kasi on a pilgrimage. When did you get back?"

"This morning. We were stranded in the floods," Pralupi answered. Looking squarely at Dhanavantri, she asked, "What news of Ghatakarpara? Is he back in Ujjayini yet?"

"He is still in Udaypuri." Not one question enquiring after the Queen Mother or her brothers or about the state of affairs in the city she had grown up in. All Pralupi seemed to care about these days was her son, Dhanavantri thought.

"Till when does Vikrama intend keeping him at the frontier?" Pralupi eyed the physician irritably, as if he was somehow responsible for Ghatakarpara's situation. "He should be in Ujjayini, learning how to run a kingdom."

"One can learn how to run a kingdom from anywhere," Dhanavantri blinked in confusion. "And to run a kingdom, one should learn to be a soldier first."

The princess twisted her lips into something that was a

cross between a smirk and a scowl. "At least I hope Amara Simha is taking good care of my son."

"Amara Simha is back in Ujjayini."

Pralupi's eyes flew open, and in their depths, Dhanavantri saw shock, rage and horror. "Ghatakarpara is all alone at the frontier?" she hissed. "What is Vikrama *thinking*? Has he gone mad?"

"There are thousands of soldiers and officers of the Imperial Army and the Frontier Guard in and around Udaypuri," the physician offered. "I don't know how Ghatakarpara could be alone at the frontier even if he wished to."

"Vikrama has lost his senses," Pralupi shook her head with vehemence. "My boy *mustn't* be at the frontier; it is not his place. Vikrama needs to be told..."

Brushing abruptly past Dhanavantri, she swept through the doorway and stomped down the shadowy passage, muttering agitatedly to herself, fists clenched in anger and distress.

* * *

A shadow appeared over the patch of sunlight that tumbled in through the open door of the armoury, making Kalidasa pause and look up from the whetstone where he had been honing his scimitar.

"Ah, Vikrama," the giant's dark, brooding face softened into a smile. "A pleasant surprise."

"I am glad it is pleasant," the samrat remarked with a smile that didn't quite make it to his eyes. He stepped into the armoury and looked around. The place was deserted – the king had already guessed as much when Kalidasa had addressed him by name – with most of the *samsaptakas* either in the training grounds, or back in their barracks after their routine exercises. A cloying scent of clove hung in the air, and

Vikramaditya's eyes went to the bowl of clove oil that the councilor was using to oil the scimitar.

"What brings you here?" Kalidasa asked, setting the sword down on the whetstone.

"It has been a while since we spoke as friends," the king shrugged lightly. He approached the whetstone, picked up the scimitar and held it to the light, feeling its edge with his thumb. "A really long while," he said for emphasis as he tested the weight and balance of the heavy sword by whirling it around in a few practised moves. The ease with which the samrat wielded the scimitar fetched an indulgent yet admiring glance from Kalidasa.

"If my memory serves me right, the last time we spoke as friends was the day Narada came calling."

Vikramaditya gazed at Kalidasa thoughtfully before nodding. "Are you done with this?" he asked, handing the sword back to the giant by its hilt. Seeing the councilor incline his head, the samrat reached for a rag to wipe the oil off his hands. "Let us get some fresh air then. The smell of cloves is stifling in here."

The sunshine that the two friends stepped into felt bright and warm on the skin, without being unpleasant. It was a welcome and uplifting day after the rains that had laid siege on Ujjayini, stirring nostalgia in Vikramaditya of the time he and Kalidasa used to roam the streets and parks of the city in quest of some exciting adventure or the other. That was before his coronation, when the burden of driving the barbarians out had rested on Vararuchi and the Acharya.

"Are you writing anything these days?" the samrat asked.

Kalidasa gave a wry smile. "The sword and the quill were never destined to bleed at the same time."

They walked for a while in silence – it seemed they had nothing much to talk about after all. Sensing the absurdity of the situation, the giant turned to Vikramaditya. "How's Vishakha?" he asked, regretting the question almost immediately upon seeing the dejection settle over his friend's face.

"The same," the samrat gave a small shake of his head. "Nothing's changed."

As if with a force of will, he faced Kalidasa. "But I am not going to lose hope," he continued, speaking partly to himself, instilling courage. "She remembered us showing her and Kshapanaka the way out of the Labyrinth, and me saving you from falling off the ledge. If she can remember once, she can remember again."

"She will, my friend." Kalidasa hoped he sounded a lot more confident than he felt. However, seeing Vikramaditya's downcast face, he said, "Do you regret sending the Heal… I mean, Shukracharya away?"

The samrat gave this a moment's thought. "Not for myself, no. Yet, I do realize many would have benefitted from his being around. Vishakha, the people of Ujjayini, *badi-maa*… you. Knowing this doesn't make it easy for me." Vikramaditya paused and placed a hand on his companion's shoulder. "For that I am sorry, my friend."

"Please don't shame me by tendering an apology, Vikrama," Kalidasa laid his own hand over the samrat's and gave it a reassuring pat. "I am already deep in your debt for everything you have done for me; an apology from you would crush me. No one doubts you did the right thing by asking Shukracharya to leave. Moreover, you heard what the raj-guru said – it is best I leave a past that had something to do with the Hunas buried deep. Ghosts that haunt cremation grounds should never be invited home."

Vikramaditya inclined his head in agreement. "When you started seeing these visions, why didn't you tell *me* about them?"

"You already had so much on your mind; I didn't want to burden you with my problems as well. I was also confused… I… didn't know what they meant… I still don't."

"Do the visions still persist?"

"All the time."

"The same ones? No changes?" The samrat looked closely at Kalidasa.

The councilor didn't reply immediately. "You know the one where I am sitting by this fire, and there is a man with a dagger and I know he is going to hurt me." Kalidasa paused to see if Vikramaditya was following him. "Well, last night, for the first time, I got a clear glimpse of the man's face. The one with the dagger, I mean. It is the same man who is chasing me on the horse, trying to kill me with an arrow. The same hard face with the *hriiz* on the forehead."

They had reached an open area next to the archery range. Vikramaditya's eyes strayed to a small, covered enclosure that had been erected in this open space, and he paused in his stride. Following his king's gaze, Kalidasa also drew to a halt.

Within the enclosure, eleven squat *kalashas* made of copper sat on a raised platform. Square pieces of red linen cloth covered the mouths of each *kalasha*, the cloth pieces held in place by strings tied around the *kalashas*' short necks. The eleven urns held the symbolic ashes of each of the eleven *samsaptakas* who had given up their lives defending Dvarka. Per *samsaptaka* tradition, the *kalashas* had been filled with sacrificial ash when the eleven warriors had first taken the Death Oath – every *samsaptaka* performed his own last rites as part of the initiation into the elite unit. Now that they were dead, their urns awaited an auspicious hour so the ashes they contained could be consecrated in the Kshipra.

"The message from Vararuchi said they made Avanti proud," said the samrat. "Chief Yugandhara is having a memorial built for them. There will be a plaque in Dvarka bearing Udayasanga's name, with the honorary title of Eternal Friend of the Anartas bestowed on him." It was Vikramaditya's turn to lay a comforting hand on Kalidasa's shoulder. "Your men will be remembered as heroes, friend."

The giant gave a quick nod, but stayed silent for a while longer. "Udayasanga was one of the best we had, and as true a friend as any," he said quietly. "The Hunas have taken too much from me. A time will come when they will have to pay for this. I wait for that time."

* * *

"Are you really sending me back to Devaloka, lord?"

Menaka's large, imploring eyes swam with hope and relief as they sought out Kubera's coal black ones, yet there was a trickle of fear in her voice, born of the doubt that this was just another of the many perverse games the yaksha loved indulging in.

The yaksha lord's head rolled sidewise on his squat, fleshy neck in what could have been a shrug or an indeterminate nod. Reclining on a round couch, surrounded by silken bolsters, the mists from Lake Alaka swirling around him like incense, Kubera continued staring at the apsara, his face hard and inscrutable. The expanse of his stomach and chest rose and fell to his breathing, but other than that, hardly a muscle moved in that great mass of flesh and hair.

"Why, my lord?" Menaka asked, suddenly afraid that she had done something to earn the yaksha's displeasure. She was Indra's gift to the master of Alaka, and it was her duty to please her new lord, no matter how abhorrent the task. "If I have failed in my duties..."

"The deal was that I could keep you in Alaka on the condition that I did what the lord of the devas wanted of me," Kubera interrupted the apsara harshly. "You are being returned because I have failed to keep my end of the bargain." The yaksha's thick lips peeled back in a bitter sneer. "If nothing else, we yakshas at least honour our word."

"Is there a message you would like me to convey to the deva lord?" Menaka asked, struggling to contain the surge of respite coursing through her body.

"Your return to Devaloka is all the message that Indra would need," said Kubera, his gaze sliding over Menaka, feasting on her curves before settling on her bare, milk-white midriff. Feeling his breath suddenly grow ragged in his throat, the yaksha shook himself with an effort and tore glazed eyes away from the tempting figure standing before him. At a wave of his hand, the mist around the apsara receded to reveal a short flight of steps that led away to the right. A small, oval coracle nudged the bottommost step, lapped by the lake's waters.

"This will take you to the far shore, where you will find a palanquin waiting," Kubera said, pointing to the boat. "The palanquin will bear you back to Amaravati. Now go – before I change my mind about you."

The yaksha lord waited for the mist to close around Menaka before snapping his fingers. This time, the curtain of mist behind Kubera parted, and from within its shifting folds two figures emerged. Both were yakshas, bear-like in build and appearance, but one walked in a broken, hobbling gait, his shoulders badly stooped and misshapen. At the sight of the deformed yaksha, a scowl spread across Kubera's face.

He surveyed the newcomers critically while they bowed to him, before fixing the cripple with a glare that would have melted stone.

"You failed," he said in a pithy growl.

"Pardon me, my lord, but I would have succeeded had the mahaguru Shukracharya not come in the way. He had cast powerful protective spells over the human queen. I could do nothing to her."

"From what I understand, Shukracharya put in an appearance very late," Kubera raised an eyebrow. "What stopped you from killing the queen earlier?"

"The king, my lord," the yaksha kept his eyes on the floor. "He is alert, fast and fearless. But I had him on the run and would still have killed the queen were it not for the mahaguru."

Kubera rose and walked slowly toward the ring of mist. A path opened before him, and he slipped through onto a marble promenade lined with perfumed fountains on both sides, their jets arcing and meeting overhead to form a glimmering archway. Yet, no water fell on the promenade, and the marble was cool but dry under the yaksha lord's feet.

"You are certain it was Shukracharya?"

"I am, my lord." The yakshas had followed their overlord, the cripple shuffling and dragging himself along. "I recognized him when he fought me. He nearly had me in his control. I had no choice but to flee, master of Alaka."

"Besides our humiliation, do you know what else your failure has cost us?" Kubera asked, his voice aching with lust and longing as he watched a small boat dwindle into the distance, tugged along by the currents and the unseen hands of mist-wraiths. "Indra had promised us Menaka and a dozen other apsaras in exchange for the human queen's life." He turned and heaped a scornful look on the yaksha. "Leave us alone."

Once they had the terrace to themselves, Kubera considered the second yaksha. "Do you believe it was Shukracharya?"

"I do, my lord," the yaksha replied. "Our brother couldn't have been mistaken. Look at what has happened to him – broken in flesh and spirit. No human could have done that to him, lord."

"The lord of the devas wants to destroy the one thing that the human king holds dearest to his heart. And the mahaguru of the asuras arrives in time to *prevent* its destruction." Kubera scratched his beard thoughtfully. "It makes me wonder what is so unique about this human king."

"Didn't the lord of Devaloka tell you, master?" the minion enquired.

"I asked, but he didn't say. And I didn't press him. Sometimes, it is enough to agree on a deal when the price is right." Kubera was silent for a moment. "But now we have to know. I want you to learn everything there is to know about this human king, and why the devas and the asuras are so interested in him. Find out if there is anything we yakshas can gain from this king's survival – or from his destruction."

Meru

The tip of the sword was inches away from Jayanta's soft, white throat, the blade quivering in Indra's hand as the lord of the devas fought to contain his rage. Jayanta's face was drained of blood, and his eyes twitched frantically between the sword under his chin and his father's face, flushed and livid under the great golden beard.

"You think you are smart enough to talk back to your father, is it?" Indra growled through gritted teeth. "You barely make it back alive from your ill-conceived adventure, and you have the impudence to teach me the responsibilities of the king of Devaloka?"

Mastering his temper, the deva lord loosened his hold on Jayanta's shoulder and stepped back. Shoving his sword back into its sheath, he whirled around to Brihaspati. "What have I done to deserve this for a son, gurudev? It has to be the impure asura blood of his mother."

The prince gave Brihaspati a sullen look, and then his gaze drifted to Narada, standing a little way behind Indra, a hint of a smirk on his lips. Jayanta's eyes flitted to Urvashi next, and a rush of shame overcame him, burying him in the landslide of his father's insults. Pains and aches from the abortive summoning of Ahi still tortured his body, but observing the expression of apathy on the apsara's face was like having a dagger driven through his ribs.

When the kinnara had borne his tortured body into Amaravati the previous night, he hadn't expected concern or sympathy from his father or Narada or Brihaspati. But he had hoped Urvashi would be there to comfort him and appreciate what he had tried to do for Devaloka. Instead, the apsara just stood there, remote and indifferent, watching his debasement.

"– the gurudev and Narada about having discovered the mantra?" His father's voice floated through the haze of anger, despair and self-loathing, and it took Jayanta a moment to realize that Indra was not through with him yet. "Amaravati could have been saved from destruction had we known about Ahi and the mantra. Do you realize that? We could have used Ahi to defend ourselves from the vyalas. Do you realize that? Of course you don't! You chose to keep Ahi a secret, and now half the city lies in ruins. But why would you care?"

"All I wanted to do was to surprise you with the Halahala, father," the prince mumbled in his defence.

"Oh!" Indra considered his son in mock interest. "Come on then, surprise me. Where is the Halahala?"

Jayanta's chin drooped to his chest and he studied his toes.

"And how exactly did you plan to get hold of Veeshada's dagger once Ahi had flattened the human kingdom? Did you have even an inkling of where the dagger was? Did you expect Vikramaditya to come crawling to you, dagger in hand, pleading for mercy, or did you intend scavenging through the rubble until you found it?" Indra paused, but only to catch his breath. "I'm sure it never occurred to you that there might have been asuras lurking around the city, waiting for an opportunity to pounce on the dagger."

The deva lord turned and walked over to one of the windows that overlooked the southern drawbridge. Hands on hips, for a full minute he watched the shadows slink off the bridge as the sun gained the sky. "Be gone, you fool," he spat, throwing Jayanta a contemptuous glance over his shoulder. "Go play with your wooden swords and blunt spears. Get lost!"

The prince cut a hurried path across the room, keeping his face averted from Brihaspati, Narada and Urvashi so they couldn't see the hot tears scalding his eyelashes as outrage, insult and hatred smothered him from all sides.

Indra's broad back stayed turned in disdain, and it was only when the patter of his son's feet died away that he swiveled to face the room. Urvashi immediately drew near, soft and quiet as gossamer. "You shouldn't be so harsh on him, my lord," she murmured. "Whatever he does is only to prove himself worthy in your eyes. He only wants to show you that he's now a man."

"Humph!" Indra gave his head a dismissive flick as he picked up a goblet of soma resting on a side table. "He only wants to show *you* he's a man," he corrected. "*You* are all that the brat wants, and he'll do anything to have you. And you encourage him with your smiles and sulks – I know all about it, so don't deny it."

"Is my lord jealous of his son?" the apsara fluttered her eyelids at the lord of the devas and ran a finger down his cheek. "And does my lord doubt my affections?"

Brihaspati chose that moment to address Indra. "Urvashi is right, lord," he said, taking two steps forward. "You shouldn't be so harsh on Jayanta. After all, we now know that the prince can summon Ahi, and that is indeed a rare talent – one we could use should the need arise."

"What good would that serve?" the deva lord asked irritably. "He might be able to summon Ahi, but he doesn't have it in him to bend the monster to do his bidding. An iron will is required to control the serpent-dragon. That is sadly lacking in Jayanta."

"His will can be tempered and strengthened like steel," the chamberlain insisted. "I can see to it that the prince masters the art of exercising control of his will."

"You may, if you think it will serve any purpose, gurudev." Indra gave an uncaring shrug. Snapping his head in impatience, he looked at Narada. "What have we done with the kinnara who took him to Sindhuvarta? I want it flogged in a public square and made an example of."

"We mustn't forget that the kinnara tended to the prince and brought him back to the safety of Devaloka, my lord," the diplomat reminded gently. "It is my humble opinion that we let the kinnara lord Tribhanu mete out a fitting punishment. These are troubled times and it is recommended we keep allies like Tribhanu on our side."

"Humph!" Indra snorted again, but the wisdom of Narada's words kept him from arguing. "Do what is necessary, but make it clear to Tribhanu that no kinnara is to help that foolish son of mine, no matter what inducements are offered..."

A looming shadow covered the doorway, interrupting the lord of the devas. Looking up, Indra saw a garuda fold its wings and step over the threshold. The scout-birds had nearly gone extinct, but fortunately for the devas, a handful had been so far to the north and the east that they had escaped the vyalas' cacophonous assault. The garuda standing at the door was one such survivor.

"Salutations, mighty lord," the garuda bowed, the words emerging from its throat in a weary croak.

"What is it?" Indra arched an imperious eyebrow.

"I bring news of the asura king Hiranyaksha and mahaguru Shukracharya, my lord. Hiranyaksha and the mahaguru arrived at Mount Meru with a contingent of asuras a little after daybreak. They have been welcomed as you had instructed, and await an audience with you."

* * *

Carried from lip to ear by traders, travelling artisans and Avanti's own soldiers at speeds that would have put town criers to shame, the reports of the extraordinary occurrences in Ujjayini had started reaching Vararuchi right after his departure from Raivata. All along the long road back to Ujjayini, information came to him in disjointed little nuggets, believable at times, unreliable or patently exaggerated at others. But over the course of the journey, the samrat's half-brother had been able to piece together a fairly accurate picture of the events that had transpired in the city in his absence.

Still, nothing had quite prepared him for the devastation that he had witnessed once he crossed the Kshiрra and entered Ujjayini by its western gate. And though over half a day had passed since his return, the dismay and disbelief hadn't yet fully left him. Even now, as he rode the capital's streets in Amara Simha's company, he couldn't help staring wide-eyed at the wrecked neighbourhoods struggling to stitch themselves back into the city's fabric.

"You would not believe how overjoyed we were to see the serpent decimate the Huna navy," he said to Amara Simha with a regretful shake of his head. "No one had any idea of what it was, where it had come from or where it went, but each one of us in Dvarka was eternally grateful to the beast for having saved us that morning. Had I only known of its true intent…" he trailed off, dropping his head in remorse for having partaken in the rejoicing.

"There's nothing to feel bad about," Amara Simha shrugged. "You had no way of knowing. And had you even known, there was nothing you could have done about it." The brawny councilor's lips twisted in a sour smile. "At least the monster did its bit of good by wiping out the Huna fleet."

They rode in silence for a while.

"Did you get to meet the Samrat?" Amara Simha asked.

"I went to see him, but he was asleep." Vararuchi reined in his horse to allow a handcart loaded with sand and blocks of stone to trundle past. "I was told he had been awake by Vishakha's side almost all night."

Amara Simha nodded. "She remembered him," he said. "Just moments before the yaksha attacked. So near, yet so far. I think that's what hurts Vikrama the most." After a moment's silence, he heaved a despairing sigh. "Had one of us councilors been with them, it might have turned out differently."

"How?"

"Our... talents. What the Mother Oracle calls *gifts*. Those might have come in handy against the yaksha."

"You really did turn into a lion?" Vararuchi turned to his companion in curiosity.

"I didn't get to see my face, but... yes, a part of me did." Amara Simha looked down at his palms and forearms, and flexed his fingers at the memory of the claws that had appeared at the tips. "Those who saw me said it was a sight."

"Just once? You haven't done it again?"

"It apparently takes practice. That's what the oracle told Shanku. The girl has been working on her gift – you must see her," Amara Simha shook his head in amazement. "It is downright creepy the way she vanishes and appears at will."

"She can go *anywhere* she wants?" Vararuchi raised his eyebrows.

"Anywhere within a radius of a few miles, yes. She must also be familiar with the place she wants to go to beforehand – she can't travel to places she doesn't know anything about or has never been to before."

"Still impressive." Vararuchi paused. "Also what Kshapanaka and Varahamihira can do."

"Kshapanaka was amazing. You know something?" Amara Simha looked at Vararuchi. "Varahamihira did a small experiment a few days ago. He got Kshapanaka to shoot a dozen arrows at a target and had the arrowheads tested. He found nothing in them – they were just plain metal barbs. Then he got her to shoot another dozen arrows, but this time he worked her rage up by talking to her about the yaksha and Vishakha. He then tested this set of arrows as well. You know what he found?"

"Venom?" Vararuchi guessed.

For a second, Amara Simha looked stricken at having been robbed of the joy of presenting his own narrative's triumphant climax. "Yes," he said with a dumpish shrug, but he recovered quickly. "Kshapanaka's gift is fueled by anger. Varahamihira thinks even mine might be. And..." he paused dramatically and edged his horse around so he could face Vararuchi. "Varahamihira thinks your leap that brought the rakshasa down in the market square is *your* gift. We have also been hearing accounts of some of the impossible things you did battling the Hunas on their ship."

"I have been wondering about it," the king's half-brother confessed. "It had me worried... it is not natural, after all. But yes, now that I see a pattern..." He looked right at Amara Simha. "How is this happening all of a sudden? Where did these gifts or whatever you call it come from?"

"No idea. I am as much in the dark as..." Amara Simha stopped as his eyes switched to a point a little above and behind Vararuchi. "Ah, look who is here," he exclaimed.

Glancing over his right shoulder, Vararuchi saw Kalidasa standing on the landing of an open stairway that led down from the two-storied building directly behind him. The giant had been in the process of descending the steps when he had noticed the two councilors on the road, and now he stood staring down at Vararuchi with a strange, preoccupied expression.

"Kalidasa, greetings..." Vararuchi said. Then, noticing the bemused look on the poet's face, he gave a mild frown. "Is something the matter?"

The giant blinked a couple of times and cocked his head to one side, as if pondering something over. "I... no, nothing," he shook his head. "When did you return?"

"Just this morning."

"What are you doing here?" Amara Simha enquired.

"One of the *samsaptakas* who went with you to Dvarka lived here," the giant answered, nodding at Vararuchi. "One of the eleven who didn't come back. He has left behind an old father and a much younger brother. They have no one else, so I dropped by to meet them."

"I am sorry," Vararuchi murmured and looked up at the house that Kalidasa had exited.

"Don't be, brother," said the giant. "He was a Warrior of the Oath, and he fought and died bravely. Let that be his abiding memory. That is what I told the old man and the kid as well."

Vararuchi inclined his head in acceptance.

"Are you returning to the palace?" Amara Simha asked. Seeing Kalidasa nod, he jerked his head. "Come along then. We're also headed that way."

"My horse is tethered on the other side," the giant pointed down an alley. "Go ahead. I will fetch it and join you."

As Vararuchi and Amara Simha prodded their mounts forward, Kalidasa ducked into the alleyway. Walking along the narrow, checkered stretch of pavement dappled with sunlight, the giant blinked again, trying to recollect a thought – *an awareness?* – that had flitted through his mind like an apparition as he had come down the stairs. One moment it had been there, a doe in the mist – *a snake in the grass?* – but the next it was gone, a shadow in the mind's eye, more imagined than real.

Kalidasa riffled through the compartments of his mind, searching for a remnant of the thought so he could pick up the trail again, but whatever it was stayed two steps ahead, eluding him.

* * *

"We are glad the masters of Patala see opportunity in collaborating with the devas."

Narada beamed a shiny, artificial smile at Hiranyaksha and Shukracharya from across the stretch of polished teakwood where the two estranged sets of Sage Kashyapa's descendants sat in negotiation.

For all the goodwill and enthusiasm that the diplomat exuded, there was a marked lack of cheer among those seated in the ornate gazebo, and the mood was edgy as Hiranyaksha and Indra missed no opportunity to glower at each other. Shukracharya and Brihaspati didn't help the situation with their poorly concealed dislike for one another, so the misty breeze that blew through the forest of Himavanta – laden with the rich scents of devadaru, narilata and a hundred varieties of wild orchid – failed to have a soothing effect on the small gathering.

"It is not a question of opportunity. It is a matter of need," Shukracharya answered curtly.

"Whose need?" Brihaspati asked in a needling tone. "Yours or ours?"

Favouring the chamberlain with a sour look, the high priest answered, "The question would have been unnecessary had you been better qualified to comprehend the problem facing us, gurudev. But as you so kindly ask, let me tell you that the need is both ours *and* yours."

Narada winced inwardly at Shukracharya's effrontery and

braced himself for a cutting retort from Brihaspati. The rivalry between the two was legendary, and dated back to the time they were pupils training together under Sage Angirasa, then chamberlain of Devaloka. Though neck to neck in talent and application, the consensus was that Shukracharya was the marginally better student – and the one most likely to succeed Angirasa as the spiritual guru of the devas. However, to the surprise of many, at the time of anointing a new chamberlain, Angirasa picked his own son Brihaspati over Shukracharya. Not one to give in without a fight, Shukracharya accused Angirasa of favouritism and appealed to the council of Devaloka to adjudicate the matter. It will never be known whether it was out of respect for Angirasa or a general reluctance to rocking the boat, but the devas refused to overturn Angirasa's decision – a costly mistake, Narada had often admitted to himself in private later.

Having staked his reputation on the challenge, Shukracharya suffered a grave loss of face – to say nothing of having earned the displeasure of Brihaspati, Devaloka's new chamberlain. Embittered by what he saw as an abject pandering to Angirasa's whim – and a support of nepotism over meritocracy – the young sage swore vengeance on the deva council and left Amaravati for Patala, where, out of spite, he offered his services to the asuras. The asuras promptly made Shukracharya their high priest, fuelling more hatred between Angirasa's former pupils.

"*Need*," Indra answered in place of the chamberlain. "You speak as if you are in mortal fear of the human king. One defeat at his hands and the mighty asuras appear to have lost the appetite to fight." The lord of the devas looked from Narada to Brihaspati, a smirk playing on his lips.

"One defeat is a little more dignified than three at a human's hands." It was Hiranyaksha's turn to ratchet up the sarcasm.

Narada felt disheartened. He had brought the two sides together to discuss peace, but there was the history of mistrust and betrayals to surmount first. Here, in this very gazebo, under the monastic shadow of Mount Meru, Puloman had died when a meeting called for peace had escalated into a war of words and got out of hand; the diplomat worried that they were heading down that same path all over again.

"You are right when you say I fear the human king cannot be defeated," Shukracharya interjected in a sombre tone that made everyone look at him in surprise. "We have learnt it the hard way, and so have you."

"A setback or two doesn't mean he can't be defeated," Indra countered, but the arrogance had suddenly gone out of his voice, replaced with doubt. "He is only human, after all."

"We sent Andhaka and a pishacha army. You sent the Ashvin Brotherhood, the Maruts and Ahi." The high priest observed the devas exchange furtive glances at the mention of the serpent-dragon, and wondered why. "One would think this would have been enough to break any enemy. But the human king still stands. I have spent a lot of time in the king's palace, so…"

"You were in the king's palace?" Brihaspati blurted, the shock making him shed his usual hostility toward the high priest.

"I was looking for a way to get to Veeshada's dagger," Shukracharya spread his hands and said with surprising candour. "It is a long story, but what is important is that I saw enough to realize he can't be defeated by you or us – or both of us together. Not right now, at least."

"May I ask what makes you so certain, mahaguru?" Narada peered at Shukracharya.

"What do you know of the Nine Pearls?"

The devas looked at one another. "The Nine Sacred

Pearls?" Indra's brow crinkled in a dubious frown. "They don't exist. Everyone knows that."

"Until not very long ago, all of you in Amaravati thought the vyalas didn't exist." Shukracharya saw the devas' faces darken at the mention of the gruesome beasts. "Until a little while ago, we in Patala believed the mantra to raise Ahi had been destroyed for good."

"So the Nine Pearls exist. What about them?" Brihaspati asked.

"Vikramaditya has a council of nine warriors. Each of them bears one of the Nine Pearls." The high priest paused to assess the three devas across the table. "I have seen and heard about how the powers of the pearls manifest in the councilors. One of them is immune to venom, another transforms into a man-lion, while a third can appear and disappear at will. I was right beside one of them when he conjured an energy shield out of thin air to block Ahi's venom. And you know the interesting thing? Most of them don't even know what they are doing, what powers they possess. They are seeing and using these powers for the first time."

"How did they acquire these powers?" Indra asked, flustered.

"They have always had these powers, only locked away safely. *I* was responsible for their unlocking," Shukracharya gave a sheepish nod. "When the Maruts came to claim Veeshada's dagger, I cast a Regeneration Spell over Ujjayini to render the king's army hardier, so they could counter the attack. Unfortunately, the spell worked too well. It stimulated the dormant power of the pearls and brought them out into the open."

"You haven't changed a bit," Brihaspati's tone was mocking, irascible. "Even under father's tutelage, you were impulsive, doing things without considering the consequences. Look where your rashness has landed us."

"Pardon me, mahaguru," Narada butted in, nipping

another heated exchange in the bud. "I fail to understand how the Nine Pearls are an impediment to defeating the king."

"The Nine Pearls are designed to protect powerful things from coming to harm – it could be anything, a place, an energy source... or, as in this case, the human king. It is not a coincidence that all nine bearers of the pearls are the king's councilors. That is the way it has been ordained. The Nine Pearls are interdependent and draw their strength from one another, growing stronger and stronger as each pearl gains in strength. It is a virtuous cycle. And the stronger they grow, the better they protect the thing they have been designed to protect." The high priest paused to let his words sink in. "See the problem we are up against?"

The sighing of the wind in the devadarus and the rush of a hidden mountain stream filled the silence that had laid siege to the gazebo. Mist drifted past the assembly seated around the teakwood table, the edge of combativeness ripped out by the sobering realization of the challenge they were facing.

"You must have seen a way around this," Indra looked perceptively from Hiranyaksha to Shukracharya. "You wouldn't have made this journey all the way from Patala just to tell us it can't be done."

"Oh, there is a way," the high priest smiled. "There is *always* a way." He looked around the table, the smile going cold on his face. "As long as the Council of Nine stays together, nothing can happen to the king. Inversely, to get to the king, we only have to weaken the force that the Nine Pearls exert on one another. We have to drive a wedge between the pearls, and then keep driving them apart."

"We break the chain that binds the councilors together... their unity," said Narada. "How?"

A wolfish smile lit up the high priest's countenance. "I had the opportunity to observe the king and the councilors closely when I was at the palace, and upon leaving Ujjayini,

I applied myself to learning everything I could about them. I have discovered deeply guarded secrets and bitter truths that can divide the king and his council – fissures that run deep, which the humans themselves are yet ignorant of, and are ours to exploit. Already, with some help from me, the wheels have been set in motion to trigger an initial crack in their unity – any moment now, *that* rift will tear into the open. That will only be the beginning, though. There is potential to split the palace right down the middle –" rubbing his hands together, Shukracharya fixed on Indra, "– but for that, I will need your help. This can be the revenge you have been thirsting for."

"Tell me what I should do, mahaguru."

Shukracharya began detailing his plot, and shedding their antagonism, Indra and Hiranyaksha drew closer in anticipation of the misfortunes that would strike Vikramaditya down.

Horseman

Water streamed off Kalidasa's head, neck and shoulders in rivulets as he bent low over the bubbling fountain, bracing his hands against its stony rim for support, staring down into the broad bowl of dark, glistening water. His reflection bobbed amidst the ripples, a dull silhouette against the starlit sky.

"*Umg'a, Thra'akha... umg'a*!"

Jump, Thra'akha... jump!

"Is everything alright, your honour?"

Kalidasa gave a start and turned. A sentry stood in the shadows at the edge of the terrace, right by the gallery that gave into the councilors' bedchambers. The soldier looked unsure, caught in two minds over approaching the *samsaptaka* commander.

"Yes... I'm fine," the giant blurted. "It's... just the heat. You may go."

The sentry withdrew with a short bow, returning to his nocturnal vigil of the palace. Kalidasa waited for him to disappear from view before making a slow, ponderous plod back to his quarters. It was hardly twenty paces from the fountain to his bedchamber, but by the time the councilor shut the door behind him, sweat had once again broken out on his brow, and ran freely down his neck and jawline.

"*Umg'a, Thra'akha... umg'a!*"

Somewhere in his sleep, just like that, he had understood what the man wielding the bow and arrow was yelling. He had also understood the words that had escaped his own lips in a shriek before the man had responded, urging him to jump.

"*Ba... unnu pa'hze!*" Father, help me!

Father.

The dark face behind the drawn bow, bronzed by the heat of the desert sun. The curly beard and the ferocious black moustache, speckled with the grey of time. The fierce black eyes of a predator that softened and glowed with pride whenever they settled on him. The *hriiz* on his forehead, strong, black and talismanic. *Ba*. Father.

"*A'po h'lumi oa, ba?*"

He remembered sitting across the ritual fire, watching his father hone and cleanse the dagger in the sacred flames as the priests sat around chanting ancient hymns to propitiate the desert scorpion. He recalled the fear creeping over him as he looked at the gleaming dagger. He recalled wondering aloud if the dagger would hurt a lot as it cut and gouged the skin and flesh on his own forehead.

"*Z'ah, z'ah,*" his father had replied with a kind chuckle. Not at all.

Examining the dagger's edge in the firelight, he had added, "*A'hiy h'lumi? Zuh te'i Ga'ur Thra'akha.*" What pain? You are Ga'ur Thra'akha, the Gift of Death itself. "*Ini amgo du'z... duz'ur Zho E'rami.*" Moreover, you are my son... son of Zho E'rami, Zho the Fearless.

Kalidasa also remembered the hunt. All of them, charging across the open plain in pursuit of the herd of deer. It had been his first hunt, and he had been brimming with excitement as his father and his men had first stalked, then cornered their prey, hunting the deer down with ruthless precision. He had been too small to wield a weapon, but the thrill of the chase had still been heady...

Then, without warning, his horse had bolted.

He had hung on to the bucking beast for dear life, and it was plain luck that his father caught sight of the crazed horse making a beeline for the dense forest at the edge of the plain. His father had given chase, screaming at him to leap off the horse before it crashed into the trees and the undergrowth. But terror had made him numb and he clung to his mount's neck, ignoring his father's commands. In a last-ditch effort, his father had raised his bow and taken aim at the horse with the intention of stopping it with an arrow.

"*Umg'a, Thra'akha... umg'a*!" Jump, Thra'akha... jump!

Perhaps it was fear, perhaps it was his father's words finally getting through to him, but he had leaped off, landing hard and bouncing and rolling... He had ended up with a dislocated shoulder; the horse disappeared into the forest, never to be seen again.

Standing in his chamber, absently towelling sweat and water off his sculpted chest and shoulders, Kalidasa suddenly recalled something else. *Smoke*. Curtains and curtains of white smoke swirling around him, filled with the smell of burning wood. And charred flesh.

He recalled lying on his stomach and looking down into a valley where some buildings had been set ablaze. He recalled watching a knot of soldiers hustle four prisoners – three women, one man, all in chains – into a granary. The soldiers had then set the granary on fire, burning their prisoners alive.

The towel dropped from the councilor's nerveless fingers. He reeled at the memory of the smoke and the blazing granary. His throat felt parched, as if the heat from those flames had dehydrated him. The room swam before his eyes, tilting steeply one way, then rocking the other. Kalidasa lurched to the nearest wall and rested his back against it, drawing support from its solidity. He bent his knees and slid to the floor.

The man whom the soldiers had pushed into the granary was Zho E'rami. Huna warlord. *Ba*. Father. Strong, unbending, holding his head high until his last breath. The women… one was his elder sister, Ei'hi. One, a widowed aunt. The third, the aunt's daughter. The women's screams issued from the granary as another sound filled his ears – sandalled feet pounding on earth, drawing closer. And all the while, his eyes on the horseman.

The horseman. The one who had ordered the granary to be torched with his family trapped inside. The leader of the soldiers. There was something familiar about him, the way he sat on his saddle, the slight slouch of his left shoulder…

That was when everything came back to the giant in a boiling, seething tide. *Everything*.

* * *

Hearing the heavy door creak on its hinges, Vikramaditya looked up to see Pralupi flounce unceremoniously into the room.

"I need to speak with you, Vikrama." The princess took three steps forward and stopped, lips pursed into a thin line, waiting for the king to respond. If she noticed Vishakha lying in her bed, pale and detached, she gave no indication of it, and she roundly ignored the two maids and the matron entrusted with the queen's care.

The samrat raised an eyebrow at his sister in surprise, taking in the fatigue that lined her face and cast dark circles around her eyes. "I didn't know you were expected in Ujjayini," he said. "When did you arrive?"

"Last night." Pralupi's manner was abrupt. "Can we talk?"

Vikramaditya glanced out of the open window. The sun hadn't quite cleared the horizon, and the mist still hung in blankets over the lake. The breeze that blew past the billowing brocade curtains bore a mild nip that sent gooseflesh along the king's arms. "It is still early. Maybe once you are properly rested..."

"I have rested enough." Pralupi crossed her arms and planted herself square so her intention was plain to everyone in the room.

Vikramaditya sighed. From as far back as he cared to remember, this was how it had been with Pralupi. Obstinate and demanding, bent on having her way every time. Age had robbed much from his sister, but regrettably, it had left her dour mulishness untouched.

With a nod, the king rose from the queen's side. He paused to give Vishakha a tender glance, bending down to tuck back a curl of hair that had escaped from behind her ear. His fingers strayed down one cheek, brushing softly against her skin, the lightest of caresses, and then he was striding away from the bed, businesslike. "Come," he said to Pralupi, gesturing to the door.

Not another word was exchanged until the siblings had crossed to a private alcove abutting a terrace at the other end of the gallery. The samrat stopped to ascertain they were alone, before turning to Pralupi. "So what new crisis brings you all this way to Ujjayini?" he asked without preamble.

"You were behind the move to have Shashivardhan declared successor to Vatsa's throne."

Thrown off guard, Vikramaditya blinked at his sister. Finally, he gave a small, noncommittal shrug.

"Why?" Pralupi's tone was waspish. "I thought we had an understanding that you would get Chandravardhan to make Ghatakarpara the next king."

"What understanding?" Vikramaditya stared at Pralupi in

amazement. "I had made it perfectly clear that I was *not* going to tell King Chandravardhan anything to that effect. I had told you that succession to Vatsa's throne is Vatsa's internal matter, and I shall not interfere with it in any way."

"That did not stop you from sending Dhanavantri to manipulate Chandravardhan into naming Shashivardhan as the next king," the princess appraised her brother with a sneer. "Isn't that interference in Vatsa's affairs? You got the Acharya to browbeat King Harihara into breaking off Rukma's alliance with Shoorasena and have her marry Shashivardhan instead. Isn't *that* interference in Heheya's affairs? Or is Rukma's marriage no longer an internal matter for her father to decide for himself?"

Vikramaditya flinched inwardly, stung by the truth in Pralupi's words.

"All this talk about not interfering in your allies' decisions is just that – talk. You have no qualms about meddling in their lives when it suits you, so spare me the moral high ground."

"You appear to know a lot about what's happening in the kingdoms of Sindhuvarta, so I imagine you would be wise enough to appreciate the reasons behind what you term as my meddling," the king replied. In truth, Pralupi had never cared much about Avanti's own politics, so the extent of her knowledge of the goings-on in the rest of Sindhuvarta surprised Vikramaditya. "I'm doing what is needed to keep us strong and united in the face of the growing threat from the Hunas and the Sakas."

Pralupi considered the king for a moment from under arched eyebrows. "The barbarians pose a real threat, yet you choose to keep my son at the frontier instead of recalling him to Ujjayini?" she unexpectedly opened a new front of attack. "You sent for Amara Simha, who has experience in fighting the Hunas, but you leave my boy at the mercy of those savages? How can you do this – he is your own nephew, *your own blood*!" The princess' voice rose at the last few words, sharp and hysterical. "Why is he even at the frontier?"

"The frontier makes one hard; the palace makes one soft. Ghatakarpara is learning to be a soldier," the samrat tried to reason, even as he struggled to control his own voice. "If the Hunas cross into Sindhuvarta, he will have to fight like one, so it is better he equips himself as best as he can. Look at it as a gift from an uncle to a nephew."

"The uncle could apply himself toward making the nephew the next king of Vatsa," Pralupi suggested tetchily. "That would be a more welcome gift."

"That won't happen. Shashivardhan is Chandravardhan's rightful heir, and now that..."

"Shashivardhan will squander everything he inherits in wine and dice," the princess spat harshly. "Everyone in Vatsa knows that. Even those in Chandravardhan's council don't trust the son to mend his ways. Only *you* are blind to that fact."

"Who doesn't trust Shashivardhan?" Vikramaditya asked, surprised. Knowing he might not get a straight answer to that, he gave a dismissive shake of his head. "I doubt you would be able to name a single councilor who doesn't have faith in Shashivardhan's capabilities."

"Yashobhavi," Pralupi took the bait.

Councilor Yashobhavi. That was whom his sister was getting all her information from. The samrat filed the information away carefully. "Does Yashobhavi have a solution to his fears?" he asked, hoping the question seemed nonchalant enough.

"He too believes Ghatakarpara would be the ideal choice as Vatsa's next king."

Vikramaditya stared, too stupefied to react. What exactly was he hearing? Was his sister making all this up to somehow nudge him into acting on her behalf, or was this the truth? How far did Pralupi's influence in Kausambi really extend? Was it just to Yashobhavi, a man whom Chandravardhan trusted implicitly, or were there other councilors in her sway as well?

"See, I told you," Pralupi looked at the king triumphantly. "Ghatakarpara is the right one to succeed to the throne, brother. It is not too late – he can still be king, if you will it. He will be welcomed by Vatsa's council, I assure you. And if you are worried about Harihara giving Rukma away to Shoorasena... well, Harihara wants a king as his son-in-law. Would it matter to him if that king is Ghatakarpara instead of Shashivardhan? My son will accept Rukma as a bride..."

"No," Vikramaditya shook his head, dazed. Then, more vehemently, "No, I can't do this. Not to King Chandravardhan."

"You *can*, but you won't," the princess narrowed baleful eyes on her brother. "Because there is nothing in it for you. You want everyone to see you as the good and just samrat, the noble friend. So what if that leads to the fall and ultimate ruination of an allied kingdom? You would rather sit back and watch than muddy your hands trying to save an ally. Your image would remain perfect and untarnished. That is all you care for."

"You can twist the facts to draw any conclusion you choose, but no..." There was hurt in Vikramaditya's voice. "This matter is closed." He turned away, unwilling to prolong the absurd argument. Pralupi, however, stopped him short.

"I want you to call Ghatakarpara back to Ujjayini," she said. In a challenging tone she added, "Or is that also something you can't do?"

"It is something I *won't* do," the king corrected, drawing himself to his full height. "My nephew volunteered to go to the frontier knowing the Hunas were coming. I will not insult his courage and self-belief by summoning him back to the palace. He went by his free will. When he returns, it will be by his own free will."

"Then you should hope nothing happens to him there,"

Pralupi warned. "If something does, I shall hold you accountable..."

A flurry of footsteps on the stairway interrupted the siblings. Vikramaditya turned to see a soldier rush up the steps, two at a time, until he made it to the landing and caught sight of the king and his sister.

"Salutations, Samrat... salutations, my princess," the soldier gasped for breath, bowing.

"We are busy," Pralupi snapped, impatient.

"Salutations, soldier," Vikramaditya overruled his sister with deliberate calm. "What is it?"

"Your honour, Councilor Kalidasa..." the soldier hesitated, his eyes shifting between the samrat and Pralupi. Seeing the samrat give a brisk, encouraging nod, he said, "The councilor demands an audience with you and the council in the Throne Room, your honour."

"The Throne Room?"

"Yes, your honour." The soldier paused, and his face went pale. "Councilor Kalidasa has invoked the Throne's Justice over the massacre of his family by the royal court of Avanti."

* * *

The Throne Room was perfectly still.

Outside the Throne Room, the palace was perfectly still.

Across the lake, the rest of Ujjayini was perfectly still.

Birds had fallen silent on their perches; the horses had stopped snorting and whinnying in the stables. The wind that had been blowing from the north all morning, weaving ceaseless ripples across the lake's surface, had dropped to a whisper, then died in adherence to everything else. Not a soul moved, not a leaf stirred. It was as if time itself had drawn to a heavy halt and was holding its breath, weighing the import of what Kalidasa had just said.

I am the son of Zho E'rami.

Zho E'rami. Zho the Fearless. Warlord of the *x'sa* line of Hunas, the most courageous and intrepid of Huna clans, whose warriors had driven a huge, bleeding swathe into Sindhuvarta during the expansion. The *x'sa* had served at the vanguard of the Huna army, leading with guts, blazing a trail so the rest of the force could follow and consolidate. The *x'sa*: the first of the barbarians to set foot in Sindhuvarta, and the last ones to be pushed back into the Great Desert.

Somewhere, someone – one of the courtiers, probably – cleared a throat out of nervousness and the enchantment broke. Suspended breaths were expelled in a collective sigh that rose and tinkled the crystal lamps overhead, and sank and stirred the dust underfoot at the same time. Feet shuffled and whispers erupted and travelled all around the Throne Room like a catching fire until the cavernous chamber was agog with satin-soft voices. Then, with near-perfect synchrony, all eyes sought out Vikramaditya, seated on the black marble throne, its gold and ivory inlays forming Avanti's sun-crest above and behind his head.

"If you are a Huna by birth, how come you are not adorned with the *hriiz*, my friend?" the samrat asked, his eyes anguished yet gentle on Kalidasa, who stood in the centre of the chamber, dark and wrathful, facing the throne.

"I would have been, had my family not been killed that day." The giant paused, and what seemed like a cross between a scowl and a smirk flashed across his face. "I don't wear the holy *hriiz*, yet mine was the life it protected that day. It is the only reason I escaped death and am standing here now."

"I don't follow you, my friend," said Vikramaditya.

Kalidasa threw a glance around and saw the confusion in the gathering of faces. "Young Huna boys have the holy *hriiz* inscribed on the foreheads in their ninth year. Everyone had been preparing for my initiation a whole week before I turned nine. Father would hone the dagger in the sacred fire and priests would propitiate the desert scorpion with prayers and sacrifices. The day I completed nine – the day of the ceremony, before the inscribing of the holy *hriiz* – I had to go into the forest all alone and hunt three animals all by myself. It is part of the Hunas' initiation rites. I left at dawn, and before mid-morning, I had killed a rabbit, a peacock and a mriga calf. I returned home happy and triumphant..." his face clouded with anger, "...to find everything in flames, everyone dead or dying. Burned and butchered by Avanti's troops. That is what I meant by the holy *hriiz* saving my life – it led me into the forest, away from certain death."

A short silence fell over the chamber as everyone waited for the king to say something. Instead, Amara Simha spoke.

"Do you remember exactly when you lost your memory, Kalidasa?" The face behind the flaming red beard was sympathetic, but also distraught.

"My father named me Ga'ur Thra'akha, councilor," the giant replied coldly. It was as if he had erected a wall around himself to guard against anyone feeling sorry for him. "Kalidasa is a name given to me by Avanti."

"Not by Avanti," Varahamihira corrected from the divan where he sat, his crutch propped against one shoulder. "The name was given by the one who brought you to this palace as his friend. Don't let the bitterness of one past memory distort all other memories."

Kalidasa shot Varahamihira a quick glance, but kept his eyes averted from the samrat.

"So do you remember when you lost your memory?" Amara Simha asked again, still kind and patient.

"I remember running away. Hiding in the forest, then finding the Kali temple at night." The giant gave his head a jerk, casting that train of thought aside as something less important. "But that was all later. Much after I saw them kill my father and sister."

"You witnessed their deaths?" Vikramaditya's expression was pained and disturbed.

"My father, my sister Ei'hi, my aunt and her daughter... I saw the soldiers push them into the granary and set it on fire. I watched all of them being burned alive." Kalidasa's fists clenched. "I also saw the man who gave the soldiers the command, the leader of Avanti's troops."

"Who was it, friend?" the king asked.

"Him." Kalidasa swung an accusing finger across the breadth of the Throne Room, and a muted gasp leaped from the assembly.

Kalidasa stared at the man standing silently to one side, arms folded across his chest, easily overlooked in the crush of courtiers. *The horseman.*

It had almost struck him the previous morning, just as he had exited the house of the martyred *samsaptaka*. Coming down the stairs, he had glimpsed the man astride his horse, his back turned to the house, chatting with Amara Simha, and a faint memory had jogged his mind.

The same poise on the saddle. The telltale slouch of the left shoulder.

When Amara Simha had hailed him, the man had turned around to look – and again there had been something vaguely familiar about him, something seen before.

The same jet-black locks, the same shape of the head and the set of the shoulders, the same cocky self-assurance.

Then their eyes had met. Yesterday, Vararuchi's eyes had smiled at him in greeting. Whereas the eyes that had turned upon him in the burning, smoke-filled valley all those years ago had been cold and hard and remorseless. But there was no doubt they were the same eyes.

Those eyes now appraised him defiantly over the expanse

of the Throne Room. They were still hard and wholly unapologetic. The eyes of an unrepentant killer.

* * *

"What Kalidasa says is true. It was me."

Vararuchi stepped forward and swept a gaze around the Throne Room before locking eyes with the giant. He remembered the day vividly. They had planned for it months in advance, drawing and redrawing strategies, working the manoeuvres in meticulous detail, checking and revising every little aspect of the attack. Everyone had known they had only one chance of storming the Huna garrison in Lava and bringing the dreaded Zho E'rami down.

That method and thinking had paid handsome dividends. They had caught the *x'sa* battalion flatfooted, and the garrison's defence had crumbled almost without a fight. Best of all, Zho E'rami, one of Sindhuvarta's greatest tormentors, had fallen to Avanti's sword that morning.

Now, as he stood in the Throne Room, Vararuchi also recollected the face looking down at him from the top of the embankment; a small, dark, soot-stained face smeared with mud, big eyes staring at him, horrified. Then the face had disappeared from view, ducking behind the embankment.

The men had later told him it was a small boy, fast and agile. The boy had managed giving them the slip and had disappeared into the smoke. He remembered having shrugged it off. He hadn't recognized him when, on returning to Ujjayini, Vikramaditya had introduced him as his new friend. Even the fact that the boy had been found hiding in a temple near Lava, with no recollection of his past, had failed to ring any bells.

That kid now stood glowering down at him, a tight mass of muscle and pent-up angst.

"You killed my family in cold blood," the words rumbled from deep down Kalidasa's throat.

"Have you ever asked around Sindhuvarta how many families your father killed in cold blood?" Vararuchi answered, not in the least bit intimidated by the giant's size. "Zho E'rami got what he deserved."

"But the women..." Vikramaditya looked at his half-brother, aghast. "Why? What harm had *they* done?"

"The Hunas and the Sakas never stopped to ask what harm *our* women and children, *our* old and infirm had done to them, Samrat. They didn't let questions of ethics interfere when they were murdering and pillaging their way through Sindhuvarta. Why did the rules have to change when it was our turn to play? The only way of teaching the Hunas a lesson was by paying them back in their own coin."

"The rules that applied to us and them could never have been the same, brother," the anguish was plain in Vikramaditya's voice. "Our fight was not for ownership of a fertile piece of land. It was about defending the sanctity of ethics and fairness and dignity – about defending humanity. Those are the values worth fighting for. If we forsake those very values in war, we become the very thing we are fighting against. We become them. Then what do we have left to fight for?"

"Fine thoughts, my king, but in reality, that is not how battles are won. At least that was not what rid Sindhuvarta of the invaders." It wasn't obvious from Vararuchi's tone whether he was scoffing at the samrat, but the atmosphere in the Throne Room had soured distinctly. "What drove the savages back was fear – fear that we could be exactly what they were. Fear is the currency they traded in, the currency they understood. Fear is how we restored the pride and dignity of Avanti."

"There is neither pride nor dignity in taking the lives of innocents, councilor," the samrat gave a sad sigh.

Vararuchi bowed stiffly, taking note of the shift in the way Vikramaditya had addressed him. When he spoke, his tone was cold and formal. "I don't dispute the throne, but I wish we could have told that to an enemy who killed every innocent in sight while plundering the kingdoms of Sindhuvarta." He paused and glanced up at Kalidasa. "Speaking of innocents, ask anyone here who wiped out the entire royal court of the kingdom of Nishada, who killed Queen Vishakha and Kshapanaka's parents. It was a *x'sa* battalion. So it may well have been your father who orphaned the queen and Kshapanaka – two innocent children who had nothing to do with your father's war."

Kalidasa gave the assembly a once-over. By turning this into an injustice against Kshapanaka and Vishakha, and insinuating that Zho E'rami might have had a direct hand in the massacre in Nishada, the king's half-brother had cleverly manipulated the sentiment of the court away from him and back against the Hunas. The glance around the room confirmed this. Kshapanaka, who had been standing quietly to Amara Simha's right, was now assessing him with a mixture of shock, revulsion and suspicion, and the assembly buzzed with the seeds of doubt Vararuchi had sown.

The samrat rose from his seat, stilling the murmurs. He stepped off the raised platform that supported the throne and took two paces toward Kalidasa.

"What happened that day was wrong, and as the king of Avanti, I am deeply shamed by it," he said, speaking slowly and clearly so he could be heard by everyone present. "I wish I could undo what's done, but I cannot. I offer you an apology on behalf of Avanti, councilor. I am sorry for the death of your family at the hands of the kingdom's troops."

"I don't want an apology."

The hiss of sharply drawn breaths, followed by an even deeper silence. No one had missed the challenge in the giant's words.

"What else can we give you then?" asked the samrat.

"Avanti can offer nothing that will repair what happened that day. Nothing can heal the hurt, so..." Kalidasa plucked the gold sun-crest medallion that hung from his neck on a slender chain. The chain snapped and the medallion came away in the giant's big fist. Holding the medallion in his outstretched hand, Kalidasa approached the king.

"What is this?" Vikramaditya eyed the medallion uncertainly.

"I can't serve this palace any longer – not with the knowledge of all that has happened. I can no longer swear allegiance to the throne that was responsible for my family's death. My duty toward Avanti ends here."

The Throne Room went perfectly still. The giant and the king stood facing each other, immobile. The silence stretched, shivered, waiting to explode into a whirl of chaos.

"No, Kalidasa..." The samrat whispered in dismay. "Don't do this. I am..." He stopped, seeing the resolve in his old friend's eye. An intolerable sadness slipped over his face. "Does it have to be this way?"

The giant only held the medallion out in response, its broken chain dangling from the two sides of his palm, glinting where its shorn ends caught the sunlight.

"This is foolishness, Kalidasa," Amara Simha stepped forward, agitated. "You are one of us. You are Avanti's *own*."

"I am Ga'ur Thra'akha, Huna by blood and birth," Kalidasa replied, harsh and deliberate.

"And all these intervening years meaning nothing to you?" Varahamihira asked from the divan. "What about us? What about the citizens of Ujjayini who call you their champion? Forget all that – what about the Samrat?"

Kalidasa did not reply. He just stood there, waiting for Vikramaditya. But the king made no move to accept the medallion. Finally, the giant took another step forward, bent down and placed the crest on the floor, by the samrat's feet. Straightening, he stepped back, squared his shoulders and looked at Vikramaditya. The medallion lay on the floor between them like an embellished stain, a winking accusation, an emblem of everything that had gone wrong in their camaraderie.

"Where will you go?" the samrat asked at last, holding the giant's gaze.

"Fate brought me to this palace, fate is taking me back." Cryptic, oblique. "Ours is not to question the guiding hand of destiny." With that, Kalidasa turned on his heel to depart.

The giant was halfway to the door of the Throne Room when Vararuchi called after him. "If you owe Avanti nothing, leave your sword behind as well." The words carried through the awed stillness of the chamber, arresting Kalidasa in his stride.

For a few seconds, the giant stood with his broad back turned to the throne and the councilors, as if in thought. His left hand dropped to the pommel of his scimitar, hanging by a belt at his waist, and his eyes followed, taking in the curve of the sheathed blade. Then, in the same motion, his gaze lifted as he turned to face Vararuchi.

"This sword was forged for me by a humble blacksmith in Udaypuri whose son's life I happened to save. This was *his* gift to me, not the palace's. There's only one way of parting me from this sword – someone will have to prise it out of my dead fingers."

With narrowed eyes, Vararuchi watched Kalidasa head for the exit. Turning to the samrat for a reaction, he was appalled to see the stricken look on his brother's face. It had hurt when Vikramaditya had openly sided with Kalidasa, chiding him for having done what was needed to protect the kingdoms of Sindhuvarta; he had felt humiliated when the king had tendered Kalidasa an apology. But the Huna had brushed the apology aside, insulted the authority of the throne – and even dared someone to take away his sword. Despite all that,

Vikramaditya was letting him walk away. All for the sake of a friendship that lay in tatters, which had failed to stand the true test of loyalty. The enemy was being allowed to win.

Something fractured and fell apart inside Vararuchi. And in that dark, depressive vacuum, resentment sent up its first bitter and poisonous shoot.

Gandharvasena

"If you are thinking of dissuading me from leaving, don't. Amara Simha and Varahamihira have both failed."

Shanku glanced at Kalidasa, sitting stiff on his saddle, staring straight ahead, his face a mask. She said nothing.

They were riding, side by side, through the streets of Ujjayini, heading in the direction of the city's north gate. Everywhere along the streets, townsfolk watched them as they rode past. The news of what had transpired in the palace had spread like wildfire. *Councilor Kalidasa is a Huna!*

There was curiosity in some faces, as if they were seeing a stranger for the first time. In others there was apprehension, and in still others, hostility. There was also dismay and grief in evidence. Occasionally, Shanku and Kalidasa encountered soldiers of the City Watch and the Imperial Army. The soldiers were, without exception, deeply respectful – some even bowed at the departing giant. The commander of the *samsaptakas* was a role model for many of them, and their awe of the warrior couldn't be brushed aside in the skip of a heartbeat.

"It is unfortunate that it had to end like this," Shanku spoke at last.

Kalidasa flicked a glance at the girl out of the corner of his eye. She faced ahead. He noticed the white, short-tailed mare she was riding, the one they had first seen in the horse market, the one that Shanku had secretly set her heart on. Three days ago, he had bought the mare as a gift for Shanku. Just three days, and it already felt like eons had passed. So much had happened in such a short time; an entire generation of memories had sprouted and borne a harvest of bitter fruit in three days.

"I would ask you to come with me, except that I know you won't," he said with a heavy sigh.

"All these years and you choose this moment to bring that up?" Shanku's voice wavered and cracked a little. With an effort, she composed herself. "You are right. I wouldn't come. My loyalty lies with my king. So should yours."

"I can't make myself do it," the giant muttered tightly. "I have seen the cruelty of this throne."

"And I have seen its mercy and kindness."

Neither had anything more to say, and their hobbling conversation broke down to a standstill. They rode in silence under the bright noonday sun. Rounding a corner, they turned into a main street. A hundred yards away, the city's wall rose. The north gate was directly ahead, at the end of the road.

Between them and the gate, a posse of thirty horsemen stood blocking their path.

Kalidasa's hand went to his sword before he realized that the men were *samsaptakas*, with Angamitra at their head. The men's weapons were sheathed, their postures non-threatening.

"Salutations, commander," said the captain, and the men followed suit.

"Salutations... men," the giant corrected himself at the last moment. They were no longer his men.

"We came to... say goodbye..." Angamitra struggled to bring the words out. "...and wish you luck, commander."

"I wish you luck too, brave men." Kalidasa let his eye dwell on every face before him.

"May I ask where you are going, commander?" Angamitra asked.

"I will go wherever my destiny takes me."

One of the *samsaptakas*, a young man, spurred his mount forward a couple of steps. "Wherever you go, we are prepared to follow you, commander," the boy said. "I definitely am."

Kalidasa's eye strayed to a fresh scar on the young man's chest, a pink, puckered line from beneath his right collarbone to the edge of his shoulder. The bright cadet whom he had nearly killed that morning in the training ground, he remembered in a flash. He recalled Angamitra speak highly of him.

"Hush, boy," Kalidasa raised his hand. "Never utter such foolish, mutinous words. You are the Samrat's men. Your job is to protect your king and your kingdom. That is why you took the Death Oath. Never forget that. And about coming with me... my battles are my own to fight, but your battles are here." He gave a heavy pause, loaded with meaning. Pointing at the gate, he said, "Your battles will come in through there. Prepare well to meet them."

Angamitra prodded his mount forward. "The men will do as you say, commander."

The giant gave a small smile. "You are a brave warrior, one of the best I have known. It is now time for you to be more than a warrior. It is time for you to lead the men as their commander. The men will hereafter do as *you* say. Marshal them well."

The captain stared at the giant, too overwhelmed for words. Kalidasa nodded once and nudged his horse, and the *samsaptakas* quietly made way for him and Shanku. They rode down the street with Angamitra and his men trailing behind, until they were in the shadow of the massive gate. While the guards bowed to them, Kalidasa turned to the girl one last time.

"I wish you luck," he said stiffly.

"I wish you luck as well in wherever your destiny takes you. Or should I say, wherever you force your destiny to take you next?"

The giant held Shanku's piercing gaze for a moment. Without answering her, he wheeled his horse around and rode out of the gate, picking up speed as he raced past the burnt-out dwellings outside Ujjayini's wall.

* * *

Aatreya was finding it hard to believe his ears.

"Since when have they been seeing each other?" he asked.

"For a week maybe, maybe from even earlier," said Governor Satyaveda. "Chirayu has been observing their meetings over the last week or so."

Aatreya grimaced and rested his elbows on his knees, steepling his fingers under his flabby chin. His eyes flitted from one corner of the dusty, rundown room to the other, processing what the governor had just told him.

"How and where did my daughter meet him?"

Satyaveda shrugged. The muted roar of men cheering and shouting filtered up from beneath the wooden floorboards. The cockfight was due to begin anytime now, and he wanted to be down there by the mud pit, watching the bloodletting. Instead, he was stuck on a divan, listening to Aatreya put forth silly questions.

"She must know who he is, right?" the merchant asked. "I mean..."

"Apparently not. Chirayu tells me that when they meet, Ghatakarpara makes it a point to pass off as a plain soldier of the Frontier Guard. He hasn't even told her his real name."

Aatreya shook his head in disbelief. As he returned to his ruminations, the governor almost heard the thoughts and emerging possibilities buzz and click through the fat merchant's mind. His daughter, the object of a prince's infatuation – *even love, perhaps?* – and not any common prince. A prince of the Aditya dynasty, nephew of the samrat himself. Satyaveda could see what an attractive proposition this presented to a greedy old pig like Aatreya, and the thought disconcerted him. He needed the merchant on his side...

"The girl is a fool to think anything will come of this," the governor spoke harshly. "She thinks her father will approve of a match with a lowly soldier of Avanti."

"But he isn't really a soldier," Aatreya blurted, confirming Satyaveda's fears.

"No, he is not. But when your daughter does discover his real identity, she would be stupid to believe that the palace would entertain a proposal for the prince from a modest millet merchant." The governor looked at Aatreya pointedly, before deciding to puncture any remaining hopes floating around in that head. "Especially one who has been trading Avanti's military secrets with the savages from the Marusthali."

Satyaveda had the pleasure of seeing Aatreya's fledgling ambitions flag and falter. "Yes, very stupid of Aparupa," the merchant nodded glumly. Snapping erect, he said, "I shall put an end to this whole business. I will drill sense into her, and send her away to her grandparents' place in Balipura, if necessary."

"No, my friend, don't do that," the governor waggled a cautionary finger. "Say nothing to her. You know how rebellious youth is. Forbid her and she will devise ways of disobeying you and meeting him. And even if you send her away, the prince might still be able to learn of her whereabouts and seek her out."

"What should I do then?"

Satyaveda brought his lips close to the merchant's ear and whispered, "Better the prince disappears, no?"

Aatreya stared at the governor, taken aback.

"Aparupa doesn't know who he is. If he disappears, poof –" the governor raised a clenched fist into the air and suddenly opened his fingers to mime a vanishing act "– well, he is a soldier. He could have been posted elsewhere along the frontier, or recalled to his garrison. He could just have tired of her and gone away without even a goodbye – that is what is expected from heartless soldiers all the time, isn't it? It will break her, but she will reconcile herself. And where will she go looking for him even if she wished to? She doesn't even know his real name." Satyaveda smiled at the merchant. "Simple, isn't it?"

Aatreya nodded. "It sounds fine, but how do we make the prince disappear just like that?"

"You forget our friends from the Marusthali, dear fellow. What wouldn't they do to get their hands on a royal hostage?" The governor gave a cunning chuckle. "The king's nephew, no less. I would think the reward for that would be more than handsome."

"How do we even do it?" the merchant asked in wonder.

"Aparupa will help us." Seeing the confusion in Aatreya's eyes, Satyaveda added, "Not that she would know, of course."

"I still don't get it."

"I do." The governor smiled and gave the merchant a friendly smack on the shoulder.

Later, sitting in the private cubicle overlooking the amphitheatre where gamecocks slaughtered one another as people placed illegal bets on the birds, Satyaveda's mind strayed from the sport in the arena to the one he was playing with the palace of Avanti.

They had denied him a place at the council table, *him* – grandnephew of chief councilor Acharya Vedavidya, and son of councilor Sagopana. A seat in the royal council had been his by virtue of birth. Yet, when the time came, they had overlooked him, picking the orphaned princess from Nishada – *a woman!* – in his place. They had made him Governor of Malawa instead, making it sound as if it were a great honour. But all he remembered was what he was *not* – royal councilor of Avanti. Later, adding insult to injury, they had appointed that treacherous Warden's daughter Shankubala as councilor. A slip of a girl, *a traitor's daughter*! Obviously, the palace had respect for neither tradition nor true talent. And then, finally, this inexperienced fool of a prince, Ghatakarpara. Benefitting from being the king's nephew, what else. *Love-struck idiot!*

Thank heavens the prince was love-struck, Satyaveda hastily corrected himself. He couldn't have dreamt of a more perfectly tailored opportunity to finally have his revenge on Avanti.

* * *

"Why didn't you stop him, Vikrama?"

The samrat didn't respond immediately. For a long while, he just sat holding Vishakha's white, limp hand, feeling the softness of her skin on his palms. He ran a finger over the jade ring adorning her middle finger, then traced the blue veins along the back of her hand, back and forth. At last, he looked across Vishakha's bed at Queen Upashruti.

"What good would that have done, mother?" he asked. "The only way of stopping him from going would have been by imprisoning him. After everything else that Avanti has done to him, putting him in chains and locking him away would be the ultimate travesty of justice." Vikramaditya shook his head. "No, mother. Giving him his freedom is the least we could do to atone for what happened."

"But you do know where he is going, don't you?" Mother and son were alone in Vishakha's bedchamber. The matron and the maids had vacated the room temporarily, so Upashruti spoke freely.

"His exit from the north gate fooled no one; even he knows that," the king nodded. "He has gone in search of his roots."

"And you know what that means. He knows every little secret of ours. Every trapdoor, every secret tunnel… he probably knows the exact number of swords in each of our armouries."

"I know, mother."

Upashruti heaved a resigned sigh. "Let us hope he doesn't altogether forget all those years of kindness we showered on him. Maybe he will respect your friendship enough not to betray us."

The samrat did not reply. The three lamps guttered, and shadows stretched and jigged along the floor and across walls. The night was otherwise silent. They sat quietly for so long that the Queen Mother began feeling drowsy, and her eyelids drew down over her eyes. Blinking rapidly, she gave a start and was about to rise from her chair to wish her son good sleep when Vikramaditya looked at her.

"Why have I failed so miserably, mother?" he asked.

"What? I don't see how…"

"I promised to protect her." Vikramaditya gestured toward Vishakha's inert form. "I failed in doing so. I took oath to protect the people of Avanti from harm. I failed in that too. My best friend came to me seeking justice. I failed to give him that. I failed our friendship. Why, mother?"

"You are being too hard on yourself, Vikrama," Upashruti spoke sternly but kindly. She came around the bed to stand by the king's side. She stroked his hair and drew his head to her, cradling it in a comforting embrace. "None of what has happened was in your control. Vishakha and the people of

Avanti... what befell them was the outcome of the devas' and asuras' greed. And Kalidasa... It wasn't *your* fault, son. You weren't even there. You weren't even king then."

"I am now, and still I failed. I fear I will fail next in honouring the trust that the Omniscient One has placed on me." The samrat placed Vishakha's hand gently back on the bed. He then took Upashruti's hands into his own and gazed up at her. "Why has everything suddenly started coming apart, mother?"

"The Mother Oracle warned us about an eclipse. This is probably the dark of the sun."

With a tired little nod, Vikramaditya let go of his mother's hands and turned to lean his head against her. Upashruti's palm brushed over his forehead, caressing the worry lines. The samrat stared into Vishakha's eyes, far away from the anxieties that beset her husband. *Had Zho E'rami actually ordered the massacre in the court of Nishada?*

"Who knows how much darker it will get before the eclipse wanes," he wondered aloud, "...if it wanes at all."

* * *

Despite the lateness of the hour, Indra's eye was bright and clear as he heard the garuda recount everything that Shukracharya had to share with the devas. The more he listened, the greater Indra's admiration for the high priest grew, and he was forced to admit to himself that the devas had probably shown poor judgment in not picking Shukracharya as their chamberlain. The mahaguru's ingenuity in plotting his moves against the human king was exemplary, and it crossed Indra's mind that he couldn't have asked for a better ally in his quest for Veeshada's dagger.

His lips curled upward at the irony of the thought. Shukracharya was no ally. Only compulsion had brought them together and was keeping them from one another's throats. The moment the need to cooperate ceased, they would go back to being bitter foes.

"So the rift that the mahaguru spoke of has indeed come to pass," he smacked his thigh in satisfaction, giving Narada a broad, triumphant grin. "The thread that binds the Nine Pearls has started fraying, as the mahaguru promised it would."

"The mahaguru says that the king's court is in ferment, and the time is right to make the next move," the garuda said. "He urges speed so we can capitalize on the hurt, confusion and despair prevailing in the palace."

"Of course." Indra jerked his head as much in assent as in a dismissal of the garuda. Then, addressing Narada, he asked, "Do we have news of Gandharvasena?"

"The prince is already here, lord. He awaits you downstairs."

"Let us meet him."

The two devas threaded through endless passageways and down infinite flights of stairs until they came to a broad gallery that overlooked an atrium with a large, glistening fountain at its centre. Water wafted up from it like white smoke, boiling over and cascading back into the pool at its base, where neon-coloured fish darted about amid fronds of wavy fern and riverweed.

A figure stood by the fountain, staring down at the fish, his back to Indra and Narada. On hearing their footsteps, the deva turned, and seeing them, he bowed deeply. Straightening, he looked at Indra, who appraised the deva with a small smile of approval. Tall and gracefully built, the deva had an easy, languid poise that bordered on the feminine. Locks of soft, brown hair framed his fair face, ripe with youth. The features were all clean, sharp cuts, as if hewn out of sandstone by a sculptor of exceptional skill. His light brown eyes harboured a lazy charm, with the capacity to enchant and melt every apsara in Devaloka.

Gandharvasena. His most potent weapon against Vikramaditya so far.

More powerful than the Ashvins, the Maruts or any magical yaksha from Kubera's court. More powerful than the primeval serpent-dragon Ahi itself. Not that Indra would ever have known, had Shukracharya not revealed the secret that made Gandharvasena so lethal and devastating. An ideal weapon for a perfect vendetta.

The deva lord descended the last flight of steps into the atrium, the smile still playing on his lips as he savoured the idea of the handsome, willowy deva rattling the foundations of the palace in faraway Ujjayini.

End of Book 2